When you least expect it

Natalie Johnson

Prologue

'Another drink, madam?'

I open my eyes and look up to see Jake standing over me with a tall glass of something bright blue, finished off with a sparkly straw and cocktail umbrella. I wrinkle up my nose, squinting to try and stop the brilliant sunshine from hurting my eyes.

'Shift, will you? You're blocking my sun!' I moan, as I lift my leg off the sunlounger to gently push him away with my foot.

I can hear the waves lapping at the shore, and I prop myself up on my elbows, taking the frightfully garish drink from his hand. I rest it on my stomach and flinch as the cold glass hits my warm skin. I look down at myself. Not bad. I'm getting quite a tan.

I take a quick glance up and down the beach. It's quiet now. The midday sun seems to have got the best of most people, but I'm a firm sun worshipper and, despite the rising temperature, there's a comforting breeze coming in from the sea that takes the edge off the Caribbean heat. I am definitely making the most of it. After all, this is my honeymoon.

'So, how is my favourite girl in the whole world feeling now?'

'Smooth-talker.' I take a huge sip of my drink, giving myself total brain freeze. Despite my avoidance tactics Jake doesn't let it drop.

'Seriously, how are you feeling?'

I swing my legs off the lounger and sit up to face Jake. His blonde hair is messy from the sea and the sand, and I smile to myself as I notice he has it tied back with one of my hairbands. There are freckles spattered across his nose from the effects of the sun, and I want to reach out and touch them but stop myself.

'I'm OK. I haven't thought about it for oh, at least thirty-two whole minutes today. I think we have a record.'

Jake nods slowly, looking impressed. He stands up, cupping his hands around his mouth, and bellows, 'Ladies and gentlemen, we have progress!'

I giggle and grab his hand to pull him down.

'Shh, you idiot!'

He sits down and the hairs on his legs brush mine (my legs that is, not my hairs). I move my leg a little, shying away slightly at the closeness, but he doesn't bat an eyelid. I can still feel the touch of his leg on mine, like the contact somehow burned my skin and left a mark.

'You're doing good, sweet cheeks, you know that don't you?' he says seriously, before leaning forward and taking a sip of my drink through the sparkly straw. I smile at his total lack of propriety.

'I know I am!' I say, swiftly changing the subject. 'I'm holding it together better than you. I'm the one who had to hold back your hair last night when you were heaving over the toilet bowl, you lightweight!'

I wink at him, and he shoves my shoulder in what he

probably thinks is a gentle push, but he's so strong I swing backwards and almost fall off my sunbed. He lunges forward and grabs my arm, just in time to save me and my drink. I sigh and bat my eyelids at him.

'You're my hero,' I say, and I mean it.

In truth, I don't know how I would have got through this past week without him. It doesn't feel like I've only known him five days. Truth is if everything had gone to plan I probably wouldn't have even met him. I would have been married for a week now. Mrs Carrie Annabel Kingston-Croft. But it's still just Carrie Annabel Kingston. I blame my parents. This is totally their fault for naming me Caroline. This would never have happened to a Savannah or an Alicia, but to Carolines everywhere this sort of thing probably happens all the time. I feel anger rise up in me, as I think about the last week. This should have been the best and most memorable trip of my life. Well, it's certainly in line as a strong contender for the most memorable. And here I am, on a beach, wondering how it could have all gone so very wrong, sharing cocktails with a man who isn't my husband, but who I only just met.

Chapter One

One week earlier

'Hello!'

Knock. Knock. Knock. Actually it's more like *KNOCK! KNOCK! KNOCK!* I roll over in bed. Go away, go away, go away. I groan inwardly. Then it starts.

'Caroline? Where are you? Caroline!'

Oh. God. My mother. And why is she *singing* the words? *Just say them like a normal person*, I think irritably. Be quiet Mum, please be quiet. Maybe if I lie here and don't move she won't notice me. She'll go away and forget she has a daughter, and there will be no more Carolines yelled up the stairs.

I hate my name. I know that might sound like a cruel thing to say and actually, that's not true, I don't hate the actual *name* Caroline, but it's just never worked for me. I never felt like a Caroline. I don't know what I should have been called, but Caroline just wasn't it. Thankfully, my wonderful dad started calling me Carrie as soon as I was born and, despite my mum's best efforts, it stuck.

My bedroom door bursts open and in she strides. I knew I should have taken that key off her. My mum is a law unto herself and an absolute force to be reckoned with.

My dad died two years ago, and ever since I've been waiting for my mum to fall apart, as I did, but it never happened. For the few weeks after his death, I would find myself looking at her like a time bomb waiting for her to explode with grief, and I braced myself for having to deal with, not only my own all-consuming feeling of loss, but the clean-up operation that was thirty-one years of marriage, a massive heart attack and an unexpectedly taken husband. But she never did. After all those years of marriage she wouldn't let her grief beat her and rob her of what was left of her life. She resolutely refused to succumb to the pain and heartbreak she was feeling.

'Your bloody father won't beat me on this one, I swear to you, he won't,' she had said on more than one occasion. Even after he'd gone, they were still fighting with each other, albeit a little one-sided now, but that didn't seem to deter my mum. They were always trying to outdo one another and it's still the same, even though he's passed away. I, unfortunately, did not fare so well. I only realise now how hard that must have been for my mum. I behaved as if I'd lost both my parents, but she was very much still here and trying to hold it together, for my sake as much as hers. I understand that now. I wouldn't speak or eat for days on end and, looking back, I realise how selfish I was being. I was so wrapped up in my own grief that I had forgotten my mum had lost her husband.

I was very much a daddy's girl, like his little shadow, and the thought of never seeing him again ate away at me.

Never hearing the sounds of him swearing at the sports on TV and never seeing him argue with my mum, then giving me a secret wink like he knew he was being bad but, shush, it was our little secret, it tore me apart and my heart physically ached with grief. But eventually, after many weeks of seeing my mum coping so well, I realised that life goes on and it was as if her strength started to rub off on me.

A few weeks after his funeral, Mum had come over to bring me a few of Dad's special things that reminded me of him. The ridiculous wool hat he used to wear when he was gardening, a small, leather coin purse that I bought for him with my pocket money one year on holiday in Spain, the dog-eared, faded photograph of me, sat on his knee as a child on my first day at school, looking as proud as anything in my shiny new uniform and my dad beaming at the camera.

Over a coffee in the kitchen, fresh tears fell at the reminder of what used to be and my mum took my hands in hers and said, 'I will always miss him, and I will always love him. But love, life goes on. And he would want it to. Just because his life ended, doesn't mean ours have to as well.'

And that was it. We never spoke about it again, but we both knew what we had to do, and I took my lead from my mum and promised to be a daughter she could rely on from then on. It was that day that I asked her if she'd give me away. I knew if my dad wasn't going to be here to do it, it had to be her and I know how much today means to her, but I can't help feeling the familiar twinge of sadness that my dad won't walk me down the aisle.

My thoughts are broken as I'm brought back to earth with a deafening, 'Goodness me! Come on you lazy thing,

WHEN YOU LEAST EXPECT IT

get up! Honestly, to think this is your wedding day and you're not even out of bed.'

She tuts to herself and shuffles around my room, picking up the debris left by me last night, trying to tidy things away. I glance at my wedding dress hanging on the wardrobe and then turn to look at the clock.

'Mum, it's nine a.m. The ceremony isn't until two. Why on earth do I need to get ready now?' I flinch as she pulls open the curtains and, as I adjust my eyes to the light, I break into a huge smile as I see my mum in her full wedding outfit, complete with hat and clutch bag. She must have been up at the crack of dawn to get dressed already.

'Oh Mum, you look so lovely.'

She really does. She's wearing a cream, linen dress down to her knees and a short, sea-green, silk jacket that matches the colour of her eyes. It's finished off with green, kitten-heeled shoes and the most impressive cream hat I have ever seen, trimmed with small, green beads, that sits on her perfectly blow-dried, honey-coloured bob. She looks beautiful. I see her flush slightly as she twirls for me, her dress swinging around her knees like a little girl.

'Do you like it? Really? I'm so glad I kept it as a surprise.' She looks down at her outfit and, as she smiles to herself, I know she's thinking of my dad. How I wish in this moment he could see her. Perhaps he can. She suddenly snaps out of her reverie, and it's straight back to business as usual.

'Well come on then. Enough about me. Get yourself up, young lady. You've got a wedding to get to!'

_____

I take a long, leisurely shower and, after doing my own make-up, I pick at one of the croissants my mum has brought with her (along with plenty of champagne) whilst sat in front of the mirror as my hairdresser, Kate, adds the finishing touches to my long, auburn hair. More importantly than just being my hairdresser, Kate happens to be my fiancé's sister and even more importantly than that, is one of my closest and oldest friends and today, *most* importantly, happens to be one of my bridesmaids. Being naturally wavy, I decided to opt for loose curls in an effort to avoid the frizz of a hot, July day. Humidity is most definitely not my friend.

'So how does it feel to think in a few hours' time you'll be Mrs Luke Croft?' Kate asks, smiling at me in the reflection of the mirror, the photograph of me and my dad tucked in the corner.

'Honestly? A little scary. But it'll be Kingston-Croft, don't forget.' I smile, a little embarrassed. I was a bit worried about my choice to double barrel my name, and I thought Kingston-Croft sounded, well, a bit snooty quite frankly, but I didn't want to lose what felt like the last connection to my dad. Being an only child, there's no one else to carry on the family name and keeping my surname will be a daily reminder of him.

Kate laughs. 'Very posh indeed, dear,' she says, unintentionally doing a spot on impression of my mum. I slump my shoulders and stick out my bottom lip before looking up at Kate.

'I still can't believe we don't get to share the same name though.'

After talking about us being official sisters ever since I started seeing Luke, Kate met a guy, Justin, in a bar near her office one evening after work. It was quite definitely love at first sight, if you can believe in such a romantic sentiment. They booked a last-minute holiday together six weeks later, headed off to the other side of the world and got married on a beach in Thailand, just the two of them, and didn't tell a soul until they got home. Hence why she's no longer a Croft.

'No wonder your mum is so excited about this wedding,' I say to Kate. 'It's the only one she's going to get since you buggered off to Thailand. I blame you for all this drama, you know?'

Kate looks apologetic and rightly so, but to be honest, I wish I had the guts to do what she did. To go on holiday and come back husband and wife, just like that. Not to say that I didn't want the big, white wedding now it was here, but had my dad not passed away, would I still have felt the need to do the traditional thing? Was one of the main reasons I agreed to it all to give my mum, and Luke's mum come to think of it, something to look forward to?

It was eight weeks ago that Kate and Justin landed in Heathrow as newly-weds, after only knowing each other for two months, and I'm not entirely sure Kate and Luke's mum has got over the shock quite yet. They are perfect together though. I knew the first time I saw them together they were meant for one another. Their love of the outdoors, their craving for adventure and their passion for cooking up a haphazard storm in the kitchen (I have to say Kate's duck à la pina colada *really* left something to be desired), as well as their quite obvious, and sometimes a little uncomfortable, passion for each other are all evidence of this. Which is the complete opposite of me and Luke, who have known each other since school and, after being asked for about the millionth time by our parents when it was going to happen, got engaged two years ago. It was just before my dad died, on my birthday. Luke threw a massive surprise party and got down on one knee in front of all our friends and family. It was really lovely, especially since my dad was there.

Snapping back to the present, I look up at Kate in the mirror. She has a deep frown across her delicate face and is painstakingly concentrating on touching up the curls in my hair when the door opens and Emily's face pops through the gap. Emily's our other best friend and my only other bridesmaid alongside Kate. Her family moved to our village, on the outskirts of Warwickshire, around fifteen years ago from Plymouth, when her dad got a job as a director at a potato factory. She still tells people it was because he got a job as chief chocolate bar designer at Cadbury's, which is not even a *real* thing. At least, I don't think it is? Maybe I should apply.

Emily spends most of her time at ours or Kate's house, despite having her own flat in Stratford. Her parents have since retired back down to Devon to a rather gorgeous, seaside cottage that we all enjoy frequenting for a week or two when they take their annual cruise around the Caribbean every summer. Plus I have to thank Emily for today, I guess, as it was her who first brought Luke to my attention. He was in our maths class, and he asked to borrow her protractor. He was gorgeous, even back then, with his black hair gelled to oblivion but he just looked *sooo* cool to our giggly, impressionable, teenage hearts.

The story goes that I was actually using her protractor at the time and, as I passed it over, the tips of our fingers touched ever so slightly and I fell head over heels there and then in

2B Maths class. It's always been an unspoken wondering, but I have my suspicions that Emily quite liked him as well to start with, although she would never, ever admit it, to me or anyone else. I often used to catch her watching the two of us together at school and then looking away shyly when she thought I'd seen.

'Hi Bride,' she whispers and steps into the room with a spin to show off her dress. 'What do you think? I must say this dress is so great, you have excellent taste.'

'No honey, you wear it very, very well.' I smile back at her and do an excited handclap. She really does. She looks stunning. I have both an incredible taste in friends and dresses it would seem. For the bridesmaid dresses I went for a gold, halterneck, knee-length dress which perfectly complements Emily's tiny frame, her poker-straight, brown hair and olive skin. Kate stops her tonging and turns to see.

'Ah, Em you look gorgeous! Damn, I'll look rubbish next to you!'

'Don't be stupid!' Emily and I both yell at the same time.

'Really Kate,' I say looking her in the eye, 'you look fab.'

While Emily is petite and dark, Kate is taller with curves to die for and short, blonde, bobbed hair.

'Really Em, the boys will be falling over themselves to get at you today,' Kate continues as she turns to me, her hands on her hips. 'There are some single men coming to this party I hope?' I raise my eyebrows at her accusingly. 'Oh no, no, no!' she quickly backtracks. 'For Em, not for me! Married woman now, thank you very much.'

I smile because, despite the fact she's only known Justin for a few months, they are totally and utterly committed to each other. I turn over my shoulder to Emily, as Kate tuts and quickly follows my head with the tongs so I don't rip out a chunk of my own hair.

'Yes, there are plenty of Luke's single mates coming. You've met most of them before, but they have blossomed since our college days, I can tell you. There is this one guy actually...'

Emily cuts me off mid sentence.

'I'm not really looking at the moment, but you know, thanks.' She looks really uncomfortable for a second. Emily is *always* looking for a man, but I can tell from her face she doesn't want me to press the issue, so I leave it. Kate, however, possesses no such discretion.

'Hang on a minute!' she throws her hand to her chest in mock horror. 'Do my ears deceive me? You, Miss Emily Friar, are *not* looking for a man?'

I look over to see Emily's reaction, trying to gauge what's going on.

'Well y'know,' she starts, playing with the hem of her dress, 'not, *not* looking, just not really...' she trails off and hangs her head at the look on Kate's face.

'Well,' Kate says firmly, 'you don't fool me, missy. You're the party girl! And the only singleton among us now, so don't you dare let me down. In fact, let's get started. Go downstairs and grab that bottle of Moët out of the fridge. It's time we started celebrating.'

'Oh grab the orange juice too,' I add. 'We can go all eighties and have Buck's Fizz.'

Minutes later Emily returns with three glasses balanced in her hands. She hands two filled with champagne to me and Kate and keeps one with what looks like straight up orange juice for herself. Emily raises her glass.

'Well cheers then. To you, Carrie.' She gives me a small smile. 'Oh and to Luke, I suppose,' she adds, her face a mixture of apology and… discomfort, perhaps? It's something I can't quite put my finger on.

Suddenly Kate starts off again, 'Oh no way, Em! There had better be some alcohol content in that glass and not just OJ? We are celebrating here!' she grabs Emily's glass from her and studies it, but Emily seizes it back and takes a sip.

'Alright, calm down, Kate! I didn't want to have a real drink in case anyone needs me to pop out again.' She nods her head in my direction, 'In case Carrie needs anything.'

I smile at her. 'Thank you, sweetie, but honestly, if we do I'm sending my mum just to get rid of her!'

'Ah well, more for me,' Kate giggles and takes a big swig from her glass, seemingly satisfied with this justification. Suddenly she waves her hand in front of her face like a lunatic. Me and Emily look at each other and start to laugh out loud, as Kate jumps up and down and takes a big swallow.

'Ooh, those bubbles went right up my nose!' she cries, rubbing the end of her little pixie nose. She walks over to my dress and picks up the long, ivory veil hanging next to it. 'Now,' she says proudly, 'let's try it on with the finished article.'

My hair looks so beautiful I'm a bit reluctant to put the veil on. Kate has left half of it down and pulled the top half back with a comb, so the curls fall gently across my shoulders.

'Hang on, hang on!' I wave my arms above my hair. 'I'm not sure I want the veil now.'

'What?' says Emily slowly, who looks as equally as horrified as Kate. 'But Carrie. The veil. It was the bit you were most excited about. It took you longer to find your perfect veil than it did your dress!'

'I know, I know, but Kate you've done such a good job, I don't want to ruin my hair. It looks so lovely as it is.'

Kate walks over and stands behind me with the veil. 'Carrie, you have to at least try it on.' Her face is etched with concern at this clearly unacceptable turn of events. I look from her to Emily, who is stood nodding on the spot, and back to my reflection in the mirror.

'Go on then,' I sigh.

'The veil is what makes you a bride,' Kate says as she fastens it to the back of my hair and steps back with a flourish. Oh. My. God. They're right. It looks beautiful. In fact, sod it, who am I kidding, *I* look beautiful. I stand up and face the two of them. Kate clasps her hands under her chin and beams at me. Emily looks, well, a bit shell-shocked actually, but it must be strange seeing your best friend in her wedding get-up. Not that I would know (cheers Kate!).

'And now,' Kate pauses for dramatic effect and does a little shoulder wiggle. 'The dress!'

Emily looks to have tears welling up and she rushes out of the room with her hands on her cheeks. Kate and I laugh at each other. Classic Emily. She's definitely the most emotional of the three of us. She loves a good cry and is quite a sensitive soul deep down. I really do have the best, best friends. When they cry at how gorgeous you look on your wedding day, a girl knows they're keepers.

Chapter Two

As I rummage around for my specially purchased 'wedding night' underwear, Kate goes over to the wardrobe to get my dress. She's necked that champagne pretty quickly, and I know she won't have eaten this morning in a bid to make sure she looks super skinny for the photos, so I am slightly concerned she is going to mess up the hair she just spent so long doing. Thank God she finished that before the champers at least.

'Er, can you manage, Kate? Maybe we should wait for Em?'

'No, don't be silly. I'll be fine. Honestly, I'm not a complete imbecile!' she says as she trips over my shoe. Jesus. What are friends for hey? *Not an imbecile just a drunk*, I think to myself but she's in full swing now.

'Right,' she instructs, 'go and get a hand towel and we'll put it over your head so you don't get make-up on your dress or mess up your hair, OK? I'll get the dress sorted. Oh, and you better take that veil off if you're wearing it, you can't put your dress on over that.'

Ah. Well, yes maybe she was a good bridesmaid choice after all, as I hadn't thought of any of that. How do people know these things? Where is this wedding manual everyone seems to have read except me?

'OK. Back in a sec. I'm going to nip to the loo while I'm there before I get trapped in the dress for the whole day and need your help to have a wee!' Kate screws up her face in faux revulsion, and I decide to check on Emily too. Plus, I know she wouldn't want to miss this bit.

The bathroom door is closed when I get to it, and I can hear Emily's voice, low and muffled like she's whispering to someone. Who on earth is she in there with? Or perhaps she's on the phone, you idiot! Yes, much more likely, Carrie. Wedding brain! I know I shouldn't, but I could tell she wasn't a hundred per cent herself this morning, so I listen up against the door.

'For God's sake this is hard for *you*? How do you think it is for me? I have to pretend nothing is wrong? I'm sorry. I can't do it. I just can't!'

Emily's anguished voice floats through the door, and I can tell from the tone of her voice she's been crying. Jesus, this sounds bad. Is she OK? My heart is beating quicker, as I shift from one foot to the other. I bet it's a guy. She loves the bad boys. She's had some absolute shockers in the past. There was this one guy, James, she dated him for three months, and he wouldn't introduce her to any of his friends or colleagues and wouldn't ever invite her to his place. Turns out, it was because he was actually a married father of two and didn't want to get busted! For a moment there's silence, until her voice starts up again.

'You just don't get it do you? You have absolutely no idea. How can I *act normal*? Everything is so far from normal it's untrue! This baby is yours too, you know. I can't do this on my own.'

Oh. Fuck. Baby? A baby? Emily's pregnant? How? Well, I know how. But, you know, *how*? And more importantly, whose? And when? OK, so some guy found out she was pregnant and now wants nothing to do with her. This is the sort of absolute classic bad boy 101 behaviour that she seems to attract, the poor love. What a scumbag. I've told her before about these guys, who want to string her along while it's all fun and games and then run at the first sign of anything more serious than a late-night booty call and phoning you a taxi at two in the morning. God, poor Em. So *that's* what the orange juice was about. What is she going to do? I stare at the door as if it's going to give me an answer and guilty lean in again. There is a quick pause before I hear her voice.

'And you can forget that because you already know I'm keeping it and that's not going to change.'

I look at the door. I'm actually feeling quite proud of her standing up to this lowlife who has clearly just suggested something she one hundred per cent does not want to do. Emily begins to mumble something, but I can't make out what. I press my ear to the wood gently, as I lean in closer and balance myself on the door frame.

'For fuck's sake!' she spits out, angrily this time. 'I can't go through with this.'

With what?

'Either you tell her...'

My brain is working overtime now trying to piece it all together. So there's another woman? God, Em, you don't half pick them.

'...or I will, Luke. I have to go. Your fiancée needs me to help her into her dress. You shit.'

And suddenly, I'm in it. At least I think I am. Am I? She said Luke, right? Maybe it's another Luke? No, his fiancée. She said Luke and she said fiancée. That's me. Emily and Luke? Emily is having Luke's baby. My best friend Emily is having my fiancé Luke's baby. No. No. That can't be it. Can it? My brain must have added it up wrong. But that's what she said. Didn't she? My legs turn to jelly, and I back against the bannister. My mum has left a disposable camera on the top, and I send it crashing down to the hall floor. It lands with an almighty bang, but I barely hear it. It seems like it's a million miles away to me. Everything is swimming, and I can't think. I can't see. My heart is racing. Luke and Emily. Emily and Luke. And a baby. Their baby. I feel sick. Suddenly the bathroom door and my bedroom door open at the exact same time and Emily freezes as she sees me, all colour draining from her face. My eyes meet hers and then instinctively drop to her stomach, then to the floor. Kate steps towards us completely oblivious to what I've just heard. I can feel Emily looking at me, but I can't move. I'm frozen to the spot, my heart pounding in my chest.

'Right,' I can hear Kate saying somewhere, 'are we getting dressed or what, chick?'

She stops in front of me and, realising something isn't right, looks at me, her face etched with concern.

'Carrie? Carrie, are you OK?'

I say nothing.

'What the hell's happened? Are you alright? Did you break something? I heard a smash. Em, what happened?'

Kate's eyes bounce between me and Emily until finally, Emily speaks in my direction.

'How long have you been there?'

I just shake my head. Emily takes a step towards me, but I shrink back from her.

'Carrie. How long have you been there?'

Kate looks at me utterly confused. 'Where have you been?' she asks, frowning.

'She's been here, I just don't know how long,' Emily says impatiently. 'Carrie. Please. How long have you been here?'

Kate throws up her hands to stop us both from speaking.

'Can someone tell me what the hell is going on?'

Silence.

'Emily?'

I vaguely register Emily shake her head.

'Carrie? *Carrie!*'

I jolt back to reality and raise my head to face Emily. There are tears streaming down her face.

'Tell her,' I say quietly.

Emily says nothing.

'Tell her,' I repeat, but more sternly this time.

'Em, what is going on? Tell me what?' Kate almost shouts as she turns to face Emily.

'I can't,' Emily says and breaks down in tears, covering her face with her hands. Kate takes a step towards her and puts her arm around Emily.

'Oh, Em. Come on, you can tell me. We're your best friends. You can tell us anything.' Kate nods encouragingly in my direction, and I almost laugh at the irony of the situation.

Then no one says anything for what seems like an eternity. It's only me and Emily that know. Well, and Luke. No one else. I could say nothing. Forget it. Move on, get married and live happily ever after. And I know that, for now, it's almost not real and that as soon as she says the words to Kate, as soon as another person hears them and it's out in the open, then it becomes very, very real indeed.

Then Emily speaks, barely audibly. 'I – I'm, I'm pregnant.'

Kate opens her mouth. Then closes it. Then opens it again and leaves it open for a second before she yells, '*What*?' No one answers her. 'Oh my God, Em, is this true? Jesus! Well you kept that bloody quiet! How exciting! I mean, I think? Is it? God! Er, who? How? I mean, a baby, that's massive! It's…' Then she stops and looks at me sympathetically.

'Oh, Carrie, I am so sorry. I'm such a thoughtless idiot. This is *your* wedding day. It's all about you today and yes, of course we are excited for Em, I mean, I think we are. Right, Em?' Without waiting for an answer she hugs Emily closer and drags me into her other side. 'But this is your day and I promise you, we promise you, it'll be about that, don't we Em? Today is all about Carrie.'

In fact, I think you'll find today is now all about Emily and Luke's baby.

'Wow, what a big day for all my girls,' she laughs, 'how brilliant! I kind of feel left out now!'

I can't stand it any longer. I'm ripping off the plaster, exposing the wound for the entire world to see and once I say it, that's it. Forever. Never to be taken back. I turn to face Kate, but not before I glance at Emily. She knows what's coming and opens her mouth ever so slightly, as if she is going to say something, but I get there first.

'It's Luke's,' I say, deadpan and Emily and Kate both stare at me. Emily with absolute terror on her face and Kate with utter confusion.

'It's Luke's?' Kate frowns but then answers her own question. 'Oh yeah, I mean of course, of course!' says Kate. What *is* she talking about? 'I meant it's yours *and* Luke's wedding day. How could I forget my big brother? Oops! Don't tell him,' she giggles.

'No,' I say, my voice steady. I lift my hand to my hair and tug off my veil, letting it drop to the floor. The look of horror on Kate's face as she sees it fall would be funny if it all wasn't so awful. I can barely get the words out, still not wanting to believe they are true, but the look on Emily's face tells me that we both know they are. 'It's Luke's baby.'

Kate frowns to herself for a second. Then looks at Emily. Then down to her stomach. Then at me. Then at the veil.

I look Emily straight in the eye. 'It is, isn't it?' I ask her, even though we both know it's not really a question.

Kate turns to Emily, shaking her head quickly as if she's trying to get her thoughts in place. 'Sorry, can I just… what the *hell* is going on? *You're* having Luke's baby?' she asks, so fiercely and bluntly that I see Emily actually wince. She looks to the floor and gives the tiniest, barely noticeable, nod of her head.

Kate grabs Emily by the shoulder and positions herself in between the two of us as if to shield me from the painful, awful, hideous truth.

'You're having Luke's baby.' This time it isn't a question. 'I want to hear you say it,' Kate demands and Emily starts to cry again.

'Say it!' I shout from behind Kate, as my vision begins to swim with tears. I don't even know where that came from, but it must be loud because it makes both of them jump and turn to look at me.

'I'm pregnant,' Emily says, her voice scarcely a whisper. 'And it's Luke's. We only slept together once Carrie, I swear,' she pleads, stepping around Kate, as much as my human shield will allow.

She must think in for a penny in for a pound, because she continues talking, whether I want to hear it or not.

'It was the night of your hen do. You know when I came back here early, because I felt ill?'

I remember. We'd been out for dinner and drinks, followed by more drinks and lots of dancing, when Emily thought she'd eaten something dodgy because she was starting to feel nauseous. It was our final dress fitting the next day, so I told her to go home to mine and Luke's, where we were all staying, and get some rest for tomorrow. I was disappointed, but I was more worried than anything. What an idiot I feel now.

'But Luke wasn't even here then. He was out with Justin,' I say confused and look at Kate for an answer, but she shakes her head at me, apparently as much in the dark as I am.

'I'd forgotten where you'd said the spare key was hidden,' Emily says. 'I think I was a bit drunk, and I didn't want to bother you because I knew you'd worry and come back early. I didn't want to ruin your night…'

Oh so you ruined my life instead, I think to myself.

'…so I called Luke. He came over and let me in.'

'But he stayed at Justin's that night? I know because he was still there when I went back home the next morning,' says Kate, looking at her in disbelief, not wanting to believe what she's hearing. Emily sniffs, tears still rolling down her perfectly made-up cheeks.

'He left after… after…' and she stops talking as she realises what she's just said. I feel sick. I don't want to hear any more, but I can't seem to move as I listen to her. 'Well, he let me in and said Justin was still jet-lagged from the holiday and that he'd gone straight to bed when they'd got in, so did I want a drink with him? I got so much more drunk, and I don't even know how it happened but, well, it did somehow, and I didn't mean it to, and the next morning everyone was there, and you and Luke were just so happy, and I just felt sick with guilt…'

'And so you should, you bitch!' Kate yells loudly, her eyes wide with anger. 'Em, just go. I can't even look at you. You need to not be here right now,' she says, suddenly disturbingly calm, to an inconsolable Emily.

Emily stands there shaking, just as I do behind Kate. I know I should be the one saying all this, but I can't move or speak. All I can think about is that this is my wedding day. To Luke. My Luke. Or so I thought. With his relaxed, carefree way and his floppy, black hair, his designer stubble. I think of his blue eyes and his big, wide smile. His square jaw and his broad, swimmer's shoulders. Then of him and Emily. My best friend. And the baby they are having. Then it all went black.

Chapter Three

I woke up on the landing, with my mother bending over me in floods of tears and Kate looking terrified holding a wet flannel to my throbbing head. What's going on? My first thought was 'it's my wedding day'. My second thought was 'Luke cheated on me'. With Emily and now she's pregnant. No, it wasn't some hideous dream. I fainted apparently. The last thing I remember was Kate yelling at Emily to leave, and I have no clue what happened after that. Where is she now? Maybe she's with Luke? No, don't think about that. It's now six p.m. We would have just been doing the speeches; holding hands and smiling at each other while our family and friends laugh along with us and revel in our newly wedded bliss. Instead, I'm sat at the kitchen table, nursing what seems to be my one thousandth cup of tea (I've let most of them go stone cold, undrunk), staring at the clock, while my mum and Kate exchange worried, nervous glances with each other.

'Carrie…' my mum ventures, 'Jane called again. What do you want me to say? I know this is awful, but I feel like I should tell her something at least…' She trails off and looks at Kate. 'I mean, it's not her fault her son can't keep it in his trousers and has ruined my daughter's life. And, more importantly, her wedding day!'

Through the fog in my brain, I still manage to pick up that my mum thinks the worst part of it is the wedding day ruining, rather than the life ruining.

'Sorry, Kate,' she continues as she turns to face Luke's sister, 'brother or no brother, he's done a terrible, terrible thing. I won't ever forgive him for it. Ever.'

Kate gives a snort. 'Don't worry, Alice, I one million per cent agree with you there.'

I sigh. 'Tell her what you like, Mum. Tell her to talk to her son.'

'Yes, I think she's probably done that by now, babe, which is why she's calling you.' Right on cue, Kate's phone starts to ring and she looks at the screen. 'And me,' she says pointedly, but doesn't answer it. 'I think you should talk to her. It might help.'

'Help? How could it help, Kate? Does she have a magical time machine where I can go back to a time when my fiancé, sorry *ex*-fiancé...' (My mum visibly blanches at this statement.) '...isn't a cheating piece of shit, if such a time does in fact exist. A time where he doesn't get my best friend pregnant, and I don't find out two hours before I'm supposed to become his wife! Because that would be super, fucking awesome!'

I realise I'm stood up, with my hands slammed on the table, so I sit back down and lift my fingers to my temples. It's the most I've said for the entire day, and I know it must be bad because my mum didn't even tell me off for swearing. I've let my mum and Kate field all the phone calls and make all the un-arrangements. I know Kate's spoken to Luke, because he's not tried to contact me and hasn't been back to the house. Although maybe she hasn't, and he's just not bothered. Maybe he doesn't care at all and he's glad it's all come out, so he doesn't have to marry me and can go and be a happy family with Emily.

I can't even bear to think what Kate said in the church. Does everyone think it's me? That I jilted him? That *I* made some huge mistake and have let them all down? What are they all saying now? I wonder if anyone knows the truth, and if Luke has told anyone else? I sincerely doubt anyone but him and Emily knew before her outpouring this morning. I even question whether or not he might have told Dan. Dan knew Luke liked me before I did. He knew he was going to propose before I did, so in hindsight, I guess he probably does know. I'm sure he does now anyway.

God, does that mean Dani knows? Dani is Dan's totally vile girlfriend or 'partner' as she calls herself, even though they have only been together for like six months. None of us can understand how someone as totally gorgeous as Dan – on the inside and incidentally the outside too – has managed to pick such a hideous human as Dani to share his life with. She's a personal trainer from some gym, owned by Satan I'm sure, where they point and laugh at you while you're forced to run naked on a treadmill with a pool of circling piranhas at the end. She actually called me three times in the months before the wedding to tell me that if I wanted any pre-wedding workout tips, she would be happy to 'get me off that couch and blast away all of that fat'. What was the exact phrase she used on one occasion? Ah that was it, 'because no one wants a jiggly bride'. A jiggly bride? I'm a size ten for goodness' sake! And OK, I'm not a sculpted athlete with a six-pack like Dani, but I know I'm definitely not fat. She will be dining out on this like it's a low-carb, fat-free, cacao brownie.

Who am I kidding, do I really care what Dani thinks? Actually, yes, I do. I care what everyone thinks right now. I don't want people to a) think this is my fault, because I have absolutely no doubt in my mind that this is one hundred per cent Emily and Luke's fault, and b) think I'm some pathetic case that can't even manage to hold on to her fiancé long enough for him to actually walk down the aisle and marry her without forcing him into the arms of another woman. Because I know that's not what happened. I know that things between me and Luke were good. We loved each other, we had fun. Didn't we? It was easy and safe and, OK, perhaps we didn't have so much in common as we did when we were younger, but aren't all relationships like that after a while? And that's not a bad thing, right? We had been together a long time, but we hadn't grown apart as some couples do. God, had we? Argh, I hate this. And I hate Luke. Everything I believed about our relationship no longer feels true. Was the whole of it one big, long lie? Was he always looking for an escape? Looking for someone else? It's made me doubt everything I knew about him, about us. I need to get out of here. I need to see him. I push back my chair causing a loud scraping noise on the tiles, which makes my mum and Kate jump out of their skins.

'I'm going out.' They look at me like I've just said I'm going to the moon. 'I need to see Luke.'

'Are you sure that's a good idea?' Kate ventures, hesitantly.

'Yes, are you sure?' my mum puts in. 'I don't want him to upset you.'

'Upset me?' I say with disbelief. 'What, you mean like slept with my best friend upset? Got her pregnant upset? Ruin my wedding day upset?'

I know I keep repeating the same things, but the more I say it the more it sinks in and I need to hear what's happening. I need to rationalise why my wedding day has gone from being one of the happiest, to one of the worst days of my life.

'Imagine, Mum, if after the day I've had, Luke could actually make me any *more* upset.'

To her credit she doesn't give me a response.

'I'll drive you,' says Kate, picking up her car keys from the worktop.

'What shall I do?' my mum asks, looking a little frantic at being left alone.

Kate puts a hand on her arm. 'Alice, you stay here, and you can field any more visitors and calls. I'll be back soon, and we can sort it all out then, OK?'

I have no idea what Kate thinks they are going to sort out, but this seems to placate my mum somewhat. I walk out of the door leaving Kate to follow me before they can say anything else.

Chapter Four

Kate wisely, either through fear or lack of knowledge of what to say, stays silent on the way. I don't even know where we are going, since I've not spoken to Luke and I don't know where he is. As we turn right at the end of the road, I realise we are heading in the direction of Dan's house. Dan is Luke's best mate and his best man, so I'm guessing Luke's still there from getting ready this morning. They lived together until he moved in with me, so the route's a familiar one. Kate pulls on to the driveway, turns off the engine and shifts in her seat to look at me.

'Do you want me to come in?'

I think about it for a second, but I don't even think I can get my legs to the door on my own.

'Yes please,' I nod.

Kate rings the bell and takes my hand in hers. I'm shaking, and my stomach feels like a washing machine. I'm not sure if it's nerves, anger, sadness or something else entirely. It must only be about ten seconds before the door opens, but it feels like the longest ten seconds of my life. Then I'm greeted by Dan, whose face is set in a look of pity, fear and what, slightly sickeningly, looks a lot like guilt.

'Carrie...' he says. He doesn't seem in any way surprised to see me, so I guess Kate texted him to let him know we were coming. I'm a little annoyed, as I had kind of hoped for the element of surprise, but I can sort of see why she did. At least this way Luke had time to stew waiting for me. Pig. I look up at Dan and, instantly, I know he knows what's coming.

'Did you know?'

He runs his hands through his hair and sighs.

'No.'

'Did. You. Know?' I say through gritted teeth. 'And don't you dare lie to me, Dan, I swear...' I point my finger at him like a schoolteacher.

Dan is, without question, one of the nicest people you will ever meet. Certainly that I have ever met. He's classically handsome, with striking green eyes, thick, strawberry blonde hair complete with a smattering of gorgeous freckles across his nose that just add to his nice guy persona. He gets a lot of people say he reminds them of Prince Harry, and I think that's actually the main reason Dani likes him, to be honest. He and Luke met at Scouts, when they were little, and have been inseparable ever since, so he became like one of the family with us all spending Christmases and birthdays together. He lost his dad when he was small, and his mum, who is also one of the nicest people ever, became close to my mum, due to her incredible support, when my own dad died.

'Carrie, I only found out this morning, I promise you.' He takes hold of my shoulders and looks me straight in the eyes. 'Luke's my best mate, but we're all like family. I wouldn't lie to you, not about this, I swear.'

He pulls me into a hug, whether I like it or not, but I'm too tired to fight it so I let him. I pull away as I feel tears threatening to fall, and he looks to Kate then me.

'He's in the kitchen,' he says to both of us.

I step forward and Kate touches my arm.

'We'll wait in the garden, OK?' She looks at Dan, who nods in agreement, and despite his actual innocence in all this, I can tell he feels guilty by association.

I open the kitchen door and see Luke sat at the table with his head in his hands. He stands the second he sees me and goes to take a step towards me until I hold up my hand to halt him in his tracks. I can't have him near me right now. He rubs his hand across his mouth and gestures for me to sit down, but I walk to the kitchen counter and lean against it. He slumps down into his chair and looks up at me, shaking his head. The silence weighs so heavy in the room, but there's no way in hell I'm going to make this easy for him by being the one to break it.

'Carrie… I… shit,' he begins. Oh, I'm so pleased to see he's really thought about what he's going to say to me. He stands up and starts pacing the kitchen. 'God, I just… I mean… I'm so, so sorry. I never meant…'

'Never meant to what, Luke?' I say, my own voice trembling as I try to keep calm. 'Never meant to cheat on me? To sleep with my best friend? To get her pregnant? To ruin the happiest day of my life? To publicly humiliate me? Lie to me? Destroy everything we built together? What Luke? What exactly did you never mean to do?'

I can feel my voice getting more and more irate, so I take a deep breath to calm myself down. He's hanging his head in shame and looks up to meet my eyes which I am sure are blazing with rage right now.

'All of it, Carrie. God, this was the worst mistake of my life, and I'm paying for it so dearly. I love you so much. I want to marry you.'

Even with tears running down his cheeks, he looks so gorgeous. He's still wearing the dark grey suit trousers and crisp, white shirt we picked out together for our wedding day. It takes all my self-control not to reach out and touch him in that moment. What a coward.

'Well, I'm sure your son or daughter will be thrilled to hear you say that when they're older. How could you, Luke? How *could you*?' I yell at him and he jumps at my outburst. He opens his mouth to speak again, but I interrupt him. Nothing he says will change my mind, nothing. He's a different person to me now. He's not the man I knew, not the man I thought he was.

'Save it, Luke, honestly. I don't even know why I came. I know exactly what you're going to say, and I don't want to hear it. You're sorry, you never meant it to happen, you love me. Well it means absolutely fuck all now. There is no way back from this. None.'

'Carrie, please just wait… What are you going to do?'

I start towards the door, and he goes to follow me out. I sigh and stop, as I turn to face him. 'I don't know, Luke, but I know what I'm *not* going to do and that's marry you.' And then it hits me. 'Actually, do you know what? I do know what I'm going to do.'

I think he thinks I'm going to slap him across the face, because he takes a step back. Oh, how I would love to, but I won't sink to violence just yet. I walk out of the front door just in time to glimpse Dan holding Kate's hand in his, and then drop it immediately when he sees me. Had it been another day I would have asked them what was going on but, quite frankly, they are the least of my worries right now. Kate jumps off the wall, while Dan flits his gaze between me and Luke looking concerned.

'Carrie, wait!' Luke calls after me, but I ignore him.

I hear Dan say quietly, 'Give her some space, mate, yeah?'

'Kate?' I hear Luke's voice call hopefully.

Kate turns to face her brother, her face like thunder, as she jabs a finger in his direction. '*You*, I will speak to later on.'

'Where are we going?' she asks, as I get in the car and we pull away from the house. I draw a long breath and try to steady my nerves.

'Right now we are going home and then on Monday, you're taking me to the airport and I am going on my honeymoon.'

'What? Carrie, what are you talking about? You can't just go!' I can hear the panic in her voice. 'You can't just leave! You need to be around people right now.'

'Actually, Kate, I think that's the last thing I need. Everyone and everything here reminds me of Luke.'

Her face looks so sad all of a sudden, as she takes in the full meaning of what I've just said.

'Sorry, but even you. And I need some space, some time to think about where I go from here. I have two weeks, all paid for, in a luxury hotel, thousands of miles from here. I'm going to go, gather my thoughts and come back and decide what to do. I don't want to be here, Kate. I can't be here. I don't want to be anywhere near Luke.' I pause. 'Or Emily.'

This is the first time I've mentioned her name all day, and I can tell from the look on Kate's face, she doesn't know what to say.

'Carrie, about the baby...' she says warily.

I hold up both of my hands to protest. 'Kate, please, I don't want to know.'

'He asked Dan to tell me, he doesn't want it. He's even asked Emily to consider having an abortion.' The words hang in the air for a second.

'For God's sake, Kate, that makes it worse not better! Jesus! Right now I can't believe this is the same man I agreed to marry, that I actually wanted to spend the rest of my life with.'

Kate hesitates for a second. 'I know. That's what I said. I'm disgusted with him.' She sighs deeply. 'God, I can't believe we are even related! I think he's trying to do what he thinks is the right thing, the thing that he thinks you'll want and getting it all wrong.'

'How on earth could he think that would be what I want? Like that's the solution to the problem? Does he even know me at all? It's too late, Kate, you know it is. He perhaps should have realised that the thing I *didn't* want would be for him to shag my best friend! Him not wanting this baby, well that just proves he's absolutely not the person I thought he was.'

I stare out of the window not quite daring to ask the question I know I'm going to have to or it will eat away at me.

'What's she going to do?'

'Emily you mean?'

'Yes. Is she going to keep it?' It. Poor baby. It's done nothing wrong, none of this is 'Its' fault and I can't even bring myself to call it a baby, just 'It'.

Kate gives a very small nod.

'Yeah, Dan said the... other option most definitely isn't an option as far as she's concerned.'

A heavy silence falls between us for a moment.

'You're going to be an auntie.'

Kate's eyes fill with tears, as she pulls over and turns off the ignition.

'Carrie, I don't know what to do. He's my brother and I hate him, but I can't just disown him, you know that. As much as I want to right now. And if he's not involved in the baby's life then, well, I have to be. I can't let it down too, it's innocent in all this. I'm sorry, but it's coming into a world that's enough of a mess as it is but, know this, I will never forgive Emily for what she's done. Ever.' She takes my hands in hers. 'I love you, you're my best friend. I'm sorry, I just don't know what to do.'

I drop her hands and pull her into a hug, my tears falling now too.

'Oh, Kate, it's not your fault. Any of this. I don't blame you. I love you too.'

'Please stay, Carrie. I don't want you to go away. I want you here where I can make sure you're alright.'

'Kate, I can't. You know I can't. This will be good. I need this. Please understand.'

'I do, it's just... Are you sure? I really don't like the idea of you being all alone, so far away, with your thoughts and no one to talk to. I don't think it's a good idea. It's not going to make you feel any better.'

'Honestly, Kate, think about it. Even if you're right, how much more shit can I feel?'

Chapter Five

I arrive at the airport in Barbados after what was one of the most luxurious and depressing flights of my life. Thanks to there being a note on my booking saying I was part of a newly-wed couple, I was greeted by two glasses of champagne in the first-class lounge and a couple's massage voucher, only to see the pitying looks on people's faces when I explained it was just me. One young girl at the counter actually gasped and threw her hand over her mouth in horror, like I was some sort of social pariah.

I hadn't even thought to call the hotel in advance to say it was just going to be me (funnily enough, my mind was elsewhere), so I was greeted by a tall, slender, middle-aged man with short hair and a close-cut beard. His hair was greying slightly at the temples, which was the only thing that gave away his age, as his face was wrinkle-free. He was wearing an incredibly smart suit, which bore the gold-threaded logo I recognised from all the literature and the website of our, sorry, *my*, five-star, all-inclusive resort on the breast pocket. He was holding a big sign that read 'Mr & Mrs Croft'. Jesus. I started to see a pattern emerging and realised this was going to happen for the entire trip. I walked over to him, and his friendly face broke into a welcoming smile as he held out his hand to me.

'Good morning and welcome to Barbados! Mrs Croft I presume? My name is Michael, and I'll be escorting you to your hotel today. Is your husband far behind you?' he asked glancing over my shoulder. Yes, try four thousand miles far behind.

'Well, no, I mean, yes. Actually, it's just me.'

I don't offer any further explanation. Michael tilts his head to one side as he considers his response for a moment.

'Ah. Well. Just you right now or just you for the whole trip?' he asks slowly. His voice has a soft Bajan lilt to it that's incredibly soothing.

'Just me. For the whole trip. And it's Miss Kingston. Carrie.'

God bless Michael. If he was surprised he didn't let it show, and he's clearly picked up on what I was trying to infer. Without missing a beat he reaches for my case and starts across the forecourt to the car park as he turns to me, smiling.

'I'm right over here. Please follow me, Miss Kingston. The drive won't take long, we should be at the hotel in around half an hour. Would you like me to call ahead and let them know of the change of plans?'

Yes, that I'm a jilted spinster with a lowlife, father-to-be, ex-fiancé. I decide on a more tactful approach. 'Yes please, that would be very kind.'

I suspect, from the reception I've been given so far, that the hotel wouldn't have let our arrival go without ceremony or occasion. I can just see them now, rushing about our room, or rather honeymoon suite, like maniacs hoovering up rose petals, blowing out candles and wheeling chilled buckets of champagne out of sight.

I don't even hear Michael make the call, as I look out of the window to take in the scenery as we pass by. Even though it's only nine thirty a.m. and the sky is fairly cloudy, it's still so bright that I find myself reaching into my bag to dig out my sunglasses. We pass a mixture of small, wooden, newly built houses, all in pastel pinks, blues and yellows, coupled with the much larger, gated homes set back from the road. They're bunched together in clusters of threes and fours, surrounded by fruit trees and tall palms. Every now and again, I catch a glimpse of the sea from in between the buildings, until we take a steep drive down towards it and reach the coastal road, following the line of the shore that takes us along the western side of the island to St James. We drive past an assortment of hotels, shops and restaurants and bars, all interspersed with white, sandy beaches and the bright blue sea. It really is picture-perfect. I let my head drop back against the warm leather of the headrest, close my eyes and take a deep breath. This is going to be just what I need.

I feel the car come to a stop, as I open my eyes, and see we've pulled into a large, turning circle, complete with a fountain in the middle and surrounded by lush, green grass. Gates on either side of the fountain bear the hotel crest of two, crossed palm trees with 'Palm Bay Hotel' written in gold across the middle.

Michael steps out of the car and opens my door. Within moments there are two extremely strapping men rushing forward to collect my bags from the boot and load them on to a trolley. Michael ushers me inside the cool, air-conditioned reception where every surface is coated with cool, cream marble and dark grey, velvet chairs populate the corners and surround a number of small tables. The effect is striking.

'This is where I leave you, Miss Kingston. Maya on reception will take good care of you from here.' He gestures towards the front desk and an extremely beautiful woman nods at Michael and gives me a beaming smile, flashing her perfect teeth. Maya has light brown, braided hair piled on top of her head in a huge bun and bright red lipstick that perfectly complements her flawless, caramel skin tone. I suddenly feel shabby and underdressed.

'I hope you have a good stay, madam,' Michael says and, although I've only said about ten words to him and known him for all of half an hour, I feel strangely sad that he's leaving. His presence was somehow calming and felt like a real comfort. 'And may I add, if I'm not speaking out of turn, try to relax. These things have a way of working themselves out. Most of the time without our realising it.'

Unexpectedly, my eyes fill with tears as they meet his. 'Thank you, Michael,' I manage, trying to hold it together, 'I'll try and remember that.'

And with that he turns and leaves.

Once Maya, who was very kind and made absolutely no reference to me being here alone thanks to Michael's forewarning, has checked me in, she walks me to the lift and up to my suite. It is the biggest hotel room I have seen in my entire life. It spans across a corner of the hotel on the fifth, and top, floor and has the most stunning views of the ocean and beautiful beach below. The bed stands in the middle of the room, with a large, velvet ottoman at its foot. Off to my right is a lounge with two double sofas – velvet again – and a huge, flat-screen TV fixed to the wall. To my left I can see the bathroom and take a step inside to investigate further. I've always loved hotel bathrooms. I don't know what it is but there's something so satisfying about them. I'm definitely not disappointed by this one. It's compete with two sinks, a huge corner bath, which looks like a Jacuzzi from the holes I can see around the sides, and a gigantic walk-in shower spanning half the wall. Two sinks. Won't be needing those!

In between the bed and the bathroom is another door with floor-to-ceiling slats across it. I look at Maya who walks over to it and opens it up.

'Your walk-in wardrobe,' she explains. *Oh yes.* Thank you very much! There is a ridiculously large amount of hanging space, shoe racks, drawers and at the end of it, a massive, full-length mirror that covers the entire wall. The bright spotlights do me no favours whatsoever and only serve to highlight how terrible I look. I vow to actually make an effort on this trip and not let myself go completely.

Maya exits the wardrobe and gestures for me to follow her out of the large, glass doors that lead off the bedroom and on to an enormous balcony. It follows the curve of the hotel, all the way round my suite, to meet the doors of the lounge and comfortably has space for two sunloungers, a small coffee table and a larger dining table with four chairs, all in a dark grey wood with cream cushions.

'Now this is my favourite part,' says Maya, bringing my attention to the centre of the balcony, between the two sets of doors. My eyes widen as I take it in and, in spite of how crap I'm feeling right now, I can't help but smile. A hot tub. It has perfect views over the sea and is large enough for around five people, let alone two. Or one.

'Wow,' is all I can manage. 'This is the most incredible hotel I have ever been in, hands down. 'Thank you, Maya, this is wonderful.'

'I hope you have a very good stay with us. You can dial zero for reception from your phone, it's nine for room service, which is twenty-four hours, and eight for the bookings desk, which takes care of any trips, tours or activities you might want to partake in. There's all the literature next to your bed, and I'll be happy to talk you through any of it, but for now I'll let you get settled and unpack. Your bags are just through there. Please do let me know if you need anything. Anything at all.'

I hadn't even noticed my luggage had arrived, I was so engrossed in my suite.

'Thank you very much,' I say resisting the urge to give her a hug. I think the lack of sleep is making me extra emotional. That and the fact that everyone is being so nice to me.

'Your wristband is right here,' she says as she passes me a bright yellow, rubber bracelet with 'Palm Bay Resort' written in gold. 'Just show this at any of our outlets and you'll be taken care of. I'll be on my way now.'

She leaves without another word, giving me a friendly smile as she closes the door behind her, and for the first time since my dad died, I feel truly alone.

Chapter Six

After a long nap, and what felt like an even longer shower, I start to feel a little more human again. I unpack, which is actually fun given the fact I have a huge walk-in wardrobe to try and fill, but I suddenly feel light-headed, which isn't surprising, seeing as I haven't eaten since breakfast on the plane and that I barely touched.

I decide to go in search of food and water and pull on my denim shorts and white, halterneck top. I look in the mirror and immediately change my top to a loose-fitting, black vest. My pale skin and the white made me look transparent. Let's give it a day or two of tanning before I chance it again.

I throw some sun cream into a bag, pick up my key card and shuffle into my brand new flip-flops, chucking the packing into the bin on the floor. Kate bought them for me for this trip. Kate. I said I would call her when I arrived, but I can't face it right now. I glance at my phone that's been charging on the side and realise I should at least let my mum know I'm here safely. I fire off a quick text.

Hi Mum, I'm here OK. Good flight, great hotel! Going to get something to eat. Leaving my phone in the room so will call tonight. C xxxx

As I exit my messages, I see I have three new emails. One from an online wedding website, congratulating me on my big day. Delete. One from the wedding venue. Ugh. Read later. And one from Luke. I'm undecided whether or not to open it and finally decide to not let it ruin my first day. Whatever he has to say isn't going to change anything, so it can wait. I came here to get away from him, so I'm in no rush to see what he wants. Besides, I like the idea of making this difficult for him and not jumping to attention as soon as he decides to get in touch.

Nothing from Emily, and I don't know if that's a good or a bad thing. I'm not sure if I want to hear from her or not. I think about it for a moment and decide that, for now, I probably don't. What would she have to say that could make me begin to forgive her? If she even wants my forgiveness that is, since she's not been in touch. Maybe all along she was waiting for me to find out, so she could have him all to herself and raise *their* child. I feel like her betrayal is almost worse than Luke's. Is it wrong for me to feel that way? All those times I've told her things, things about our relationship, the times I've bitched about Luke when he's annoyed me, and when I've called her straight away when he's done something lovely and I was bursting with excitement to share it with someone. Has all the advice she's ever given me been part of some big agenda to steal my fiancé?

I feel sick. I suppose it didn't seem like that from that fatal phone conversation I overheard, I admit. Deep down, I think I know that's not what it was but, right now, I'm too angry with her, and it's still too raw for me to think logically about it. God, I need a drink. Luckily, I have a magic, little wristband that allows me to go straight downstairs and acquire just that.

As I take the lift down to the bottom floor I can't help but feel a tad nervous. This is the first time I've ever been on holiday on my own, and the scale of what I've signed up for by coming away to a place I don't know, for two weeks all alone, has finally hit me. What the hell am I doing? I can't just run away and think it will all be fixed when I get back. No, stay calm, it's fine. This is going to be good for me. I need the space. I don't want to be anywhere where Luke could possibly try to see me, and I definitely don't want to be near Emily. The thought of bumping into either of them – alone or, even worse, together – would be too much to bear.

Oh God, should I just go back up to the room and stay there for two weeks? I wouldn't have to leave, they have a TV and Wi-Fi and room service. I'd be fine. I wouldn't even have to get dressed or anything. I could sunbathe on my balcony and no one would ever know I was here and, most of all, I wouldn't have to talk to anyone and explain why I'm here alone. In fact I *don't* actually have to tell anyone why, at least, not the real reason. I could be writing a travel piece for a magazine, or something like that, and be here researching hotels and resorts on the island. Perfect! Christ, is that the best backstory I can come up with? How depressing. In my made-up, fantasy life that's what I went with? I really *do* need a drink.

I'm jolted to my senses by a loud *bing* as the lift doors open, and I step out into the foyer. As I turn to my right, and towards to the reception desk, I see Maya and head over to ask her advice on somewhere casual and low-key to eat because I really don't fancy sitting at a table, fine dining alone, when I see her chatting to a tall, blonde, shirtless man with his back to me. He's leaning on the desk and whatever he's saying is making her laugh out loud and shake her head. He's wearing bright red board shorts and has a tanned, muscular back, huge thighs, toned calves and looks, from what I can see from the rear, a little bit *Baywatch*, to be honest. His body is super athletic and I find myself suddenly wishing I'd made more of an effort in the gym pre non-wedding. I go and stand next to him and, for some reason, I don't dare to look up. He's much taller than me, but at five foot two it's not hard, and I feel intimidated by his obvious confidence. Well, that and his annoyingly attractive back. Maya looks to me immediately on my arrival and gives me a friendly smile.

'Hello, Miss Kingston, how are you? Everything OK with your room?'

'Yes thank you, it's wonderful. I'm feeling much more human now! I was just wondering where I could grab a bite to eat. Nothing fancy, just a sandwich from a bar or something. Oh and it's Carrie,' I say, feeling really at ease in her company.

'Of course, Carrie.' She gives a very small nod of her head that makes me feel like royalty and reaches down below the front desk to pull out a small, colourful card which she unfolds on to the desk.

I can feel Baywatch looking at me, but I still daren't look up at him. His presence is very unnerving, and I'm finding it hard to ignore his gaze. I can almost feel the space between us buzzing. I feel him shift, so he's facing me, and as the air moves between us, my arm prickles slightly at his close proximity to me. Maya pulls out a pen and points down to what I can see to be a small map of the resort.

'This is reception here, where you are right now,' she says circling an area on the very bottom of the map, 'and if you walk down this route and through the path with the tall palms, you'll come to The Coconut Shack which does bar food and drinks all day long. You can't miss it, it's just before you get to the beach, and you'll see the large pool to your right and the waterfall plunge pool and hot tubs to your left.' She draws circles all over the map as she speaks and looks up at me. 'OK?'

'Er, yes I think so,' I say, swivelling the map around. 'I'm sure I'll find it.'

'I'll take you.' Baywatch suddenly speaks, and I'm surprised to hear he sounds British. I immediately look up, totally forgetting my earlier nerves, and I'm met with the most incredible pair of, what can only be described as, golden yellow eyes I have ever seen. I stare at him unable to speak for a moment. God, this man is gorgeous with a capital G. And possibly even O, R, G, E, O, U, S as well. Even more so from the front than from the back. He's tanned, clean-shaven and has thick, messy, bright blonde hair, no doubt bleached from the sun, that he's pushed back off his face to reveal those captivating eyes that seem to be completely disarming me.

I've been with Luke as long as I can remember and never has another man caught my attention, but something about Baywatch has my stomach churning and my pulse racing. It's like the air is alive with electricity, and I feel my cheeks heating up. What the hell is going on?

'Er…' I say, looking at Maya for some sort of assistance as, apparently, I've lost the power of speech. She gives an almost imperceptible shake of her head, and then regains her composure.

'Miss Kingston,' she says with a sigh, 'this is Jake.'

Baywatch/Jake grins down at me, his hands on his hips. He looks like some sort of half-naked superhero. My eyes flit across his pecs and his well-toned stomach, which reveals a well-defined six-pack, until I realise he's watching me, and I quickly look away. Jesus, what's *wrong* with me? I've just been jilted by the supposed love of my life, and yet here I am drooling over some complete stranger like he's a slice of cake I'm about to devour. Get a grip.

'He's our...'

'I work here,' he says, interrupting Maya. 'Come on... Carrie, wasn't it?'

He bends his arm towards me to imply I should link mine through it, but I just stare at his huge biceps curled in front of my eyes.

'No, no, really. I'll find it. I'm a big girl, I don't need an escort,' I say, shaking my head in protest and holding up my hands. I'm aware that came out harsher than I intended so I smile, trying to come across less of a moody, ungrateful cow. 'I just mean, I don't mind getting lost. There's lots to see, I'll be fine.'

'Well, if you're sure! But if you change your mind I'm a great person to get lost with.' He gives me a totally brazen wink and is seemingly unperturbed by my rebuffal.

Was he flirting with me? Don't be ridiculous, Carrie, I've just seen him charming Maya, and he's quite clearly got a way with the ladies. I watch as he bows extravagantly to her before flashing me a dazzling smile and heading off through the doors to the terrace. I watch his honed body disappear off into the bright sunshine. What does he do here, I wonder? He looks like a lifeguard, but has the body of a personal trainer, and is dressed and tanned like he works on the beach. Maybe he's part of the water sports team or something?

I try to think back to my relationship with Luke in the early days. Granted we were teenagers, so it was a different kind of attraction back then – like a boy band infatuation – but has he ever made the hairs on my arms stand on end? I mean, he must have done at one point, I'm sure, otherwise I wouldn't have agreed to marry him, right? I know Luke's good looking, but maybe I got too complacent and didn't see it. Maybe I wasn't attentive enough, didn't fancy him enough. Maybe that's why he went off with Emily. No, this is *not* my fault, I remind myself. No matter what was happening in our relationship, nothing will ever excuse his behaviour. I hate that I'm second-guessing all the aspects of our lives together now. *Did* we have problems and I just didn't see them? I mean, we did disagree on some of the things for the wedding and, now I think about it, most of the things Luke suggested were nothing like I'd imagined my wedding day turning out. I suppose I caved on some things because of our parents and, well, I got swept up in it all and went along with most things just to keep everyone happy. But was *I* happy? Now I don't even know.

I think of my mum and dad and Kate and Justin. Two solid couples. At least I thought the latter were until I saw her and Dan looking shifty the other day. Something that, despite my own troubles, has been playing on my mind. Were Luke and I like my parents? Could I see us getting old together, really and truly, now I think about it? I honestly don't think I ever really looked that far ahead, which I know sounds ridiculous as I had agreed to marry him, but because we had been together so long, marriage just seemed like the logical step for us. Oh, why did I seem to have all the answers to these questions before? Perhaps it's because I never actually asked myself the questions and was just plodding along, blissfully unaware, thinking this was how life was supposed to be. Maybe it takes something like your fiancé sleeping with your best friend, and finding out on your wedding day, to truly be able to take a look at your life and assess it for what it really was. For everything I thought it was, it now seems to be the complete opposite.

As a growl in my stomach turns my attention back to the job in hand, I decide to stop obsessing over Luke (that and stop my daydreaming over Baywatch) and head off to look for the bar. I wave to Maya, who's now on the phone, and slide on my shades, as I wander outside. The heat of the midday sun hits me immediately, in contrast with the cool, air-conditioned hotel foyer. It's blissful to feel the warmth on my skin, and I look up to see the cloud from this morning has cleared and the sky is bright blue. I follow the path that Maya marked out for me and, despite Baywatch/Jake insinuating I needed an escort, I find it straight away.

The Coconut Shack sits right on the beach where the edge of the pool area meets the sand. It's a large, round, well, shack I suppose, made entirely from wood and the bar follows the curve of the building and goes all the way round it in a full circle. There are a number of wooden tables and chairs that sit under its large canopy, circling all the way round the building like a moat. I head to the bar and pick up a menu, as young guy, in a dark red polo shirt sporting the familiar hotel logo and beige shorts, pops out from a door in the middle of the building and meets me as I get to the bar.

'Good afternoon, ma'am. Welcome to The Coconut Shack! What can I do for you today? You thirsty? Hungry? Or all of the above?' he claps his hands and rubs them together in anticipation of my order and gives me a big, eager grin. 'I'm Dale and your wish is my command, miss.'

I laugh at how incredibly happy and upbeat he is, as I take off my shades. He has deep, brown eyes and short, tight dreadlocks that stick up off his head about half an inch and wiggle as he bounces around. He's cute but in a 'this is my cute, younger cousin' sort of a way. He's probably in his late twenties but has a baby face that makes him look much younger.

'Hello Dale, I'm Carrie,' I say politely, 'and I'm all of the above. What can you recommend?'

'Well it's all good, my dear,' he says passing me a menu and pointing to a dish halfway down. 'But the fishcakes are definitely worth trying at some point, so no time like the present. How does that sound? Am I floating your boat?' I laugh at his shameless, but ultimately harmless, flirting.

'You're the boss,' I say, smiling back at him. 'And I'm happy to take your recommendation on cocktails too, that is if it's not too early?'

'Hell no, girl!' he yells, slapping his thighs like he's in panto and beaming at me. 'You're in the Caribbean now. There ain't no such thing as too early. Or too late for that matter! You leave this to me.'

As he jogs off with all the enthusiasm of a puppy, I pull up a bar stool that faces out over the beach and climb up on to it. *Damn, I really should have brought a book to read so I don't look like such a loner*, I think as I glance around. I didn't really think this whole travelling alone thing through, did I? But, in my defence, I have had other things on my mind. I look down to the beach and the sea looks so inviting, I decide to take myself off to give it a quick inspection.

'Er, Dale…?'

Suddenly a head pops round the corner.

'Hey, you rang?'

'I'm just going to take a quick walk on the beach. I'll be back in a few minutes, is that OK? I'll just leave my bag here, there's nothing valuable in it.'

'Hey, take as long as you like, girl. I'll keep your drink iced. You have no fear when Dale is here!' and his head darts back in.

I step down off the decking and make my way through the cluster of cabanas and sunbeds, that match the ones on my balcony, and head towards the bright blue sea, its surface sparkling as the sun bounces off it, reflecting its rays back to shore. I head straight down to the water and feel suddenly calmer as a wave breaks and washes over my feet and ankles. I turn and walk along the beach, parallel to the sea, and look up at the hotel trying to spot my room. I see it immediately, as the huge balcony is a total giveaway and it's the only one of its kind on this side of the hotel. I feel rather smug, knowing that's where I'm staying. I look back out to sea and can see a huge cruise liner making its way around the coast. Now that would have been pretty cool, to disappear off on a ship in the middle of the ocean, then there would have definitely been no way anyone could have found me. I feel a sudden presence behind me, and I know instantly, without turning around, who it is.

'So where's the lucky fella then? If you were my wife I wouldn't let you out of my sight.'

I turn around slowly to see Jake beaming at me. Luckily, he has shades on, so I'm not forced to look into those pools of golden loveliness.

'Excuse me?' I say raising my eyebrows and my voice at the same time.

'Come on, he can't be bored of you just yet! I know they say marriage makes things boring, but you can't have driven him away already?' He's grinning away to himself, and I'm getting more and more confused, not to mention angry.

'What the hell do you mean?' I say crossly, suddenly losing my cool. 'And who the hell do you think you are?'

Now it's his turn to look confused.

'Woah! Take it easy, I was only joking…! To say you've just got married, sweet cheeks, you're a tad tetchy. I'd have a word with that husband of yours if I was you. Does he know you're going to be this much trouble to live with? I mean, I actually kind of like it, it's very sexy…' he laughs.

He's hit every raw nerve in my body, and it opens the flood gates. I burst into tears, and he looks horrified. He instantly steps towards me to envelope me in a huge hug, whether I like it or not.

'What are you doing?' I ask between my sobs, my voice muffled against his skin. I gently try to push him away, but he holds me tight and, if I'm honest, he smells divine, like coconut and saltwater, so I'm not actually trying very hard. My cheek is pushed against his chest, and his skin is hot to the touch. I feel like my whole face is on fire. He gently releases me but doesn't completely let go, as he looks down, his face full of concern.

'Are you OK? Has someone hurt you? Is it your husband?'

'What are you talking about? I don't *have* a husband! Who told you I did?'

'You did. Well, your shoes did.'

I automatically look down at my feet and then back up to him even more confused now than ever. 'What *are* you going on about?'

'Look!' and he points to the sand where I've just been walking, his eyes wide. I put my head in my hands following his gaze and see footprint after footprint marked with *just* and *married* that's been imprinted on the sand by the soles of my flip-flops.

'Oh, bloody Kate!' I actually growl, as I hop around and pull off the traitorous footwear, hurling them on to the sand like a mad woman. I take a deep breath and bury my hands in my hair. He gently cups my elbow and runs his hand up my arm making my hairs stand on end. I wish my body would control itself, but I don't seem to be in any control of anything right now by the rate these tears are coming.

'Look, I'm not exactly sure what's going on here, but I think you could use a drink and a chat. So please, just come with me and try not to yell any more, OK?'

I can hear the smile in his voice, and I risk a look up at him. He has his sunglasses pushed into his hair and his eyes are dancing as they look at me. He nods towards the bar. Hell, I think to myself walking barefoot across the beach, what have I got to lose?

Chapter Seven

My tears are still in full flow as I follow Jake down the beach, back to The Coconut Shack. It's like a switch inside me has flipped, letting all the emotions from the last few days come flooding out, and I can't turn it off. He puts his hand on the small of my back, as he guides me to a table away from the beach where it's quieter. It's an incredibly intimate gesture, and I wonder if he doesn't realise or just doesn't care that he's touching a complete stranger.

He waves his hand silently at Dale who responds with a nod of the head and disappears. Jake pulls out my chair, and I slump down into it. He doesn't say anything, as he takes the chair opposite mine, but I can feel him staring at me, as he allows a silence to settle between us to give me some time to compose myself. I'm aware of two drinks being set between us, as I finally look up at him.

'Sorry,' I sniff, smiling gratefully as he passes me a napkin. 'It's been a rough few days, and I think it's only just hit me. I'm never normally like this.'

'That's OK, I'm not judging. You obviously needed a good cry. Are you ready to tell me what's happened? I'm not forcing you, but I'm a good listener, and I promise you can trust me. It won't go any further.' He pauses, but I don't respond. 'Come on, it's your holiday right? Don't start it like this. You're meant to be having a good time. Let's get whatever's bothering you sorted, and we can enjoy ourselves. No one deserves to be this upset.'

I'm vaguely aware that he said *we* not *you*, and my stomach does another involuntary flip. I reach forward and take a long sip of my drink which tastes very much like a strong rum punch. It's sweet, sharp and delicious. I sit back in my chair and take a deep breath, as I tell him about everything that's happened and he listens patiently. He doesn't interrupt me once, he just lets me talk and talk and talk until I give him a rueful smile.

'And, well, there you have it. That's about the long and short of it.'

He pushes his hair back off his face and leans forward on the table. He exhales slowly, blowing a long puff of air out of his lips, and my eyes are drawn instantly to his mouth. 'Well, fuck.'

'I know,' I reply.

He doesn't say anything for a long moment, and I wonder what he's thinking.

'Let's get some food.'

'What?' OK, I didn't think he was thinking *that*.

'Food. You need to eat. Dale,' he calls over in the direction of the bar, 'what's on the menu today?'

'Well, your date ordered fishcakes, but I, er, wasn't sure when was a good time to serve them…'

I smile at his thoughtfulness. 'Now would be lovely,' I say, as I realise I am actually starving. All this woe works up a real appetite.

'Make that two,' Jake adds. Dale gives a little salute and heads off again.

Jake sighs, and as I sit forward leaning my elbows on the table (my mother would be horrified) I notice he mirrors my action.

'Look, I'm really sorry about what I said on the beach. I had no idea that… well, I had no idea.'

'It's OK. Really. You didn't know. I'm sorry I had such a meltdown. Thanks for being so nice. I think I needed to get it all off my chest. All my friends and family are caught up in it too so to talk to someone else, I think it's helped.' And I honestly do.

'So, what are you going to do?' he asks hesitantly.

'Well, me and Luke are over. For good. All the trust has gone, and I've realised that maybe things weren't as perfect as I thought they were. I was just going along with what I thought my life should be, without really stopping to think if it was what I wanted. I mean, even if we didn't love each other like we should have done, surely he should have respected me enough not to shag my best friend?'

'Yes, I would say so.' Jake reaches for his drink and clinks the edge of his glass against mine. 'Cheers.'

'To what?' I ask, wondering what on earth I could have to celebrate.

'To you. You're going through a rough patch. But that's all it is. You're going to come out the other side of it, you know that don't you? And you'll love your life and yourself better for it at the end. I don't claim to know you well or know this Luke guy, but no one deserves to be treated the way he treated you. It sounds to me like he was all set to go ahead and marry you, when he knew all this was going on, and that was OK by him. He was willing to potentially screw up your life and give you no say in the matter whatsoever. He sounds pretty shitty to me.'

'I just keep overthinking everything all the time. Going over and over the same stuff. And I hate that. The more I think about it, the less I'm hurt over Luke, which sounds stupid because I had said I'd spend the rest of my life with him, but I'm more hurt by the loss of my best friend. You always think your friends are going to be the constant in your life, no matter what happens. I must sound mental. I'm sorry, I don't know why I'm telling you all this.'

'Because I asked. And it does no good to go over it in your head alone. Trust me. Talking about it is better than not, even if it is hard right now. But friends aren't always rated as the people who you've known the longest. That doesn't make someone a good friend. And I know that from experience.' He takes a long swig of his drink, as I digest what he's just said. I'm suddenly aware that he's taken my hand in his and is slowly running his thumb over my knuckles. I go to withdraw my hand, feeling embarrassed at the contact, but he holds it tighter and it forces me to look up and meet his gaze, his face serious.

'You've been dealt a bad hand, gorgeous. I know you've got to get things straight in your head, but you can sit here for days, weeks, months even, going over it, trying to piece it all together. Or you can just say fuck it and move the hell on.'

He shrugs his shoulders and smiles at me as he releases the hold on my hand. I can still feel his touch on my skin, as I stare at the spot where he's touched it.

'Is that what you'd do?' I ask quietly.

He smiles gently. 'Yes, gorgeous, that's exactly what I'd do.'

He stretches back in his chair and raises his arms above his head, as my eyes wander down to the line of hair that disappears down the top of his shorts. Christ, he is really hot. I don't know if it's because of the physical contact he keeps dishing out – which he is clearly so unfazed by – or because, quite frankly, I'm enjoying the attention, but I can feel a few, tiny butterflies dancing in my stomach. My daydream is broken by Dale placing two plates of delicious-looking fishcakes and a basket of sweet potato fries in front of us.

'God, I'm starving,' I say digging my fork straight in. I catch him watching me, as I shove a huge forkful of food into my mouth and quickly cover it with my hand, embarrassed. His mouth turns up at the corners, and he digs into his food.

'So how long are you staying then?' he asks me, casually popping a chip into his mouth.

'I'm booked in for two weeks, and I only arrived this morning so I have plenty of time left.'

'For what?' he asks as his lips curl up at the corners again. Is he laughing at me?

'For… you know, anything…' I mumble feeling slightly flustered.

'Oh yeah? Well sounds like the world's your oyster, sweet cheeks.' He tilts his head to one side and narrows his eyes at me. 'You ever been jet-skiing?' he asks out of nowhere.

'No, but I've always wanted to!' I answer honestly. Whenever I've been away on holiday, I have always sat on the beach longing to try the jet skis. We all usually went away in a group. Me, Luke, Kate, Emily, Dan and whoever his latest conquest was at the time, that was our holiday squad. Aside from the few city breaks me and Luke did together, we always went as a group. Luke was definitely *not* into water sports. He thought they were too dangerous and didn't trust any of the equipment apparently. Now I think he was just being a wuss. To be honest, I was surprised when he picked Barbados as a honeymoon destination, since he repeatedly says he gets so bored sat on the beach, but I've always wanted to come, and I have a strong suspicion this was more Kate's doing than Luke's. Breaking my thoughts, Jake suddenly stands up, sliding on his shades, and pushes back his chair.

'Tomorrow. I'll take you. Meet me here at say ten a.m.?'

'Well, I'll have to see if I can fit you between self-pitying and wallowing in despair. I'm terribly busy.'

He winks at me and turns to leave, giving Dale a high five over the bar as he passes.

'Tomorrow,' he calls over his shoulder and disappears towards the pool area at a jog. I feel a little disappointed at the abrupt way he's ended our lunch, but I presume, from what he and Maya said, that's he's most likely at work right now.

Looking at my watch it's almost three p.m. Definitely time I called home or my mum will be completely freaking out. I decide to head back to the room, call my mum and take a look at some of the things-to-do leaflets Maya left in my room before I head down to dinner. Alone. Not a prospect I am relishing, if I'm totally honest. I may need a few more rum punches before that one. Dale heads over to our table as I stand up.

'Excellent recommendation. The fishcakes were delicious, thank you.'

'No worries at all. I'm glad you liked them. See you've been making friends already?' he says with a raise of his eyebrow. 'Only been here a few hours and already got yourself a lunch date! That's quick work. Even puts my moves to shame.'

I laugh and shake my head. 'No, it was more of a therapy session than a date. I'm not sure how it happened really.' Does Dale really think it's a date?

'Ha! That's normally *my* line of defence. Did I hear a second date tomorrow too? Damn, you're on fire!'

'It's only jet-skiing. And he's just being nice because he works here and I'm a paying guest. It's really nothing more than that.'

But something at the back of my mind, and in the pit of my stomach, tells me I'm not one hundred per cent sure I totally believe it.

Chapter Eight

I don't quite know why, but I'm really dreading calling my mum. In fact, no, that's wrong, not my mum, I'm dreading calling home. Being away from home means I can almost pretend nothing happened and try and forget all the awfulness. Any link to home, even my lovely mum, is a reminder of why I ran away in the first place. God *did* I run away? Is that all I've done? Ran and left all my problems behind that in two weeks I'm going to have to face? My mind drifts to the thought of Luke and Emily, and I quickly push them to the back of my mind. Maybe Jake was right, why go round and round punishing myself with what-ifs and what could have been? Luke and I are over. For good. As is my friendship with Emily. There really doesn't seem much reason to look back and all the reason in the world to look forward.

I think to my non-date with Jake tomorrow and feel the butterflies wake up once more. I know he's only being kind to me, especially since it was sort of his fault I burst into tears on the beach on the first day of my holiday, and I don't want to mistake his thoughtfulness for something it's not. He's an obvious flirt, and not just with me that much is for sure, but I can't deny the ridiculous things my body seems to do of its own accord in his presence and it makes me a little uneasy. I know I'm emotionally vulnerable right now, probably even a little, dare I say it, needy, so I must remind myself not to read more into it than what it is, even if he is totally gorgeous.

Back up in my room, I grab my water out of my bag, unplug my phone and settle myself on one of the sunbeds on the balcony. Two messages from Kate, a missed call from my mum and a message from Emily. I know I have to read it and, as I open Emily's message, my heart is thumping and I feel sick at the prospect of her having been in contact.

> *Carrie, I hardly even know where to start. I know nothing I say will change how you feel about me, I can't even bear to look at myself right now. I can't begin to express how horrible I feel, or go any way to make it better, but I am so, so, so sorry for everything I've done. I made one huge, stupid mistake, and I've hurt the one person who means the most to me. I know you won't ever forgive me, and I don't blame you. I will never, ever forgive myself for what happened, and I never meant for you to find out how and when you did. It was unforgivable. I don't know what the future holds for me now, but please, please know I never meant to hurt you. You were, still are to me, my best friend, and I love you so much. I will never forgive myself, Carrie, but I just needed to tell you, needed you to know that I'm so sorry. I don't expect I'll hear from you again, but if you ever want to, you know where I am. I will always want to hear from you. I'm so sorry for all of this mess. You're the*

*best person. You deserve only good things. I'm so
sorry it was me who contributed to taking your
happiness away. I'm just so sorry.
All my love, always. Em. Xxxxxxxxx*

I wipe away the tears running down my cheeks and draw
my knees up to my chest, hugging them to me tightly. She's
right. I will never forgive her. How could I? I'm so hurt by
her disloyalty, her complete and utter betrayal. I know the
tears I am crying right now aren't for me and Luke; they're
for me and her.

The more I think about Luke the more I keep coming
back to the same thought. I did love him but it was friendship
and comfort and years of history that kept us together, even
the security and familiarity of him when I lost my dad. He
was safe. And that's what I needed then. But I suddenly
realise that that's not enough, is it? To be married and to
be really in love, it needs to be more than that, to commit
to each other wholly and truly. Reading Emily's message, I
understand that it's not losing Luke that's making my heart
hurt, it's losing Emily.

I'm so angry with him, and I am beyond hurt that our
relationship meant so little to him that, after all these years,
he would cheat on me. With Emily of all people. Not some
random stranger but with someone that he knew would
hurt me the most. That's what I find most unforgivable
from him. He's not only destroyed our relationship, but
also mine and Emily's. I feel exactly the same about her
too. That she had to choose *my* fiancé to climb into bed
with and, by doing so, she knew she would ruin not only
my relationship with Luke, but our friendship as well, and

it clearly meant so little to her that she went ahead and did it anyway.

I take a swig of my water and lift my face up to the sun taking a few deep breaths, composing myself before I call my mum. Once I feel ready, I bring up her number and hit dial. She answers on the third ring.

'Carrie?'

'Hello, Mum, yes it's me.' Just hearing her voice brings me out in a big smile.

'Did you get there OK? Is everything alright?'

'Yes, I'm fine. Got here fine, hotel is gorgeous and have been down to get something to eat. Mum, I've got a hot tub on my balcony!'

'Gosh, how lovely! Is the weather nice? And are you OK, love? I do worry, you know.'

'I know you do, Mum. I'm alright. I'm just going to take some time out, gather my thoughts and I'll be ready to face it all when I get home.' I stand up and head to the edge of the balcony looking out on to the sea. 'It's gorgeous here, Mum. I can see the sea from my room and the resort is all enclosed, so it's really safe. I don't even have to leave here if I don't want to. You have nothing to worry about. Have you heard from anyone?' I ask, knowing she will understand my inference of anyone to mean Luke or Emily.

'Er, Jane came over for a cup of tea yesterday. She's mortified, Carrie. She feels so, so awful about everything. She said she feels responsible for raising a son who could behave so badly, but I told her we didn't blame her. I hope that was the right thing to do?'

'Of course, Mum. No, I don't blame her at all.'

Jane had been like a second mum to me, and I know she would be totally devastated by her son's behaviour. 'She didn't make him be unfaithful. No, Mum, the blame falls solely on him and Emily.'

There's a pause on the line before my mum speaks. 'Speaking of which, she came round last night. She didn't know you'd gone away and had presumed you wouldn't have been at your house, so she came here. I didn't let her in, but I was very good and managed to not lose my temper completely. I told her, in no uncertain terms, she wasn't welcome here and that I knew my daughter well enough to know you wouldn't want anything more to do with her and so to please leave you alone. I'm not even sure why she came. I don't think she was either, to be honest.'

Hmm. No Luke then. I think he's probably too terrified of my mum to show his face – and he's probably right on that one.

'Yeah, I had a message from her. Apologising,' is all I can mutter back to my mum.

'Lovey, you know no one thinks this is your fault, don't you?' she says sadly. 'This is nothing you did. You can come back and hold your head high, love. You've got nothing to be ashamed about. Nothing at all.'

Tears fill my eyes instantly, and I blink them away. 'I know, Mum, thanks. I'll be back soon. I just need to not be there for a bit. I'm already glad I came, I know I made the right choice.'

'Well I'm glad you're feeling a bit better, love. We go through ups and downs, life doesn't always go the way we planned but we are still here, still breathing. You pick yourself up, dust yourself off and get on with it. There's nothing else to do, Caroline.' And I know she's not only making reference to me and Luke, but to the loss of my dad too. It's a solid reminder that no matter how crap things seem right now, I've been through much worse.

'Oh, Mum,' I sniff, 'thank you. I'm doing surprisingly alright. I had a good cry today, and I feel much better, things seem much clearer.'

Even the message from Emily and hearing she's been to see my mum, can't undo the benefit that my outpouring with Jake had.

'I'm going to call Kate but will be in touch in a couple of days. Love you, Mum.'

'I love you too, darling. You take care, OK?'

We hang up and, knowing that she had booked the day off work to recover from the wedding, I decide to video call Kate so I can show her the suite. She picks up almost immediately, and her smiling face pops up on my screen.

'Carrie! It's so good to see your face. I know it's only been, what, like a day, but I miss you already! Tell me it's all totally horrible and you're coming home right now. Don't make me jealous!'

I laugh and instantly feel better for calling her.

'Here, check out my view!' I flip the camera round and give her a panorama shot from the balcony. 'Not bad, hey?'

'Not bad? It's gorgeous! Oh, I'm so glad it's a lovely place. Not that it was ever going to be anything but with me helping plan.' Ah, so it was her doing, I knew it. 'How are you, babe?' she asks. 'You doing OK?'

'Yeah, I'm alright. I had a wobble earlier on today, but I'm OK now. I'm actually feeling much better about things. I know it's over, Kate, I just need to start moving on.'

'Wow, Carrie that's… are you sure you're OK? It's only been a few days.'

'I know, but what's the point dwelling on the past now? I know I'm probably still in shock, but a bit of distance has helped. It's over, Kate. So over. Now I just need to get on with it and start getting my life back on track. I know it will be easier said than done, but I also know that's what I have to do. I can't go back to him, Kate, you know that.'

'No, I know you can't. Nor would I ever want you to. Brother or no brother, I don't blame you.'

'Hey, is that Carrie?' I hear a voice in the background, and Dan's face pops up behind Kate.

'Hey, Kingston!' he beams at me, his hands on Kate's shoulders, I notice. Normally this wouldn't have even registered with me but something has been playing on my mind since I saw the exchange between them in the garden the other day. 'How's Barbados treating you so far?'

'Hey, Dan. What are you doing there?' It sounds more accusatory than I meant it to. 'I mean, what are you guys up to?' I say, lightening my tone.

'Oh, I just popped in for a cuppa and a bit of cake. There's a lot flying about.' He laughs then suddenly realises how totally inappropriate his joke was.

'Jesus, Dan.' Kate rolls her eyes and I actually laugh.

'Oh shit! Carrie, sorry. I'm an idiot. Too soon?' He grimaces and looks utterly ashamed. I start laughing with him because it's so awkward and awful that it's actually funny.

'It's fine. It cost a bloody fortune, so you might as well enjoy it.'

'I'll call you later, OK?' Dan says to her and drops a kiss on the top of her head, as he does when he says bye to all of us, but this time I find it more intriguing than I normally would. I see her eyes follow him as he leaves.

'Where's Justin?' I ask innocently but secretly hoping she says he's home so I can stop panicking that something untoward is going on.

'He's gone into work today. He had the day booked off like we did but thought he might as well save his holiday, so he went in.'

'Oh, OK.' She would never cheat on Justin. Would she? With Dan of all people. Although, I never thought Luke would cheat on me but there we go. God, what an awful thing to think. I am a terrible friend. I inwardly curse Luke for making me think the worst of his sister. I know her and Justin are solid but, deep down, I also know something isn't quite right. We both go silent for a second before Kate bounces back as though nothing happened.

'So, anyway, take me on a tour of this suite will you, lady!' she instructs me.

Kate oohs and aahs in all the right places as I take her round my huge room and is especially impressed with the massive hot tub. 'Blimey, that's amazing! Now I really wish I'd made you take me with you.'

'It is pretty special,' I agree. 'I guess if you're going to feel crappy what better place to do it than here? I'm going to put on a nice dress and go to dinner on my own tonight, have a drink at the bar then come back to my room and watch movies with this massive bed all to myself.'

'Good for you, sweetie. Any plans for tomorrow?'

'Er, no, not really. Maybe the beach and pool, that's about it. I might check out some of the trips and water sports at some point.' I don't know why I feel the need to hide the fact I'm meeting Jake. It's not like there's anything to it but, for some reason, I don't feel comfortable sharing it with her right now.

'Sounds good. Keep in touch, honey, yeah? Love you lots and miss you.'

'I will. Love you too. Love to Justin.'

I hang up, grateful that we didn't talk about Luke or Emily. Sometimes you just need a chat with your best friend to cheer you up, but I can't shift the feeling that I know we are both keeping something from each other.

My message from Emily, and the phone calls to home, almost make me forget I still have an email from Luke to read. *Might as well get it out of the way*, I think. I tap it open and sit back on the sunbed.

> *Carrie,*
> *Please know this is the hardest email I've ever had to write, and I'm so sorry I couldn't sort myself out enough to say it all to your face when you came over to Dan's. You deserve so much better. This is all one million per cent on me. I can't believe that this is happening and, even more so, that it's of my own doing. You're the one constant thing in my life, the one I could depend on, and I let you down in the worst way possible. I can't get my head around that all the years we had together can be over, just like that.*

Yeah, well, they are pal, so you better get used to it. Can't get his head around it? Like he hadn't even considered that us breaking up was going to be an option?

I am so, so sorry for what I did. And for everything that's happened since. I don't know what the future holds for me but (and I'm so sorry because this is going to be as hard for you to hear as it is for me to write) Emily wants to keep the baby. I told her I will support her financially as best I can but that I can't promise I will be there for her and the baby in any other way. I need some time to think. Carrie, I wish I could see you. So much. To tell you how much I care about you and that I never intentionally set out to hurt you.

Care about. Not love, I notice.

Kate and Dan have both told me you're certain that it's over between us and, as much as I can't bear the thought of being without you, I understand what I would be asking of you if I asked you to stay with me, and I understand that I can't. I don't know what is going to happen in the future. I know I have a lot of bridges to build, and I would like to start with you, the most important person in all of this. I love you Carrie and I am so, so, SO sorry that I've fucked all this up. You're amazing. The most beautiful, kind and brilliant person. And I'm a complete idiot. I really hope we can sit down face-to-face and talk about all this soon. Love always, Luke. XXXXXXXXX

Yes you're right, Luke, I *am* all those things and it's a real pity you didn't realise that before you shagged Emily. So he's not asking me to get back together with him, but he does want to talk. Part of me is relieved, but the other part is annoyed. Doesn't he want to fight for me at least a little bit? Even if I have no intention whatsoever of going back to him, it would still be nice to think I meant enough to him for him to try. But who am I kidding? I know I don't really want that. I just want him to let me go.

I sit there for several minutes rereading the email, at least three times, considering what to do now. What are my options? I know deep down that I can't just ignore it and pretend he didn't send it, because he did. I don't want to sit down face-to-face with him, even though I'm going to have to at some point, I suppose. Luckily, the house is mine and all in my name. I used some money I received when my dad died as a deposit and, even though we were engaged at the time, both Luke and I agreed to put it in my name only. Thank God. The last thing I would want now is to get embroiled in a whole heap of red tape trying to get that sorted. I stare at the screen for a moment longer willing it to give me an answer and then start typing.

Luke,
Go crawl into a hole and die, you piece of shit.
All the best, Carrie xx

OK, maybe not.

Luke,
Let me be very, VERY clear when I say this, all of your apologies, however well intended, mean absolutely nothing to me. You betrayed me in the

most unthinkable way, and I will never forgive you.
Ever. Any relationship we had ended the moment
you decided to sleep with Emily. What you do from
here on in is no longer my concern, but I will say
this – step up and be a man. Do the right thing.
Try not to be as shit of a dad as you have been a
fiancé. I'm saying this, not for you or Emily, but
for your child who, as much as it kills me to think
about it, does deserve better from you. Please have
your stuff out of the house by the time I get back.
Anything you leave, I'll take to the charity shop. I
don't expect you to contact me again. Any messages
or emails you send me will be deleted without me
reading them. You didn't email me to make me feel
better, you emailed me to make yourself feel less of
a total bastard. I won't ever forgive you, Luke, but
I am absolutely ready to forget you.
Carrie.

I reread what I've written and feel rather proud of myself. Is it too harsh? No. Under the circumstances, I think he's done well not to get more of an earful. Keep it calm and classy. I feel myself about to cry, and the tears fall silently as a sense of relief floods through me. I had been dreading Luke getting in touch. And Emily. And now that they have and I've dealt with it, well with Luke at least, I feel some sort of closure. Like a huge weight has been lifted. For the first time since the wedding day, I feel like I can breathe.

Chapter Nine

I spend the next couple of hours either reclining on the balcony or escaping the heat by lounging in my suite. The phone calls home have drained me somewhat, and I didn't feel like venturing out any further. Despite my earlier relief, I still have a nagging sensation that I haven't yet responded to Emily. I know I don't have to, but I want to close the door on the whole saga as much as I can. I take a while to think of my reply, feeling sick at the thought of responding to her. After much pacing up and down the balcony, I finally decide to keep it as level as I can.

> *I don't want you to be sorry, I want you to be a good enough friend not to have done it in the first place. If you have any respect for me at all, you won't contact me again.*

I pause, my thumb hovering over the send button. *Oh, sod it,* I think and press send. All things considered, she's got off rather lightly too. I head inside, throwing my phone on to the bed as I pass and go and run a bath before going out. The size of it means it takes an inordinately long time to fill, so I go back to take in the views from my balcony. The pool area looks gorgeous, and I decide to give it a road test tomorrow after jet-skiing.

I can see the waterfall plunge pool just down to my left and think that's the best bet for a loner like me, as opposed to the larger pool that's surrounded by people. As I look across at the expanse of sunloungers scattered here and there, I spot a pair of red shorts and flash of blonde hair. It's currently sandwiched between two very tanned, very pretty girls, one blonde and one dark, whose bikinis seem to be made up of postage stamps held together by string.

Jake's sat on the end of one of their sunbeds and is laughing as the girl sits back, her long legs crossed to make room for him. The other one throws her head back at something he's just said and touches his leg as she does so. I suddenly feel a stab of jealously, which is utterly absurd, but as he stands up to leave I can't help but admire his well-honed body. No wonder they are falling all over him. God, is that what *I* did? No, it's definitely not. I was emotional, upset and I'm pretty sure all the instigation of lunches, jet ski dates and touching came from him, not me.

I see the two girls give him a wave as he turns to leave them but, as he does so, he suddenly looks up, directly to my balcony and straight at me. I instantly want to turn and run, embarrassed that I've been caught watching him, but that would be too obvious, and he's already seen me now. He doesn't wave, but I see a wide smile spread across his face and then watch him disappear through the palm trees towards the beach. Oh great. So now he thinks I'm a complete stalker spying on him! Although, to be fair, I was being super nosy. He's clearly not short of admirers. And rightly so, I concede.

He's definitely a rare specimen, with his eyes and his hair and multitude of muscles. Jesus, maybe I was stalking after all. I turn and head inside, to get ready for dinner, before I get myself in any more trouble.

I feel very nervous as I take the lift down to the ground floor, towards the main dining room of the hotel, and have to muster all my courage to walk into it alone. The hotel information told me that a poolside bar offers similar foods to that of The Coconut Shack and that there's a more formal restaurant situated on the first floor. There's also a popular seafood grill on the far side of the complex, owned by the hotel and part of their all-inclusive offering, but it's just outside the resort and also open to the general public. Maybe I'll try that one soon if tonight goes well. And by goes well, I mean just get through the evening without crying or making a fool of myself. I don't want to stick out too much so decided the buffet option would be the safest bet for my first night, since I've already tried out The Coconut Shack.

I try and walk with purpose, as I show my wristband to the lady stationed by the doors of the dining room and give her my room number. She smiles and tells me I can pick any table, inside or outside, and help myself to the huge selection of international buffet laid out when I'm ready.

It's a huge room with high ceilings and bifold doors that open out on to a terrace and garden area, around the side of the hotel, with the edge of the beach visible at the end point of the lawn. A warm breeze blows through the room and, despite the early evening heat, leaves it feeling airy and comfortable.

I choose a table in the corner of the room, where the inside meets the outside, and settle myself down there. I remembered to bring my Kindle with me and a magazine I picked up at the airport, so I drop both of these on the table feeling secure they'll be safe. The room is about half full, which I was hoping would be the case, hence my coming down to eat at six p.m.

I wind my way through the tables and to the large buffet situated all along one side of the room. Everything looks delicious, and I'm unsure where to start. Fruits, cold meats and a huge variety of salad options follow on to the hot main meals. Baked sweet potato, cornbread and plantain are a few that catch my eye, along with local dishes such as flying fish and chicken with Bajan hot sauce. There really is something for everyone's taste, but I opt for flying fish with rice and a salad for now and promise myself some fruit and coconut ice cream for dessert. It is my holiday after all. I have to stop myself using the word honeymoon as it couldn't be further from what this is.

I don't fill my plate too much, as I'm still feeling pretty full from the fishcakes at lunch, but I still can't help but think I've had a classic case of eyes bigger than my stomach. A couple of people catch my eye on the way back to my table, a mother with a small boy hanging from her leg and an elderly lady helping her husband choose between chips and rice (she won, he's having rice), give me warm smiles and make me realise that I'm worrying for nothing. Most people are nice by nature and probably won't even notice I'm here alone. It's not like I have 'jilted doormat' tattooed on my forehead or anything, but I decide that I would rather be 'honeymooning' alone than be here with Luke, having just married a lying cheat.

I'm so clumsy by nature and, trying to draw less attention to myself not more so, I'm concentrating on weaving through the tables and trying impossibly hard not to spill any food from my plate, when I glance up and see Jake sat at my table, kicking back in a chair with a huge grin on his face. Instantly, my heart starts beating faster, and I can't help but smile back.

'I'm sorry, sir, but this table is taken,' I say to him seriously, as I put my plate down and pull out my chair. He leans forward and takes a piece of cucumber off my plate, popping it into his mouth.

'Sorry, I'm eating now, I couldn't possibly move.'

He's wearing a pale blue polo shirt and beige shorts with tan loafers. His hair looks damp and, even from across the table, he smells like clean linen and soap.

'You look lovely,' he says genuinely, and I feel my face start to heat up.

I'm wearing a knee-length, black sundress with a tie waist and crochet details at the hem and neckline.

'Thanks, I wasn't sure how formal it was so...' I trail off as I realise I'm about to start rambling. Why the hell would he want to know about my fashion choices? 'So, to what do I owe this pleasure?' I ask. 'Have you finished for the day?'

'Something like that,' he says, popping another piece of cucumber in his mouth. 'And no one should eat alone.'

'Well, I'm afraid I'm going to be doing quite a lot of that this holiday, so you best get used to it. You can't be here for every meal.'

'Well, I've made lunch and dinner so all that's left is breakfast...'

I'm not sure if it's meant to be as flirty as he makes it sound, but I blush instantly and have to look out of the window as I can't meet his eye. I feel him watching me, as I brush a strand of hair off my face that's been blown free from my ponytail by the breeze.

'Seeing as it's your first night in Barbados, I wondered if you wanted me to show you around the resort?'

'That's really sweet of you but, honestly, please don't feel you have to babysit me. I'm not going to have another meltdown, I promise. You're working anyway, aren't you? You have better things to do than show me around. What is it that you do here again?'

He leans over again, this time armed with a fork, and spears a chunk of flying fish then shoves it into his mouth. Most people would feel very uncomfortable with a near stranger eating off their plate, but there's something about him that makes the whole thing feel like the most natural thing in the world. He shrugs before answering.

'This and that.' He pauses before continuing. 'I look after things, make sure everything's working, anything that needs sorting, I try and sort it. That kind of thing.'

'So, like a sort of... handyman?' I say, trying not to make it sound derogatory. He bursts out laughing, and I'm not sure why it's so funny, but at least he doesn't seem to be offended.

'Ha! Yeah, why not? Yes, sweet cheeks, I like that. Handyman.' He reaches over and spears another piece of fish.

'Shall I just go get you a plate?' I ask, raising my eyebrows

'Nah, this is more fun.' He winks at me. 'Come on. Eat up and I'll take you on a grand tour.'

'And I'm guessing by now I don't get a choice in this?'

'Nope,' he grins. ''Fraid not.' And down goes a slice of plantain.

I finish my dinner, well, what's left of it since Jake seems happy enough eating the majority of it off my plate. I don't say it, but I'm quite grateful, as I realised pretty fast I wasn't going to be able to finish all of it, as delicious as it was.

'But I wanted some dessert, I was on a promise to myself for some of that coconut ice cream,' I moan, as he stands up and holds out his hand. I'm unsure whether or not to take it but, perhaps against my better judgement, I do. The moment his skin touches mine I feel a heat spread across my cheeks and down to my chest. I really wish this would stop happening around him, it's becoming very embarrassing. I'm sure he's noticed the effect he has on me. I let him pull me up off my chair then, conscious we are amongst guests and he's an employee, drop his hand to my side as soon as I'm upright.

'We can have dessert later, sweet cheeks,' he says with another one of his butter-wouldn't-melt smiles, and I avoid eye contact with him completely as I start to blush again. I'm pretty sure by now that he *is* flirting with me, and I'm not sure how to take it or where to look. I mean, I'm enjoying it, I can't lie, and he clearly has an effect on me. Now I think about it, I honestly don't ever remember Luke making me feel giddy at his touch. I don't know what it is about Baywatch that draws me to him.

I internally reprimand myself for being so incredibly stupid and reading far too much into it. I've just got out of a whole, big mess of crap and this is me overthinking his flirting for something else. At least, I think that's what it is, but Luke and I were together since forever, so I'm completely out of the game when it comes to meeting men. *I have no idea*, I think, despondently. He catches my eye, and his lopsided smile makes me smile back in return.

'I'll give you the tour, then I'll buy you ice cream at The Coconut Shack, OK?' he says innocently as I raise my eyebrows.

'Oh, I'm so flattered since it's all-inclusive,' I say, as he gallantly holds out his arm towards the terrace for me to lead the way.

'Ladies first.'

'Are you always such a gentleman?' I ask him, as we step outside into the cool, twilight breeze.

'Definitely not, sweet cheeks,' he says, as he looks down at me. 'Definitely not.'

I blush from the top of my head to my feet.

Outside, the trunks of the palm trees are covered in fairy lights, winding all the way up to the leaves, and all the paths leading around the resort are dotted with white, swinging lanterns. There's the noise of the cicadas that I've always loved so much, and I can hear the soft waves in the distance. It's really quite enchanting at this time of the evening, and I feel myself unwind a little more. Jake leads me around towards the front of the hotel, past the on-site spa and fitness centre.

'You should treat yourself to a massage, or something, while you're here. Make sure you pamper yourself. This is your honeymoon after all.'

I see him look at me, as he tries to gauge whether or not it's too soon for him to have made a joke, but I smile at him with a roll of my eyes.

'Oh yes, what an incredibly lucky lady I am!'

'Hey, not everyone gets a grand tour by yours truly,' he says, pushing open the door to the spa area and ushering me through.

'Wow,' I whisper as we step inside. 'I didn't know they had an indoor pool here. This is gorgeous. Does it get used much?'

'Not so much during the day, but sometimes if it's dark on an evening. We get quite a lot of people using it to do an early morning swim before the outdoor pools have heated up properly. They are never actually cold out here, but people tend to do their lengths in here for some reason, maybe because it's a bit bigger. Or if we have a thunderstorm quite a lot of guests will come and hang out here until it's passed.'

'I can see why they like to. It's so peaceful.'

The entire place is decorated in pale cream tiles, and arches surround the room under which huge, round sunbeds sit, bedecked by a thin layer of chiffon curtain. Each one hangs from the ceiling to cover the beds like the canopy on a four-poster. There's a soft, jazz tune playing through the speakers, and the faint scent of vanilla and coconut drifts through the air.

Jake walks over to one of the beds, parts the curtains and lies down, stretching his arms above his head causing the bottom of his T-shirt to rise up and reveal his tanned stomach and the telltale border of a pair of black Calvin Klein's. He lets out a deep sigh, and I shift awkwardly from one foot to the other, not quite sure what to do with myself. As he speaks, his voice echoes around the room.

'This is one of my favourite places in the hotel. Come see.' He nods at the space on the bed next to him. I hesitate wondering whether getting on to a bed, albeit fully clothed, with a man I don't really know is a very good idea. He props himself up on his elbows and looks at me.

'Honestly, sweet cheeks, I don't bite.' He smiles and tilts his head to one side then continues more seriously. 'You're safe with me, I promise. I'm sure this is what they all say, but I'm actually a terribly decent chap. You can trust me.'

And despite only knowing this very charming man a few hours, and having absolutely nothing to base my judgement on apart from my gut instinct and a few heavy pointers that he seems like a bit of a ladies' man, I know he's telling the truth. I do feel safe with him. My gut told me to trust him earlier today, and it's doing the same thing now. Although the way it's let me down lately, I may need a stern word with this instinct of mine about the whole 'yes of course this wedding is a good idea' scenario. I walk over and sit down next to him lying back on my elbows to mirror his pose.

'Lie back, look.' I do as I'm told and suddenly take a sharp gasp of breath, as I see what he wanted to show me.

'Oh, God, that's gorgeous.' The pale grey blue ceiling is covered in hundreds, no it must be thousands, of tiny, almost too small to see, white, twinkling lights, slightly varying in sizes, that glisten and look like real stars set in the roof. 'I can see why you like it in here.'

'I often come here late at night after a particularly busy, or bad, day and just lie here and look up at this. It calms me somehow.' This is the first time he's spoken about himself without it being a response to a question I've asked him, and I realise that I want to know more about this man, who I seem to have so quickly struck up this weird, intense friendship with.

'What after a busy day handy-manning?' I say with a smirk.

'That's the one,' he nods and turns to face me. 'There's much more to me than just that you know. The job does not maketh the man.'

'What? That's not even a saying!' I laugh. 'No, I'm sure chatting to pretty girls all day is rather taxing for you as well.'

'Ha! So you were watching me?'

Bugger.

'No, I was looking at the view and you happened to get in the way...' I say feebly.

'Yeah, yeah. Whatever. I was just being friendly,' he says holding his hands up in defence. 'They're guests here, and I have to be nice to everyone.'

'Oh, so I'm just another guest you're being nice to?' Even though I'm smiling I know I sound petty, and I hate myself as soon as the words leave my lips. What business is it of mine what he does? And why do I even care? 'Sorry. I don't know why I said that. It's nothing to do with me. I think I'm still a bit on edge,' I frown.

'No, sweet cheeks, that's not it at all. You're different.' He stands up and I follow suit, blushing again.

'You barely know me,' I tell him.

'And yet, here I am,' he says gesturing out with his arms. 'Look, it might not seem like it to you right now, but there are not many sane blokes who would pass by a chance to hang out with a babe like you.'

I laugh out loud, as we walk towards the door. 'A babe? I don't think I've been called a babe since I was about sixteen.'

'And that, babe, is part of your problem. Come on let's go, the night is young and so are we!'

'Are you always this corny? Tell me now so I know not to have any cheese before jet-skiing tomorrow. I'll have had quite enough of it from you by the end of the day,' I tease him.

'Come on, everyone needs a bit of cheese in their life.'

'I might be lactose intolerant.'

He laughs leading me back outside. 'But you're not. Now let me show you the rest of the hotel before you slip into some sort of dairy-induced coma.'

I spend the next hour being given what is, honestly, a really good and helpful tour of the resort. I no longer feel like the new girl in class. Jake has shown me everything the hotel has to offer, and the best way to get from one place to another, so I'm not wandering around looking lost the whole time. I tell him as much as we end up back at reception and make our way towards The Coconut Shack, for what I can only hope is my promised dessert.

'So have you worked here long?' I ask, keen to know more about the man who has so passionately shown me his place of work. He knew every inch of this place like the back of his hand. I've barely got a word in edgeways for all his pontificating.

'You could say that, yeah.' He pauses, but I resist filling the gap. Now he's talking I want him to continue which, thankfully, he does. 'My dad has always worked in hotels, and it was just sort of natural for me that I followed in his footsteps. I looked up to him all my life; he was a great man, a great father. I was born in the US but went to school in England and then when he died, four years ago, I came here.'

'Oh, I'm so sorry to hear that. My dad passed away a couple of years back too, so it's just me and Mum now. We were very close. I miss him every day. What did he do, your dad?'

'The same as what I do. I have a sister who lives in Paris but my mum's still in England. In Kent. She's retired though, so she manages to fly out to see me quite a bit. She loves it here as you can imagine.'

'I can. And that's good that you still see her lots. I bet she misses your dad.' As much as I'm glad I've got him talking about himself, I really don't want to get into a conversation about our late fathers. I feel far too tired and emotional today, so I opt for a change of subject. 'So why Barbados then? What made you choose here? Or is that a silly question?'

'I mean, come on, it's Barbados, what's not to love, right? But the job came up and it was the right time and place, so here I am.'

'And whereabouts do you live? Nearby? I didn't see much on my drive in, and I don't know the island at all.'

'It's OK, I'll show you round. Again.' He glances down at me briefly with a smile. 'And I live here.'

'What, *here*? At the hotel?' I say surprised. 'I didn't know they had staff quarters here.'

'They don't, but there are a few of us who live on-site and I happen to be one of them.'

'I guess the nature of your job means you need to be close for any urgent calls and emergencies at any time of day or night?' I ask and he tilts his head, as if in consideration, but doesn't answer. I'm worried I've offended him again so continue to ramble on. 'I suppose, being a five-star resort, the guests aren't the sort to put up with a blocked toilet in the middle of the night, are they? God, sorry. If that's even your job, I don't know...' I trail off embarrassed. Damn it.

'Well, let's just say I do deal with a lot of shit, sweet cheeks. Now, can I tempt you with the dessert I promised? Maybe even another rum punch?'

'You're fast becoming a very hard man to say no to,' I say, not realising how it comes out.

'What excellent news,' he grins back at me, his yellow eyes twinkling all the way to the bar.

We sit down on the bar stools and are served up the most divine bowl of coconut ice cream by Dale, along with an even more potent (and rather large) glass of rum punch. I don't get to do any more deeper digging on Jake, as Dale is in full-blown puppy mode regaling us with stories of the day's exploits at The Coconut Shack.

Apparently a girl and her boyfriend had an almighty row, and she threw a drink over him and stormed off. Then later, Dale saw him consoling himself with the very attractive wife of a casino owner, whose husband leaves her here most of the time while he plays golf and conducts his business meetings on the island with a bunch of Americans. Dale seems to think this other woman may have been the cause of the row in the first place. I'm quite thrilled to hear this news, as awful as that may sound, but it does make me feel like less of an abject failure at life in general, to know that it's not all sweetness and light for everyone else out here either. As I sip, who am I kidding, down, the last of my drink, I stifle a yawn.

'I know it's only just gone nine p.m., but it's definitely past my bedtime.' I push back my stool and wave a goodnight to Dale.

'I'll walk you to your room,' Jake says, making to follow me.

'Really? It's just there.' I point up to my balcony. 'I can actually see it from here, I think I'll manage. Besides, I've had a very good tour of the hotel, so I know I won't be at risk of getting lost.'

'It's on my way home,' he shrugs.

'No it isn't!' I narrow my eyes at him. 'There are only two suites on the top floor, you told me that less than two hours ago, so I know you're lying. But thank you for my tour. And for making my first night here not totally shit.'

'Not totally shit. Hmm, I'm not sure that's exactly the result I was hoping for, but I'll take it. And hopefully, by the end of tomorrow and jet-skiing, you might have had an only two per cent shit day.'

'Well, that's all any of us can hope for I suppose,' I reply with a small laugh. 'Goodnight, Jake. I'll be here tomorrow at ten.'

He bows theatrically to me, making a few of the other guests turn and stare at us, as I roll my eyes. 'Goodnight, fair maiden, sleep well.'

To my absolute surprise he grabs my hand and pulls me into a hug.

'Until tomorrow,' he says looking down at me. I pull away from him gently and leave without a second glance, despite every fibre of my being willing me to look back once more. I can feel his eyes on me all the way down the path until I turn a corner and realise, I've been holding my breath.

As I get to my room I can't help myself and go out on to the balcony – keeping well out of sight this time – and look down towards where I've just come from, just in time to see Jake and the blonde girl from the sunbeds today walking down to the beach.

Chapter Ten

I set my alarm for eight a.m. so I can get up, take a quick shower and grab a small breakfast before I go jet-skiing. I have no idea what suitable attire is but, presuming I'll be flung in the sea at some point, I decide to go with a black, one-piece swimsuit with a low back and cut out sides, mainly to try and avoid losing either a bikini top or bottoms along with my dignity.

I remember once in Corfu on the beach, Kate was hit by a particularly forceful wave and both her boobs popped out of her bikini top. Whilst trying to shove them back in (she does possess a rather large pair, much to my envy), she got knocked off her feet again and ended up flashing her bum to the entire beach. After that day, I soon learned that the sea and skimpy items of clothing don't mix.

The thought brings me back to Jake and the blonde, and I wonder whether or not any of her skimpy items got lost on the beach last night. Not your business, Carrie, I remind myself. He's just a friend. In fact, he's barely that, he's a charming hotel employee paid to look after the guests. And today is certainly not a date.

I slap on some sun cream, pull my hair up into a bun and, after putting on some denim shorts and a bright yellow cami top, I head to breakfast in the dining room feeling much more confident than I did last night.

I sit at the same table as I did yesterday evening and, after ordering a coffee from one of the waiters, go and grab two pancakes with a small drizzle of maple syrup and a side bowl of watermelon. I didn't want anything big, since I'm going to be bobbing about on the ocean, but this just hits the spot and, as it's only just coming up to nine a.m., I sit back and enjoy a second cup of coffee, as I do a spot of people watching.

I try and tot up who I've seen so far that I recognise. The young mother and toddler are on the far side of the restaurant making their way out to the beach, followed by a man, who I assume is her husband, and a little girl of around six. No sign of the old couple today. She's probably got him doing lengths or some aquarobics before breakfast, the poor soul, and my mind wanders back to the pool with Jake last night.

The thing about being at home was everything reminded me of Luke, and I realise that having had Jake show me around last night, everything here now reminds me of him, although in a much less 'feel like you could throw up or punch someone at any moment' sort of way. It also dawns on me that I've not woken up feeling upset or angry like I have every other day since *it* happened.

See, I knew coming away was going to be a good thing, I think to myself with a celebratory sip of coffee. Just at that moment, a scrape of chairs automatically draws my attention to look over in the direction of the noise and to a table a few over from me. It's the two girls from the pool, and I can see the blonde Jake was with last night. I hear a thick, American accent as she speaks to the brunette across from her.

'Like, you have *no* idea, I mean he was just, like, amazing!' she shrieks and giggles manically which sets off Brunette like some sort of chain reaction. 'He knew all the right things to say, and I've never known a man be so attentive before. It was like he really cared, you know?'

'Oh my God, Bryony. Like, I can't even! I mean, he's so hot too!' Brunette waves her arms about like a lunatic, and Bryony, the blonde, laughs her head off.

'Yeah, he's hot but, you know, he's like… I dunno, kinda, just so…'

'What like *normal*?' Brunette suggests whispering the word 'normal' as if he has some contagious disease.

'Oh my God, Amy, that's it. You are, like, *so* smart! He's so *normal*. I mean, when I started talking about Christian he wasn't even impressed. Or like, even jealous?' Bryony is incredulous at this fact, and I wonder who the hell Christian is, and what has Jake got to be jealous about?

'Amy, honey, you know me, I'm not a complicated girl.'

Yeah, no shit, I think.

'But really, he was so, like, *whatever* about it.'

'Er, yeah?'

'Yeah.'

OK, this is like trying to understand two Martians. I have never come across two people who say so much but actually don't say anything at all. It's like being in *Clueless*. They both turn to their plates of food, well I say food, but Bryony has one slice of watermelon, *one*, and Amy has two slices and some strawberries. I watch as Bryony picks up her piece and takes a tiny nibble, then pushes her plate away and sighs like she's just eaten a Big Mac.

I get up to leave and purposefully avoid passing their table. They both look immaculate, even at this time in the morning, and even though I actually made a bit of effort this morning, I still feel like crap next to the pair of them. I smooth my hands over my bun instinctively and suck my stomach in that little bit harder. I have half an hour before I'm due to meet Jake, so I take a wander towards The Coconut Shack but take a right turn as the path forks and detour over to the pool area. I've not been down here yet and, although I've seen it from the balcony, it's a huge space with three swimming pools of varying shapes and sizes. It's populated with, what I've noticed are, the trademark Palm Bay Hotel sunbeds, with tables and chairs around the outside edges covered by large umbrellas. There are a few people out here already but plenty of the beds are free.

On a sudden whim, I sit down on the closest bed and pull off my vest. Twenty minutes in the sun might just be in order, plus the last thing I want is to be waiting for Jake and given a grilling by Dale if he's around. I don't want to seem overly keen, although he quite clearly knows I've nothing else to do.

The sun instantly heats my skin, and I feel my body slip further into holiday mode. I hear the shuffle of flip-flops pass me and open my eyes to see a girl occupy the sunbed but one away from me. She's wearing a bright orange bikini with a huge, wide-brimmed hat and long, black hair falling down her back. She's tiny, even smaller than me, and has a pretty, elfin face. She sees me looking over, and I give a little wave.

'Morning. Lovely day isn't it?'

'Hi,' she says, giving me a small smile which doesn't quite reach her eyes. 'Yes, I suppose it is.' She glances up at the blue sky and back to me, smiling feebly again.

'I like your bikini. That colour is lovely on you,' I say with a smile. I don't know why I'm still talking to her, as she quite clearly has something on her mind, but she looks sad, and I get what that's like.

'Oh really? Thanks. I thought I might look a bit satsuma-ish.' She laughs and I join her.

'Not a satsuma in sight, I promise. When did you arrive?' I ask her. She seems nice and, although I'm sure she's not going to be here on her own, it might be nice to have someone to say hello to or get a drink with sometimes maybe.

'This is my fourth day. We're here for two weeks.'

'Who are you here with?'

'My ex.' She grimaces at me and rolls her eyes.

'Your ex? Wow, how did that happen?' I say with raised eyebrows.

She takes off her hat and pulls her hair up into a bun with a big sigh. I sit up and lean forward towards her, ready for the story.

'Well, he wasn't my ex when we arrived, but I found out, last night actually, that he slept with someone else, on the second night of our holiday. Yes, *this* holiday! I was still a bit out of it with jet lag and a bit too much sun, so I went to bed early, and he got chatting to some woman after I left and ended up shagging her on the bloody beach. Can you believe that? What a shit. And she's bloody married!'

'Jesus! God, I'm so sorry. What did you do?' I say, feeling incredulous that this story is almost as ludicrous as mine. She looks embarrassed for a second.

'I'm not proud of it, but I'm afraid I made a bit of a scene last night. I threw my drink all over him, in the bar, when I found out. Actually, you know what? Scratch that, I am proud of it. He's lucky he didn't get a punch in the face the way I was feeling. But I am a bit bothered about what people must think, there were loads of people about, they'll all know, and now I look like the crazy girlfriend for lobbing my cocktail over him.'

Ah! So *this* is the couple Dale was telling us about last night. The cheating boyfriend and the, very valid it would now seem, drink thrower.

'I don't think anyone one would blame you for throwing your drink over him, or even punching him in the face for that matter. He definitely sounds like he got off lightly with just a soggy T-shirt. So what did you do after you gave him a soaking? I hope it was with something very sticky and pink?'

She pulls a face at me. 'Would you believe it was a 'Sex on the Beach'?'

I have to bite my lip to stop the smile escaping over the awful irony of the whole debacle.

'Sorry,' I say ashamed of myself. 'It's absolutely *not* funny. I shouldn't laugh at all.' I meet her eyes but am pleased to see she's started smiling too.

'No, it's OK, that bit is actually pretty funny,' she says and gives a little, but sincere, laugh. 'What is it they say? If you don't laugh you'll cry, right? Well anyway, after drenching him the best I could, I grabbed all his crap from the room and threw it into the corridor and told him to absolutely, one million per cent, go and do one!' She slams down a bottle of sun cream as she finishes her outburst. 'He's moving to another hotel because that's cheaper than changing his flight to get home, but we are finished as far as I'm concerned. This was kind of a make-or-break holiday for us. We've been together for two years, on and off, and it's not been great the last six months, so I thought some time out might be good for us. Or, you know, not.' She sighs and gives me a sad smile with a shrug of her shoulders.

'Bloody hell, I'm really sorry. That's awful.'

'Ah, it's OK. Well, I mean it's not, but honestly, it wasn't working any more, us being together. I just feel like such an idiot, you know?'

'Well actually, yes, I know *exactly* what you mean.'

I proceed to tell her my story, and she listens intently, making all the right noises in all the right places and even throwing her hands to her mouth at the really good/bad parts. She is an excellent audience.

'God, and I thought *my* life was bad! Ouch. Sorry, I didn't mean it to come out like that,' she says looking mortified, but I laugh at her phrasing.

'Don't worry, I know what you meant. And you're right. It's a mess, I just have to concentrate on clearing it up. I need to look after myself and get on with it now, move forward. We both do.'

I look up at her with a smile which she returns sincerely. It's been a long time since I've made new friends, as our little group was so established, but what the hell. She seems really nice, and we are both in the same boat by the sound of it, so I decide to take a step towards my new life.

'Listen, I have to be somewhere in a minute, and I don't want to seem like I'm being forward or anything, so please feel free to say no if you'd rather not, but what are you doing later on? I wondered if maybe you might fancy getting dinner together this evening? You know, rather than us both sitting and eating alone.'

Her face lights up, and I know instantly I've done the right thing.

'Oh my God, I would love that. Yes! Thanks so much. I was worried about looking like a total loner.'

'You and me both. Shall we meet at The Coconut Shack at, say, seven thirty then?' I smile at her and get up to leave. 'I'm Carrie, by the way.'

'I'm Rachel, and yes to later on. That sounds perfect,' she beams at me. 'Thanks so much.'

'No need to thank me, you're coming to my rescue too. So nice to meet you, Rachel. I look forward to our date later.' I laugh.

'Me too. And I tell you what, we'll have much more fun without those two-faced, shitty blokes of ours.'

'I don't doubt it. Enjoy your day,' I chuckle at her, as I head off to the beach thinking how much I like my new friend.

Chapter Eleven

I see Jake immediately as I make my way down the path to The Coconut Shack. With his massive frame, perched on a bar stool, and his ultra-blonde hair, you can't help but notice him. He's wearing white shorts, which show off his tan to perfection, and I suddenly feel self-conscious again and I pull my beach bag across my body. He's talking to Dale and laughing heartily at whatever's just passed between them. The sight of him sets the butterflies loose in my stomach again, and I take a moment to hide behind my sunglasses so I can stare at his perfect form. I am terrible.

'Hey!' Dale's voice breaks through my secret perving and makes me jump, even though they couldn't see me looking. I push my glasses on to my head and can't help but gawp as Jake stands up from his stool and reaches his arms high above his head in a long, drawn-out stretch. He really is the most perfect specimen, and I have to tear my eyes away and blush slightly as I realise Dale has quite obviously clocked me this time. He catches my eye, and I can see him smirking slightly. I recover my composure just in time for Jake to stick out his arm and draw me in for a one-armed hug.

'Here she is! You look gorgeous. Dale, check out my date,' he says with this arm still slung over my shoulder and making no moves to remove it. The tips of his fingers are hanging tantalisingly close to my chest, and I'm trying so hard to concentrate on not blushing. Dale smiles at me but chivalrously avoids looking me up and down despite Jake's prompting.

'Hell, you don't need to tell me, I know a beautiful girl when I see one.' And he winks at me.

'Oh, please.' I say rolling my eyes in mock outrage, as I laugh and look up at Jake. 'I thought it was just you with the cheesy lines?'

'Dale learned all his best moves from me, isn't that right young Jedi?' This time it's Dale's turn to laugh, and he waves an arm in our direction as Jake steers me towards the beach.

'Catch you later, bud,' he calls to Dale over his shoulder, as I turn my head and give him a friendly wave.

'Have fun you guys. And Carrie, don't let him get you into any trouble!'

It might be a bit late for that. The beach is starting to get busy with guests, and I'm acutely aware of Jake's arm still around my shoulder. I'm not sure if I love it or if I'm uncomfortable with it in the presence of other hotel guests, but as soon as he releases me a moment later, I'm disappointed and crave the contact again. I push my shades on to my face and smile as the hot sand tickles between my toes.

'What are you grinning at?' he asks.

'Oh, nothing and everything. I love the warm weather. It's so rare back home, and I know it sounds like a total cliché, but just feeling the sand between my toes makes me so happy. I always loved the beach, even as a kid. It brings back good memories.'

'Like?' Jake asks, and I'm happy to reminisce.

'When I was at primary school, every year, me, Mum and Dad would drive down to Torquay for a week's holiday in the summer. We would go to the beach every day, even if it was raining. We lived so far from the sea, it was such a novelty for us.

'I remember once, being huddled behind a windbreak in the tipping down rain, with a bit of plastic tarpaulin over our heads, and laughing until we cried because it was so ridiculous and rubbish, but so fun. I used to love those holidays.'

A warm feeling grows inside me. It was something I looked forward to every year. Just the three of us. Getting fish and chips, and Mr Whippy ice creams, and chasing after my dad as he tried to get the kite going along the beach. At the end of the day, we would walk along the Princess Pier, and I would pretend I was an actual princess and that there was a sea monster trying to capture me. Dad would be the knight trying to slay him. I was thinking about taking my mum back there one year, but not yet. The memories would still be too painful without Dad. I'm still deep in thought when Jake takes my hand and squeezes it, before letting it fall back to my side. He doesn't say anything, but I can feel him looking at me.

'It's OK. I'm not going to cry again, promise.' Well, at least not right now.

'I know you're not, sweet cheeks, you're a tough cookie. But anyway, you'd be allowed to cry about missing your dad, just not about jerks who can't see a good thing when it's staring them in the face.'

I smile at him, and he peers over his sunglasses and winks at me with a huge smile. My butterflies are off again, but no sooner have they taken flight, I remember seeing him last night with Bryony the Blonde and what she said at breakfast. Should I say something about it? Why would I? It's not like he owes me an explanation or anything, and I would just embarrass myself. Before I can stop myself the words are out of my mouth.

'So, what did you do last night?' What is *wrong* with me?

'What, you mean after you abandoned me in preference of your bed?'

'Ah well, you've not been in my bed have you?' I reply without thinking. 'It's a dream come true.'

'I most certainly haven't, sweet cheeks...' he almost growls at me, and I mentally kick myself for walking straight into that one. It would appear I'm so out of practice, talking to men, that I can't seem to stop setting myself up. Still, I allow myself a small smile as I get a sudden image of that tanned body against my crisp, white sheets. OK Carrie, calm down. I'm behaving like a teenager, but my brain just won't behave when I'm around Jake. And judging by the heat blazing in my cheeks, my body won't either.

'Last night I was doing my standard knight in shining armour routine,' Jake explains. 'One of the guests, actually, it was one of the girls I was chatting to when you were perving on me from your balcony yesterday, was crying, and I mean actually sobbing, over an earring she'd lost on the beach. Apparently they were Cartier and cost more than most people's houses, so she was beside herself.' He rolls his eyes.

'So you were consoling her as well? You do have a thing for sobbing ladies then,' I say, only half teasing.

'Not consoling, no. I left that to one of the lads from the fitness team, he's got a rather large soft spot for her. Though

God knows why, she's actually really annoying.' He looks at me, his face suddenly serious. 'Don't repeat that though, she stays here a few times a year and is just about to star in a film with Christian Bale, so she might bring some A-listers here in future if she makes it big. I tried not to be star-struck when she said his name, but I actually loved him as Batman!' I raise my eyebrows at him, and he shrugs his shoulders and laughs. 'What can I say? My guilty pleasure. So anyway, I went to help her look for it on the beach, and was just about to give up, when Dale came running down to say it had been handed into reception by another guest. She's very lucky, I never thought for a second she'd find it.'

I take a moment to process all of this. Christian? So she was talking about Jake not being impressed with her Hollywood mates. And he was helping her look for her earring on the beach, and she was upset so that's why he had his arm around her. I can't deny the rush of relief I feel, and I suddenly realise I might just like him a tiny bit more than I'm letting on to myself. Just as a friend, of course, and I hastily try to shove the butterflies back into their cage.

The sudden touch of his hand on the small of my back does nothing to quell that sensation, as he guides me across the sand and points to a spot further down the crescent-shaped beach to a collection of jet skis, what looks like a big, inflatable banana and a huge blow-up disc floating in the water. There are four jet skis sat on the edge of the sand, and a little hum of excitement zips through my body as I clap my hands together.

'Eek, I'm so excited!' I chirp sincerely to Jake. 'I've always wanted to do this.'

'Are you nervous?' he asks.

'No, not at all.' I pause before continuing, 'Why? Should I be?'

'No, not at all.' He smiles, repeating my words back to me. 'I'll look after you. I'll let you into a little secret,' he says and leans down to whisper into my ear. 'It's not my first time.'

I bat him away with my hand, frowning at him.

'You're terrible,' I say, but I'm laughing and starting to enjoy his playful banter more and more as I get used to it. I have to admit, I'm having fun and after the past few days, it feels amazing.

Jake introduces me to Theo and Greg, two ridiculously buff guys who draw him into a man hug and shake my hand politely.

'You can leave your bag with the guys; they have a locked trunk they keep valuables in. It'll be safe with them.'

Neither Theo nor Greg say anything but both smile and nod at me, so I hand it over with a thank you before suddenly realising I'm still wearing my clothes.

'Oh, my clothes...' I say to no one in particular, and Theo hands me back my bag with another smile as he and Greg politely turn away and busy themselves with readying the jet skis. I look at Jake, who is just stood staring at me, and I blush. *Is he really going to watch me undress?* I think, slightly mortified. We stay like that for the longest moment, and he seems as lost in thought as I am. He holds out his hand to me all of a sudden, and I'm not sure what he wants me to do with it.

'Want me to hold your bag?'

'Oh! Yes please,' I stutter handing it over and sigh gratefully when he turns his back to me and goes to talk to the boys. I quickly peel off my shorts and top, folding them up together, and walk over to Jake reaching for my bag as I get close to him, but as I get within a couple of steps of him he suddenly turns around, and I end up planting my palm straight on to his abs.

'God, sorry!' I whip my hand away embarrassed, but he just laughs and drapes his arm over my shoulder again.

'Any opportunity to feel me up, hey, sweet cheeks? Don't worry you'll have plenty of time to wrap yourself round me when we're out.' I stuff my things into my bag, and he hands it over to Greg. I'm suddenly really nervous, and I know that it's more about being in such close proximity to Jake, rather than travelling at high speed across open water with a nigh on stranger. He suddenly frowns and looks down at me, his face serious.

'Shit. You can swim can't you?'

'Yes, I can swim, don't worry. I wouldn't have said yes otherwise, would I?'

'You might have been ready to throw caution to the wind just to spend some time in my company. Right, Theo will get you fixed up with a vest and then on you hop.' He winks at me.

I hold my arms out wide, while Theo takes out a vest and I slip into it. I do up the buckles across the front, and he checks them for me, nodding, and gestures off towards the jet ski. Talk about the strong silent type. I head over to where Theo directed me and stand there, unsure what to do with myself. Surely I don't get on it until it's on the water? Luckily, Jake saunters over, and he and Greg begin to push the machine off the shore. Once in the shallows, Jake places one foot on the back of the jet ski and pushes himself up, as Greg beckons for me to do the same and I take his outstretched hand to help me. I manage to get on fairly smoothly, and Jake glances at me over his shoulder as Greg pushes us further out.

'Alright back there?'

'Yes, fine thanks,' I squeak, as I take a deep breath and realise I'm actually more nervous about the jet-skiing part of this adventure than I first thought. I smile as I realise I've just called it an adventure. But I feel like it is. And let's be honest, when was the last time I had one of those? Sadly, I can't remember. Suddenly the jet ski roars to life, and I instinctively grip my legs tighter around the seat and do my best to tighten my arms around Jake's firm body. I can still feel his muscles even under his life vest.

'Hold on back there,' he yells over the thrum of the machine I can feel vibrating beneath me. 'Yell in my ear if you need me to stop, OK?'

I nod then realise he can't actually see me so shout, 'YES!' over his shoulder.

Then, without any further warning, I feel a sudden jolt and cling tighter to Jake as the jet ski pulls away from the shoreline and we race off into deeper waters. We keep what I imagine is probably a relatively slow pace until we clear the line of buoys at the edge of the bay and meet the open water, then Jake tilts his head back so I can hear him a little better.

'Hold on back there! And don't worry, you can grab on as tight as you like, you won't get any complaints from me.'

I smile and acknowledge my understanding by gripping him as tight as I can and leaning my head into his back. I suddenly imagine that we don't have the life vests separating our bodies and feel a flush in my cheeks at the thought of being pressed up against him in such close proximity. On second thoughts, it's probably a good thing we have them in the way.

I don't have much time to daydream as Jake squeezes the accelerator and we lurch forward. I let out a little squeak as we bounce over the breaking waves and head further out to sea. I risk a glance behind me and can see Greg and Theo getting smaller and smaller as we push on, away from the beach.

'Hang on!' Jake shouts, and I hold on as hard as I can as we begin to turn parallel to the shoreline. As we straighten up, I lift my head from where I've nestled it into Jake's back. We've travelled much further than I thought and I can no longer make out the shapes of people on the beach, but I see the hotel looking like a tiny house opposite where we are. I can just about make out my balcony.

As we bounce over a wave, and I feel myself lift a couple of inches from my seat, much to my dismay, I squeal again. I grip my thighs together as hard as possible to try and anchor myself to the seat, and I hear Jake laugh from in front of me and we increase in speed again as we fly across the sea.

After what feels like ages, but must only be a few minutes, we slow to almost a standstill, bar the movement of the waves, and the noise of the engine dies down. I worry for a second that something might have happened and start to panic that we are stranded out at sea, until Jake turns around to face me. He's wearing a huge smile and it's completely contagious as my face breaks into a grin.

'Come on then,' he says nodding towards the… handlebars? I think that's what they're called.

'Come on where?' I ask looking around. I'm a strong swimmer, but I don't fancy getting off this far out.

'Your turn.'

'I'm sorry, my *what*?' I ask, terrified that I already know what the answer is.

'To drive. Come on. Come up front.'

'Jake, I can't drive a jet ski! I wouldn't know what to do.' No. I can't do this.

'Of course you can. It's easy. I'm right here. I'll show you what to do and we are far out in open water. There's nothing to crash into and if we fall off, we fall off. Here, look.' He lifts a red coil that's attached to his life vest and runs all the way to the front of the jet ski. 'This is the key. If we fall off, the ignition shuts down and we get back on. No dramas.' He unclips the key coil, and he grabs my hand looking me straight in the eye. 'Trust me, Carrie. You can do anything.' I go a deep shade of pink.

'I think that's the first time you've used my name,' I whisper quietly and drop my eyes to my hand in his.

'What, did you think I'd forgotten it? And actually it's the second, if we're counting.' He smiles at me and tugs my hand. 'Come on. I'm putting my life in your hands, and if I'm OK with it, so should you be.'

'Oh, don't say that,' I groan, and I stand up cautiously trying not to rock us too much. 'That only makes me more nervous.'

'Right, step forward, and I'll shuffle to the back. Grab on to me,' he instructs.

I swing my right leg over the seat and hold on to Jake's shoulder as I shuffle my feet along the side, but as he wriggles to the back of the jet ski, the shift in weight suddenly throws me off balance and I feel myself tilt backwards. With a shriek I suddenly lean forward and throw my left leg over the seat to stop me falling ass first into the sea, which leaves Jake and me face-to-face, as opposed to back-to-face like I'd planned. My right leg is slung over his and our bodies are only a few inches apart. I feel my heart thumping in my chest, and my breathing is suddenly slow and deep to match his.

His hair is damp from the spray, and he's pushed his shades up on to his head so I can see his eyes in all their perfect glory. He's still for a moment and then slowly tilts his head, and I watch his eyes roam all over my face before he brings them back up to meet mine. I feel a surge through my stomach as the back of his hand brushes against my thigh, and his touch feels like it's set my skin on fire. Our eyes are locked, and I suddenly forget we are on a jet ski in the middle of the sea and that I've know this man for a matter of hours. I feel something that I can't ever remember feeling with Luke, or anyone else I've ever met for that matter. And the worst part is I don't know what that feeling is. I know in my own head it sounds like a complete cliché, but I feel a connection of some sort. It's like he can see into my soul and soothe it. And right in that moment, I want him to kiss me. I want to feel his lips on mine and to lose myself in him and forget about everything.

What the *hell* am I doing? I scold myself internally for being so ridiculous. I'm only feeling this way because of what's happened. If I came across Jake on another path in my life, I wouldn't have given him a second thought. OK, maybe that's a lie. I swallow and bite my lip and for that very moment, I think he actually *is* going to kiss me. And I know I would let him.

'Oh bollocks,' I sigh quietly, my eyes not leaving his, and I don't quite realise I've said it out loud until he lets out a deep laugh and throws back his head.

'Enjoying the view?' he asks, and he slides his sunglasses back down and puts both hands on my waist. Or what would be my waist, if it wasn't covered by my life vest. And I thank God that it is, I daren't breathe. 'As much as I'm enjoying this, we can't stay here all day, sweet cheeks.'

He lifts me gently as I steady myself on the front of the jet ski and attempt to turn myself the right way, without getting myself into trouble this time. I feel a wave of relief and disappointment as the moment passes by, and he's back to his playful banter. Ass first into the water sounds like the much safer option right about now.

I manoeuvre myself so I'm finally facing forwards and stare blankly at the handlebars. Jake reaches round, clips the key to me and places both his hands over mine as he leans forward to guide them. I feel his breath on my ear as he speaks.

'Now, very gently squeeze the controls on the handlebars.' Ha! I was right. 'There are no brakes, so easing off will eventually bring us to a stop, OK? You turn in the same way you would a bike, but don't do it too sharply or we'll end up in the sea. Right, ready?'

'Not at all, but I'm here now so I don't really have a choice.'

'I'm right here. There are no boats, no swimmers, you'll be fine. Just squeeze and go, OK?'

'Squeeze and go,' I repeat. I mean, how hard can it be? Very, very gently I squeeze the controls on the handlebars and we lunge forward. I let out a little scream and let go, clasping my hands together at my chest so I can't do any more damage.

'It's OK, it's OK,' Jake laughs as he places his hands back over mine and guides them back to the handlebars. 'Let's try again. Easy does it. A little less pressure and once we get going, I'll take my hands off, alright?'

I nod meekly and gently start to squeeze my fingers around the controls again as I feel Jake do the same. My heart thumps nervously but we begin to move forward slowly, and I feel more confident that I'm not going to throw us both into the water. Jake squeezes his hands tighter, his fingers closing over mine, and we pick up speed.

'I'm going to let go now, you'll be fine. Keep your hands steady and no sudden movements, OK?'

'OK. I got this,' I say, more to myself than to Jake. I do as he said and gently increase the pressure of my fingers feeling us move through the water.

'I'm doing it!' I say gleefully, and I hear him laugh behind me.

'Yes you are, sweet cheeks,' he says softly into my ear as he puts his hands on my waist. I stiffen at his touch, but he only laughs again. 'Health and safety purposes, gorgeous, don't panic.' Hmm. Indeed.

As my nerves start to subside the thrill of me actually driving a jet ski fills me with excitement. I squeeze harder on the controls and feel a jolt of exhilaration as we pick up our pace across the waves. The spray and wind are hitting my face, and I can taste the salty tang of seawater on my lips. I break into a huge grin, as I begin to turn us out to sea. The jet ski bounds over the water, and we bounce in our seats. Holding the handlebars steady, I release the pressure of my fingers so I don't throw us off as we turn. Suddenly Jake lets out a loud whoop from behind me, and I laugh as he squeezes his grip on my waist.

'Go you!' he shouts, and I can feel my smile spread from ear to ear. This is the most fun I have had in such a long time, and I don't want it to end. As my confidence builds, I begin to turn us across the ocean, zigzagging over the water as I drive us further along the coastline. After a few minutes of letting me do my thing, Jake leans forward.

'We're coming in towards the Bridgetown port,' he calls out, and I look towards land to see the harbour coming up in the distance. 'Swing her round slowly, in a wide arc, and we can head back up the coast to St James.'

I nod and begin to slowly twist the handlebars to the right, careful not to take too sharp an angle and throw us off. The whole jet ski tilts towards the water, and I straighten up as we round back on ourselves. It's not until we are fully upright, and steady, that I realise I've been biting my lip in trepidation of throwing us into the water.

'I did it!' I yell excitedly as I bounce on my seat in joy. 'And we didn't fall off!'

'Have faith, sweet cheeks, you might just surprise yourself.'

I feel him plant a light kiss on the back of my head and know he's not just talking about jet-skiing. I can do this. I can get over this mess, get over Luke and losing Emily, and move on with my life and be OK. I know it's going to take a lot more than jet-skiing but it's a start. A start at a new me, a me that's all mine and not Luke or anyone else.

Jake shouts instructions in my ear to guide us back up the coast and into the beach, all the time reassuring me how great I'm doing, but my nerves are gone and I feel a real sense of triumph. As we near the shoreline he reaches over and puts his hands over mine again to guide us in, and Theo and Greg wade out to the shallows to meet us as Jake cuts the engine. He gets off the back, as they hold it still, but before I can begin to climb off, he puts both hands on my waist and lifts me off the jet ski into the shallow water. I rest my hands on his broad shoulders to steady myself and, as he lowers me on to the water's edge, he dips his head so his gaze meets mine.

'You, young lady, are amazing.'

I perform a curtsey and bat my eyelids at him whilst I unclip my vest and hand it to him.

'Why thank you, kind sir.' He holds out his arm and I slip mine through it, without any of the earlier hesitation I felt about being in his company. 'I had a very good teacher.'

'I wonder what else we can teach you while you're here…' he says quietly, and I don't respond. A silence hangs in the air between us, and I deliberately don't look at him as I know I'm blushing. Again.

'So what are your plans for the rest of the day?' I ask in a bid to break the tension.

'What do you mean? You're my plans.' It's such an innocent comment but the sincerity of it makes me almost well up, and I have to blink back a couple of tears.

'Well, I guess I'm all yours.' His eyebrows shoot up at this comment, but I ignore him. 'Oh, except I have a date tonight.' I see the briefest frown flit across his face, but he recovers immediately.

'A date, hey? So I've got some competition for your attention then have I? I better up my game.' Oh, please don't, I pray silently. I'm not sure I would be able to cope. I'm just about managing to keep control of my blushes without any extra ammo coming my way.

'So come on, tell me all about this date then.' He tries to sound disinterested, but I can tell from the tone of his voice that he's a) not used to not being the centre of attention and b) that he doesn't like to share. I decide to put him out of his misery.

'Actually, it's with a girl. And don't you even *dare* say anything.' I wag my finger at him as he falls about laughing.

'You're making it too easy, sweet cheeks,' he laughs, as he pulls me into another one-armed hug, almost crushing my skull with his biceps. 'Let me say bye to the guys then you can fill me in on what you've been getting up to while you've been away from me.' He winks and heads over to Theo and Greg, who have been busying themselves with the jet ski, handing over our vests. I follow him and retrieve my bag from Theo while saying my own thanks, to which they nod and still say absolutely nothing in reply. Perhaps they've never seen a girl before. Or maybe they see Jake with so many they don't bother to converse with them any more.

'You hungry?' Jake asks. 'Fancy brunch back at the hotel?'

'Yes, that sounds like a very good plan, even though I did just eat breakfast. Does that make me a total pig?'

'Absolutely not,' he smirks, 'you're girl after my own heart.'

The butterflies take fight and I bite my lip, hoping that he's wrong.

Chapter Twelve

We walk slowly back along the beach, at the shoreline, letting the waves break over our feet as they wash in and out. I fill Jake in on my new friend Rachel, and he pulls all manner of faces as I give him the low-down on what's happened with her and her ex.

'I know who she means. The other woman. They stay here a lot. She's…' he tails off, and I suddenly have an uneasy feeling in my stomach.

'She's what?' I ask.

'She's not someone who likes to take no for an answer. She has a lot of money, well her husband's money, coupled with a lot of time on her hands. You rarely see them doing anything together here. Have you heard of Luis Mendoza?' I shake my head in reply and he continues. 'Well that's her husband. He's a Brazilian millionaire. A casino owner predominately, but he has a lot of fingers in a lot of pies. Most people think they have the measure of him; rich, older man, young wife, they make assumptions, but he's one of the kindest men I've ever met. He ploughs thousands of dollars into charities in Brazil. He came from nothing, made all his own money, so he likes to try and give something back.

'He could easily afford his own place on the island, but he always stays here, in the exact same room, every time he comes to Barbados. I think it reminds him of his first wife. He was married to her for almost twenty years before she died, and she was his world. They used to come to this hotel all the time, so Michael tells me, and then she died and a matter of months later, he met and married Katya. He was lonely, I suppose. There's no way he couldn't know about her not-so-discreet liaisons, but he turns a blind eye and pretty much lets her do what she wants. I mean, everyone knows what she's getting out of it but him...' Jake shakes his head.

'Perhaps he doesn't want to get old alone,' I say, 'and sharing his life with someone is better than sharing it with no one, no matter who they are and what they do.'

'Is that what you think?' he asks, his voice low and even, stopping and turning to face me.

I think about his question before answering with absolute conviction. 'No. That's not what I think at all.'

I know in my heart and soul that if I was asked to pick between being married to Luke, knowing what I know, or being alone for the rest of my days, I would always pick the latter.

'Being in a bad relationship can sometimes feel lonelier than actually being alone,' Jake says in an unexpected moment of raw honesty.

'And you know this from experience?' I ask warily.

'And I know this from experience,' he answers sincerely. Although he's just been open to share this little nugget of information, I already know better than to push it any further, and I know that was the right decision when he changes the subject again.

'Luis always throws a bit of a party when he's here; it's kind of a tradition. It's for both staff and guests, but the guests usually dip out quite early, so everyone ends up letting their hair down a bit. The next one's on Friday night. You should come, and Rachel too. It's good fun.'

'Will his wife be there?' I ask. 'I don't want to bring Rachel along to something where she's going to end up having a fist fight with his wife.'

'Ha!' he barks loudly. 'No chance. She thinks these things are way beneath her, like she's mingling with the peasants or something. Rachel will be safe, I promise.'

'Do you and Katya get on?' I ask, knowing that what I actually want to know isn't what I've just asked.

'Sort of, yes. On the surface, she can be very charming.'

Oh, I bet she can, I think.

'But she's real trouble. I try my best to stay away from her if I can. I have to be polite, of course, but I attempt to have nothing to do with her any more.'

Any more. The words hang in the air between us, and I have to bite my lip to save myself from blurting out the words again as a question. Jake feels it too and glances down at me, while his hand rubs the back of his neck sheepishly.

'She, er, she had a bit of a thing for me, I think, when I first met her.'

Really? I can't think why.

'She used to follow me around and try and corner me on my own.'

He sounds like a scared teenager being pinned by a cougar, and I almost laugh at how worried he sounds. She must have traumatised him.

'Nothing happened between us,' he says quickly. 'Although it wasn't through want of her trying. It got really awkward for a while, but she soon set her sights on some other unsuspecting victim.'

'Jake, look,' I say, stopping and turning to face him, 'you don't have to explain yourself to me. Really.'

'I want to, sweet cheeks. I want you to know not all guys are bad news.' He absent-mindedly takes hold of my hand and brushes my knuckles with his thumb. He stares at our hands linked together and is silent for a moment. It's almost as if he doesn't realise he's touching me. 'You can trust me. I know I said it before, but I mean it. It's important you know that.'

'Why?' I ask, unable to hold back any longer. 'Why is it so important?'

He runs his hands through his hair and looks out to sea, and I sneak a cheeky glance at his body. Sigh.

'It just is. But if you're letting me take you out on seafaring adventures you've got to have a little bit of faith in me, right?' And just like that the moment's passed and we are back to the usual playful banter once more.

He carries on down the beach for a couple of steps, and when I don't follow him immediately, he turns to looks at me. What am I doing? I chide myself. I keep reminding myself that Jake's job is to keep the guests happy and entertained and that I'm not special in any way. But why does he make me feel so much like I am? Like no one matters but me. He's probably had a lot of practice pursuing female guests, and I have no doubt that many of them will have succumbed to his irresistible charms. And he is *so* charming. Charming, funny, handsome. He's gorgeous. But why can't I shake the feeling that there's something more, something unspoken, that I can't seem to put my finger on that's passing between us. I can feel a connection to him. I felt it the first time I saw him, and the first time our skin touched, and every time since. I know how incredibly naïve and stupid it sounds, as I only met him yesterday, but I already feel like he knows me.

He walks back towards me and stands a matter of inches from me, and I sense it again then. Something palpable between us, so real I can almost touch it. I don't know if he feels it too but we stay that way for a moment, so close but not touching, until he gently strokes the outside of my arm.

'Come on, you,' he says simply.

We walk back along the beach in silence until we are almost back at the path that leads up back towards the hotel.

'Look, I hope you don't think this is being too forward,' he asks me. Ha! I think it's a bit late for all that. 'But how would you feel about room service on your balcony? I know the menu pretty well and could get the chef to rustle you up anything you fancy that's not on there. And the view's pretty great from up there.'

He winks and, although I'm nervous about having him in my room, I know I've nothing to worry about in his company. I also realise he might not want to be seen out and about with me, and I understand why. To be honest, I'm a little nervous about being in his company too much around the hotel and the other guests. The last thing I want is for him to get into trouble.

'That sounds great. You shall be my first guest,' I say with an air of ceremony.

He raises an eyebrow at me with a smirk.

'Oh, your *first* guest, hey? I'd better make this good. Set the bar high enough and I could well be the only one you'll need...'

Cue burning cheeks.

We walk up the path towards the hotel, and I'm looking around to see if anyone's seen us but nobody gives us a second glance. Maybe I'm being paranoid. This might sound terrible, but most people probably don't even know who he is, they might have seen him around but they don't know he works here. One person that does know, however, is Maya, and as we reach reception I make towards the lift, but he stops at the front desk.

'I won't be a second,' he says and jogs to the desk, leaning over it as Maya takes a call. I carry on waking towards the lift, unsure what else to do, and hit the call button. I see Maya put the phone down and say something to Jake, but I can't hear what. He laughs, and she raises her eyebrows at him and glances over to me. I feel instantly embarrassed, as he's clearly told her he's going up to my suite, and I'm desperate to yell 'I'm not a total slut. Honestly, it's just brunch!' But she smiles at me, and I give her a lame, little wave as I shuffle, self-consciously, from foot to foot. Jake walks towards me and turns and blows a kiss to Maya as he nears me. She rolls her eyes, but she's smiling as she does it. She seems to do a lot of eyebrow raising and eye rolling around Jake, I note. And she definitely looks like someone who has got the absolute measure of him and also takes none of his crap.

He joins me at the lift just as the doors open. It's empty, and he holds out his hand to let me step inside. I enter and turn to face the open doors, with my back to the mirror on the wall. I step to the side slightly, as I expect him to stand beside me, but he walks in and stands there, straight in front of me, facing me with his back to the door. His chest is at my eye level, and I look up to see him staring down at me.

The doors close behind him with a *bing* and the lift begins to move upwards. I'm suddenly very aware that I'm still only wearing my swimming costume, my clothes stashed away in my bag, and he's only in his swim shorts. We stand that way for a few seconds before I can no longer bear the tension building between us, and I look away. At that moment he takes his hand and twists a loose piece of my hair around his fingers before letting it drop back down to my face. I risk a glance up at him.

'Sweet cheeks, I...'

BING.

The lift doors open and he pauses for a moment, like he's wondering whether or not to carry on talking, but he moves to the side to let me pass. I instantly wish I'd done more squats in my life, as I pray he's not looking at my bottom. Don't flatter yourself, Carrie, he's not interested in your bottom. But I have a sense his eyes are on me, and I want to curl up in a ball.

'Sweet cheeks indeed,' he says very quietly, and deeply, in that growling voice. I whip my head around and scowl at him, but I can't help the smile (or the blush) that creeps on to my face. *He was checking out my bum.* And wasn't repulsed by it, it would seem.

'Eyes on the road, mister.' I point towards my door and stand still, my back against the wall until he's passed me. He saunters past, his face grinning, and another deep frown that I throw his way makes him laugh.

My stomach is churning slightly, as I slide the key card and push open my suite door. I know it's only brunch but it feels like more than just that in this moment. Aside from the jet-skiing earlier, I'm struggling to remember the last time I was alone like this with a man who wasn't Luke. That's because you never have been, Carrie, I remind myself. Then I'm hit with a sudden wave of panic. God, what if he thinks I'm going to sleep with him? What if he expects it? I know what he said on the beach, and I do trust him, but what if I'm so out of practice I've missed all the signals and he thinks he's coming up here for a quickie? I mean, he's gorgeous, and I would be lying if I said my thoughts hadn't drifted there a couple of times. If this is what he wants would my body take over all rational thought and just give into his touch? My heart starts beating faster as I realise I've frozen on the spot, my hand still holding the door open to my room. I feel Jake move a step closer behind me, and he takes over holding the door and slowly turns me around to face him.

'Just brunch, sweet cheeks, don't look so worried,' he says very gently, his tone light-hearted and with a sincere smile on his face. I relax instantly and exhale.

'I wasn't...' I trail off because we both know what I was thinking, and now I feel completely stupid and embarrassed that I even thought it. I don't think for a minute he would take advantage of me in any way, shape, or form, and Lord knows why I would even begin to think he would actually want to. Just because he's flirting with me, doesn't mean he wants to *sleep* with me. Jesus, I feel like an idiot right about now. Thankfully, Jake changes the tempo again, as he claps his hands, rubbing them together, and strides past me, straight to the room service menu on the bedside table.

'Now, what do you fancy?' he asks, as he reclines on my bed and raises his eyebrows at me. Despite me having just freaked out, I'm happy we are back to business as usual. He looks divine on those crisp, white sheets and, in that second,

I wonder why I was worried about him wanting to sleep with me at all.

'You pick,' I say with a laugh and shake my head at his last comment. 'I'm just popping to the bathroom. Won't be a sec.' My costume is pretty much dry, but I take in my bag and slip on my shorts over the top so I'm not feeling quite so exposed while we eat. I don't want to put him off his dinner. Although the way he flirts with me at every given opportunity, I'm not sure he would care if I sat there naked. I pull down my bun and redo it before splashing water on my face to get rid of some of the salt. I notice my freckles have started to come out, and I've already picked up a bit of a tan from this morning.

After getting dressed in my shorts and putting on a slick of lip balm because you know, what the hell, I head back to the main room to find it empty and see Jake leaning out on the balcony, his back to me. I walk out to join him and take a glance at my phone on the side. A message from Mum and one from Kate. I think about opening them for a moment but, worried they might ruin my day in some way, I ignore them for now.

Jake must hear me coming, and he turns round as I step outside. His arms are stretched out along the edge of the balcony as he leans back against it, baring his entire torso. I give a half smile and push my lips together hard to stop a grin spreading across my entire face. He is quite the specimen. I don't know why, but I have the sudden urge, for the first time since we met, to walk up and put my arms around him. His easy way has made me feel so comfortable that I'm worried I'm starting to blur all the usual, appropriate boundaries. I get a hold of myself and take a position next to him on the balcony, looking out to sea, at which point he pulls me into a hug. So much for keeping my hands to myself. My hands feel tiny compared to his muscly back, and I let out a big sigh as I just let him hold me for a second. Why does his touch feel so good, and why does my body seem to respond to it so much? I sigh deeply, getting a little lost in the moment, and he pulls away from me.

'I had fun earlier. Not that this isn't fun,' Jake says, gesturing around him with his arms. '*You're* fun, sweet cheeks. I like being around you.'

I'm taken aback by this little confession and don't really know what to say.

'So what food did you order?' Was that really the best response I could come up with?

He smiles at me and gives a small shake of his head with a sigh, as if he didn't quite want that part of the conversation to be over. But the way he says some things, they make me get so nervous around him. Good nervous. But nervous all the same. I've just come out of my heap of crap with Luke, and I'm worried I'm not in a healthy position to make rational, well thought out decisions. I know I'm totally overthinking this, he's not asked me to marry him. He's not even kissed me yet, and here I am worrying about having non-existent feelings for each other. I push the thoughts to the back of my mind, determined just to enjoy it for what it is. But half the problem, I realise, is that I'm not totally sure *what* it is. He seems to captivate me in a way I've never known, and I don't know what to do with it. I turn my attention back to him, as he starts reeling off a ridiculously long list of food that he's ordered for us.

'...and so I thought you must like something in all that lot.' I just nod enthusiastically having absolutely no idea what he's just said. 'Shall we get this baby going, what do you say?' he asks, sounding excited. I look around, momentarily confused, until my eyes follow his line of sight and fall on the huge hot tub.

'Oh no, no, no. No *way* are you getting me in that thing!'

'What? So you're more than happy to get on a jet ski with me and go racing off over the open ocean, but climbing into what's essentially a large bubble bath is scary?'

No, I think to myself, *the scary thing is being in what's essentially a large bubble bath with* you.

'Jake, it's not even twelve o'clock!' I stutter, as if this is some sort of explanation for not getting in a hot tub.

'It's not filled with tequila, you know?' he teases, totally ignoring my protestations and walking over to it. He leans down to one side of it and flicks a switch, as it springs to life with a mass of bubbles.

'The food will be another ten or fifteen minutes. Hop in.' He's already climbing the two small steps up to the tub and swinging his leg into the water. Oh Lord, I have to get undressed again, don't I? I should have just left my bloody shorts off.

I stand with my arms folded self-consciously, trying to put off the inevitable. Jake's chest height in the water, looking super relaxed, with his shades covering his eyes. He tilts them down like a schoolteacher and looks at me over the top. I know instantly that he knows why I'm hesitant and there's that sensation again. That he already knows what I'm feeling.

'Sweet cheeks...' he begins slowly, and takes that moment to take off his shades and drop them on the edge of the hot tub, lifting himself out of the water and striding towards me. I burst out laughing at his grin and his over-egged swagger. He knows exactly what he's doing, and I have to admit, he's irresistible.

'Don't be shy now.' He winks at me and shakes his head, flipping his hair back and forth.

'You are such an idiot,' I say, unbuttoning my shorts and stepping straight into the hot tub. He smiles smugly, mission accomplished, and sits back down.

'See? That wasn't so hard, was it? And for the record, you have nothing whatsoever to be ashamed of.' I blush deeply and glance at him out of the corner of my eye.

'Thanks,' I mumble, embarrassed.

I turn my head, looking out at the view. From where I'm sitting I can see the edge of the swimming pool and, on the other side of the path and surrounding trees, the roof of The Coconut Shack that leads out to the white sand and bright, azure waters. It's idyllic, and I still can't really believe I'm here. That I did it. Coupled with the fact that it's mid-morning, and I'm sitting, half-naked, in a hot tub with a nigh on god. *Ha! Fuck you Luke*, I smile smugly to myself.

'What are you daydreaming about?' Jake's voice breaks my thoughts, and I know he's been watching me.

'Oh, just admiring the view.'

'Really? Me too.' He grins, and I'm about to whip my hand across the water and splash him for making such a comment, but something about his suddenly serious tone stops me, and he doesn't take his eyes from mine. I briefly look away, but his intense stare draws me straight back in, and my eyes return to meet his. So deep and so unusual. So new, to me, and yet looking in them now, they feel so familiar. They really are quite unsettling. I feel like there are many things I could say, but I'm not sure where to start, so I decide to just not say anything at all.

'Sweet cheeks, are you happy?' he asks me which takes me a bit by surprise. Even more surprising is that I answer, without hesitation.

'Yes, I am. And I actually am, I'm not just saying that. Being here, it's better. And you,' I pause and smile warmly at him, 'you help. Being around you helps. And I know it's stupid, because I hardly know you at all, but that's just how it feels. Despite what's happened and the fact that I know I really shouldn't be, I am.'

I stop there because I know I'm starting to ramble, and I don't want to get swept away in it all and say something stupid. I'm still a bit emotional, but something about Jake makes me want to spill my feelings. I am happy here now, but I admit to myself that I'm also uneasy about what my future holds.

'I'm leaving in two weeks, Jake. What am I going to do when I get home?'

'Two weeks is a long time. And you don't have to do anything. Do you guys have a house together?'

'We do, but it's my house, in my name. I emailed Luke to tell him to get out, so I'm hoping he's gone when I get back. If not, I can stay with my mum until he is. I just want a clean break now.'

'So Luke's been in touch?' he asks warily. I tell him about the messages and my subsequent replies.

'Well done, sweet cheeks. You're amazing.'

'Jake, I'm not amazing, I'm just… being practical, logical. I'm…'

'Amazing,' he shrugs. 'Dress it up how you like, but not many people would have handled this the way you have.'

'What, you mean by running away?'

'You didn't run away, you needed space, and who wouldn't? No one can blame you for that.'

'Yeah, but I came on my honeymoon! Who does that? What was I thinking? Was this the worst idea ever? Sorry. I don't actually expect you to have answers to these questions. I'm more asking myself than anyone.'

I realise I've been gesticulating wildly and splashing water everywhere, as Jake wipes his face and takes hold of both my hands.

'Carrie, look at me. It's going to be OK. That part of your life, it's done, you don't ever have to go back to it.'

'You make it sound so easy. At the end of the day, well, at the end of two weeks to be precise, I'm going to go home and then what? You won't be there to distract me from everything, and I'm going to have to fall back into my normal life, only this time, it's missing a huge chunk in the shape of Luke and Emily, and I don't know how to do that, Jake.'

Well, this took a bit of a turn, I muse as my eyes fill with tears. Five minutes ago I didn't think I would be sat in the hot tub crying. There were a fair few thoughts that crossed my mind, but crying wasn't one of them.

There is a long pause before Jake speaks, a small hint of amusement in his voice.

'You find me distracting?'

'No! I mean yes, you do distract me, but I don't...' I trail off. 'Yes. Yes, I find you distracting.' God, I'm just unravelling in front of his very eyes. I put my head in my hands. 'For whatever reason, you seem to bring out my worst traits.'

'And they are?' he asks with mock cautiousness.

'Being too honest and rambling!'

He laughs and slides over to me, taking my hands away from my face and holding them in his.

'It's been a matter of hours since we met, but in that time you've shown more sense of character, more strength and more genuine sincerity than most of the people I've ever come across. And if those are your worst traits, I think you're doing alright.' He cups my chin in his large hands and slowly and gently rubs the outline of my bottom lip with his thumb. 'What is it about you?' he asks with a frown on his face, although I'm not sure he's asking me as much as he's asking himself. I force myself to look at him and put my hand up to cover his. I gently move it away from my face, and my stomach flips at our touch, leaving me feeling giddy and sick all at the same time. I can still feel the space on my face where his hand was, and I wish I hadn't moved it away. But I almost feel I'm *too* happy. Like I've replaced the empty feeling of the last few days with Jake, and when I leave I'm going to have to face it for real, like being here is sticking a huge plaster over the wound that I'm going to have to rip off in two weeks' time.

Suddenly there's a loud *TRING!* and I jump out of my skin, squeezing Jake's hand in an involuntary response to what I can now calculate is the doorbell, signalling the end of the moment and the arrival of our food. Jake gives a little huff, and it's the first time I've seen his face look annoyed, but he recovers immediately and beams at me.

'Food time!' he says excitedly, as he leaps out of the hot tub and puts his hand out to help me.

'Why do I feel like Red Riding Hood when you say that?' I say narrowing my eyes at him with distrust.

'Ha! Tasty indeed!' he growls back in my direction.

He grabs a towel, that's been placed on the sunbeds by housekeeping, and throws another one in my direction, wiping his face and torso on his way to open my door. Without a moment's hesitation, I note. I'm suddenly worried at what the hotel employee on the other side is going to think about him being up here in my room, but I soon realise that Jake clearly doesn't and he greets them like long-lost friends, ushering them through the doors and into the suite. A middle-aged man and young girl wheel in two huge tables full of silver platters, followed by a teenage boy carrying a tray laden with a cafetière, teapot and fruit juices of varying colours.

'Just here is great,' he says and directs them over to the space by the open doors. They wheel the tables over and open up the leaves from underneath, spreading the platters out as they do so. Then, in sync, they all turn to look at me, and I plaster an awkward smile on my face feeling like I've been caught doing something I shouldn't.

'Thank you so, so much.' I say weakly, and Jake shakes each of their hands in turn and reiterates his thanks.

'Thanks George, you're a star,' he says to the older man. 'Have a great day, guys.'

'You too, sir. Ma'am,' replies George, nodding at me politely. *What a gent*, I think. They all take another swift look at me and then back out of the room sheepishly. I don't know what they look so awkward about. They certainly aren't the ones shacked up, half-naked, with the hotel handyman. George closes the door behind him, and I walk over to the tables where Jake is already unveiling silver platters. He holds the top of one of the metal domes and lifts it off with a flourish to reveal a huge plate of scrambled eggs and smoked salmon with bagels.

'Ta-da!'

'Bloody hell, Jake, this looks delicious. How much food did you order?'

'Madam, please be seated,' he says in a terrible French accent.

'Merci beaucoup, c'est magnifique. Je suis très impressionne,' I reply without missing a beat, and Jake shoots back a wicked grin.

'Mais bien sûr. Mes talents sont infinies,' he says, smugly.

I throw back my head and let out a loud laugh.

'Touché.'

He passes me a plate and carries on removing the rest of the covers. My stomach gives a rumble right on cue. It all smells divine.

'So French, hey?' Jake grins at me, as he scoops up some pancakes with bacon and maple syrup, loading them on to his plate, popping a piece of crispy bacon into his mouth as he does so. He licks his fingers, and I wonder how he can make the most innocent gesture seem so bloody sexy.

'Oui.' I smile oh-so sweetly, spooning some of the bagel and eggs I was just eyeing up on to my plate. 'My dad was a French teacher at my high school. He taught me all I know,' I explain, and I smile at the memory of me and Dad driving my mum crazy singing along to the CD of French songs in the kitchen. And the car. And the lounge. 'And you?' I ask him.

'Well working in the hotel trade, the odd language comes in handy.'

'So you speak more than one?'

'I do,' he nods.

'Oh come on, stop being so coy!' I tease as we step out on to the balcony, and I sit down at the table. The sun is blinding against the white floor and walls, and Jake walks over to the corner of the balcony and pulls over the huge, square parasol so it shields our table. I stare at his arms as they flex around the heavy furniture and tilt my head to the side. Swoon. I raise my eyebrows at him, as he still hasn't answered my question, but he just gives a little smile and brings out the tray of drinks, setting them down on the ottoman and passing me what looks like a cappuccino.

'I speak French, Spanish, almost fluent Italian and a little German.'

My eyes widen. 'Holy crap, Jake, that's amazing! Where on earth did you learn to speak all those?'

He shrugs non-committally. 'School. My dad. My mum. Work. Mostly from work actually, the guests I mean. It's amazing what you pick up.'

'So have you worked abroad a bit then? Hmm. God, this is gorgeous,' I mumble through my full mouth, ramming another piece of bagel in and not even caring that I must look incredibly unattractive right now.

'I worked in the UK for a while, but the hotel was a big international chain so a language was kind of a prerequisite, and the same in the States. But I did work in France and Switzerland for a couple of years too, so I've picked up a bit along the way.'

'It sounds like you've picked up a *lot* along the way. That so impressive. Didn't you want to do anything else with it? Sorry, that sounds awful, doesn't it? I just mean with all those under your belt, the world was your oyster. You could have had your pick of jobs.'

He smiles knowingly at me and takes a swig of my cappuccino without a moment's hesitation.

'I love what I do. Really. I wouldn't swap my job for anything. It's what my dad did, and it makes me feel closer to him, like I'm continuing his legacy in some way. No need for you to worry about what's under my belt, sweet cheeks.'

He walks over to the table and brings me a bowl of fresh fruit and a basket of salt bread rolls. I break one in half and take a bite out of it, groaning at the soft, springy centre.

'Seriously, why is all the food here so damn good? I'm going to be the size of a house by the time I go home. I don't need to worry about bumping into anyone, they won't recognise me at this rate.'

Home. There it was again. A constant reminder that I still had unfinished business to deal with. Despite the finality of my messages to Luke and Emily, I knew, deep down, that it wasn't going to be that easy.

'So anyway, what about you?' Jake asks me. 'What do you do?'

'Actually, I'm self-employed.'

'Pray tell, doing what?' He leans forward in his chair, sharing my bowl of fruit.

'Seriously?' I say with mock irritation. 'Has anyone ever told you you're the worst dinner companion ever? Do you ever get a second date?'

'You can tell me later,' he smiles. My heart quickens slightly, but I retain my composure.

'This isn't a date,' I giggle. 'We're two friends having breakfast.'

'A half-naked breakfast in a hotel suite on a tropical island.'

'Do you ever get bored?' I ask exasperated but blushing.

'What of making you blush? Never, sweet cheeks. Never.' And the look he gives me is one that I can only describe as pure sex, which does nothing at all to help with the intense colour in my cheeks. Damn it, so he has noticed. OK, now I'm really mortified.

'Ah, this is too easy,' he chuckles and shakes his head.

'Oh, I'm so glad you find mocking me so very amusing,' I say folding my arms across my chest like a grumpy toddler.

'I'm not mocking you, don't be cross.' He grabs my hand and gently pulls it to unfold my arms. 'And you're not amusing, you're funny and you're gorgeous and I love it,' he adds like it's the most natural thing in the world for him to say. Christ, I almost thought he was going to say love *you* for a second there. I really am getting carried away now. Yes, let's ask him to marry you next, Carrie! Ready for babies, Jake? Step right up!

'Anyway, stop trying to distract me,' he scolds, 'you were telling me about your work.'

'I'm a freelance proofreader and transcriber,' I tell him, happy to be back on safer ground. 'I work mainly for universities and colleges. They send me what they need me to do, I do it, send it back and they pay me for it. I work from home; well I can actually work from anywhere. I do a bit of translation as well with my French. People always say it sounds so boring, but I like it. It gives me a sense of achievement. I like to get something rough round the edges and make it perfect. I like seeing something unfinished and turning it into the finished product.'

'So you like things rough round the edges, hey? I'll bear that in mind,' Jake drawls at me.

'I think we both know there's nothing wrong with your edges,' I mutter, unable to help myself, which earns me a winning grin and a raised eyebrow from Jake. 'What, you think you're the only one who has banter?' I say, as I stretch my arms over my head and cross and uncross my legs in a theatrical manner. Jake bursts out laughing, and I giggle. What's come over me? I'm throwing all inhibitions out of the window, and for once I feel great about it. I think I've got a case of something they call 'the fuck its'.

We graze on the buffet for a while longer before Jake asks me if there's anything I'd like to do.

'Not really. I don't know what there is to do here, but I'm not that bothered. I'm quite happy with just hanging out. I need to relax, I think.'

'Whatever you want, gorgeous. We can do nothing. Or everything.'

I daren't risk looking at him, as I know I'm bright red all over and the butterflies in my stomach start whizzing around at just the thought of doing *anything* with him right at this second.

We leave the table, and he makes a call down to room service to let them know we've finished eating (although I stole a salt bread roll and pot of jam for later) and together, we wheel the tables back out into the hallway for George and his team to come and collect. I don't bother getting dressed or covering up because, quite frankly, that ship has sailed by now. He really doesn't seem to care which puts me even more at ease. I think of all the times I've changed in the gym, hiding behind my towel, and how I would cringe to myself on my previous holidays at revealing myself in a bikini, even in front of all my closest friends. Yet now, in front of a total hunk who does incredibly strange things to me and can make me blush with just a look, I'm, for want of a better phrase, letting it all hang out. I grab my sun cream from my bag, settling myself on one of the sunbeds and turn to look up at Jake, and he's taken up his spot leaning back on the balcony.

'Can we just do this?' I ask scrunching up my nose and squirting a big blob of sun cream on to my hand and rubbing it into my arms.

'What, rub lotion into each other? Hell yeah, I'm up for that.' And he stalks across the balcony making me feel like a gazelle waiting to be pounced on. I point a finger at him and put on my best stern face, which is very difficult while he's looking as if he's going to swallow me whole.

'You stay over there and keep your hands to yourself!'

'You're a tease and you know it,' he chuckles good-naturedly. 'Want me to do your back?'

'Take one more step and I'm calling security to have you removed from my suite,' I giggle, but he just laughs and takes the bottle from my hand, walking behind me.

'I am security, I'm afraid, so your pleas will fall on deaf ears. OK, that's not strictly true, but they won't come anyway. Marcus owes me money from our last poker night.' I hear him squirt some cream on to his hand, and he tosses the bottle on the bed beside me, and I tense with anticipation of his touch.

'I love how you know everyone here. And that you all seem to be mates with each other. It feels like a real family, it's so nice.'

At that moment I feel his hands move on to my body, and he rhythmically beings to massage the sun cream into my shoulders, neck and back. I take a deep sigh and roll my head from side to side to allow him better access. His hands are so large they cover most of my upper body, and the feel of him moving back and forth over my bare skin is so hypnotic. My skin feels like it's glowing where he's touched it. I bite my lip as he moves further down my back and under the tie of my costume. I arch my back automatically, as he spreads his fingers very slightly around my waist. Then suddenly, he stops.

'There. All done.'

I let out a long breath and manage to say a timid, 'Thank you,' before he sits himself on the sunlounger next to me and flashes a wicked grin in my direction.

'Do you want me to do your le…?'

'I can manage, thank you very much,' I say quickly, cutting him off, but I can't help the smile that sneaks into my voice. There's just something about the way he is, that no matter how annoyed I try and get at his incessant teasing and flirting, I just can't.

We spend the next few hours lounging on the balcony and fall easily into periods of companionable silence. We talk more about my childhood holidays and my parents, and he tells me stories of his time in Europe and the places his work has taken him to. He avoids the topic of his actual job, and I wonder whether it's because I've made him embarrassed about it, but I begin to grasp that he's really not bothered about such things and I stop worrying.

Thankfully, we also avoid the subject of Luke, and I'm grateful we seem to have made an unspoken agreement to stay on safe ground with our topics of conversation. I'm exhausted just thinking about it and it feels good to have a normal conversation. Well, as normal as normal can be on a balcony, in the sun, on my honeymoon with another man.

Later in the afternoon, Jake goes down to the bar and returns with a jug of rum punch and some bottled water, plus some tapas-style nibbles. It's easily the most relaxed I've felt in weeks, even in the run-up to the wedding, and I feel a gush of emotion when, after dozing off in the sun, I wake to find Jake's positioned the parasol over me so I don't burn.

'Hello, sleepyhead.'

'Oh God. Jake, I'm so sorry.' I push myself up into a sitting position. 'How embarrassing. Could I be worse company? Between lamenting my mess of a life and then actually falling asleep on you, I'm sure you could have thought of better ways to spend an afternoon.'

He smiles at me, his face lighting up. 'There was nowhere I would rather have been. Trust me. If I wanted to leave, I would have.'

'Oh, charming!' I say grabbing one of the cushions on the beds and throwing it at his head which, annoyingly, he catches and lobs right back.

'You're very cute when you're asleep, you know?' He takes a swig from a bottle of water and a sudden image of him dowsing himself in it, letting it run all over his body like some sort of Diet Coke advert, pops inappropriately into my head. OK, now I'm blushing just *thinking* about him. I need to drench myself in water by the sounds of it. Get. A. Grip. One afternoon in a man's company and I've lost all self-control.

'Please say you weren't watching me sleep, I may curl up in a ball and die!' I cringe.

'Not watching,' he laughs. 'I'm not a complete stalker. Observing, rather.'

'Same difference,' I tease. 'Stalker.' But he smiles at me and pushes himself off the sunbed.

'I didn't want to leave when you were sleeping, but I do have to go for a while. Sorry. Work.' He looks rueful and runs his hands through his hair. 'I know you have dinner plans but I might see you later?'

'Well, I have nowhere else to go but here so… What time is it, by the way?'

'Just gone four p.m.'

'Four p.m.!' I yell, alarmed and jump off the bed. 'Jake, I've been asleep for hours. Why didn't you wake me? You must have been so bored. I'm so sorry.'

'You clearly needed to rest, and you looked peaceful. I was just happy here in your company. Really, it's fine.'

As if to prove it, he comes over to me and slides one hand around the back of my neck. I tense slightly and move my head back a tiny fraction, which he acknowledges with small smile. He tilts his head down to me and his lips gently brush my forehead.

'Until tonight,' he drawls with a mischievous grin.

'Seriously?' I say, exasperated and feeling rather hot all of a sudden. 'You don't have to try and charm my pants off all the time, you know.'

He laughs loudly. 'I think it's safest for all of us if I don't say anything in response to that.'

I stay rooted on the spot until the door closes behind him before I fling myself on the sunbed and let out a long sigh. I hear my phone ringing and, irritated, get back off the sunbed and retrieve it from the side in my room. It's a call from Kate. I don't answer it because I don't want to lie to her about what I've been doing, but I can't bring myself to tell her I've spent a day in such close proximity to Jake. In fact, I'm not sure I want to mention his name to her at all.

Chapter Thirteen

I don't venture out again but decide to stay in my suite, to catch the last few rays of sun on the balcony, before I get ready for my dinner with Rachel. I even manage another dip in the hot tub, which is fun, but I have to admit, far less so without Jake. Funnily enough the view really isn't quite so good.

I've spent nearly a whole day with Jake, and now I'm feeling more confused than ever. Apart from the conversation we had about me going home, I hardly thought about Luke at all. For much of the day I felt like we were almost on holiday *together*, and it's made me feel a little on edge. It sounds ludicrous but he's so easy to be around, and I can't ignore the fact I do think I might actually fancy him a bit. But, in a friendly sort of way. I don't want to jump into bed with him but could happily spend an evening in his company having dinner, maybe some drinks. OK, so I've made that sound like a date with someone I fancy.

Oh Lord. I haven't fancied anyone in so long, I've forgotten what it's like. I actually take a gasp of breath as I realise that I've just admitted to myself that I didn't fancy Luke. But surely I did? I mean, we were getting married. I must have? Mustn't I? I'm not going to do this right now, I decide. I really should call Kate now I've composed myself (and my story) a bit.

I start to run a bath and sit cross-legged on the bed to FaceTime Kate. I purposely ignore my emails for now. She doesn't pick up, so I head towards the bathroom and, just as I get there, I turn on my heels as my phone starts ringing.

'Hello, darling!' She beams at me as her face comes on to the screen. 'Sorry about that, I was on the phone. I'm just on my lunch break, good timing. You alright?'

'I'm good, I'm good. Weather's lush, food's great, beaches are awesome. I went on a jet ski today!' Oh crap. Why did I let that slip out? What is my problem?

'Get out! That's awesome! Was it fun? Was that with the hotel?'

'Yeah, so much fun. I loved it. It was just down on the beach right by us.'

'Wow. So cool. What are your plans for tonight?'

'Not much, I made a friend today. A girl called Rachel who just broke up with her boyfriend. On this holiday, would you believe? So we are teaming up for dinner later, a sort of losers-r-us Caribbean convention.'

'Don't be daft, you're nowhere near being a loser in any way. That's sounds really nice. Good for the pair of you,' she says seriously. 'None of this is your fault, Carrie. You're doing amazing and, honestly, I can't believe how OK you sound.' She gives a small laugh. 'It's really weird, you sort of look better than I've seen you for ages. I know you must feel awful still, but you're doing so well.'

I feel a bit annoyed at her patronising tone but remind myself she's just being nice and to not be such a bitch. What do I expect her to say? As much as I wish she would, we can't ignore the topic really, can we?

'Er, thanks. I think it's just the sun.' My face tries to grass me up, turning a shade of pink at the thought of Jake.

'Carrie, listen. I spoke to Luke, and he's devastated about what's happened. He's so sorry. I know this doesn't change anything, but he does care about you…'

I cut her off, as I really don't want to hear any more.

'Kate, look, he *really* doesn't. He might say that, but if he really did he wouldn't have done what he did. We are done. Nothing you say will make me change my mind or feel any less disgusted with him.'

'I know,' she says quietly. 'I was chatting to Dan just now, and he said Luke's really messed up about the whole thing.'

'And I'm not? Kate, I know he's your brother, but I really can't believe you're siding with him in all this.'

'What? Babe, no, how can you say that? That's not what it is, I'm just saying, Dan said Luke's not coping very well, that's all.'

My anger is at risk of boiling over, and I'm barely keeping it in check. How dare she?

'Kate, he cheated on me. *With Emily.* Just think about that for a second. Truly process that information. Do you really think I care about how he is feeling right now? Like he's some sort of victim in all this! And anyway, what the hell is with you and Dan at the minute?' I spit. OK, so that's not how I meant this to go at all.

'What?' she says far too quickly, and I immediately note the defensive tone in her voice. 'What do you mean?'

'Kate, I know you,' I say more softly, 'and I know him. Something's not right. I don't know what's going on, but I know there's something.'

'So, you think something's happened between me and Dan? That I'm cheating on Justin. Is that what this is?'

'Kate…'

'Carrie, I can't believe you would think that! So let's get this right, Luke cheats on you and, because I'm his sister, I get tarred with the same brush?'

'Kate that is *not* what I said.' *But it is what I meant*, I think guiltily.

'Look, I know that you're going through a lot, but how dare you accuse me. I don't think we should talk about this right now.' I see her eyes fill with tears. 'I'm going to go. I'll talk to you later.'

And with that her face disappears from the screen and she hangs up. I throw myself back on the bed in exasperation and cover my face with my hands. Well, that didn't exactly go to plan. My stomach churns and, still feeling on edge, I go to check on the bath. Despite her adamant protestations, and as awful as I feel thinking it, I still don't believe she's telling me the whole truth.

———————————————

My bath goes some way to making me feel slightly more normal, although right now, I have absolutely no idea what normal is, even my old normal with Luke, that certainly doesn't feel like any of that was normal either.

I decide to dress up a bit for my dinner with Rachel and enjoy taking my time getting ready. Something tells me I'm not going to see Jake again this evening, so I won't have to worry about him thinking it's for his benefit. I leave my hair to dry in the sun and, thankfully, it behaves and falls into loose waves rather than the usual frizzy mess I get at home. It's too hot for make-up, so I embrace my freckles that have appeared after my day in the sun and leave my face bare apart from a slick of lip gloss. I pull on a pale pink, sleeveless shift dress with a deep V at the front and a pair of strappy, tan wedges before spritzing myself with perfume and a liberal application of insect repellent. I know from past experience that I'm the insect equivalent to a tub of Ben and Jerry's. After today there is no way I am taking my phone with me, but I do give my mum a text.

Hi Mum, made a friend today! A nice girl here on her own too, so we are having dinner together tonight. Been a good day – relaxed and did some sunbathing. Maybe beach tomorrow, not sure yet. Hope all's OK there. I'm feeling alright. Love you lots and lots. Will ring you tomorrow. Xxxxxxxx

Bless my mum, I know she will be worrying, and I've just grabbed my bag to walk out of the door, when I hear my phone ping. Presuming it's her, I go and check it.

Kingston – give me a shout when you get a chance. Hope Barbados is awesome and you've not flung yourself off the balcony yet, ha, ha! (Don't bother you're far too cute.) Jokes, obviously! Not about being cute, about the balcony. Sorry, I'm not very good at this, am I? So yeah, give me a ring. Love ya. DJ. Xxx

Dan. Well this just gets weirder and weirder. I smile at his rambling message and sadly realise that I won't get to spend as much time with him as we always have. I want us to stay in touch, but I just assume that, in the split, Luke will get Dan. Will I get Kate? Or will he get her too? My stomach clenches at the thought of losing another friend. I'm not sure I've done myself any favours with our last chat. I look at the time. Six fifty-three. No time to call Dan now. I don't want to keep Rachel waiting on her own, but I am very intrigued about what he has to say. I do a mental count back in my head. There will still be time later on, even with the time difference. I toss my phone on the bed and then, unable to leave it, pick it up and place it on my bedside cabinet. Just because my life is a mess, doesn't mean my room has to be.

Downstairs, Maya's still on reception, and I give her a wave as I make my way outside and down the path towards The Coconut Shack. The air is blissfully warm and the fairy lights on the palm trees send an enchanting glow across the gardens. One of my favourite things about being on holiday are the sounds. The waves on the shore during the day and the hum of the cicadas at night. I can hear a soft reggae beat coming from the direction I'm headed which is abruptly broken by my name being yelled from behind me. I spin round and see Rachel tottering towards me on pair of grey, chunky heels wearing a strappy black playsuit covered in banana leaf print.

'I am so glad I caught you,' she pants, as she reaches me and links her arm through mine. 'I hate walking into somewhere on my own or, even worse, being sat there waiting like I've been stood up. How are you? Gosh, you look so brown already. What have you been doing today?'

She fires off questions at a million miles an hour, turning to look at me as she speaks. 'You look so nice, by the way, love the dress.' She gives me a little squeeze close to her. 'Listen, thanks so much for asking me out tonight. I was dreading the rest of the trip, but thank God we bumped into each other. OK, now I'm rambling, I think I've had too much sun already! Anyway, you were telling me what you'd done today.' She takes a breath and I giggle at her.

'I'll save it until we sit down, shall I?' I reply and nod in the direction of Dale waving us over.

'OMG. That's the barman who was here the other night. The one I made a right tit of myself in front of with Ben. He is so cute as well. Oh man, I'm such a loser.' She slumps her shoulders, and I laugh at her melodramatics.

'Come on,' I nudge her in the direction of the bar, 'I'll introduce you.'

'You know him?' she looks at me, shocked.

'Let's just say we have a mutual friend.' I give her a look that tells her there is way more of a story behind my comment, and her eyes widen.

'Now this sounds like a story that needs to be accompanied by a bottle of something. Red or white?'

'White?'

'You read my mind. Now introduce me to my future husband, and you can fill me in.'

Dale and Rachel make eyes at each other like a pair of teenagers when I introduce them, and Dale makes her day when he says he was about to make her another drink to throw over Ben. He shows us to a table at the far side of the restaurant, right next to the beach. The wooden fence that surrounds the outside eating space is lit by large, burning torches from which strings of fairy lights hang between, swinging in the light, sea breeze. I look around as we settle ourselves at the table and whisper conspiratorially behind my menu at Rachel.

'There are loads of couples here. I didn't even notice until now. Thank God I found you.' We giggle at each other.

'Maybe people will think we're a couple. We would probably have more luck together than we'd have with men if our recent track records are anything to go by.'

'Let me know if you want me to snog you over the table to make Dale jealous,' I say with a straight face.

'Do you think it would?' she asks eagerly, until we both bursts into fits of giggles again. We hide behind our menus and hurry to regain our composure, as Dale comes over to take our order.

'My, my, my! You two look like you're getting into trouble already. And you've not even invited me to join you yet,' Dale says with a wink at Rachel, which sets her off again. 'What would you both like?'

We just about manage to compose ourselves enough to do a quick scan of the menu and give him our order, but after he came up trumps with the fishcakes, we go with his suggestions and end up with coconut shrimp to share for a starter, tuna steak for me and grilled mahi mahi for Rachel, all rounded off with a bottle of crisp, white wine. He throws us a bright smile and bounces off, his short dreadlocks shaking up and down as he goes.

'He is so nice,' she says dreamily. 'Doesn't he seem lovely?'

'He does. Very much. And he seems quite taken with you too.' We glance towards him and catch Dale looking over, throwing one of his megawatt smiles in Rachel's direction. 'You after a holiday romance are you, hey?' I tease her. 'Don't waste much time do you?'

'You bet I am! I'm not wasting another second on that loser. I'm definitely from the school of thought that the best way to get over a man is to get under another one.' I snort loudly and almost spit out my wine. 'Anyway, I'm young, free and single now.' She flicks her dark hair over her shoulder and her grin reaches across her face, her eyes twinkling. 'Who doesn't love a holiday romance after all?'

I don't say anything but scrunch my nose up, pulling a face.

'*Oh!*' she chuckles. 'Sounds like there is much more to this story than I thought. OK then, spill.'

I take a big gulp of wine and tell Rachel everything. I figure, why not? It's not like I can talk to anyone else about it, and I need to offload and get someone else's perspective. I need to make sure that, in my slightly vulnerable and emotional state, I'm not totally making up the chemistry between me and Jake.

I finish filling her in just as our food arrives, and a waitress places our starter between us. Rachel looks at me, contemplating what I've just said, before ripping the head off a huge shrimp and popping the rest into her mouth. I suppress a laugh, and she wiggles her eyebrows at me before saying smoothly, 'You should see what I can do to a bloke.'

I burst out laughing and follow suit, grabbing a prawn as she leans forward on the table.

'Well, I'm no expert...'

'I doubt that's true, but go on,' I interject with a chuckle.

'But he is most definitely into you. And not just wants-to-get-into-your-knickers into you. I mean properly into you.

If it was just about getting you into bed, he would've made a move by now, but he hasn't.'

'Yeah, he hasn't because he's not interested,' I say wagging my finger at her and devour another shrimp, but she shakes her head.

'No, he's not made a move because he cares about you. He knows you've been through a lot and doesn't want to rush you and ruin it. It's exactly because he *is* interested in you that he's not done anything yet. Although it sounds like it's killing him.'

'Oh, I don't know.' I let my head flop back as I lean back in my chair. 'How can I be even thinking... whatever it is I'm thinking about Jake, when I've just come out of a relationship, nearly a marriage, with Luke?'

'Because you haven't just got out of that relationship. Literally you have, but by the sounds of it, and I don't think you knew it until all this kicked off, but you and Luke maybe wasn't all you thought it was. Perhaps on reflection, regardless of Emily and the baby and the cheating, you guys shouldn't have actually been getting married anyway, because deep down, you both knew it wasn't right. People cheat because, yeah they're shitty people and most of the time because they are too cowardly to end the relationship they're in, but also because their current relationship isn't what it was when they got together.

'Look at me and Ben. That's a classic example. It's easy to get comfortable and even easier to let things run their course. The hard part is admitting it's not right.'

I run my index finger around the rim of my wine glass and glance out into the darkness hanging over the beach.

'Do you really think that?'

'Like I said, I'm not an expert, but that's exactly what I think. And for what it's worth, I think you think it too. You just don't know it yet.' She smiles warmly at me.

'Thank you,' I say, rapidly blinking back the tears I feel stinging my eyes.

'Hey,' she leans over the table and puts her hand over mine, 'life is too short to be sad. Especially when you're as gorgeous as you and in a place like this.'

'That's what Jake said,' I laugh.

'Well he sounds like a very smart man,' she beams and takes a big swig of wine, before filling up both our glasses and returning the bottle to the cooler next to our table. 'Things happen for a reason. And it usually turns out to be for a very good reason indeed. Maybe this Jake guy is that reason. Just because you and Luke had been together for years and years doesn't mean that your relationship was any more real than the one you have with a man you just met. It doesn't work that way.'

'We're just friends,' I sigh, unsure what else to say and smile up at the waitress that comes to clear our plates.

'Yeah, course you are,' Rachel says wryly. 'For now.'

Chapter Fourteen

After dinner, which is completely delicious and very, very fun in Rachel's easy company, we polish off another bottle of wine and perch ourselves on the stools at the bar. I happily play third wheel to Rachel and Dale making eyes at each other, and despite my current precarious situation, it's very sweet to watch her flicking her hair back and forth and the way he keeps glancing over at her while serving other customers. I wish I could be a bit more blasé about it all, like her, but I'm just not sure I'm programmed that way. Maybe I need a bit of reprogramming. I suddenly feel myself blush slightly, as I think about how Jake would have responded to that sentence if he were here. As I predicted, I've not seen him since he left this afternoon.

After a couple of hours at the bar and a few more cocktails later, I decide to call it a night.

'I think I'll stay here for a bit if you don't mind?' Rachel asks coyly, twirling her hair around her finger. 'Dale said he finishes at midnight and asked if he could buy me a drink.'

'A drink, hey? He is a fast mover,' I grin back at her, but she suddenly grabs my arm, looking worried.

'Carrie, do you think I shouldn't go? Does it look bad if I say yes to a drink? Do you think it makes me look, you know, easy? Or worse, desperate! He knows what happened with Ben and… Oh, just tell me what to do!' She looks at me wide-eyed then suddenly laughs before I have a chance to respond. 'God, sorry. What am I like? Overthinking it much?'

I give her a hug. 'Well firstly, yes you are. He seems very nice. And I mean actually nice, not just flirting to have his way nice. Secondly, I do feel that, in the current situation, I am really not qualified to give advice.' I spread my hands and shrug my shoulders making her giggle. 'And thirdly and finally, it's only a drink. No one could begrudge you a drink with a handsome man, could they? Have you got your phone on you?' She nods and rifles in her clutch bag pulling it out. 'Here, take my number and text me when you get in, OK? What's your room number?'

'OK, good plan,' she agrees. 'I'm in three two three.'

'I'm in the Bay View Suite, on the top floor. Swing by if you need to.' I hand her back her phone after entering my number. 'And have fun! We're on holiday after all. Shall we do breakfast tomorrow, and you can give me a full debrief?'

'Yes please, that sounds perfect. Meet in the dining room at tenish?'

'Tenish it is,' I nod. 'See you tomorrow. Thanks for such a nice night. It's been just what I needed. Here's my cue to leave.' I nod behind her at Dale, grinning from ear to ear, as he saunters past us.

'See you in the morning,' she smirks.

I head back up the path towards the foyer, which is largely empty, apart from a middle-aged couple and their teenage children checking in on reception. For once, it's not manned by Maya but by a tall, blonde, Scandinavian-looking girl with a welcoming face and bright, white teeth that stand out against her deeply tanned face. Between me and Rachel it's hard to forget people do actually come here for a nice, relaxing holiday. As I head over to the lift, the main entrance doors open and Michael, my driver from day one, steps inside the foyer, carrying a set of car keys and heading in the direction of the main desk.

'Michael!' I call waving cheerily in his direction.

'Good evening, ma'am. Are you enjoying your stay?' he says with a smile and small nod of his head.

'You know what? I really, really am.' I smile back at him. 'Although I am afraid I've been making the most of the hotel, and of the room, and haven't even thought about venturing further afield yet. I'm going to have to make an effort to get out and see the island soon.'

'Well, if you would like to see more of Barbados, it would be my pleasure to take you on a tour.'

'Michael that would be wonderful! I would love that. When do the tours run? Should I book it with reception?'

'Well they do have bus tours, but I would be happy to take you around myself.' He leans in and lowers his voice. 'Off the record, the tours are great, but they don't show you the *real* Barbados, as I would call it. It would be my pleasure.'

'That sounds perfect.' I smile gleefully. 'Are you sure? I wouldn't want you to get in any trouble or anything?'

'Not at all. I have a day off tomorrow, and my wife is at work all day. She's a nurse at The Queen Elizabeth, so if it's not too short notice I could take you then?'

'That sounds lovely,' I reply. Then add, 'Oh, I met a girl earlier today, and she's on her own here too, so would you mind if I invited her along as well?'

'Not at all. The more the merrier.' He has such a kind smile that meets his eyes, and I return it immediately.

'Great. Is it too late to go at say eleven thirty? We arranged to meet for breakfast at ten? And please let me know how much we owe you, so I can have it ready for tomorrow.'

He raises both hands and shakes his head.

'Nothing at all. My welcome gift to the island for the both of you. Spending an afternoon talking about my beloved Barbados in good company is more than enough payment for me.'

'Are you sure? I can't expect you to drive us around all afternoon for nothing!'

'I wouldn't have offered if I wasn't sure. Besides, I have a daughter similar to your age. I would like to think that if she went to a strange place, she would have someone looking out for her too.'

I place a hand on his arm briefly, then remove it as I realise he is still at work and I don't want to get him into any trouble since he's doing us favour.

'Michael, you are far too kind. So, is half past eleven OK?'

'No worries, Miss Kingston. If you don't mind meeting me across the road? Just outside the bakery on the parade of shops, would that be alright?'

'Perfect. We'll be there. Goodnight, Michael. And thank you again.'

He smiles and nods before heading over to reception and talking to the blonde on the desk. A man, who looks like a young Barack Obama, emerges from the back office and is handing over some paperwork to the family I saw checking in moments ago. I hit the lift button then wonder if I should go back and tell Rachel but figure she'll pick up my message if I text her when I get back to my room.

In the short ride up to my floor I think how much I've enjoyed my day. There is no way, when I got on the plane to come here, I thought I would ever feel as happy and relaxed as I do right now. Then as the doors open and I walk to my suite door, I feel a small niggle of nerves creep into my stomach, as I realise I still have to talk to Dan.

I change into my pyjama shorts and vest and pull my hair up into a bun. Opening the doors to the balcony, I step out and survey the night-time vista. The sound of raucous laughter spills up from the terrace below, and I can still hear the slow thrum of music from The Coconut Shack. Which reminds me to text Rachel about tomorrow. I head in and pick up my phone to see a missed call from Dan and message from my mum telling me she's been to visit Dad's grave and said hello from me. The thought of her standing there telling him what's happened makes my eyes swim with tears. I text her back a quick *Thank you. Love you Mum xxx* then message Rachel about tomorrow and compose myself before hitting Dan's name to call him back. It rings and rings and, with a surge of relief, I think that it's about to go to voicemail, until he suddenly picks up.

'Kingston! Hello darling, thanks for calling.'

'Hello Dan,' I say with a smile, and I realise how good it is to hear his voice. We've always been close and, with neither of us having any siblings of our own, have always had what we would describe as a brother/sister relationship.

'Give me a sec; I'm just pulling up at the house.' I hear the noise of the car engine cease and a door slam followed by the jangling of keys. 'I'm here, chick. You OK? How's Barbados treating you?'

'Well, the weather's awful and the hotel's just a total dump,' I say sarcastically, and he laughs.

'Tough life, hey?' he replies, to which we both fall silent after realising the irony of his comment. 'Fuck, sorry. I told you I'm bad at this.'

I head out to the balcony sitting cross-legged on one of the sunbeds.

'It's fine, really. I'm surprisingly OK. I'm hoping this isn't just a state of shock and that I'm not going to have a complete meltdown. Actually, I kind of did have one of those, thinking about it, but I am trying to be logical about the whole thing.'

'And where has this logical approach led you then?'

'I'm not sure yet. I think I'm still on the journey. This is in no way me letting Luke off the hook, but maybe we shouldn't have been getting married anyway. The fact that he had the inclination to cheat on me in the first place well, maybe we had issues and we just hadn't realised it.'

'Wow,' he says with a sigh. 'That is pretty logical. I can't really believe you're taking this so well.'

'Oh, believe me, I am *not* taking it well. I've done a fair bit of crying over the last few days, but it's done now, Dan. Nothing I do will change that, and as far as my relationship with both of them is concerned, it's well and truly over.' I lie back on the bed and gaze up at the deep, inky sky dotted with stars. 'I just want to move on. I want this part of my life to be over. That might sound cold, but I can't go back to how it was before, everything is different now.'

'But, us,' he sounds genuinely sad, 'we're OK, right? You do believe that I didn't know?'

'Of course we're OK. You didn't sleep with my best friend too, did you?' I say in a tone so he can hear the smile in my voice.

I meant it as a joke, but he laughs nervously before he speaks. 'Look, thanks for calling me back. I wanted to see if you were doing OK, but I wanted to talk to you about something as well.'

I'm not sure if this is going to be about Luke, Kate, both or neither. I hold my breath, waiting for him to continue.

'I saw Emily yesterday.' My stomach lurches, and I sit up immediately. That I *wasn't* expecting.

'Go on,' I say quietly.

'Kingston, I know Kate won't tell you any of this because she thinks she's doing you a favour by not telling you things that might upset you, but I think you deserve to know all the info, have all the facts. It's only fair. You're the one who's been shit on here.'

'OK...' I say slowly, unsure what's coming next. Dan takes a deep breath.

'She knows your friendship is over, that you'll never forgive her. And she understands. She told me about your message. For what it's worth, I'm with you. I would be the exact same way.' He pauses, and I hear him expel a deep sigh. 'She's keeping the baby, Carrie. And she said that it's up to Luke if he's involved or not but that she's not asking him for anything. She doesn't want a relationship with him. Whether she did, I don't know, but not now anyway.'

'Is that because he doesn't want the baby?' I whisper, pressing my lips together into a hard line.

'Honestly, no he doesn't. But we've talked, God, have we talked it over and over, and he's going to step up and do what he has to. I know it's hard to hear, but it's the right thing for him to do. Emily is terrified about what his family thinks, and she doesn't know how it's all going to work out, but it's important he's in this baby's life. It's his responsibility. He's made enough of a mess of everything as it is, this is the least he should be doing.'

'When is she due?'

'March. She's around three months. She said she'd been for a scan. Look, Carrie, if you don't want me to tell you any of this I can stop. I just… You're not here, and I wanted you to feel like…'

'Dan, it's OK,' I say, softly. 'Thank you. I want you to be honest with me.'

'OK, well if you're sure,' he says with caution, and I hear him draw a deep breath.

'She said she didn't chase Luke, that that night just happened. And I believe her. I think she's always been jealous of you in some way. You had the guy, the house, the friends, the perfect life.'

I let out a laugh of derision. 'Yes, so fucking perfect.' I let the tears fall as Dan continues.

'She didn't set out to sabotage it, that's what I mean. She was trying to explain to me why it happened, but I honestly don't think she knows. I know it doesn't help and that the baby will be a constant reminder of what they did to you. You deserve so much better than this, gorgeous girl. Luke's moved his stuff out of your place. I made sure it was all gone so you have nothing to worry about and…' he stops and the silence hangs between us.

'And what, Dan?'

'Kate took your wedding dress, and all the other bits, to your mum's. She didn't think you would want them there when you got back.'

'Thanks. That was thoughtful. I hadn't even thought about any of that stuff. Not a great welcome home.' I give a half laugh which falls totally flat.

'Carrie, I know you guys had a row.'

Ah.

'Do you know what about?'

'Yes.'

Double ah. I've started so I may as well finish.

'So what's going on, Dan? I know something's happening, and I know it's none of my business, but I can't cope with any more secrets or bombshells, so whatever it is…'

'It's not what you think, OK? And by that, I mean if you think we're having some sort of affair, then it's most certainly not that. I wouldn't do that to Justin, you know how much I like the guy. And I know your judgement is a little skewed at the minute, so I can forgive you for thinking the worst, but we blokes aren't all total pricks, you know?'

I smile and realise how relieved I am to hear it from Dan too.

'So what is it? Is Kate in some sort of trouble? Are her and Justin alright? You guys seem to be with each other all the time at the moment, and I may have jumped to conclusions a teensy bit, but I know I'm not totally off the mark.'

'Kingston, I promise you now, we are not sleeping together or seeing each other. It's nothing like that. But you should talk to Kate. She's having a rough time of it too what with one thing and another.'

'Why, what's happened?'

'Well aside from her brother being in the running for the most hated man in Britain, that's something you need to talk to her about. You will won't you? There's enough bad feeling flying about without you two falling out.'

'I will, I promise. Thank you, you're a good mate. But listen, Kate told me you said Luke was really in a bad way.' I wonder whether this line of questioning is wise, but I've come this far I might as well get it all out now. 'What's he said? About all of this I mean?' I ask him.

'Besides what I've told you? He's devastated he's lost you from his life. He kind of echoed what you said about maybe things not being right between you guys, but he always thought that, no matter what, given all your history, you'd be in each other's lives. Now he knows he's lost you forever. That's what he can't get his head around.'

'Yes, well he has, Dan. Of that I *am* certain. So he's going to have to get used to life without me, because I'm not going to stick around and be his mate through all of this just so he can feel better about himself. All these years, Dan. How could he?' I sniff loudly and wipe my eyes.

'I wish I could give you a hug,' he says gently, and I laugh.

'Anything to get yourself a trip to Barbados. But me too. You always did give the best hugs.' Although Jake's putting up a pretty good challenge to that title.

'I'm always going to be here for hugs, OK? This doesn't change anything between you and me. You know you're like the annoying sister I never wanted.'

I laugh out loud and hear him chuckling all those thousands of miles away. If anything, this just makes me feel even sadder, because I know it's not true. I can't expect Dan never to talk about Luke when I'm around, and I know I won't be able to avoid the topic of the baby for long with him. Eventually, conversation will drift that way, and I just don't want to hear it. Not now and maybe not ever.

'I love you, Dan. Why can't Luke be more like you and less like Satan?'

He laughs his lovely, deep laugh, and I smile at the sound. As tough as this call has been, I feel a little more closure creeping in, and it's a relief.

'I'm not sure the world's ready for two Dan Jones's just yet. There's only so much gorgeous the female population can take. Look, I best shoot, Dani's on her way over. Some yoga mat crisis she needs help with apparently, so God only knows! Give me a text if you need me, OK? I'm right here at the end of the phone.'

'Ooh, sounds like a fun night for you! I will, I promise. Big hugs, we'll chat soon.'

'Definitely. Take care, you. Love ya.'

I set my phone down on the side and look back up at the sky, staying that way for I don't quite know how long, but I start to get goosebumps as the sea breeze picks up, so head inside and close the balcony doors behind me. I lie on my bed and close my eyes, too tired now to even get under the soft, white sheet, and begin to drift off to sleep until a loud knock on my door startles me.

After my initial second or two of fear, I realise it's probably Rachel coming for a date analysis, so I jump up and fling it open without even looking through the peephole. I do a sharp intake of breath as I'm greeted by Jake, clad in a navy suit, tan shoes and a white, open collar shirt, leaning coolly against my door frame. My eyes drift up to meet his and his gaze locks me in immediately, holding me for a moment before I drop my line of sight to look at his perfect mouth as he speaks.

'Can I come in?'

Chapter Fifteen

Before I have chance to answer, he pushes himself up off the door frame and wanders slowly past me into the room.

'It would appear so,' I mutter, as I let my eyes drift over his frame. Oh Lord, he looks heavenly. His suit is perfectly fitted and looks expensive, and the snob in me wonders how he could afford such a bespoke-looking suit on his wages. He walks straight over to the balcony, pulling open the doors and striding out to the edge before resting his forearms on the railing and dropping his head slightly. OK then.

I walk over to him and mirror his stance. I can tell something's wrong, and I gently touch his upper arm where his suit is tight from the bulk of his muscles. He turns to look at me, his eyes searching my face, hesitating on my lips for a moment longer than necessary.

'Come here,' he says softly and envelopes me in his arms pressing me tightly to his chest. The material of his suit feels silky smooth to the touch, and I can hear the deep thud of his heart pounding. He takes a deep breath, and what I am sure is a smell of my hair.

'You smell gorgeous,' he says after a long pause, then he releases me, holding me away from his body slightly, dropping his gaze forward again to meet my look.

His stare and his touch, plus the fact I've been stirred from a half sleep, brings me out in goosebumps.

'You're cold.' He strokes my arms but looks past me out into the distance. I don't tell him that I'm not remotely cold, in fact quite the opposite. 'Let's go in inside.'

He follows me in, and I walk through to the lounge and sit myself on one of the sofas. I expect him to sit on the other one, but he doesn't and I have to move up to allow space for his massive frame. I'm not sure I like this version of Jake; it's unnerving to see him so serious. More so than when he's making me blush from head to toe.

'Jake, are you alright?'

'I'm sorry, sweet cheeks. I'm fine. Really, I'm fine.' He smiles at me and puts his hand over mine, squeezing it gently. 'I just had a rough meeting, that's all. I wanted to see you. You make me smile.' And right on cue he gives me a beaming grin from ear to ear and, relieved to see the normal Jake make a return, I give him one straight back.

'Well, good,' I say getting up off the sofa, 'because only one of us is allowed to be an emotional wreck right now and that, buddy, is my crown to wear. Don't come in here with your *rough meeting* talk and think you can snatch it away from me. You've got to earn this baby!' I point to my head at my invisible crown, and he laughs, slipping off his jacket and laying it across the arm of the sofa. I widen my eyes at him. 'Oh, staying are we? Make yourself at home, won't you?'

'What, are you throwing me out? Is that why you're on your feet?'

'No, I was going to be a good hostess and ask if you would like a drink from the minibar? I figure I can stretch to some overpriced beverages.'

He stands up, making his way over to me, and we stand there for a second until he chuckles and shakes his head. 'You've no idea where the minibar is have you?'

I look around the room and place my hands on my hips. 'Er, nope. Not. A. Clue.' Jake laughs again, and I hit him on the arm. The fact that they are completely solid and my hand just bounces off doesn't go unnoticed by either of us.

'You're the expert hotel worker. Go on. Lead the way.'

His lips curl up at the corners. 'Let's play a game.'

I roll my eyes. 'Oh please God, no.'

'Come on. Hot or cold?'

I fold my arms across my chest, but he just stares me down.

'For goodness' sake,' I snap, and I feel like stamping my foot but resign myself to the fact that, no matter what, he's going to get his way. 'Fine.' I walk over to the large sideboard down one wall of the lounge that houses a desk and stand in front of the cupboard, staring at him pointedly as he resumes his position on the sofa.

'Cold.' He's smiling like a kid on Christmas, as he stretches out. I take a begrudging step forward in front of the next cupboard.

'Hotter.' Another step forward. I'm stood in line with where he's sat on the sofa, and he whispers it again. 'Hotter.'

I take a moment to assess the situation. He looks heavenly. He's here. We are quite clearly passing some sort of flirty banter between us. I'm single, and you know what? I am going to treat myself to some light entertainment. Smiling sweetly, I take a step towards him.

He breaks out in a huge grin as it dawns on him that it's game on.

'Hotter,' he growls.

I see his eyes twinkle, and I'm spurred on by his response to my obvious flirting. What am I doing? This isn't me! Or maybe it *is* me; I've just not met this girl yet. I'm kind of loving her. I take a deep breath, realising I have to commit to this idea now I've decided to go through with it, even though half of me wants to run and hide. I advance on him again and the distance closes between us.

'Hotter.' He stands up, and my heart starts beating at an alarming rate as I feel my cheeks burning. I wish the doors to the balcony were open. Step. We are almost touching, and I dare myself to look up at him. He leans down, his short stubble brushing across my cheeks. The hairs on my whole body stand on end, and I breathe deeply as he whispers, soft and low into my ear.

'Burning hot.'

I place my hand on his chest and take a very small step backwards.

'You know what they say about playing with fire,' I manage to say in a whisper, and I bite my lip. He draws away from me a fraction, his eyes roaming over my face once more.

'I don't want to get my fingers burned, Jake,' I say honestly. My voice is low and breathy. He takes my hand and places a gentle kiss on each of my fingertips. I watch him as his lips delicately meet my skin, electrifying each place he's touched. He brushes a stray piece of hair behind my ear and gives me a look that seems to burn right through to my soul.

'And you didn't even want to play at all,' he says with a wink. He breaks out into a smile, and I do too, the energy between us subsiding slightly, for now. I don't know how he does that. Even when he puts me on edge, he puts me at ease in the same breath, and it's so disarming I don't know how to react. Today, we seem to have flicked from mates to more and back and forth again several times, although I can't define the more part as anything other than some ridiculous levels of chemistry at the moment.

'It's in the cupboard under the TV,' he says, straightening up and nodding his head behind me. I practically sprint away from him and yank open the cupboard to see a white-fronted fridge with a selection of champagne flutes, wine glasses, tumblers and shot glasses above it. I pull on the handle, as the vacuum of the door resists then gives way and opens. There is a huge choice of soft drinks and alcohol, but my eye is drawn to a full-sized bottle of Dom Pérignon in the door. I decide to throw caution to the wind, something I seem to be doing a lot over the last forty-eight hours, and pull it out, waving it at Jake with a mischievous grin.

'Do you dare me?'

'Sweet cheeks, do you know how much that bottle costs?'

I look at it in my hands and shrug. 'At home it's about a hundred and fifty quid?'

'Yes, but in a hotel minibar you're looking at double that. Maybe more.'

'What, you mean you don't know all the prices off the top of your head?' He walks over to me, taking the bottle out of my hand and placing it back in the fridge door, pulling out a bottle of white wine with a label I don't recognise.

'Let's start small. We have two weeks to build up to the champagne. Besides, you never know what we might want to celebrate.'

'So we're working our way through the minibar one day at a time?'

Jake laughs, grabs two glasses and takes them over to the coffee table.

'Well, I can think of much worse ways to spend a holiday. Hand me the corkscrew, there should be one on the top of the fridge by the glasses.'

I peer in, locating the corkscrew, and hand it to him.

'Is it too late to be opening a bottle of wine?' I say sounding like the least fun person, possibly ever. He clearly thinks the same thing, as I see him suppress a smile.

'I think you'll be OK. You've not got far to get to your bed.'

When he says things like that they almost sound like a threat, and he looks at me through his long lashes.

'Do you have work tomorrow?' I ask, taking the glass he's offered from his outstretched hand. I take a large gulp, and the cool liquid goes a little way to dousing the heat that seems to have taken over my body in his presence.

'I do. I have to be up early. I'm breaking all my own rules here.'

'You have rules? These sound interesting.' I tuck my legs under me on the soft, velvet sofa and turn to face him, leaning on the cushions with my elbow.

'Well, the first one, of course, is don't talk to strangers.'

'Failed at the first hurdle,' I say taking a sip of wine and smirking at him. 'What else?'

'Oh, don't get into hot tubs with beautiful ladies, protect yourself from jet ski-driving harlots...' I let out a gasp of mock affront, as I grab a cushion and hit him with it.

'Seriously though, I don't do this all the time, despite what you might think.'

'Do what?' I dip my toe into the shark-infested water unsure of how it's going to go.

'Let myself get this close to anyone, let alone a guest at the hotel. I just…' he pauses and takes my hand. 'I just want to hang out with you all the time,' he sighs and looks up at me. 'You're so fun, you feel like a breath of fresh air, and I want to breathe you in all the time. I've never had any friends like that before.'

And there it is. The F-word. All the flirting and banter is just that. We're friends. I *need* to not read anything into it. This is just his personality, I just haven't ever seen him like this with anyone else because we're always on our own together. Am I that needy? Have I just clung on to him like some sort of loser limpet? But, he asked me out, and he came here tonight, and there is no way on earth anyone could deny we have some sort of chemistry, even if we are just friends. I need to change the subject.

'You're looking very smart. This meeting, was everything OK? Was it something formal to do with work?' Something suddenly dawns on me, and I get a sinking feeling. 'Oh, Jake, it's not me is it? No one's said anything about you spending time with me?' To my relief, he smiles.

'No, of course they haven't, I've had time off. It's fine.' But I notice he doesn't answer my question as such. We both lift our glasses and simultaneously take a drink, reflecting each other's movements. I see him glance at his watch and then look back at me.

'Jake, you can go if you have to, it's fine,' I say, throwing him a lifeline. 'Don't feel you need to stay if you have to be somewhere.'

He leans forward and kisses me on the forehead then drains his wine glass, standing up from the sofa and stretching lazily.

'I need to work tomorrow, but I'll find you at some point, OK?'

'I'm actually going on an island tour tomorrow afternoon so won't be back until later on.'

'Is that with Michael?' he asks with a small frown, and I wonder if I should tell him or not.

'Er, yes, but please don't say anything, I don't want him to get into trouble with the management,' I say hurriedly, but relax as he smiles at me.

'Of course I won't. Michael's such a good guy; you'll have a great time.'

I follow him as he strides towards the door, turning to me before he opens it.

'Thanks,' he says simply. I shrug my shoulders and smile up at him, wondering if I should give him a hug, but something stops me and he doesn't reach out for me again.

'Sleep tight, sweet cheeks.'

'You too.'

The door closes behind him and, as I walk through to the lounge to put the wine back in the fridge, I notice he's left his jacket behind. I pick it up and jog to the door, knowing he'll be waiting for the lift, but as I step out of my room, he's nowhere to be seen. I frown. Weird. As I turn back inside, I hear the latch click from behind the door of the suite opposite me.

With a sinking feeling in my stomach, I drop the jacket on the sideboard and climb into bed, leaving the glasses and wine bottle sitting abandoned in the lounge.

Chapter Sixteen

After a fitful night's sleep, I wake up feeling more tired than when I went to bed. It's the worst night's sleep I've had since my almost wedding day and even more unsettling is the fact that, no matter how I might try to deny it to myself, I know it's because of Jake. More than anything, I want to go to reception and ask Maya who's staying in that room, but I know I can't without giving her a good reason. Besides, she's far too professional to reveal any personal details of the hotel guests. I've not seen anyone come in or out for the last couple of days, but I know that it's basically a mirror image of my suite and that it's most certainly not going to be cheap. I wonder, for a moment, if it's Bryony the Blonde and Amy the Brunette, but I would definitely have heard them by now, and I'm sure they would have been telling anyone who would listen that they were staying in a suite. Ugh, I hate this. Maybe this is why I stayed with Luke so long and ignored any signs, so I didn't have to deal with all this stupid, man angst.

I shower and pull on a strappy, red sundress with a bold Aztec print and slip into my flip-flops. I get to breakfast just before ten and spot Rachel out on the terrace, nursing an espresso cup, her face hidden behind humungous, black sunglasses. Her hair looks tousled, and she's wearing a black maxi dress, which I get the feeling may be reflecting her current state. I head to the table and pull out the chair opposite her, letting the legs scrape along the tiles with a grating screech. She raises her head slowly and, even with her glasses, I can tell she wants to murder me. I snort with laughter and lift the chair off the floor, placing it gently down and take a seat. She takes a sip of her coffee before placing it down on the saucer, inordinately slowly, making the smallest *clink*.

I spread my hands on the table in front of me and say in the cheeriest voice I can muster, 'So, how was your night?'

She takes a deep breath, and I smirk back at her, as she raises a shaky hand to touch her glasses, just to check they are still there even though they've not moved a millimetre from her face. Her voice is husky and low when she speaks.

'From now on, I am not allowed to make any decisions for myself. You are my chief decision maker, because I clearly cannot control myself and am on some sort of self-sabotage mission.'

I laugh out loud and she winces, touching her hand to her head, which just makes me laugh even harder.

'I'm sorry,' I try as hard as I can to stifle my laughter, 'it's not funny. Can I get you anything to eat?'

She pales instantly and puts her hand over her mouth, slowly shaking her head.

'More coffee then maybe?' I suggest, gently. She nods, a movement so small I hardly notice it, and I wave to a waiter passing our table.

'Two espressos please, a cappuccino and could we get a large jug of iced water as well?' He nods his understanding and heads off inside.

'Carrie, I am so sorry, there is no way I can sit in a car today. Do you mind if I don't come? I'm really sorry.'

'Don't be daft.' I smile and give her hand a quick squeeze so she knows I mean it. 'It's fine. To be fair, I don't fancy spending a day cleaning up your vomit from the back seat of a car in this heat.'

'God, don't. I feel so ill. It's not big and it's definitely not clever.' Rachel folds her arms on the table and leans her head on top of them, making me laugh again. She raises her hand instantly to silence me, and I press my lips together tightly. I lower my voice and whisper gently.

'Drink your coffee, go back to bed and we'll catch up later when you're in a fit state to fill me in on all the details of last night. Let me guess, rum punch?'

'Don't. Even. Say. Those. Evil. Words.'

I throw back my head laughing and see Bryony and Amy sauntering in. To my annoyance they sit at the table one over from us. I'm sure they do it on purpose, although what that purpose is I'm not yet sure, because there are loads of spare tables. They both scrape their chairs on the tiles, wittering on loudly and screeching together at some inside joke.

'Like, don't even!' Bryony sits down and signals the poor passing waiter with a triple click of her fingers. He gives her an appropriately disgusted look then begrudgingly makes his way over.

'Two Americanos,' she snaps without looking at him. He catches my eye, and I give him a small eye roll skyward, making his lips curl up infinitesimally, as he turns and heads back inside. They are both wearing tight, almost identical, bandage dresses and Amy is sporting a huge sun hat whilst Bryony's tiny head is swamped by massive, black sunglasses with Dior emblazoned down the side in neon pink. They look like two characters in 'Guess Who?'.

'It was so embarrassing!' she continues. 'They were at the bar, like *all* night. I saw them, and she was downing shots and drinking like, *gallons* of that punch stuff like it was going out of fashion. It's, like, literally the most fattening thing to you can do to your body, you know? Seriously, what is *wrong* with some people? And she was talking to the guy who works here, I mean like *works* here, works here.' She flicks her hair over her shoulder, and Amy nods looking wide-eyed.

'Totally. And it gives you wrinkles. And…' she lowers her voice and leans forward over the table to Bryony, '…*cellulite*.'

Bryony shakes her head solemnly and sighs, with a fleeting but pointed glance over to our table at Rachel.

'It is just so sad, Amy. So sad.'

I see movement from Rachel's side of the table, and she lifts her head slowly, turning it in their direction, with a look of rage on her face so violent, I think for a moment that she's about to lob a chair in their direction. She looks at me over her sunglasses, her teeth gritted.

'Remind me when I don't feel like death that I need to go and shave those bitches' heads in their sleep or something.'

By half past eleven I'm waiting outside the bakery, after picking up a couple of bottles of water and three coconut turnovers for me, Michael and one for Rachel for later. I'm not sure what car to expect, but I am mightily surprised when a sleek, black Range Rover Evoque pulls up beside me and Michael opens the door, stepping down on to the pavement.

'Good morning, Miss Kingston.' He smiles at me politely, but I hold up both hands, one still clutching the bakery bag.

'Michael, I am only getting in this car if you promise to call me Carrie from now on. Do we have a deal? I also have a coconut turnover here that I will hold as ransom until you do.'

He smiles warmly and lets out a gentle laugh.

'Carrie. My apologies. Will your friend be joining us?'

'Ah, yes. About that. She is feeling a little… under the weather this morning, so thought it best to stay in bed for now, so it's just me if that's still OK?'

He gives a slow nod of understanding, but I can see his lips turn up ever so slightly at the corners as he tries to suppress his smile.

'Something to do with Dale's rum punch I believe,' I whisper to him.

'Ah yes. I have to say it's beaten many a man. Even me once.' He winks at me, and I laugh. 'Shall we?' he asks, and opens the rear door for me to step in.

'Oh. Would it be OK if I sat up front? I mean I understand if you would rather I didn't,' I add hurriedly, 'it's just seeing as Rachel's not coming…'

His face breaks out into a grin, and I can see he's pleased at the suggestion.

'That would be lovely. I would like that very much. In which case…' he walks round to open the passenger door and I climb in, letting him close the door behind me. I love how he seems such a gentleman, and I realise that he reminds me of my dad and the way he treated me and my mum. He was always holding doors open for us and helping my mum in and out of the car. I only realised it as I got older but, although it may have been an old-school way of doing things, it showed his respect for women and I loved him all the more for it.

Michael gets in the driver's side, and I turn to him, as he starts the engine and pulls off.

'Thank you for doing this today, Michael, it was very kind of you to offer to show me around. And this is a beautiful car. I've never been in one before.'

'Not at all. Like I said, it's my pleasure. She is a beauty isn't she?' I see his hands run over the soft leather of the steering wheel. 'I'm sorry to say she's not mine. I told a friend of mine I was taking you out today, and he suggested I borrow his car. Travel in a little luxury and you get a better vantage point from up here. I have to say, I jumped at the chance to drive her for the day.'

'Well, I'm glad we could help each other out then,' I say with a smile, which he returns with a gentle nod of his head.

'Is there anything you would like to see particularly and I can make sure to include it on our tour?'

'No, not really.' I take my sunglasses out of my bag and slide them on to my face. Although the dark tint on the windows does a lot to help with the sun's glare, it's still too bright for my eyes which are more accustomed to grey, dull, British weather. 'I'm embarrassed to say I have no idea about what the island has to offer, so I'm very much happy to let you lead the way.'

'Excellent. Well, I had a chat with my wife last night, and we agreed on a few places for your first time in Barbados. From here I thought we could go to Saint Thomas, to Harrison's Cave, it's a tourist spot, but good to see. Then up to Saint Peter to Farley Hill, you get some great views up there, then down to Bathsheba Beach in Saint Joseph and then head to

Lemon Arbour and get something to eat if you fancy, before we head back to Saint James.'

'OK, so cave, views, beach, food? I think you might just have described my perfect day out.'

He laughs, his kind eyes crinkling at the corners, as a grins breaks over his face.

'I thought we could drive up the coast a little, take the scenic route if you have the time?'

Despite the air con, a warm sensation settles over me, and I wriggle into the cream leather of the seat, the sense of calm that seems to come from being in his presence soothing any unsettling thoughts of Luke, Emily and even, dare I say it, Jake. I glance out of the window, as the blue sea whips past us.

'Right now, Michael, I have all the time in the world.'

Chapter Seventeen

Michael and I spend a perfect afternoon taking in the island. The tram ride down into Harrison's Cave was incredible and made even more exciting as I've never been anywhere like that before. It took us an hour to tour the caves, and the still, blue pools reflecting the naturally sculpted rock formations helped to calm my spirits further and was a welcome refuge from the heat of the day. Afterwards, we drove inland some more to take in the incredible views from the ruined house at Farley Hill. We sat on a bench, tucking into our turnovers, and Michael told me about the fire that ruined the old house in the sixties but it ended up adding to the appeal of the place. Apparently, its gardens are often used for weddings. Thankfully none were taking place today, so I was spared *that* awkward moment.

My favourite part of the trip was the beach at Bathsheba, its huge rock formations, sitting idly in the shallows. We walked along the coastline, Michael telling me about his work and his family, including how he met his wife, May. They were childhood sweethearts, and he had to ask her out at least five times before she finally agreed to go out with him. May demanded, however, that if he wanted a second date, he had to bring her flowers next time and make sure he paid for a milkshake. She sounds like my kind of woman. Now, as it approaches five p.m., Michael and I sit in The Village Bar at Lemon Arbour, perusing the menu that hosts a glut of Bajan delights, looking out over the parish of Saint John. We both opt for the daily special of cornmeal cou-cou and salt fish, which I hoover up with gusto.

'Michael, this is amazing, I can't believe how good the food is out here! It puts the UK to shame, it really does. I said to Jake, I'm going to be the size of a house by the time I leave.'

The way I thoughtlessly dropped Jake's name into conversation unnerves me. Will Michael think I'm just another notch on Jake's bedpost, even though nothing's happened between us? Does he even know we've been spending time together? I look up at him and see a flicker of something pass across his face, and I feel the need to explain myself.

'He's been good to me since I arrived. He showed me round the hotel and made sure I wasn't on my own when I first got here. I know he's just being friendly, but he didn't have to do all that. I was having a bad time of it.' I know I sound like I'm defending our relationship, which, now I think about it, is exactly what I'm doing. 'My last relationship didn't exactly work out, and it's all so complicated. Or maybe it's frighteningly simple. I'm sure you've gathered some of this but…' I take a deep sigh. 'I'm not sure what's going on, being here, it's been so…' I pause and look at him, my shoulders sagging. 'I'm sorry, I'm not explaining myself very well here, am I?'

Michael shifts slightly in his chair and briefly looks out over the landscape, towards the sea, before turning back to me.

'Miss Kingston, Carrie...' He corrects himself quickly at the scowl on my face and smiles his reassuring smile. '... you are your own woman, a grown woman at that, and you certainly don't need to explain yourself to me. I met my wife when we were thirteen years old, and I've never looked at another woman since. May was it for me. I knew the moment I laid eyes on her that my world would never be the same again.' His face is filled with love, the fine lines etched with the memories and laughter he's shared with her. 'But it doesn't always happen that way. Sometimes the one we're meant to be with doesn't arrive in our life right away, sometimes it takes a little time. Maybe you don't meet them until you're forty, fifty, hell, even seventy!'

He laughs at the look of horror on my face. 'I'm not saying that's going to be the case for you, what I'm saying is that the relationship you just got out of, he wasn't the one, because if he was you'd still be with him. And the person you're meant to be with is still out there, waiting for you, because you've not met them yet.'

I wipe away a solitary tear from my cheek and look away embarrassed at the show of emotion.

'Life is about taking chances, making good of the hand that life throws at us, but don't miss out on something because it doesn't fit with what you think perfect love should be. There's no such thing. Love is love and that feeling, that unexplainable connection, it hits us when we least expect it and we're helpless to do anything about it.

'I was lucky, I've had May for a long time, but I know, no matter what, I would have found her eventually. Just don't give up. Like I said, they're out there, Carrie, you just might not have met them yet.'

His words hang in the air, and he looks at me intently for a minute before picking up his glass and taking a slow sip of water, wiping the ring of condensation from the table with his napkin. As he sets his glass down he gives a small shrug of his shoulders and a soft smile.

'But what do I know, hey?'

'Oh, Michael,' I say with a small laugh. 'I think you know far more than you're letting on. But that you're also far too discreet to say.'

'It is what it is,' he chuckles, and then says more seriously. 'Carrie, he's not what you think, he's such a good man. I've known him a long time. I knew his father too.' This piece of news surprises me.

'You knew Jake's dad?'

Michael nods. 'I did. He is like him in so many ways. But one thing they shared, more than anything, was their passion to not do things in half measures. When they do something, they do it with all their heart and soul.'

'Thank you, Michael. For being so honest with me. I would never get this kind of frankness from anyone back home. I think that's why I like it here so much.'

'Telling the truth is easy; it's lying that takes the effort.'

'Your family are very lucky to have you,' I say, meaning every word.

'Ah, I tell them that every day but do they listen?' I laugh and he joins me. 'Shall we head back, if you're ready?'

I pick up my bag and place it on my lap taking one last, long look over the island out to where the sea meets the sky; the brilliant blue colours nestled side by side on the horizon. A smile spreads across my face, as I turn back to him.

'Yes, I think I am.'

Back outside the bakery, by the hotel, I thank Michael with a very big hug, which takes him aback a little, but I didn't feel like shaking his hand was enough after the day I've had.

'Today has been so great on so many levels,' I say sincerely. 'Thank you so much for using your precious time off to show me around. Barbados is beautiful.'

'It was my pleasure,' he says. 'It was a treat for me too. The thing about living here is that I don't go out and actually *see* the island any more. You often forget to stop and take a look at what's right under your nose.'

He gives me a knowing smile, which I return with one of my own.

'Thank you. I'll see you soon hopefully. Oh! Will you be at the party tomorrow? Jake invited me and my friend.'

'Perhaps. Although I prefer quiet nights in nowadays.'

I laugh. 'Me too, but I am on holiday after all.'

'Well, enjoy yourself, they're great fun.'

'We will. And I'm sure I'll catch you around the hotel soon.'

'I'm sure you will.' And with that, he gives me another one of his signature, gentle nods.

I finally find Rachel horizontal on one of the sunbeds by the waterfall pool under the shade of a huge parasol. Her sunglasses are still firmly planted on her face and, although she's ditched her black maxi dress, she's draped a black sarong over her bottom half in a dramatic fashion, its ends blowing in the breeze giving it the distinct look of a shroud. I'm not sure if she's asleep, so I touch her arm gently, and she jumps out of her skin with a yelp, her sarong slipping to the floor and her shades sliding down her nose.

'Holy crap, Carrie! You scared the life out of me. Bloody hell.' She leans up on her elbows, as I try to stifle my laughter.

'Sorry,' I say still giggling. I haul her to a sitting position and perch on the end of her sunbed, as she curls her legs up to make some space.

'How was your day?' I ask her, taking the turnover out of my bag and handing it to her. 'I bought you a present if you can manage it?'

'You are an angel,' she says pulling the wrapper off with her teeth and taking a big bite. 'This is the only thing I've eaten all day and, man, I am so ready for it.' She licks her lips with enthusiasm. 'Oh, bloody hell, this is delicious. Where did you get it?'

'From the bakery across the road. I am so going back there tomorrow for fresh supplies. So, you've made it through the day then?'

'Just about.' She blows out her cheeks, expelling the air in a long breath. 'Honestly, it was seriously touch-and-go for a while. There was definitely more than a couple of moments I thought I was actually going to die.'

I laugh out loud.

'Oh dear. Have you seen Dale?'

'No, not all day. I don't think I could face him. I have a *very* hazy memory of last night.' She screws up her face and flops back on to the sunbed throwing her arm across her eyes.

'Come on,' I say, 'I have an idea.'

'Now this was a very, very good idea,' says Rachel, as she stretches out in the hot tub, taking a long swig of water from her bottle on the side. 'I seriously cannot believe this is your room. Sorry, room-s. And this view! Blimey, Carrie, it's amazing. I'm so jealous!'

'Don't be too jealous, this was supposed to be the honeymoon suite that I was sharing with my devoted husband, and we all know how that turned out don't we?'

'I know, but what a consolation prize. And you don't have to share it all with some man. It's all yours,' she points out.

'You're right, it is.'

Rachel raises her water bottle and nods towards mine, urging me to do the same. We knock them together, meeting in the space above the bubbling water.

'Cheers!' she says happily.

'Cheers! And what are we toasting?'

She tilts her head to the side, momentarily considering it.

'To us. To me, to you. To sisterhood in the face of adversity. And to new friendships and new beginnings. And to never letting alcohol pass my lips again!'

I almost spit out my water with laughter.

'Now that is something I know you don't mean!'

'Well, definitely the rum punch then,' she concedes.

'OK, so what actually happened last night? I need to hear the events that led to your demise.'

She places her bottle of water back on the side and moves a little closer, as we settle down to dissect our previous evenings.

'After you left, the bar started to empty pretty quickly, and there were only three or four tables left. Dale kept slipping me different cocktails, some of which I am sure weren't actually legal, and me, like the gullible idiot I am, didn't quite think they would be so bloody potent. I wasn't drunk then, I can hold my own, and I am certainly no lightweight. My brother's a rugby player, and I can drink most of his team under the table, no joke. But then Dale finished for the night, and we took a jug of rum punch down to the beach, so we were away from any guests. We didn't think it would look very good, him drinking with me after work, so we snuck off.'

'And what exactly happened when you were sneaking then, young lady? Did you guys kiss?'

Rachel looks sheepish and nods slowly at me. I can see the smile creeping over her face that she's trying, and failing, to keep hidden.

'I knew it! OK, so did you guys do more than just kissing?' I probe.

I'd forgotten how fun it was to sit and chat about boys. There comes a time in your life it seems silly to ask your adult friends 'Did you snog him?' but really, as girls, that's actually all we want to know. We might ask about his job, house, car, future prospects, or past relationships, but if we could only ask one question, I bet that, nine times out of ten, it would be that one.

'We might have,' she giggles, blushing furiously.

'You hussy!' I shriek playfully and splash her with water, sending her into a fit of laughter, as she holds her hands up to defend herself.

'What? I didn't sleep with him!' She narrows her eyes, and a wicked smile plays on her lips. 'Yet.'

I splash her again and this time she retaliates, sending us both into hysteria. Within about ten seconds we are both breathless from laughter and our hair is dripping wet. It takes us a few good, deep breaths before we finally regain our self-control.

'So you didn't, yet. But you want to...' I say in a sing-song voice.

Rachel smiles coyly. 'I might do. But I am a lady, so I shan't tell.'

I guffaw at her in the most unladylike manner.

'Yeah, course you are.' I stand up and reach over to grab two towels from the chair next to the hot tub and pass one to Rachel to wipe her face.

'Thanks. He's really fun. And he's got a pretty firm bod under those hotel issue garments, I can tell you that.'

'So are you seeing him again? I mean aside from when we bump into him at work. Have you guys arranged a second date?'

'Kind of. He asked if I would be at the party on Friday, because he wasn't working that night, so we agreed to see each other there. You are coming aren't you? Don't leave me on my own!'

'Of course I'm coming. I told Jake I would.' I proceed to tell her about last night's visit from him and about what I saw, or didn't see, in the suite across.

'Hmm,' she ponders for a moment. 'He's the handy guy, right? So he could have been going to fix something.'

'Dressed in a suit, at gone midnight?'

'OK, fair point.' She frowns and pouts her lips as she's thinking. 'Why don't you ask him? I don't know what else it could be.'

'I don't want him to think I was spying on him or for him to think that I care.'

'But you do care,' Rachel says with a laugh. 'And you were trying to give him his jacket; you weren't doing anything wrong there. I'm guessing his jacket is still here? Why don't you go and give it to him later?'

'Yeah maybe,' I say. 'Although I wouldn't know where to find him.'

'I think we can both agree that he seems to seek you out like a homing device, so I wouldn't worry. He will be around later, you watch. He left his jacket, didn't he?' She reaches up and secures a section of long, dark hair that's come loose from her crocodile clip.

'Yeah, by accident.'

'It's like Cinderella,' Rachel says, dreamily. 'She leaves her shoe behind and that way, she knows the prince will have to see her again to return it. Whether he meant to or not, he wants an excuse to see you.'

'If you say so,' I sigh, and then change the subject. 'Do you want to eat? I'm pretty full still from lunch but will come down with you if you want something?'

'Nah, I'm good. The turnover was all I would care to risk. I'm feeling much more human but don't want to push my luck.'

'No worries. What are your plans for tomorrow? I was going to go to the beach if you want to come?'

'Of course I'm coming. What the hell else would I be doing on my own like a loner? Sorry, you're stuck with me now.'

'That's fine by me,' I laugh. 'And I'm pretty sure *you're* stuck with *me* not the other way around.'

'Let's call it even,' she grins.

There's suddenly a very loud knock at the door, and we both jump a little, our heads whipping round in that direction.

'Well, well, well,' says Rachel smugly. 'He's right on time. I told you.'

'It won't be him,' I say, as I jump out of the hot tub, giving myself a quick dry off with the towel before wrapping it around me. Despite what I've said, my heartbeat has quickened in my chest, and I know if I open the door and it's not Jake I will feel distinctly disappointed. I realise I do want to see him. I pad across to the door and hold my breath, my face breaking into a smile as I open it to reveal a flash of blonde hair and deep, yellow eyes gazing down at me. He's here. And the relief washes over me. Why do I want to see him so much? But it's more than that, I *need* to see him. I'm drawn like a moth to the flame, and I know I'm playing with fire, even getting involved as a friend, because I don't know where it might lead. But for now, I'm going to just enjoy his company and his very aesthetically pleasing form. The grin on his face flips my stomach, and he walks into the room planting a kiss on my forehead as he passes.

'Do come in won't you?' I say, sarcastically. 'Should I just get you a key?'

He turns to me, as he strides into the lounge, calling over his shoulder.

'Now *that* is something I can get on board with.'

'What are you doing?' I scurry after him gripping my towel to me. 'I have company.'

He's crouched down in front of the fridge, but his head shoots up, a frown on his face.

'You do? Well, aren't I the third wheel then?' His tone is light, but he stands to look at me with a wavering expression. 'Why are you wet? Were you… in the hot tub?' I see a flash of anger in his eyes, and I realise, he's jealous.

'I was actually.' After a long pause I decide to put him out of his misery. 'Rach?' I shout, and he visibly relaxes a moment later as she pops her head around the lounge door.

'Oh, hello!' she says with fake surprise and a wide-eyed innocent look on her face. She stares at him for a second suppressing her smile and looking at me with raised eyebrows. I guess he has this effect on most people. Jake crosses the room and holds out his hand to her.

'Pleasure to meet you, Rachel.'

'Yes, yes you too.' She trips over her words taking his hand in hers and clutching on to her towel with the other one.

'I hate to barge in like this. Would you ladies like a drink?'

I scoff loudly. 'Yes, you really look like you hate to barge in. And stop manhandling my alcohol!' I snatch yet another bottle of wine out of his hand, the replacement that's been put there by housekeeping. I take a moment to look him up and down slyly.

He is wearing white Nikes, above the knee beige, chino shorts and a short-sleeved, white polo shirt. He looks like he's been working, although his outfit is crisp and clean as though he's just put it on.

'A day at a time I said.' He grabs the corkscrew and sets to work on opening the bottle, his biceps taut as he screws it down into the cork.

'Rachel, would you like a drink, honey? Seeing as apparently we are opening the wine,' I sigh, smiling but with a hint of exasperation in my voice. She grins broadly at me then looks to Jake and back to me.

'Er, no, I have a date with my bed soon, I think.'

I raise my eyebrows at her, and she shakes her head as she understands my inference.

'My own bed,' she laughs. 'I'll leave you both to it. I'll just grab my clothes and be on my way. Beach tomorrow?'

I nod. 'I'll text you in the morning.'

She blows me a kiss. 'Very nice to meet you, Jake. I'll see you around.'

'You most certainly will.' He gives her his most dazzling smile, and she turns to leave with a little wave and knowing smirk in my direction.

As Jake pours two glasses of wine, I hear the door close, as Rachel slips out, leaving us alone. He walks to the sofa and settles himself in the same spot as he did last night.

'I'm just going to get out of these wet things,' I say gesturing down to my towel.

'Need a hand?' he smirks.

'I think I can manage, thank you very much.' As I turn to leave, he starts to get up off the sofa, a wicked grin on his face. I spin around, pointing my finger at him, trying my hardest to turn my smile into a stern look.

'Behave!' I giggle, and he sits back down. 'I'll be back in a moment. Go make yourself useful and turn off the hot tub.'

As I head towards the bathroom I grab my denim shorts and a loose fit, off-the-shoulder T-shirt to throw on and turn on the shower, rinsing my body quickly and jumping out. I redo my ponytail and head out to find the balcony doors half open, and Jake leaning against the balustrade outside.

'You really love it out here, don't you?' I ask him, picking up my wine glass from where he's brought it out and deposited it on the table. He doesn't look at me, but continues to gaze out to sea.

'I really do. It's probably why I like the roof of the spa so much. It's the night sky here, the sounds, the darkness. I'm drawn to it. A bit like I am to you.' He takes a mouthful of wine and glances over at me.

'You left your jacket the other night.' I know it's lame, but I don't know what else to say. The electricity between us thrums so intense that I'm surprised I can't hear the sound of it. He turns his body to face mine and, in a movement that's completely involuntary, I take a very small step towards him.

'I know,' he says, his voice low and steady.

'Jake, I don't want you to get in trouble. With me I mean.'

'We aren't doing anything wrong. You're a guest.'

'And you're a hotel employee. I don't want to be the reason you get sacked or disciplined or anything.'

'You won't be, I promise. Trust me, OK?' He takes my hand and gives it a squeeze. 'Did you have a nice day? I know Michael enjoyed himself.' Had Jake seen us come back, I wonder, because I know it's Michael's day off.

'It was truly brilliant. I know this might sound really weird, but he's really...' I struggle to find the word. 'I don't know, just very...'

'Calming?' Jake suggests.

'Yes!' I say laughing. 'That's the only word I can use to describe it. How does he do that?'

Jake joins in. 'He's a lovely man. He's become a bit of a father figure to us all here. Everyone goes to him for advice. Like the hotel agony uncle.' He falls silent for a moment, as though contemplating his next sentence. 'Any news from home today?'

'No, nothing. I'm trying to keep my phone out of reach at the moment. It's rather liberating.'

Right on cue a jaunty electronic tinkle emanates from Jake's pocket, making us both jump. A deep frown line sets on his face, as he pulls it out looking at the screen.

'You have got to be kidding me,' he mutters angrily to himself. 'I'm so sorry, sweet cheeks, I really do need to take this.'

I shake my hands in a dismissive manner. 'Of course, it's fine,' I say far too cheerily. 'Go ahead.'

He steps inside, and I know I should stay where I am and tune out the conversation, but I can't help but eavesdrop.

'What, now? No. No chance. You'll have to deal with it.' There's a pause as the person on the end of the phone speaks.

'Jesus!' he says loudly, making me start, and I sit down on one of the chairs in an attempt to look less conspicuous. 'No, not until next week. No. Absolutely not. Ask Anna, she will be able to handle this. This is what I pay her for, for Christ's sake. Yes, call me later.' Another pause. 'Not without Anna's say-so. Yes. OK. Bye, Jackson.'

He goes quiet, and I try and arrange myself in what I hope is a casual I've-not-been-listening-to-every-word-you've-said pose.

'Everything OK?' I ask smiling, trying to sound as jovial as possible, as I take another sip of wine. He runs his fingers through his hair and sits down on the chair opposite me, swirling his wine around in the glass.

'I hope so, yes.' He smiles at me, but his face is taut and etched with anxiety. 'Carrie, thank you.'

I'm shocked at his words and frown back at him with a small laugh. 'You're thanking me? Jake you're the one who pulled me out of the pit of despair I was in when I arrived, which I can't quite believe was only a couple of days ago. You kept me busy, made me laugh. What on earth are you thanking *me* for?'

'Because you arrived here and I don't know what it was, but you were so…' He looks around as if searching for something. 'You're like a breath of fresh air. I have a lot of friends here, but no one quite like you.' He laughs and shakes his head. 'You're the funniest person I've ever met.'

Now it's my turn to laugh.

'Me? Jake all I've done since I got here is cry on you.'

'That's not even remotely true. You threw your flip-flops at me on the beach, you stuffed your face with fishcakes.'

I swipe my arm at him, as he throws back his head in laughter, and I can't help but join in.

'I did not throw them *at* you,' I protest through my laughter. 'OK, I may have thrown them in your direction. And anyway, I'm sure I was actually crying at that point so that doesn't count.'

'See?' Jake says, standing up. 'You make me laugh. More wine?'

'Yeah, why not? Some of us don't have to work tomorrow.'

'Rub it in why don't you,' he calls from the lounge.

'Were you working today?' I ask and suddenly flinch as he drops the cold bottle on my shoulder, making him laugh. 'Laughing *at* me doesn't count,' I admonish him, and I push him with my foot as he passes. Then, with lightning reflexes, he grabs my ankle with his free hand and holds it there for a second, the touch of his hand on my leg making my breath catch in my throat. His eyes are alight as he sets my foot on the floor, slowly brushing up my calf as he moves his hand away.

'Now, now. Play nice.' He winks at me pouring us both a full glass. 'And yes, I was working. And yes, it was fine. Tiring, but fine.'

'What sort of things did you have to deal with?'

'Really? You actually want to talk about work? Of all the things?'

'I'm interested,' I say honestly. 'Especially since you work here. I'm keen to know all the behind-the-scenes gossip.' My thoughts stray to the mysterious Anna and Jackson from his phone call, and I wonder again what Jake meant when he said he pays her to deal with it? I guess I am doing a little digging. I know we have shared a lot, but I don't feel like I'm in a position to ask him, even though I'm dying to know.

'There really isn't much. Dale's the one with all the gossip. I try to keep out of it as much as possible.' He looks uncomfortable.

'I'll have to go ask Dale to reveal all your secrets then,' I tease and he smiles, but it doesn't quite reach his eyes. I know well enough now to not say anything else. I don't know why, but I feel like he's hiding something from me. He picks up his glass and downs its contents in one go.

'Hard week?' I laugh, with a look of surprise on my face.

He rubs his hand over his stubble and sighs. 'Something like that. I'm going for more alcohol, are you in?'

'Challenge accepted.' I drain my glass and stand up, suddenly a little light-headed. Maybe I should have eaten after all. I look at him through narrow eyes. 'You're not trying to get me drunk are you?'

He glances over his shoulder as he heads back inside. 'Is that a problem?'

'I'll have you know, I could drink you under the table,' I shout through to him, although now I'm a little nervous. I hear the clink of glasses and there's a threatening glint in his eyes as he emerges with a bottle of Grey Goose and two shot glasses, plus two bottles of Banks beer. Oh crap.

By ten thirty, I can no longer remember Jake's name, or my own name for that matter. Or the name of where I am.

I know it's warm and there are stars. Which are spinning. I hear a distant voice and turn towards it to see a man lying down on the sunbed next to me.

'You are gorgeous,' I point at him. 'And you're so tall. I wish I was so tall. Like a giant. A big, huge, woman giant, and I would step on stupid men.'

He finds this hilarious, as do I, and we collapse into fits of giggles.

'You!' he points back at me and laughs, swaying as he attempts to sit up on the sunbed. 'You are so tiny!' He begins to tiptoe round the balcony which makes me snort with hysteria. 'Like a teeny, tiny, mini person. I want to put you in my pocket and keep you forever and ever.'

He comes over to my sunbed and takes my face in his hands. 'So sweet. Like a honey flower.'

'No, not a honey flower.' I shake my head stating this like it's the most obvious thing in the world. 'A honey*bee*, and if you get too close I will sting you!' I poke him with my finger and he pretends to cry out in pain, but then he stills suddenly, his face greying. He stands up and runs in the direction of the bathroom. I point and laugh at him yelling, 'Winner!', as I stumble in behind to see him heaving over the toilet bowl. Then I feel desperate to go and help him.

'Oh no.' I rush over and stroke his hair back from his face, feeling suddenly sober. 'Are you alright?'

He nods slowly, his face pale and clammy.

'I don't feel too good,' he mutters, as he heaves again, and I grab his blonde hair, holding it back from his face with my hand. He takes some deep breaths to steady himself, and my hand drops from his hair to his face, for a brief moment, before I quickly withdraw it. 'I'm OK, it's passed. God, I need to lie down,' he groans and gets to his feet and heads out of the bathroom.

I nod, not wanting him to leave, but as I stagger to my feet and follow him out, I see he's lying on my bed, fully clothed, his eyes shut tight. I shuffle over to him.

'Jake!' I hiss. 'Jake!' I shake his massive arm and can't resist giving it a little squeeze while I'm there. His breathing has slowed, and I watch as his chest rises and falls gently. Laying my hand over his heart, he doesn't move. 'Jake, you can't stay here,' I whisper without making any real attempt to rouse him.

I flop myself down on the bed next to him and lean back on to the pillows with a resigned groan, the room spinning slightly around me. I close my eyes to try and stop the dizzy feeling creeping over me and fall into a deep and peaceful sleep.

Chapter Eighteen

I wake with a start, completely disorientated and with a thumping head, and begin trying to piece together the mayhem from the night before. My first thought is Jake. I turn, far too quickly for the state that I'm in, to find the bed next to me empty. My first thought is disappointment. My second is I'm going to throw up. I leg it to the bathroom and all of the last night's bad decisions come rushing back to greet me.

I crawl back into bed, taking a sip of water from the bottle sticking out of my bag, and check my watch for the time. Three forty-five a.m. I close my eyes and fall back to sleep instantly.

It's another hour and a half before I wake again, feeling unexpectedly OK. I sit up tentatively and risk going all the way when I'm sure that my stomach can hack it and I'm not going to be sprinting back to the bathroom. My head is throbbing slightly, but I'm no longer tired. In fact, I feel wide awake. I rifle through my bag looking for my paracetamol, knocking two back with the end of the bottle of water by my bed. I try standing and amble out on to the balcony, thankful that we managed to shut the doors last night or I'd be waking up bitten to death by bugs.

The fresh air is a welcome relief, and I settle down on the sunbed, curling my legs up to my chest as I lie on my side, breathing in the fresh, morning air. I notice the shot glasses on the table and the empty bottle of Grey Goose. Jesus, no wonder I was ill. It's only then I see the four bottles of beer and empty white wine. Ah. That would explain it then. Drinking on a relatively empty stomach, in the heat, is not the best idea I've ever had.

I think of Jake heaving over the toilet bowl. At least he was in a worse state than me. How does a guy of his stature manage to be such a lightweight? A welcome breeze wafts over my body, and I stay that way for a while. Awake, but still thinking about the night before. We had talked about our families mainly and a little about home. I don't think we talked about Luke and Emily, and I certainly didn't cry. I talked about Kate and Dan. Oh. Shit. *Kate.* I move as quickly as my head will allow and grab my phone. Sure enough there's a message from her. I open it, already knowing what it's going to say.

I don't know what the hell is going on, but you seemed to be having a VERY good time last night. I called so we could talk but clearly you are far too busy for that right now. Carrie, I'm worried about you. Hooking up with random guys while you're smashed off your face? Really? I know you've been through a lot, but I don't even know the girl I saw last night. Call me when you're ready to have a proper conversation. And when you've sobered up. K.

Oh God, this is all I need. I can't remember exactly what happened, but I know she FaceTimed me. Did Jake have his shirt off at that point? Crap, I think he did. Why the hell did he even *have* his shirt off? I can imagine why Kate may have jumped to conclusions. But really, why does she even care? OK, maybe that's unfair of me, but I feel like she wants me to be moping and just because I'm not behaving how she would, then I'm wrong. It's like she doesn't want me to be over it. Not that I am, but I think I can excuse myself a blowout. I'm *pretty* sure nothing happened between me and Jake, although I can remember looking at him when he was lying on the bed and wanting it to.

I need to do something and right now that something is go for a swim. I slip on my plain, black bikini and my dress from yesterday that's slung over the chair in the walk-in wardrobe. I grab a towel and some water and slip out of my room, attempting to gently close the door behind me, and come to a halt when I see Jake, quietly slipping out of the suite opposite me. He's wearing last night's clothes but with flip-flops instead of trainers. I freeze and watch him hold the door as it closes so it doesn't slam. He almost jumps out of his skin as he sees me, my door closing behind me with a loud *clunk*.

'Good morning,' I say curtly and make my way to the lift. I have no doubt in my mind that whoever's in that room, he spent the rest of last night with them.

'Sweet cheeks, wait…' he paces behind me, and my eyes prick with tears making me feel even more of an idiot than I do already. I hold my hand up and cut him off.

'Jake, I've already told you, you don't need to explain anything to me. OK? We're friends, I get it. Really, it's fine.' I turn to press the button on the lift, and he grabs hold of my arm gently.

'Carrie, just listen. Wait, please. Whatever you think it is, I can promise you it's not.'

I try not to be irrational and crazy, but inside my heart is beating out of my chest, and I know the sick feeling I have is nothing to do with last night's alcohol.

'I don't think it's anything, Jake. I'm not about to start questioning what you do. You don't owe me an explanation but please, whatever you have to say, just don't lie to me.'

'I think we both know that's not true. I do owe you an explanation. Come with me, please.' He looks down at me his gaze travelling up and down my body, smiling gently, the yellow in his eyes slightly dull from our ridiculous exploits last night. 'Where were you going, by the way?' he says with amusement, and I can't help but smile at him.

'Swimming.'

'Swimming?'

'Yes, swimming,' I say folding my arms over my chest.

'Just come with me for a minute, then you can be mad at me all you like, I promise.'

'I'm not mad at you, Jake, I just…' He presses a finger to my lips and pulls me into the lift that's just arrived. There's silence in the lift, but not an awkward one. I turn to him, his huge frame filling the space, and in that moment, I want him to pull me into his arms.

'Well, I think we are both surprisingly spritely, all things considered,' I say in an overly formal tone.

He laughs and shakes his head.

'I was not at four a.m. Let's just say all of last night came rushing back to me, in the literal sense.'

I laugh screwing up my face. 'Me too.'

We must have been awake at the same time. I think of me in my room and Jake, just across the hall, climbing out of the bed he most likely shared with someone else. That feeling of nausea rises up again, and I take a long, deep breath trying to quell the sensation that I know has nothing to do with my hangover.

'What the hell were we doing last night?' I can't help but laugh and give my head a shake, as I look at the floor.

'I think we may have lost the plot for a bit there. I blame it on the stress we've been under,' Jake says grinning back at me. 'I blame you. You've got me losing all my inhibitions.' And I can't help wondering if he actually has any inhibitions at all.

As we reach the bottom floor, he leads the way towards the reception desk. It's currently unoccupied, but I know there's bound to be someone close by to attend to any guests. He's taking purposeful strides, and has to wait for me to catch up, before he walks behind the desk and holds open the door leading to what I presume is the back office. It actually leads out to a large room with a number of smaller offices branching off from it in a semicircle. It's a super modern design, all glass walls and frosted panels with sleek, white furniture and grey, leather chairs. A large glass table in the middle of the room is empty but for a huge vase of flowers, and it looks fancy enough to be another reception area, let alone the back offices of the hotel. The tall blonde from reception the other day starts as Jake wishes her a loud, 'Good morning'. She clutches her hand to her chest, recovering herself, and with a quiet 'Good morning' back, hurriedly collects her papers from the copier, rushing past us to the main desk.

Jake takes my hand in his tentatively, but I don't pull away, and I let him lead me around the glass table to the back of the room, where the largest office is housed. There's a silver plaque on the door engraved with *J Holden, Group CEO.* Jake pulls out a bunch of keys and opens the door. I hesitate unsure what to do next.

'Jake, should we be in here?' I look around. 'I know it's still early, but what if someone sees us? Well, someone else,' I add, worried that we've already been busted in here by the blonde.

'I keep telling you to trust me. I wish you would.'

'My trust has been pushed to the limits lately, so I'm sorry if I seem a little on edge,' I grumble pettily, as I walk through the door and take in the room.

A sleek, silver Mac sits atop the black, wooden desk with a grey leather chair nestled under it. Two of the grey, velvet sofas sit opposite each other framing a low, glossy white coffee table just in front of it. There's a large unit to one side that I presume houses files and paperwork but, apart from that and a large lamp in the corner, the room is a lesson in minimalist chic. Jake sits on one sofa and gestures for me to sit opposite him.

'Jake,' I hiss, 'what are we doing here?'

'Just sit down, sweet cheeks.' I shuffle over to the sofa and perch on the edge as if this is less incriminating than reclining full length on it. We stare at each other for what seems like the longest time.

'OK,' Jake starts, and I can't help but feel ill with nerves. He spreads his hands on his knees and takes a deep breath. 'I've not been totally honest with you about things.'

'Jake please, if this is about last night, or this morning rather…' I pause. 'I heard you go into the suite opposite the other night too, when you left your jacket I came out to give it to you and… If you're seeing someone, and I mean look at you, why shouldn't you be? But if you are then, I'd just rather know.'

He laughs, and I feel myself on the brink of tears for a second, before pulling it back and getting my emotions in check. Being hung-over and tired certainly isn't helping.

'Sweet cheeks, the suite opposite yours, I was in there last night when I left you and the night before, but it's not what you think. Baby, it's my suite. That's where I live.'

'What?' Now *that* I did not see coming. 'You live there? How? Sorry that sounds awful, but how?' I sigh feeling guilty that I implied he was too far beneath having a nice place to live. But can he blame me? I know what that room's like, and I know how much it costs per night, so how does he manage to wangle *living* in it? Then something comes to me.

'Jake, are you seeing someone who works here? Someone high up, I mean?'

'Sweet cheeks, put down the stick, turn it round and pick it up at the right end. I live there alone.' He runs his hand over his stubble and rests it over his mouth. When he speaks I can hear a smile in his voice. 'The sign on the door.'

'What, group CEO?' I frown at him and then suddenly, like a light bulb over my head, the head of the number one idiot on the planet, I get it. My mouth goes dry as I say the words, my voice barely a whisper.

'Oh my God. You're J Holden. *You're* the group CEO.'

His eyes meet mine and we stare at each other.

'Jake, why didn't you tell me?' I frown at him, annoyed that he lied yet relieved it's nothing else I was worrying about.

'I'm sorry, sweet cheeks. I know I should have just come out and said it. It's no big secret, obviously, but I just didn't know how to after we first met in reception that day.'

'There were plenty of opportunities,' I say. 'All those times I talked about your job. God, you must think I'm such an idiot.' I flail my arms about as if to emphasise just how stupid I am. He comes over to my sofa, sitting down next to me.

'People can be a bit weird once they know about my job.' He sees a look in my eyes that I tried desperately to hide and tilts his head towards me. 'No, not just women.' It's incredibly irritating that he already seems to know me so well.

'Seriously, Carrie, I know I should have told you. I would have, I promise. It's just, when I met you, we hit it off so well, and you had all this other stuff going on. I didn't want to add to everything you've got to think about by bringing it up.' The cogs in my brain are whirring, piecing it all together.

'The car,' I say loudly, feeling as if I'm just about to crack an incredibly tricky jigsaw. I narrow my eyes at him. 'The Range Rover. It's yours, isn't it?'

He smiles and tilts his mouth to one side in a guilty look. 'Er, yeah. Yeah, it is.'

I smile at him gently still trying to process the information and how I feel. I can see a look of worry flicker across his face, and it's slightly reassuring to see he cares what I think, that it's not just me.

'Jake, I'm not mad at you. I can see why you kept it from me, but I just wish you'd said something. What do you think I would have done? You keep telling me to trust you, but you didn't even trust me with this.'

He looks hurt at my words and takes my hands in his, shaking his head.

'I do trust you. I've been stung before. I just wanted you to get to know me first, and not have this idea of me in your head once I told you.'

'You thought your job would have made me not want to hang out with you?'

'Yes, I do. I know you care what people think, and I didn't want you to be worrying about them thinking anything *untoward* was going on.'

I understand what he's trying to say and, annoyingly, he's right. I would have been bothered by people thinking I was schmoozing up to the manager, especially seeing as I'm a woman here alone.

'So, you're the manager of this and how many other hotels?'

'I'm not manager of this hotel, as such, but I do oversee the running of the group. I… er, I own it. I have one hotel here, Miami, London and we are hoping to open another in the next five years. Probably in Dubai, a few factors depending. Our main head office is actually in Miami, but I work better out here, and I can do everything I need. Emails, video calls, conference calls, it's not hard. And it's a short flight over there. I fly back and forth at least two, more like three, times a month. My dad built the Holden Hotel Group, this was his baby, his dream, and now it's mine to take care of.'

I exhale long and slowly, sitting back on the sofa.

'Woah. Jake, that's amazing'

He beams at me.

'Do you think?'

'Yes, of course. What a better way to honour his memory than carrying on his work. He would be so proud of you,' I say sincerely, giving his hand a squeeze. I can see my words have touched him, and his eyes glaze slightly. Then he pulls me into him and breathes deeply into my hair.

'Thank you.'

'For what?'

'For being so great.'

I pull away from him gently, trying to calm my rapidly beating pulse.

'Come on, big shot, you can get me some breakfast. I need to eat before Rachel sees me and starts abusing me for being hung-over. I may have laughed a little too hard at her yesterday.'

'Deal. Actually, do you want to eat in here? I can go fill us some plates?'

'Can we? That would be great; I probably look a right state. Hold on, is that why you don't want to take me to breakfast? You don't want to be seen in public with me?' I narrow my eyes at him accusingly, despite my smile.

'You, sweet cheeks, are radiant. Every day.' He winks at me and makes for the glass door of the office.

'Liar,' I reply, pouting with mock affront.

'Make yourself at home,' he laughs and disappears in the direction of the main reception. I fling myself full length on the sofa, figuring what the hell? I really didn't think the morning was going to go that way. I'm still a little annoyed he didn't mention this piece of information earlier, but I'm more irritated with myself for being so relieved the big reveal was what it was, and not that he was involved with someone else. Someone else, I chide myself. He's not *involved* with me. Just because he's opened up about this, it doesn't change anything between the two of us. I stare at the white ceiling, wondering what Kate would make of all this.

Chapter Nineteen

It's seven forty-five by the time we finish breakfast, which turned into more of a picnic on the coffee table in his office. I feel much more human, and the morning's revelations from Jake have only opened him up more. He talks animatedly about the business his father dreamed of, and how he's longing to build it up and keep it prospering. Which it is currently doing in abundance. They seem to have more and more A-listers turning out to stay in Miami, their biggest hotel, and a few of them have been to the Barbados hotel. I get very excited when he tells me that Ryan Reynolds and Blake Lively actually stayed in my suite last year for a week.

Because it's a smaller boutique hotel, it appeals to the celebrities as it's not swarming with paparazzi like some of the bigger and more well-known, luxury resorts. He says how he would like to be in London more, developing the business there, and my stomach does a little flip at this statement. Would that mean there may be chance we could meet up again in the future? As friends, of course.

Now I know what he really does for a living, it's fascinating to hear about Jake's lifestyle and, I have to admit, I am somewhat envious, although I know it's hard work.

Obviously, I don't know exactly how much money he makes, and he's taken care not to give a thing away, but I can tell from certain things he's let slip in conversation that money isn't something he has to worry about.

As he spoke, I realised I could watch him all day long. He's truly captivating. His yellow eyes draw me deeper every time they lock with mine, and his wide, genuine smile puts one on my own face without even realising it. Reluctantly, Jake and I part ways in the quiet reception which is, thankfully, still fairly empty. For some reason we both stand there, as we say goodbye, not sure what we are supposed to do, grinning at each other.

'I'm going to the beach today, probably with Rachel so...' I tail off not wanting to ask to see him even though all I can think about right now is when I'm going to see him again. He smiles and for the smallest second, he touches my fingers with his.

'I'll come find you later on,' he tells me, putting me out of my misery.

'You always say that. Another one of your late-night calls?' I laugh with raised eyebrows.

'Definitely not. I'll see you later, sweet cheeks.' And with that he heads off outside the main entrance stopping to talk to two of the concierge on the door.

I make the decision to go back to my room, take the bull by the horns and call Kate.

'Carrie, what's wrong? Are you OK?'

'Kate, where are you? You sound like... Oh crap! I am so sorry, I didn't even think. I'm such an idiot. Go back to sleep, it's OK, we'll talk later.'

'Hang on. Let me go into the spare room.' I hear her bedroom door creak, and I imagine her crossing the landing and settling down into the spare room, where Luke and I spent so many nights.

'I'm here. Are you alright?'

'Yes, I was just so eager to speak to you I didn't even think about it being like, what? Three in the morning there?'

'Spot on. But it's fine,' she pauses, 'I've not been sleeping great lately.'

There's silence on the line.

'Kate, I'm sorry for what I said about you and Dan.'

'No, *I'm* sorry. I should never have sent that text. I felt so awful afterwards and...' she sighs. 'I just feel so stuck in the middle, and I have all this other stuff going on, and all anyone wants to know is how you are, and I can't answer them, because I don't know. I don't even know how my best friend is after my brother tried his hardest to screw this all up for everyone.'

'Kate, stop. It's OK. I'm sorry I called when I was drunk the other night. That's not how I wanted it to be.'

'Honey, you don't have to explain it, you can do what you want. I just want you to be safe. Who was that guy?' She gives a short laugh. 'Nice choice, by the way.'

I can hear the grin in her voice, and I can't help but laugh too.

'His name's Jake. Kate, nothing's happened between us. He's been so nice to me since I arrived. I cried on the beach, and he bought me lunch. He actually owns the hotel.'

'No way? He only looks about our age!'

It's then I realise I don't even know how old Jake actually is.

'Carrie, listen, if you've slept with twenty men since you arrived, no one would blame you. Alright, maybe not twenty but, I get it, OK? If you *had* slept with someone then you have every right to. Yes, it would be weird, but you don't need mine, or anyone else's, permission. You can do what you like.' There's a pause, like she's wondering if she should say what's about to come next. 'And, Carrie, I know you say nothing's happened, but you've only been split up from Luke a few days, so please be careful, OK? I know you were both drunk, but I saw the way he looked at you, the way he watched you. He was captivated by you.'

It unnerves me that she's just used the exact words I would use to describe what Jake does to me.

'I know, Kate, and I don't think that. But thank you anyway, for saying that. He's been a shoulder to cry on.'

'A big, tanned, muscular shoulder by the looks of it,' she interjects with a giggle.

'To be honest, Kate, I've needed it, and I didn't think I would. I thought coming away would mean I didn't have to think about it all, but it's only made me think about it more. I *needed* to talk about it all, and it's so hard with you because you're so close to it, but Jake's an outsider with no ties to any of it. I needed someone not involved, you know?'

'I understand,' she says quietly.

'No matter what you say, he's still your brother, and I get that you can't just switch that off. Things haven't been right between me and Luke, I see that now. That doesn't excuse what he did, but I've finally started to realise that. It does make it easier knowing that the end result is the same, that we shouldn't really have been getting married.'

There's another sigh from down the phone, and I wait with baited breath for Kate to speak.

'Now I think about it, I think you're probably right. You guys *were* more like best friends, I suppose. I just wish it hadn't happened like this, maybe then there would have been some hope for us all to still be friends too. But I know that's never going to happen,' she quickly adds. 'Carrie, I don't ever want you to be unhappy.'

'I know this may sounds like madness, but I'm truly not unhappy. I'm a lot of other things. Angry, hurt, embarrassed and just, sort of, sad I guess, about the way it's all gone down, but am I actually unhappy? I don't think I am.'

'For what it's worth, I feel all those things too, and it didn't even happen to me. Bloody Luke. What a prick. I'm so sorry.'

'It's not your fault. Not even a little bit. Kate, listen. I didn't just call to talk about me. What's going on with you? Please tell me. I know it's not about you and Dan, and I'm so sorry I even thought that. I don't want you going through this on your own, whatever it is. I know everything's a bit weird right now, but you're my best friend.'

'Am I still?' Kate says softly. 'I wasn't sure I was.'

My eyes fill with tears, and I laugh through them, 'Of course you are.'

'You too, Calvin.'

I let out a loud bark of laughter at her use of my nickname, and I can hear her giggling. When we were at school, Carrie Kingston soon became 'CK' and the rest is history. I think Kate and Luke's nana actually thought my name was Calvin Klein for about two years as it's all she used to call me.

I want her to open up to me, but I don't want to push her, so I give her the chance to decide where to take the conversation and leave it up to her. She takes a deep breath, and I press my lips together, hoping she still trusts me enough.

'So, you should probably know, you were right about one thing. I have slept with Dan.'

I don't say anything, but my heart is beating at a million miles an hour.

'Carrie?' she says quietly.

'I'm here.'

'We slept together, but it was a really, *really* long time ago. I was seventeen. He'd come over to see Luke one night, and Mum and Dad were out and Luke had gone to yours. We got talking and drank blue WKD and, weirdly, we talked about you and Luke having sex, which *everyone* was talking about at the time. So Dan was like, yeah it must be really awkward, wouldn't it be great to just get the first time over with and out of the way. And, well, we kind of just decided that, yeah, it would. So we… well we had sex,' she states matter-of-factly.

'We lost our virginity to each other and, honestly, it was absolutely perfect. I can't put into words how special it was, and that sounds like the corniest thing ever, I know, but it was. We both agreed afterwards that no one would ever know. That it would stay between us. And it has. Luke doesn't even know.'

'Kate, I…'

'Just let me finish,' she says, and I can hear her voice crack slightly. 'Afterwards it was totally normal. I was worried it would be weird, and it just wasn't at all. So everything was cool and fine, until about a month later.' She lets the words hang in the air, to let me catch up.

'Oh God,' I say tears springing to my eyes as the realisation creeps in. 'Oh, Kate.'

'Yep. Pretty much pregnant.'

'What did you do?' I ask my voice barely a whisper.

'Well, Dan was amazing. He said whatever I wanted to do, he would stand by me and my decision. We agreed we would work things out, even though we weren't together. He would work as much as he could and asked if he could move in, so he could help with the baby.' She lets out a small laugh. 'It all sounded so easy back then, so simple, when clearly it was going to be anything but that. So that was it, we were actually going to have a baby. Except well, we didn't. I don't know what happened but we, I… I lost it. I was eleven weeks pregnant. I know because it was just before the first scan. We hadn't told anyone, we agreed to wait until we knew everything was OK and to buy us a bit of time to get our heads around it.

'Then one Saturday morning, I woke up and I started bleeding. Really heavy, like a period, and I knew straight away, I could just feel it. I got the bus to the hospital, because I didn't know what else to do, and Dan met me there. I had a scan, and they did some tests and, well, that was it, there wasn't going to be a baby any more, it was gone and no one could tell me why. These things happen they said, you're only young, you'll have plenty more chances to have kids. Like that all made it OK. Because I was seventeen it was fine I was having a miscarriage, because this wouldn't be my only opportunity to get pregnant, so why was I so upset? But the fact is I don't have plenty more chances. In fact, I don't have any.' She pauses and sniffs down the phone. 'Justin can't have children.'

And I have no words to say to her that could possibly make it better.

'I knew. When we met. You know he had leukaemia when he was little? Well, it's because of the treatment. I was fine with it, honestly I was. He was enough for me, and he told me straight away, and we discussed what our other options might be, which is *the* weirdest thing to be discussing on your third date, I can tell you. But he was open and honest, and I was already in love with him by then so it was too late anyway. And I was OK with it; I still am, but…'

'The baby,' I say flatly.

'Exactly. It's just brought it all back, and I feel like I'm somehow being punished for my past mistakes, getting pregnant at seventeen.'

'Kate, it was an accident not a mistake. It wasn't your fault that what happened, happened. You could never have known how it'd all unravel in the future.'

'I know, you're right. It's just made me so mad, Luke being so irresponsible with this baby and not manning up right away. Plus, it drags up old memories, which is why Dan's been around so much. Justin knows, of course. I told him everything when we were having our very first chat about wanting kids, but I don't want to talk to him about it, as I know he already feels guilty about not being able to give me a baby, even though I've told him it's about having a family not about me being pregnant with his child, it's about us together. But Dan just gets it. He went through it all with me, and it was just the two of us back then, no one else knew, and we never said anything. I think it's brought it all home for him too when we thought it was something that was long in the past. I suppose I'm never going to forget it, am I? Neither of us will.

'So now you know why I said what I said about being there for this baby. I want to make it feel loved and like it has a real family, because our baby never had that chance. And even though the circumstances are less than ideal, this baby has the chance ours didn't.'

'Oh, Kate, you could have told me. I hate the thought you went through this and I didn't even know. I knew I loved Dan, but I love him even more now. Oh, I wish I was there to give you a huge cuddle.'

'Me too. Well, I actually wish I was there rather then you being here,' she adds with a small laugh. 'And you're so right about Dan, he's always been so good with everything, so good to *me* too. There was a time after it all happened, way before Justin, I thought me and him might, you know, but it wasn't meant to be. It was our shared experiences that brought us together, and I loved him. Not like that, but we've always had that connection of what we went through. That's probably why you thought something was going on, because I suppose it always has been. We do share a secret; it just wasn't what you thought.'

A huge feeling of guilt settles over me. Why had I jumped to conclusions like that? In hindsight, I know it was Luke that had made me so suspicious about it, when in another life I wouldn't have thought twice about anything going on between Kate and Dan.

'Kate, I am so sorry, I feel awful. I can't believe I said what I said to you. You know, under normal circumstances, I would never think that. Luke's got me all suspicious and untrusting. I almost hate him for that more than anything, that I'm projecting his mistakes on to all of you.'

'Calvin, it's OK. Really, I understand. I'm so glad you know now, though. I feel like a weight's been lifted off me.' I can hear the smile creeping back into her voice, and I'm happy and relieved that she's confided in me and that things are OK between us.

'And what about you and Justin?' I ask her carefully. 'Have you talked any more about having a family?'

'No, not at the moment. There seems to be so much happening right now, but we will, in time. I know it will happen for us somehow, someday, it's just working out how we get to that.' She sighs again. 'It is what it is, Carrie, nothing can change it. Anyway,' she says with a distinctly brighter tone, 'are you OK? Apart from getting smashed with handsome strangers, how is your holiday going?'

'Good,' I say flopping back on the pillows. I glance briefly at the dent in the pillow next to me, still visible from the shape of Jake's head pressed into it last night. 'I had a tour yesterday, which was fab. Got to see more of the island and eat the most yummy food. All I seem to have done since I got here is eat. And drink. I swear the rum punch is lethal. It needs some sort of health warning.'

'Er, yes, I did see the effects of that, remember?' she laughs, and I hear her stifle a yawn.

'That wasn't even the rum punch, that was vodka, the punch is even worse!' My stomach turns just thinking about it. 'But listen; go back to bed, honey. We can talk properly later. I'm sorry I woke you.'

'Well I'm not. Not one bit. I'll ring you tomorrow, well, today.'

'Sounds good,' I smile. 'Sleep tight, again. Lots of love.'

'You too.'

We each blow a kiss down the phone and hang up. I stare at the ceiling trying to process the crazy amount of information I've been barraged with since I woke up this morning. Jake, Kate, Dan, Justin. It swims in my head until I feel dizzy just thinking about it all. A relaxing day is definitely in order, and I'm keen to catch up with Rachel too to see what she got up to last night, but I'm not sure I can take any more revelations this morning. I roll over, burying my head deep into the pillow, and fall straight to back sleep.

Chapter Twenty

The sun is streaming through windows by the time I wake up and, glancing at my phone, I see it's just after eleven o'clock. I don't know if it's the extra sleep or the fact that I don't have any conspiracy theories racing around my brain, like I have for the past few days, but I feel like I'm properly rested. I see a message from Rachel that reads:

> *Having a day on the beach if you fancy it? Dale pulled some strings and I have one of those cool cabana thingies with two huge beds, you know like they do on TOWIE when they go to Marbs? Maybe see you in a bit…? I want all the juicy deets from last night!! He is an absolute DISH by the way (which you failed to mention missus!!) Will discuss more later! Rach x x x x*

Even though I'm only going to the beach, I take a quick shower to wake me up properly and wash away the last bit of fog from the night before, dressing in a turquoise, tropical print bikini and a plain, black playsuit over the top. I grab my beach stuff and make a detour to the bakery where I pick up four turnovers and two huge slices of something called pound cake, which I'm not sure what exactly it is but, quite frankly, it's cake so how wrong can you go? I feel like I'm going to regret Michael introducing me to this bakery by the end of the holiday, at least my clothes will at any rate. The heartbreak diet they call it, don't they? When you lose weight due to the stress of it all. Well no chance of that here.

Once on the beach I spot Rachel almost immediately, not least because I hear her first, shrieking with laughter at something Dale's just said to her. He's walking past with a tray of empty cocktail glasses. Never too early in Barbados, remember?

'You've been busy,' I say as I reach her, nodding towards the tray as Dale gives me a wave.

'What?' she says looking guilty. 'What do you mean?'

'Well I was talking about the empty cocktail glasses,' I giggle, 'but clearly you've been busy with something, or some*one*, else?'

'How dare you insinuate such a thing,' she says fanning her face like she's stepped right out of *Pride and Prejudice*. 'I didn't even see him last night.' She pulls a face, and I can see she's disappointed to have missed out on an evening in Dale's company. 'He was working late and, to be honest, I needed an early night. So we will have to rely on you, missy, for our daily dose of debauchery. We don't want people thinking we're actually upstanding members of society after all.'

We laugh together, and I shake my head, stripping down to my bikini and settling myself on the plush, cream bed armed with my bottle of sun cream.

'Oh, I don't think there's any chance of that just yet, last night put paid to that. And you are not going to believe what happened this morning.'

Over the course of the day, I come to realise that Rachel makes the best audience ever when you have a story to tell and, luckily for us both, I seem to have stories in abundance at the minute. Half the time I feel like I'm on the stage performing, as she hangs on my every word, feeding back vocal responses to each part of the story. At one point, she bounces up and down on her sunbed with such vigour that she almost falls face first into the sand.

The more I chat with someone else about it, the less bothered I am that Jake didn't tell me about his super job. I probably would have treated him differently, and I know there is no way I would have let him get as close to me as I have. But now he is, I have to admit, I like the connection that's grown between us, seemingly by its own accord, and I seem powerless to stop it. I'm not even sure I want to stop it, whatever *it* is.

We have a lunch of deep-fried calamari with a light and creamy garlic dip and decide to treat ourselves to some strictly non-alcoholic fruit punch, which all goes to pot when it's Jake who delivers it, shirtless, in pale blue shorts. I can smell the alcohol before I even taste it, and as Rachel's still at the bar, no doubt flirting up a storm with Dale, he sits on Rachel's sunbed and gently asks me how I am. Although right now that question could be related to a plethora of things. He leaves as she returns, heading back to whatever shirtless task he's in charge of today, and I watch him strut up the beach stopping to say hello to a few guests on the way. I see Rachel watching me watching him, but I ignore the smirk on her face and concentrate on my tan.

We do nothing else for the rest of the afternoon except chat and sunbathe, punctuated with a few dips in the cool, blue ocean. Rachel is great fun, and I know that, no matter what, this is one relationship that will most definitely continue once the holiday's over.

At around four in the afternoon, Dale brings us over a couple of Banks beers, which it would have just been rude to refuse. After taking far too long to drink them, we agree to meet up in the dining room for dinner at seven and head off to our respective rooms to shower, change and chill. I put in a phone call to my mum who rattles on about Ann down the road having been to Barbados on a cruise, and isn't it funny, she passed your hotel, said it looked very nice, very swanky and posh etc., etc. To be honest, I didn't mind one bit, it was nice to hear my mum's voice chatting away like normal, and she actually sounded pleased I was away rather than freaking out about the whole me being on my own that she was on the verge of doing.

I plait my hair to one side and decide to wear navy blue palazzo pants with a cream vest and tan, gladiator flats. I am definitely picking up a tan and made good progress on the beach today. I stare at myself in the mirror of the walk-in wardrobe for a moment. Do I look like someone who found out their best friend was pregnant by their fiancé on their wedding day? I smile at my reflection and decide that, no, I don't. Not even remotely. I look like someone having a great time on holiday, who is about to go have a quiet dinner with a friend. Although between Rachel, Dale and Jake I know that's highly unlikely. Which only makes me grin even more.

'So what's the deal with this party tomorrow?' Rachel asks, as we finish up a slice of coconut cake and vanilla ice cream for our dessert. 'Who's the guy throwing it again?'

'Some Brazilian billionaire according to Jake,' I reply. 'Luis Mendoza. I've not heard of him before, but Jake says he's a good guy. Self-made and gives a lot of it away to charity.'

It's only then I realise that Rachel probably doesn't know that Katya is Luis's wife. If there's even a chance she's going to be there then I need to forewarn Rachel.

'About tomorrow...' I start feeling a little nervous on how to broach this. 'Jake said it's unlikely she'll be there, but Luis's wife, Katya her name is, that's the er, the woman who Ben went off with.'

'Oh, this just gets better and better!' she actually laughs, exasperated, and I'm relieved she seems to be OK with this latest revelation. 'Oh, whatever,' she says, taking a large slug of wine. (Yes, the alcohol-free day is really working out well for us.) 'You know what? She's welcome to him. She's probably done me a favour, to be honest. I'm sure this won't be the first time he's strayed and it wouldn't have been the last. Does her husband know what she's like? She's hardly been discreet has she?'

'Apparently so. Jake said he was lonely after his first wife died, and he likes her company, so he just kind of overlooks her extramarital activities.'

Rachel snorts and gives a look of derision. 'Men are so dumb sometimes.'

'So you're definitely OK to come? Even if she does turn up? Jake said it's for staff and guests but that it ends up being a bit of a staff drinking session by the end of the night. I'm sure there will be plenty of opportunity for you to catch up with Dale...'

'Drink and cute boys? Sign me up! So, come on then, what's the deal with you and Hercules now? Have you guys even kissed yet?'

I laugh long and hard at her nickname for him, and it's made even more funny because I can see just what she means. His strong, muscular body, over six foot frame and his blonde hair all completed with his chiselled jaw and deep, yellow eyes. He really is godlike. I realise I'm blushing at the thought of him just as Rachel calls me out on it.

'Ha!' she yells, pointing at my pink cheeks. 'You're so hot for him!'

'Shh!' I hiss back at her. 'Someone will hear you!' My eyes scan the dining room, but there is no one paying us the least bit of attention. As I look outside I can see Amy and Bryony sashaying across the terrace and down the path towards The Coconut Shack. I wonder if they will be at the party tomorrow, but think I already know the answer is going to be a yes.

'Do you even care if anyone hears me? Are you really bothered what people think?' Rachel says draining her glass and making to stand up and leave. I think about this for a second. In all honesty, I am never going to see any of these people again, probably Jake included, I conclude sadly. So it doesn't really matter what they think or say, does it? Or am I just making up excuses to justify my connection to Jake?

'No, I'm not bothered,' I reply, as we link arms and automatically start down the path that Amy and Bryony took moments earlier.

'Have you noticed that we seem to automatically migrate to alcohol when we're together?' I giggle at Rachel. She lets out a groan and laughs.

'We are the most tragic pair on this entire island.'

As we round the corner we see Amy and Bryony in the distance, draped over the bar and fawning all over Dale. I squint my eyes at them as we move closer.

'Is she… is she actually twiddling his dreadlocks round her fingers?' I say incredulous, and I see Dale smiling but looking very awkward, even more so as he spies me and Rachel. He does his best to extricate himself from Bryony's literal grasp as swiftly and smoothly as possible.

'Scratch that last statement!' Rachel declares. '*They* are the most tragic pair on the island. I've seen them throwing themselves over anything that moves.'

'You mean throwing themselves all over Jake and Dale. Do you think that's why we dislike them so much?' I say with a wry smile.

'No,' she says defiantly. 'OK well, yeah, maybe. But whatever, come on. We're a million times better.' And she strides off towards them with intent.

I'm seriously glad she's on my team sometimes. I scurry to catch up with her, and I'm not ashamed to admit it's because I don't want to miss a second of what's about to unfold.

To my joy, as soon as Rachel reaches the bar, Dale diverts all his attention to her, giving her the most gorgeous smile, much to the dismay of Bryony and Amy who, from the horror on their faces, look like they've both just been slapped round the face by a doughnut.

'Well don't you have quite the tan!' he grins at her. 'You're looking mighty fine this evening, if I may say.' Rachel blushes slightly, and it's still visible under her tanned cheeks. It makes me smile to see him paying her so much attention.

She nestles herself on a bar stool next to Amy and pats one next to her for me to join her. Dale holds up a jug, indicating he's about to fill it with rum punch, and we both nod and say 'Yes please' in unison making us fall into a fit of giggles, as Dale shakes his head with a smile.

While he goes to busy himself rustling up some ill-advised alcohol for us, Rachel turns to me and says in an overly loud voice, 'Gosh, Carrie, do you think we should drink this? I mean, I heard that drinking gives you wrinkles. And I think it was facial hair too.'

I snort loudly, and my shoulders begin to shake as I try not to burst into a peal of laughter, which isn't helped by Rachel theatrically flicking her dark hair over her shoulder as she continues.

'It can also make you less attractive, you know? Actually make you *uglier*. And how would we ever get the boys to like us if we were ugly? You don't think I'm ugly, do you, Carrie?'

I manage to compose myself and mutter through my giggles, 'Rachel, you are so beautiful.'

'Oh. My. God. Thanks!' she sighs, throwing her hand to her chest. 'But no, you're the most beautiful.'

I go to open my mouth to play along but she jumps in, grabbing my hands before squealing loudly.

'No, you are! Oh my God, OK, we are both the exact same amount of beautiful.'

I can no longer contain myself and burst out laughing, in what I'm sure is the most unattractive manner to Bryony and Amy who are sat looking on dismayed but also not entirely sure if we are joking or not.

Rachel swings round on her chair to face them both and says in the sweetest voice she can muster, 'OMG, hi! We are just about to get some rum punch, would you like to join us? You guys don't look like you're having any fun *at all*! Did you know frowning can give you wrinkles too? You want to be careful.'

Bryony's hand flies to her forehead in an involuntary movement, and I squeeze my lips together to prevent another loud laugh from escaping. Bryony makes a repulsed sound in her throat before sliding off her bar stool and grabbing her sparkly clutch bag from the bar.

'Aw, you're leaving?' Rachel says, sticking out her bottom lip. 'That's a shame. We were just about to start discussing the benefits of being a total bitch to other women to get what you want, and I *really* wanted your opinion, but that's OK, another time.'

Amy gasps and looks shocked, while Bryony narrows her eyes and looks like she would like nothing more than to slap Rachel around the face. Especially since Rachel's just sat there grinning at her, looking like she doesn't have a care in the world. Bryony gives a nasty smile, and I don't know why, but with a horrible sick feeling in my stomach I know in an instant what she's about to say, and I'm powerless to stop her.

'No wonder your boyfriend cheated on you. And just so you know, you're welcome to Dale, he's not really my type. And since I slept with him last night, I'm not really interested in him any more.'

She smiles sweetly and gives a little wave of her hands before spinning on her heels and making to leave. To mine, and Bryony and Amy's surprise, Rachel starts laughing. Bryony looks confused, as do I, but Rachel steps down from her bar stool and takes a step towards Bryony.

'You're lying,' she says simply.

'I am not,' Bryony snaps back.

'Yes, you are.'

'Fine. Don't believe me then, but why would I lie?'

'Because,' Rachel starts slowly, 'you're a bitch who thinks the world revolves around you, and you're so insecure that the only way you can feel good about yourself is to make other people feel bad about themselves which, quite frankly, is one of the most hideous traits in a person. And I know you didn't sleep with Dale last night, and do you know how I know?' She pauses for effect, and Bryony's face pales, even under her deep tan. 'Because I did.'

Rachel smiles and hops back on to her stool, just as Dale plants the jug of rum punch down in front of us.

'Thank you,' she says politely, pouring herself a glass and taking a ladylike sip, as Dale escapes, quick sharp, to serve some other customers. I stare, open-mouthed, at her before raising my hand and giving her a high five. I think for a second Bryony is going to stamp her feet like a toddler and have a tantrum, but she lets out a little squeak and stalks off in the direction of the hotel, leaving Amy clip-clopping off behind her in her skintight dress.

'You, lady,' I say to her, 'are awesome. And in so much trouble!'

She laughs pouring me a drink and giving hers a nonchalant stir with a mixer from a little pot on the bar. She flutters her eyelashes and throws a little pout my way.

'I don't know what you're talking about.'

I raise my eyebrows so high that they almost catapult off my forehead.

'How could you not tell me you guys slept together? We were at the beach all day! And dinner!' I say, laughing incredulously and giving her a gentle punch on her arm.

'I know, I know. I'm sorry. But today wasn't the right time, you'd just found out about Jake and your poor friend Kate. I reckoned this could wait for another time.'

I smile and give her hand a squeeze. 'You didn't have to do that. I bet you've been bursting all day long.'

'I kind of have,' she giggles. 'I was desperate to tell you, if I'm totally honest.'

'Come on,' I say, slipping off the stool. 'Let's grab a table, and you can give me all the gory details.'

'You'll definitely need another jug of this stuff if that's the case.' She smirks at me, and I wonder if I'm about to regret my willingness to listen to her and Dale's shenanigans.

After two jugs of what is, by comparison, relatively weak rum punch (I am holding Dale responsible for his inclination to keep bringing us alcohol), we are some of the few remaining guests left in the bar. Dale tells us there are a lot of flights that go out tomorrow, so it's usually quite quiet on a Thursday and Friday, hence the decision to have the party tomorrow night.

'So you'll have a fresh batch of victims to unleash your rum punch on will you?' I laugh.

'Hey, I'm just giving the people what they want.' He holds up his hands and gives Rachel a wink. 'I'm needed in the restaurant upstairs, so I'll maybe see you later on?' he asks her sounding eager.

She gives an unconvincing coy look. 'Well, you know where to find me.'

'I sure do,' he replies with a dazzling smile and a kiss on her hand. 'See you later, Carrie. Don't keep her up too late, that's my job.'

I nod and wave, mid drink, as I see Rachel beaming from ear to ear.

'You like him,' I sing to her, 'you want to kiss him, you want to marry him...'

'Oh shut up!' She bats me away with a smile. 'I do like him. He's fun, very, very fun and a perfectly pleasant way to fill my evenings.' We both laugh out loud at her statement.

'We both know it's not big romance, we're just having a bit of fun. It's a holiday fling, that's all. Unlike you.' She looks at me pointedly over her glass.

'I'm not *flinging* anything. I've said it a million times, we are just friends,' I tell her again.

'Whatever. I don't know who you are trying to convince, me or yourself, but I ain't buying it, lady. And I know, deep down, neither are you. I've seen him look at you. Trust me, that's not how mates look at each other. No matter how you feel about him, from his side, there's definitely something there. And I know you feel it too, because you're turning pink.'

My hands fly to my cheeks and she chuckles.

'See? You can say what you like, but your body knows. You guys want each other. Fact.' She leans back in her chair with an air of triumph.

'How can you be so sure? I mean, how do you know? And I'm actually asking this as a genuine question. It's only ever been Luke for me. He's all I've known, and I don't know if I'm reading this whole thing wrong. What if I'm getting carried away because I've just been dumped?'

'OK, look,' starts Rachel, spreading her hands on the table, 'you haven't just been dumped. You have, and this is what we call it in the business, dodged a bullet of epic proportions.' She gesticulates wildly with her arms to try and emphasise just how big. 'He didn't dump you, he lost you through his behaviour of supreme bastardness. I'm actually an expert on that scale. I have a chart we can refer to, if you like?'

I laugh at her and run my hands over my hair trying to calm some of the frizz I'm sure is taking hold. The night is hot and humid, and I always seem to get even warmer when I start thinking about Jake.

'Carrie, I don't really know Jake and, to be honest, I hardly know you, but I'm going out on a limb here and saying that we've shared enough alcohol and gossip about boys to officially call ourselves friends.'

'We are definitely friends,' I say giving her hand a squeeze and smiling warmly at her. Now I think about it, Rachel's probably the best friend I have right now. And Jake. She smiles back, her eyes twinkling.

'So, in my official capacity as your friend, I am telling you, just go with it. Don't overthink it. Nothing's happened between you guys yet.' She hesitates and narrows her eyes at me with a pout. 'Has it?' she asks accusingly.

'No, nothing's happened,' I say trying not to let my mind wander to thoughts of the something and keep it on the nothing. 'If it had, I would be freaking out so much I'd have to come and tell you immediately. In fact, I might just end up telling the first person I saw.'

She laughs raucously and bangs her hand on the table.

'Why would you be freaking out?'

'Because,' I say spreading my hands out in front of me, 'think about it. I've never been with anyone except Luke. We were teenagers when we got together, so consequently I've never *been* with anyone else, in every sense of the word.' I really hope she's got my drift, and that I don't have to spell it out any more.

'You mean he's the only guy you've ever slept with? Then you definitely need to see what you've been missing.'

'Honestly, Rach, the thought terrifies me.'

'It does?' she frowns. 'Why?'

'Because I don't know what I'm doing. I mean, I know what I'm doing, but I'm not experienced am I? Not like Jake will be.' I think about how many women Jake must have been with, and I feel a stab of jealously cut through me.

'That's exactly why you don't need to worry.' Rachel shakes her head at me as if I'm totally missing the point. 'He's going to be a total pro. You won't need to worry about a thing. The sex was good with Luke right?'

I bite my lip, looking around, worried someone will have heard us but, again, it's just me panicking. I seem to be paranoid beyond belief that someone will realise we are talking about Jake. I think about Rachel's question for a moment, although the thought of Luke and I having sex is now a disturbing and nauseous thought. Especially now I know that I'm not the only person he's ever had sex with.

Luke and I had good sex, right? I'm pretty sure it was. Although, as I've just said to Rachel, I haven't got anything to compare it to. I lower my voice and whisper to Rachel.

'We didn't have sex loads, but no one does, do they? And I suppose it was fairly routine, but we knew what each other liked so it wasn't particularly adventurous. But it was nice, I suppose.' I trail off slowly, realising how totally lame my sex life sounds and feel slightly mortified.

I sneak a look up at Rachel's face, already knowing the exact look she's going to be giving me. And, yep. I am correct.

'You *suppose* it was *nice*?' she manages to stutter through the obvious disgust at this statement. She slowly lays her hands on the table in front of her and takes a deep breath. 'Right, I am only going to say this once.'

I screw up my face, wincing, as I know what's coming.

'You should never have to suppose sex is something, it either is or it isn't, there is no middle ground. And, it should never, ever be nice. Wild, hot, loving, gentle, earth-moving, mind-blowing, leg-shaking, intense, terrible even, sometimes, but never should it be nice. I'd rather it was terrible than nice! Nice is so... so...' she frowns as she searches for the word.

'So beige?' I offer up.

'Yes!' Rachel yells, pointing her finger at me. 'That is the exact word. Beige. Carrie, you deserve so much more than beige. You shouldn't be with someone who just gives you mediocre, meh sex. I'm not saying it has to be all *Fifty Shades* or anything, but it has to be at least worth having. Seriously, you should never aim to marry someone who only makes you feel nice. You need so much more than that.'

I slump my shoulders and lean back in my chair rolling the base of my glass round and round on the table.

'I hadn't ever really thought about it before. I mean it wasn't terrible, but...' my voice peters out again, as I'm reluctant to offer up the words. 'It was OK,' I say, weakly, then look up at Rachel's face and add, 'OK is the same as nice isn't it?'

'Yep,' she says proudly, taking a big swing of her drink and folding her arms across her chest.

'I don't know why we are even talking about this,' I reply, more to myself than to Rachel, and I do my best to stop the redness creeping up my face once more. 'Like I said, nothing's happened.'

Rachel grins widely at me and raises her eyebrows skyward. 'But when it does, I bet you are in for an absolute treat.'

Back in my room, after we manage to limit ourselves to the one jug of punch and a cocktail each, I bid a slightly giddy

Rachel goodnight. There was a distinct eagerness that flitted between her and Dale as they said a far too brief goodbye, which I am sure translates to more of a 'see you in your room when I get off'.

I check my emails but only a find of couple of non-urgent, work-related ones that I fire off responses to letting them know I'll be back to work in a couple of weeks. That's what I love about my job, the flexibility and my lovely, loyal client base I've built up over the years. Obviously, no one I work with knows what's happened, and it's a relief to have one part of my life that's been untainted by Luke and Emily's mess.

There's also a message from Kate that's a simple smiley emoji and some kisses. I don't know if her or Dan have been in touch with Luke and Emily and told them not to contact me or whether it's my messages to them that's done the trick, but either way, I'm pleased to not have to deal with it. I send her a *Ditto* back accompanied by some kisses.

I check the time, reluctant to make the same mistake I did with Kate, and once I've worked out it's a sensible time to phone home, I call my mum to check in. We have the nicest, most comfortable chat since before the non-wedding day. I don't feel like a jilted bride any more, and she sounds happy and relaxed, not worrying about her wayward daughter who's absconded to sunnier climes. I ring off, excited about the rest of the trip and do my best to dissuade myself it's on the back of my conversation with Rachel about Jake. I half expect him to drop in and see me, but when it gets to half past midnight and I still haven't seen him, I decide to go to sleep, feeling a little flat.

I lay awake in bed for far too long listening for the sound of his door, like some total stalker, but at some point I drift off to sleep, my head swimming with a million thoughts of Jake.

Neighbour, CEO, hotel owner, saviour of damsels in distress, drinking buddy, uber-hunk and, to top it off, completely and utterly irresistible.

Chapter Twenty-One

'So how dressy is this party anyway?' Rachel asks, before we part ways after another long and tiring day at the beach.

Before I can answer she stretches her arm out and places it next to mine.

'Look at us, we're getting proper brown. How come you're browner than me and I've been here longer? I need to up my tan game.' Without waiting for an answer she's off again. 'So what are you wearing tonight?'

'I don't know. I haven't really thought about it, to be honest.'

'You haven't seen Jake in over twenty-four hours and you haven't even thought about your outfit?'

She's right. The last time I saw or spoke to Jake was our brief moment on the beach yesterday. We don't have each other's phone numbers, and I haven't seen him at the hotel all day. The only way we know what's going on tonight is because Dale gave us the info when we passed him on the way back from the beach just now. I can't deny that my stomach is churning at the thought of seeing Jake again. With both nerves and excitement. I know he's working, and I can't help but wonder if the phone call he got the other night has something to do with his absence.

'I was thinking a black jumpsuit,' I tell Rachel. 'Something to cover my legs if we are outside all night. I can't bear the thought of getting bitten.'

'Good plan,' she agrees. 'I'll go grab a shower, pick up my stuff and come up.'

'Perfect, see you soon.'

We agreed to have a proper, old-school girl's night, and she's coming up to the suite so we can get ready together. I don't know what it is about Rachel and Jake. Maybe it's the circumstances or the holiday vibe, but it feels like I've known them both forever, not just a few days. The more I think about having to go home, the sadder I feel.

I've just stepped out of the shower, with my hair dripping wet, when I hear a rap on the door. I grab a fresh towel off the rail, cursing myself that I've managed to pick one of the smaller ones, that barely covers my body, rather than the huge bath sheets they provide. Oh well, it's only Rachel. She's seen me in a bikini, so I don't think she will mind me in my state of undress. I tiptoe out of the bathroom to let her in.

'That was good timing,' I yell through the door, yanking it open, 'I've just got out of the sh...'

I stop suddenly, as I'm greeted by a pair of yellow eyes that drink in my appearance and roam over my half-naked body, like a kid seeing their presents on Christmas Day.

'Oh Jesus. Jake!' I say slightly hysterical, as I pull at the very revealing towel, trying my best to get it to cover more of my body. The trouble is when I tug at one bit, it seems to expose another area all together. His grin stretches from ear to ear, and he actually has to press his lips together to stop himself smiling any more. Despite me being practically naked, he steps past me, without another word, then halts just a few paces from the door and turns to face me.

I'm still hopping from foot to foot, trying to work out what to do with myself, when he says in a low voice, 'It looks as if I timed this perfectly. And if you tell me you are naked under that towel I can't promise I will stay over here.'

I know my face has gone scarlet, and I'm powerless to do a thing about it.

'Don't you take another step, mister,' I say feeling furiously hot and bothered. 'Wait there.' I shuffle backwards to the walk-in wardrobe, dropping my towel and pulling on my beach playsuit that's hanging over the back of the chair.

'Please don't get dressed on my account,' he calls from behind the firmly closed door.

I can hear the smirk in his voice, and he's still smiling as I step out, fully clothed this time.

'Shame,' he says with a shrug of his shoulders and another quick flick of his eyes over my body.

'And to what do I owe this pleasure?' I ask with a smile. He's here. And the overwhelming excitement and happiness I feel at seeing him is as unexpected as it is terrifying, despite his unscheduled visit and my embarrassment at being caught unawares.

'It felt like I hadn't seen you for too long, and I wanted to, before tonight. You're still coming, yes?'

I nod. 'I am.'

He takes a step towards me and pushes a piece of hair back from over my shoulder my whole body electrified at the briefest touch of his skin on mine. He's wearing a white polo shirt, navy trousers and tan leather shoes that look very expensive.

He smells divine and, as he pushes his hair out of his face, I chance a sneaky look at his body, and I am suddenly desperate for him to touch me again. The connection between us fires to life as he does just that, and reaches out and cups my face with his hand. I can't help myself and lean into it, my hair standing on end, brushing my cheek against his rough palm, the very corner of my lips touching his skin as I do. He quickly withdraws his hand and takes a deep breath, and I watch as his tongue very slowly and purposefully licks his bottom lip.

'I better go,' he says, and takes a step back, as if he doesn't trust himself to be that close to me any longer.

Quite frankly, I don't trust myself right now. I am desperate to feel his skin on mine again. My entire body prickles at just the thought.

'I'll see you soon,' he says quietly, and leaves without another word, leaving me standing there feeling disconcertingly turned on by our little encounter. I know that if Jake had made a move on me just then, there is absolutely nothing I would have done to stop him.

Voices coming from outside wake me from my fantasy, and no sooner has the door closed there's a knock on it again. This time I know it's Rachel, and I let her in seeing Jake's door to his suite close behind him. She dances in with an armful of clothes, clutching a bottle of something that look suspiciously like champagne.

'I am totally ready to party!' she exclaims, as she heaves everything down on to the bed and disappears into the lounge, presumably to get some glasses. 'I thought we could have some bubbles while we get ready,' says Rachel as she strolls back through.

'Well, the last time I did it was the morning of my non-existent wedding, so let's hope tonight goes better than that,' I say and the look of regret on her face makes me laugh rather riotously. 'Rach, it's OK, don't look so worried, I'm fine. Look at me, making jokes about it and everything. I must be making some progress, right?'

She walks over to me and gives me an unexpected squeeze, which I return, never one to turn down a hug.

'You are a complete babe and I love that you're just like, "Oh, you think because you tried to screw me over on our wedding day I'm going to lie down and cry about you? Well think again, loser. I'm going on an awesome holiday, will make some new friends and will meet the actual man of my dreams." In. Your. Face.'

She clinks her glass heartily against mine, and we both lose some champagne over the rim.

'I'm not sure it's quite like that, but I do like the in your face bit.' I slide on to the bed and curl my legs up under me. 'Can I tell you something?'

Rachel frowns, shoves a load of her clothes out of the way to make some space, and matches my position on the bed. She takes both my hands in hers and looks gravely serious for a moment.

'I meant what I said. We are friends. You can tell me anything.' A wave of affection for her washes over me, and I smile warmly at her.

'Now I feel silly because you're being so nice, and you're going to think I'm a total nightmare.'

'I would never think that. I promise. Go on. You can talk to me,' she says.

'I feel like I should feel guilty for having, whatever it is I'm having, for Jake and, Rachel, I just *don't*. Luke and Emily do keep popping into my head, but most of the time, I just sort of don't think about it. And now I'm worried that makes me a bad person. Shouldn't I be a crying mess? My fiancé and I just broke up in the most humiliating way possible, and my best friend's pregnant with his baby, and I'm over here rocking the whole, "let's have another cocktail and perv on the hunk across the landing" vibe. What's wrong with me? Why aren't I a total, broken wreck? Am I a bad person?'

'What? No,' Rachel says with real conviction in her voice, grabbing me by both shoulders and then letting go suddenly. 'Sorry, I didn't mean to manhandle you.'

'Please do, it's the most action I've seen in weeks,' I lament and she laughs.

'You don't need to feel bad about anything at all, Carrie. The fact that you're not a sobbing mess doesn't mean you don't care, or that you're not hurting. It means you're dealing with it.' She pauses for a moment looking at me with a sad smile. 'Sometimes, it's just not meant to be. You and Luke sound like you had been together so long you'd forgotten why you were together. And that whatever you'd grown into, it wasn't enough to keep you together, not long term. Like I said, I think a part of you isn't sad, because you know it's the right thing for you two not to be together. Even if you couldn't see it before. Does that make any sense at all?'

'It does, I hope you're right. So you don't think I'm a horrible person?' I say anxiously.

'You're the least horrible person I know, and I know some serious shockers.' She rolls her eyes and I can't help but laugh.

'Thank you,' I say, pulling her into a hug. 'Shall we make a start on outfit choices for tonight?'

'Let's. I have no idea where to start, hence why I brought up most of my suitcase.'

She pulls out a couple of dresses holding them up against her. One's a slinky, red halterneck with a slit up to her bikini line and the other, an electric blue bandage dress that I would have to have myself sewn into.

'Which one do you think Dale would appreciate seeing me in the most?' she muses swapping the dresses in and out for one another.

'I think Dale would like to see you most out of either,' I reply, and we fall into a fit of ridiculous giggles. 'But for argument's sake, let's say the blue.' She discards the red one on the floor and picks up another outfit from the bed.

'OK, and now which out of *this* one and the blue?' I look at the mountain of clothes piled on the bed. Then back to her. Then back to the pile.

'Hang on,' I say, 'I think we're going to need more wine.'

'I can't walk in these sodding shoes,' Rachel complains, as we head down the path to The Coconut Shack and surrounding beach where the BBQ is being held. The air is already thick with the scent of the grill drifting towards us, and my stomach gives a loud rumble.

'You look amazing, Rach. And anyway, you can take them off once we get to the beach.'

'That's true, once Dale has seen me in the whole outfit, who cares. I still wish I'd worn flats like you.' Right on cue, she stumbles and grabs on to my arm. 'Sorry, I think I'm just going to concentrate on putting one foot in front of the other for now. Thank God we didn't drink any more, I'd be crawling down this path right about now if we had.'

'In light of which, shall we get something to eat first before we embark on the cocktails?' I suggest.

She throws back her head in laughter, almost felling herself in the process.

'We are so predictable, aren't we? Let's find Dale so he can see my outfit and I can take these ridiculous shoes off.'

Luckily for Rachel, Dale isn't at work tonight and is stood by the BBQ chatting to one of the guys I've seen serving at breakfast. He spots us almost immediately, which isn't hard considering Rachel's bright blue dress and that fact that she looks like a model in it. His eyes widen as he takes in her appearance and excuses himself immediately, walking straight over to us.

'Wow,' is all he can say. I look between them and suddenly feel very awkward, a bit like the only fully dressed person at a nudist beach.

'Dale, I think this is the first time I've seen you speechless,' I laugh.

'Hell, I think it might be the first time I have been,' he stutters.

'I'll leave you guys to it. I'm going to get some food. Catch up with you later?'

Rachel puts her hand on her arm and looks guilty.

'You don't have to leave, we'll come with you.'

'Rach, it's fine. Look how many people there are. I'm sure I can find someone to talk to. Promise.'

'Are you sure? I don't mind…'

I hold my hand up to stop her mid flow. 'I promise I can look after myself.'

She leans in and drops her voice so only I can hear.

'Yes, but can you keep yourself out of trouble?' She winks and I feel my face beginning to go pink.

'No worse than you seem to be doing,' I giggle back at her, with a brief nod to Dale that only she notices. She gives me a quick hug, and the pair of them scurry off to a dark corner of the bar and are ladling out rum punch quicker than you can say hangover.

I do a scan of the crowd and see Michael standing next to the BBQ swigging from a beer and looking happy and relaxed. I snake my way through the crowds towards him, and he looks up from his beer and greets me with a smile.

'Good evening, Miss Carrie.' He gives me a small gentlemanly nod of his head, and again I'm overcome by his comforting presence.

'And to you,' I say with a smile and a small touch of his arm. 'Are you having fun?'

'I'm ashamed to say I am. But I'm a home bird,' he says with a shrug. 'May and I, we've done all this.' He surveys the crowd of revellers with a knowing glance. 'It's my time for sitting down relaxing, taking the world at a slower pace, you know?'

'That actually sounds perfect right now,' I say, as I take the proffered bottle of beer from his outstretched hand with a grateful smile. 'Quiet nights in, with no drama.'

He shakes his head with a small laugh. 'Don't wish your life away, Carrie. There will be plenty of time for you to sit back and put your feet up. Right now is not that time. Trust me.'

I suddenly flinch and suck in my entire midsection, as I feel a broad hand snake around my waist and press firmly across my stomach. A low growl in my ear tells me immediately who it is, not that I was ever in any doubt.

'Quiet nights in, hey? Sounds good to me.'

My hair stands on end as his warm breath brushes the back of my neck, and I only relax once he's removed his hand and casually slung it over my shoulder. I know my cheeks are pink, but it's more out of embarrassment of Michael witnessing Jake's display of obvious intimacy, rather than the act itself. He holds out his hand to Michael who takes it, and they exchange a warm glance of what can only be described as affection towards each other.

'Michael, I need you to look after my girl for me while I speak to Luis for a moment.' He turns to me piercing me with his eyes. 'Don't go anywhere. I'll be back soon.'

Without waiting for a response, he strides off through the crowd to a table that's been set up to incorporate two of the large cabanas on the beach. It's currently occupied by a big group of people that I can only assume contains Luis and his entourage. I look at Michael feeling flushed.

'I'm not *his* girl. We're friends,' I tell him with a nervous, and what comes out as a very pathetic, laugh.

I know I'm banging out the same line to Michael as I have before, both to him and to anyone who even implies there might be anything more than a platonic relationship between me and Jake, but I'm not sure what else to say. Jake's manner, and the way he doesn't care who sees him with me, both excites and unnerves me all at the same time. My stomach churns at the thought of his hand pressed against my body, and I press my lips together, my own hand unconsciously moving to the place his was only moments before.

'Of course you're not,' he says looking at the floor and taking a sip of his beer. A smile plays on his lips, and I narrow my eyes at him. He takes one look at my face and laughs out loud this time. 'Like I said, it is what it is.'

Keen for a change of subject I glance around me.

'This food smells delicious. What time does the buffet open?'

'I'd say right about now.' And he gestures to a small line of people that have begun to form a not so orderly queue on the other side of the BBQ. It's only then I notice the huge table stretching right around the outside of the building. It's heaving with various hotplates manned by hotel staff who stand, waiting like nervous soldiers, weapons in hand, ready to do battle with the hungry masses.

'Is it rude if we get in the queue right now?' I ask Michael, giving him a nudge.

'You're in the Caribbean,' he says, his accent suddenly thicker than usual, 'you don't get there soon, you don't get fed!'

I grin and follow him, as we weave through the crowd towards the ever-growing line. I do a quick search over my shoulder for Rachel and Dale, but they're nowhere to be seen. That sounds about right, I think to myself with a smirk. It'll probably be hours before I see them again.

As we make our way across the sand to the end of the queue, I'm helpless to try and keep my gaze away and my line of sight drifts to Jake and the man he's talking to. I can tell he's tall, even though he's sitting down, and has a thick head of dark hair topping a tanned face. He's still good-looking, even though he must be in his early sixties, and his clothes and gold watch, that I can spot even from over here, tells me that he must be Luis Mendoza. To my surprise, he's not how I thought he would be at all. I was imagining a small, round, balding man, I guess matching my stereotypical billionaire image, but this man is so far removed from that. He's flanked by a couple of burly looking guys who must be some sort of security team, and he's laughing and engaged in animated conversation with Jake who is smiling back in return. He doesn't spot me watching him but, not one to miss a trick, Michael confirms my suspicions.

'That's Mr Mendoza with Jake. He's a very kind man. He's done a lot for the hotel in terms of bringing in business and is very generous to the staff. I'm sure Jake will introduce him to you later.'

I scoff as Michael passes me a plate and we settle in line.

'I'm sure he won't. Not if he's as important as you say.'

'I think out of the two of you, you're the important one, Miss Kingston.'

I overlook his use of Miss Kingston on this occasion, as my head is flooded with thoughts of Jake. For some reason, tonight more than usual, I feel drawn to him more than ever. Despite how I try my mind keeps wandering back to him, and my whole body feels on edge, like it's waiting for him to be close to it again. I shake my head and try and focus. Get a grip, Kingston. Get. A. Grip.

Chapter Twenty-Two

'Seriously. I can't eat another thing, or I am going to explode. You'll have to roll me into the lift. That's if I fit.'

Michael laughs and leans back in his chair, as I do the same. After loading my plate with food, we found a table just to the side of the bar which was quieter and a little tucked away from the throng of people spilling out on to the beach, most of who I recognise from around the hotel. Unfortunately, our secluded little spot well and truly blocked my view of Jake, which set me more on edge than I was already. I know I keep glancing around to see if I can see him, and despite me trying my hardest to make it look innocent, I know Michael has noticed. We've been joined by Maya who looks particularly gorgeous tonight with her long braids loose around her face and in a bright turquoise, flowing maxi dress. She's not wearing a scrap of make-up, and her natural beauty and flawless skin is seriously envy inducing.

They're both the height of discretion and understanding throughout our meal, and they welcomingly avoid the topic of Jake, or any questions about my life back home, sticking to neutral topics. Maya pushes her plate away from her with a sigh and takes a sip of her water. No wonder she looks so radiant. My blood has probably been replaced by rum thanks to the last few days.

'You think I would learn,' she groans. 'I always overeat at these things. A classic victim of my eyes being bigger than my stomach. If anyone sees me near that dessert table, you have my permission to wrestle me to the ground.'

'Only if you do the same for me,' I say, and we laugh together, leaving Michael shaking his head. She sits up suddenly in her chair, flicking her braids over her shoulder and looking around with a frown.

'Has anyone seen Dale?' she asks with a small huff. 'He was meant to meet me, but I've not seen him. Seriously, this is the last time I let him get away with letting me go home on my own. That boy is on his last chance.'

I freeze, a sense of dread washing over me. Dale and Maya? Oh God, not another one. What am I supposed to do? Do I tell Rachel? Do I tell Maya? Unless she knows already? He's hardly been discreet, but she certainly doesn't sound like someone who knows her boyfriend's been sneaking around with hotel guests behind her back. Oh, bloody hell. Luckily for me, Maya doesn't seem to be looking for an actual answer, as she stands up from the table abruptly.

'I'm going to find him and tell him I'm making my own way home. I refuse to spend another night off running around after him.'

She huffs off and disappears into the crowd and, for a split second, I feel relieved until I realise the horror that could come from her actually finding Dale. With Rachel. Should I try and find them and warn them? It's unlikely they will be anywhere in public, so I'm praying they've gone back to her room. There is no way Maya would think to look there.

I relax a little and decide to use the opportunity to quiz the all-seeing, all-knowing Michael about this recent revelation.

'Wow, Maya and Dale!' I say as nonchalantly as possible. 'I had no idea.'

'Yeah, she tends to keep quiet about it to be honest, what with them working together,' Michael laughs. 'She gives him a hard time, but she loves him dearly, and I know she wouldn't change him for the world. Despite how she moans about him sometimes. You know, they live together and work together, so they must have a pretty good relationship.'

'Gosh, they live together?' I say, unable to hide my shock. It must be serious then. A million thoughts run through my brain at lightning speed. Unable to make sense of them all, I take a long sip of my drink. Why didn't Jake say anything, so I could have warned Rachel off? Suddenly, I'm furious with both him and Dale. Knowing what he knows about both mine and Rachel's recent relationship woes, he still thought it was OK for Dale to cheat on Maya, right under her nose? I feel sick to my stomach that he would let this happen without a second thought for the consequences. Unless, he doesn't know. Perhaps, because he's the boss, they kept it from him. I pray that's what it is, and that he's still the man I thought he was. A good man, like Michael said. And for one thing, I would trust his judge of character more than anyone right now. *Please* let him not know.

'Do you think she'll find Dale?' I say, with a nervous laugh, desperately hoping the answer is no.

Michael's face breaks into a broad grin, and he pushes himself up out of his chair.

'I'm not a betting man, Carrie,' he leans down towards me and whispers, 'May wouldn't let me get involved in such a fool's game, but I would bet all I had on that boy not getting out of here without Maya tonight. She knows him better than anyone, meaning she knows how he thinks and knows exactly where to look for him.' He laughs and I plaster on a fake, and slightly, manic smile. 'Please excuse me for a moment,' he says, and I stand automatically. 'No, no don't get up. Your date is here.'

He gives me a wink, and I spin my head around to see Jake sauntering over to us his whole demeanour full of intent. It feels like my whole body pulses just at the sight of him, the electricity surging through me. Even though I can't stop thinking about Maya and Dale, and I'm angry that Jake might have known, my traitorous body says another thing entirely. He beams at me, as he reaches the table and bends to kiss my head, placing his broad hands on both of my shoulders.

'There she is,' he says softly, and I feel him breathe in deeply through my hair. His scent tonight is intoxicating, and it's all I can do not to throw myself at him. Tonight, the electricity between us is thick and almost palpable.

'Jake,' I say seriously, shrugging his hands off my shoulders, 'I need to talk to you.'

He pulls up the chair next to me, a deep frown on his face, as he reaches to the ice bucket in the middle of the table and pulls out two more beers, handing one out to me. I shake my head, and he replaces both of them. He either doesn't fancy drinking alone, or the look on my face tells him I'm not in the mood.

'Sweet cheeks, what's up? You've got me worried.'

'Jake, did you know about Dale and Maya?'

'Dale and Maya?' He looks confused for a second. 'What about Dale and Maya?'

'Er, the fact that they live together.'

'Yes,' he says slowly, dragging out the word, 'I knew. Why, what's the problem?'

'And you didn't think it might be prudent to maybe mention it?' I hiss trying to keep my voice down.

'Why would I mention it?' He lets out a small laugh. 'No offence, but I don't see how that's of any concern. Or any of our business.'

I let out an incredulous, and disappointingly unattractive, snort. I cannot believe he is being so blasé about this. Could I really have got him so wrong?

'OK fine,' I say crossing my arms in front of me, 'It's none of my business, but don't you think Rachel might have wanted to know? Did you really think it was OK for her and Dale to go swanning off, doing God knows what, when he's living with Maya?'

'Sweet cheeks, I'm not sure how...' He stops suddenly, and his shoulders start to shake with laughter.

'Jake, I don't see what could be so funny,' I say crossly, even more annoyed that he appears to be taking the situation so lightly.

'Sweet cheeks, Maya and Dale. Yes, they live together, but that's because they're brother and sister. They're not a couple!' He laughs again, shaking his head, as I open my mouth then sag defeated in my chair. Brother and sister?

'But Michael...' I start then I pause and think. Michael never actually said they were a couple. In fact, he said nothing of the sort, I just instantly jumped to the wrong conclusion. 'Oh God, now I feel like an idiot,' I groan, as Jake continues to chuckle away. 'Will you please stop laughing at me?' I scold and bat his hand away as he reaches for mine.

This just makes him laugh even more, and I'm powerless to resist his strength, as he grabs both my hands and holds them in his.

'Oh, you are so funny. Did you really think Dale is one of the bad guys? And that I would condone it?' He looks a little hurt, and now I feel super guilty for ever thinking he would think such a thing was OK. 'I thought you thought more of me than that.'

'Jake, I do,' I say hurriedly, squeezing his huge hand in mine. 'I'm just in a suspicious frame of mind at the moment. I'm sorry. I don't think you would let that happen, no.'

'But you did for a second. I told you to trust me. I just don't know why you won't.'

'I do, I'm sorry.' I hang my head feeling shameful, and I'm full of regret about how I automatically thought the worst of Jake. 'I'm such an idiot.'

'You're a gorgeous idiot though,' he says, and I meet his eyes to see he's smiling. I notice he's doing that thing he does and rubbing his thumb over the back of my knuckles. He leans in close to me and, for the second time that evening, I think he's going to kiss me. But for the second time he doesn't.

'I'll let you off, just this once,' he winks, 'but you have to make it up to me.'

'That depends on what you have in mind,' I say in a much more suggestive way than I intended.

'Well for starters, I don't like sharing, even with Michael, so as your punishment, you aren't allowed to leave my side for the rest of the night.'

Gosh, what a hardship.

'I think I can manage that,' I say shyly. He stands, and I take hold of his outstretched hand without hesitation.

'I'd like to introduce you to Luis. I've been telling him all about you.'

'All about me?' I say, worried.

'Not all *that* about you. That's all in the past. No, just about how great you are.' He says it so easily, I barely notice it as a compliment.

'In that case, lead the way,' I say with a sassy shake of my head and, with my hand still in his, Jake begins to lead me through the crowd. He's barely taken two steps when he stops and looks down at me, his expression unreadable. He doesn't say anything, but just clasps my hand a little tighter and flashes me his gorgeous smile, making my heart race.

As we weave through the throng of people, I know I have a stupid grin on my face, but I don't even care what the other guests might think. I only have another ten days left here, and I'm never going to see any of them again, so who cares? I think this evening I am well and truly throwing caution to the wind.

As we reach the beach and make our way to Luis's spot, I can't help but feel a little nervous. This man is incredibly rich and incredibly powerful. I also know from Michael and Jake that he's good for business, so with my track record of putting my foot in it and getting the wrong end of the stick lately, I'm hoping I can keep it together.

There's less people down here now, and one of the burly guys is sat down chatting intently to what looks like a younger looking version of Luis, with the tan and the lean physique, but apart from the two of them, the billionaire sits alone sipping on a glass of champagne. Luis spots us approaching and smiles warmly, standing to receive us. He stretches out his arms and, rather than the formal handshake

I was expecting, kisses me on both cheeks. I look up at Jake to gauge his reaction, as I'm not sure how to take it, but he just grins and nods encouragingly.

'Carrie, Luis Mendoza. Luis, this is Carrie Kingston.'

Luis's face is still plastered with a dazzling smile, and his kind face puts me at ease immediately. There's a spattering of grey hair and lines around his dark brown eyes, but he could pass for a much younger man than I suspect he is. I'm having a hard time seeing why Katya seems to think she's so hard done by.

'Hello, Carrie. What a pleasure to meet the young lady who seems to have had such an effect on our dear Jake.'

I giggle and glance at Jake who is rubbing his hand across the back of his neck and looking decidedly sheepish for once.

'Let's you and me sit down and have a good chat, shall we,' Luis continues with a mischievous glance in Jake's direction who shakes his head with a light-hearted laugh.

'I'm going to get more champagne,' he says with an air of resignation and signs off to me with a wink and a point of his finger at Luis. 'Now I know you'll take care of her for me Luis, just don't take *too* much care of her, OK?'

Luis just shrugs and leans back on the cabana cushions gesturing for me to take the seat beside him, which I do somewhat gingerly.

'Don't worry about us. Now, Carrie,' he turns to me and hands me a glass of champagne, 'tell me, what do you think of the hotel? You're enjoying your stay, yes?'

'Very much so,' I say relaxing somewhat. 'I've been very well looked after. The staff are quite something.'

'Aren't they just? They are one of the main reasons I keep coming back here. That and the memories this hotel holds for me.'

'Yes, Jake told me you've been coming here for a long time.'

'Too long' he says rolling his eyes skyward. 'Makes me feel old to think how long. Do you know I used to come here with my first wife? She loved this place.' He sighs and looks out to sea, which is in darkness but the soft rush of the waves breaking on the sand echoes up towards us. 'Every morning she would come down here to the beach and walk along it as the sun rose. I would often wake to an empty bed and find her down here. I always said she was at her most beautiful at that time of the morning in that sunlight. But truly, she was beautiful every minute of every day.'

I start to feel myself welling up at his words, and my voice cracks as I speak.

'You must miss her very much.'

'I do, but my work, it keeps me busy. And Katya,' he laughs, 'she certainly keeps me on my toes.'

I'm unsure how to respond to that statement, so I smile in what I hope is an encouraging and friendly way, but Luis is clearly no fool.

'Ah, I know what they all say. Why is a young thing like her wasting her youth on an old man like me? But, believe it or not, she's good fun. And we know where we stand with each other. I am under no illusions. I mean, of course she is surely with me for my sparkling wit and dazzling smile, no?'

'Well you seem to me as if you're younger than some of the young men I know!' I say, and Luis claps his hands on his knees roaring with laughter in delight.

'I can see why Jake likes you so,' he says with a raise of his eyebrows.

'Oh, we're just friends,' I say as an auto response to his question. He places his glass down on the table and shifts so he's facing me.

'I don't have many friends, Carrie. Doing what I do, even my personal life becomes business. But I have to say, I don't look at my friends that way.' He nods his head in the direction of the hotel, and I see Jake making his way across the beach towards us, two bottles of champagne in hand. 'Not even the ones as pretty as you,' he whispers with a wink.

I watch Jake as he moves towards us, his tall muscular body, his beach blonde hair and chiselled jaw.

'People keep saying that. About the way we look at each other. What does that even mean?' I say, my forehead scrunching into a frown. I don't know why I've decided it's a wise idea to seek relationship advice from this man but, right now, he seems like as good an option as anyone.

'Because it's the one thing you can't fake. Your words, actions, they can all be fabricated. But the way you see someone, the way you look at them, *really* look at them, you can't make that up, nor can you hide it.'

'Thank you, Mr Mendoza.'

'Luis, my dear please, my friends call me Luis and any friend of Jake's is most certainly a friend of mine. Jake!' he calls and stands up opening his arms to greet him. 'And you brought the party! Excellent!'

Luis claps Jake on the back with such vigour that, even with the size and stature of his frame, he almost sends him lurching forward into my lap. Luis very graciously moves to the side to allow Jake to sit beside me, his thigh brushing against mine as he begins to open the bottle of champagne and pour us a glass each.

'To new friends,' Luis toasts. We clink glasses together and take a sip, Luis almost downing his in one go.

'Now, Jake, this situation in Miami,' Luis addresses him, 'you're sure you don't need my help, no?'

'No more than you've given me so far, thank you. I appreciate it, Luis. I owe you.'

'You owe me nothing of the sort. Have Anna speak to my office first thing in the morning so we can iron out all the details. Now please excuse me one moment.' He glances at his watch. 'I must make a phone call. Someone, somewhere in the world is still at work.'

Silence falls between Jake and I for a moment, and we both glance at each other with a nervous smile.

'Well, this is all rather nice,' I say sounding ridiculously like my mother.

'I don't do nice,' he says with a wicked glance in my direction.

No, I bet you don't, I think to myself crossing my legs automatically.

'Sweet cheeks, I...' Jake runs his hands through his hair. 'Will you have dinner with me tomorrow night?'

'Dinner? Yes, of course I will. I'd love to. Was that all you wanted to ask me?'

'Yes. OK, good.' He's rubbing his palms on his knees and looks distinctly out of sorts.

'Jake, is everything alright?' I ask, wondering why he suddenly seems so nervous. A flash of doubt crosses his face, but a moment later it's gone and he's back to his beaming grin.

'It's fine. Works been... trying,' he says struggling to find the right word.

'Is that what Luis was talking about?' I'm keen to know more, but I don't want to seem nosy even though that's exactly what I am.

'Yeah, we had a bit of trouble at the Miami hotel. You've heard of Alexander Steele?'

'Er, have I? I love him!' I say with way too much enthusiasm. 'I love those *Professor's Son* movies!'

Alexander Steele is the absolute hottest thing in Hollywood right now. He landed a film franchise called *The Professor's Son*, a sort of Indiana Jones meets Dan Brown, where a young, unassuming librarian is left a sort of quest by his estranged father in his will, and it turns into a hunt to find some undiscovered treasure or something like that. He always gets the prize and the girl, and his perfect six-pack has won over a legion of fans worldwide.

'He's like, proper A-list famous,' I say excitedly, cringing when I realise how much I just sounded like Bryony and Amy.

'Yeah well, I'm afraid I'm not such a fan,' Jake grimaces. 'He was staying at the Miami hotel while doing some film promo and, apparently, got into some sort of mega row with his girlfriend.'

'Cara Porter,' I interrupt unhelpfully earning me a glare from Jake. 'Sorry, carry on,' I mutter.

'And they ended up trashing one of the rooms. And I mean not low-key in any way shape or form, I'm talking furniture off the balcony, into the pool, that sort of thing.'

'Jesus,' I say quietly, 'that sounds really bad. Although, they say there's no such thing as bad publicity, right?'

'I'd definitely agree with you under normal circumstances, but it's common knowledge that Cara has a pretty abundant coke habit and that's really not something I want associated with our hotels. One of the headlines read *Cara's Cocaine Meltdown* and there are hundreds of pictures of the hotel online. The manager there, Jackson, he called me the other night to let me know, and I've had Anna, she's head of publicity and PR for the group, working around the clock to do some serious damage control.'

'Right, well, yes. When you put it like that I guess it's not totally ideal. What will you do?'

'I might have to go out there, Carrie,' he says looking at me through his long lashes.

'Oh, right OK,' I say instantly feeling deflated at the prospect of him leaving for a few days. Or longer, perhaps. Recovering slightly, I manage to say brightly. 'Well of course you have to go, that's understandable. I'll be fine here.'

Why did I say that? Like he's worrying about leaving me when the reputation of his hotel might be in danger.

'I just wondered…' he wrings his hands together, and his nerves seem to have returned. 'I need to make a call to Jackson later, but if I have to go, will you come?'

It takes me a moment to realise what he's said, and I stare at him.

'Sorry, what?'

'Come. To Miami. With me.'

Yes that's what I thought he said.

'OK.'

Jake's head flies up, and he looks at me open-mouthed.

'What?' he asks.

'OK, I'll come.'

'You will?'

Oh no, did he just ask me to be polite, and now I've said yes he doesn't know what to do?

'Er, yes. I mean, that's if you are actually asking me.'

He reaches for me and clasps my hand in his.

'No! I mean, yes,' he laughs sheepishly. 'No, I'm not, not asking you. And yes, I very much am asking you. I just thought it was going to be harder than that to get you to come.'

Now it's my turn to laugh.

'What do you mean?'

'I had this whole speech planned, and now I don't get to use it.' He shrugs as he spreads his hands in front of him.

I reach out and touch his thigh, before I realise I've done it, and quickly remove my hand, stunned at how tiny it looks. I can't help myself, and I grin at him.

'Oh please, *please* let me hear the speech,' I tease him.

'Well actually, I was hoping I could just take off my shirt and that would be enough.'

'I've seen you with your shirt off and, quite frankly, you'll have to do better than that.' As I speak, I reach out and shove him on the shoulder, and he grabs my wrist playfully as I do, raising his eyebrows at having caught me. He gently pulls me towards him, and leans in his lips dangerously close to my neck, and whispers in my ear.

'Then I'll have to see what else I can do,' he slowly pulls away and looks me dead in the eyes, seeing all the way though to my soul, 'won't I?'

Instinctively, I lean the slightest fraction forward and release a long, slow breath. Time seems to freeze between us, and I can feel it, sense it, his longing, his need to kiss me. But we stay that way for what seems like an eternity, but in reality, it must just be a couple of seconds. I see his eyes dart down to my lips for the smallest second and without thinking bite down on my bottom lip.

'Jake,' I whisper. It's not a question. I just want to hear his name on my lips.

He clears his throat, and sits up straight, the spell between us broken. Unexpectedly, he stands up and then just as unexpectedly sits back down again and turns to me.

'You'll really come?'

I don't know why it was so easy for me to say yes. I don't know why out of everything I've been overthinking lately, this decision, this, that is actually quite a big one, you know, leave the country with a practical stranger and go to a strange place where you know nobody and most likely spend the night, this I decide is as easy as picking out what I want from the buffet for breakfast.

'I may be mad but, yes, I'll come.'

Jake tilts his head to one side, considering me for a moment.

'I know I'm going to regret asking this, but I can't help myself. Why did you say yes? And please don't change your mind!' he adds quickly, holding up his hands.

I laugh. 'I'm not going to change my mind. I've said I'll come, and I will. And I don't know why.' I say honestly, with a sigh. 'I guess, overthinking's got me nowhere, so how about not thinking at all and just doing?'

'I like this Carrie.' Jake winks at me earning him a smile in return.

'Plus,' I say with a roll of my eyes, 'you're not the worst company ever, I suppose.'

'You know just how to massage a man's ego don't you?'

'Ha!' I scoff, 'I think we both know your ego needs absolutely no massaging at all.'

'I think the less we discuss you massaging anything of mine the better,' he says quietly into his champagne with a raise of his eyebrows.

'Lord! Do you ever have a day off?' I groan, through my laugher. I see Luis making his way back over to us with yet another bottle of champagne, despite the fact we still have an unopened one sitting on the table. He dances over to us, looking a bit like the embarrassing uncle at a wedding, and I smile warmly at him. He may have billions in the bank, but you can't buy cool.

'How are we getting on, my friends?'

'I'm excellent,' says Jake with an air of triumph. 'Because this lovely young lady has just agreed to come to Miami with me this week.'

Luis clasps his hands together and shakes them firmly in a salute celebration.

'What wonderful news! Oh, Carrie, you will simply love it. How exciting indeed.'

'I've agreed to go on a little trip not to marry him,' I tut with a giggle at Luis.

Jake leans into Luis and says conspiratorially, 'Well, at least not this week.'

Then they both start laughing like a pair of idiots, and I can't help but join in.

'You're both as bad as each other!' I tell them.

'I think she means as good!' Luis laughs, and I'm actually starting to get a bit hysterical, even though it's not even remotely funny. My uncontrollable laughter seems to set them off even more which only makes me laugh more. What a set of morons we must look like. And I don't care. I'm laughing and happy and, right in this moment, I love my life. This life, this strange new life I'm beginning to start rebuilding for myself.

After taking a few swigs of champagne to compose ourselves, the giggles seem to subside. Luis is wiping the tears away from his eyes.

'I don't even know why I am laughing!' he exclaims looking like he could start off again at any moment. 'How is it you say? I have got the giggles?'

'That's exactly what we say,' I laugh. 'And don't worry, I have them too.'

'Laughter is one of the greatest things you can share with someone in life,' he says with a smile and a small glance between me and Jake that only I notice.

I see a small group of men and women making their way over to us, and Luis gives them a wave and jovial yell of something in Portuguese. I notice one of them looks vaguely familiar, and I presume I must have seen her around the hotel. She's stunningly beautiful and is wearing a tight, red bandage dress that clings to her curves and is carrying a pair of expensive-looking heels in her hand, as she moves effortlessly across the sand. I notice the red soles of her shoes identifying them as Louboutins. She swings them back and forth, and I deduce that it's more about her showing them off rather than anything to do with it making the sand easier to walk across. She shakes out her waist-length, blonde hair and, from the way she's holding court with the rest of the group, I know that she must be Katya, Luis's wife.

She oozes confidence and is undeniably beautiful which immediately puts me on edge. She once made a move on Jake, and instantly I feel jealous and also incredibly inferior, which is ridiculous, and I mentally kick myself for letting myself feel that way. New Carrie. Confident Carrie. I take a deep breath and plaster a smile on my face, as they reach us. I thought she wasn't coming? I do a quick scan of the bar and, luckily, see no sign of Rachel. Hopefully she's still too occupied with Dale to surface any time soon.

As if sensing my discomfort, Jake leans into me.

'That's Katya,' he says without bothering to clarify which of the women he's referring to. It's completely obvious who she is.

I try to sound as casual as possible, 'I thought she wasn't coming?'

'She wasn't,' Jake says somewhat grudgingly. 'I doubt she'll stay long. She doesn't usually show her face.' He frowns a little and his smile slips very slightly, but he soon recovers and gives my hand a little squeeze for which I'm grateful. I suddenly feel out of my depth in this group. My eyes wander back to her, and she's shimmying between the tables towards Luis. His eyes light up, and he stands opening his arms to her. She leans up on her tiptoes, tilting her perfect cheekbones up to him to let him kiss her, which he does, willingly, on both cheeks.

'Here is my darling!' Luis coos, and Katya bats her eyelashes at him and cups his face in her hands, rubbing her nose against his. For someone who didn't know what they know about her, anyone would think she was the smitten wife. She certainly puts on a good show. Maybe he doesn't know about her indiscretions after all.

Katya turns her gaze to Jake and gives him a sickly-sweet smile. He stands and, for some reason, I feel compelled to as well. She holds out her hand, and I'm not sure if she means for him to shake it or kiss it, but I'm pretty convinced it's the latter. To his credit, he reaches out and shakes it then leans in and gives her a swift kiss on each cheek.

'Jake,' she drawls in a smooth and thick, Eastern European accent that I can't quite place. 'How wonderful to see you. I hope you and my husband have been behaving yourselves?' The look in her eyes says that she would love nothing more than to misbehave with Jake, and I am reminded a little bit of the wolf in Red Riding Hood. Except this time, it's the wolf wearing the red dress.

'Of course,' Jake replies politely and turns his body to open the group up to me. He places his hand on the small of my back, and I see a flash of shock and what is quite clearly anger pass over Katya's face as she gives me a sweeping glance from head to toe.

'Katya, this is Carrie. Carrie, Katya Mendoza.'

'Nice to meet you,' I say in my most polite voice with a smile as sweet as I can manage.

'Likewise,' she replies looking as friendly as she can, but she can't quite manage to hide the coldness in her voice. There is a slight pause as the four of us stand awkwardly, not quite sure what to do or say next until, thankfully, Luis breaks the tension.

'Would you like a drink, my darling?' he asks Katya, reaching for the champagne, but she places a hand on his arm stopping him.

'No thank you, my love,' she purrs, shaking out her hair again, 'I just came to let you know we are leaving.' She leans up and kisses him on the mouth but their lips barely touch, and she pouts in an exaggerated manner.

'Have fun, won't you? You're on the guest list, VIP, and Matteo will be with you. He will take care of you.' Luis nods to an incredibly burly man stood slightly behind Katya that, surprisingly, I hadn't even noticed before. Matteo nods back, and then I notice his eyes flit momentarily to Katya, who meets his in return. It's only for split second, but that one look tells me everything I need to know. Matteo isn't just her bodyguard, they're sleeping together.

'Of course, I am in good hands. Don't wait up, my love,' she says with a giggle. Katya turns and nods to Jake.

'Jake, a pleasure to see you. Look after my beloved husband for me, won't you?'

'As always, Katya,' he replies, and I wonder why, after saying they got on, there appears to be some real tension in the air this evening. I have a suspicion that it's about me. Whether it's my affiliation with Rachel that she's discovered and feels unsettled by my ability to spill the beans to her husband at any given moment, or my closeness to Jake, I don't feel like we are going to be friends of any sort any time soon. Or in fact ever. She glances at me once more with a look that, this time, I really can't place.

'Goodnight, Carrie, how very nice to meet you.'

I almost laugh, because it's clear from every fibre in her being this is a massive lie. So I decide to play her at her own game.

'You too, Katya, you too,' I say, most emphatically, as I reach for her hand and give it a small squeeze. She looks taken aback, and her face falters ever so slightly. 'I love your dress, by the way.' I decide to throw in for good measure.

Ha! That really does it! She looks like her face is about to split in two with the ginormous smile she's glued on to it. She opens her mouth to say something but just nods and turns to leave with another swift kiss on Luis's lips. I see her look up at

Matteo through her long lashes, and his mouth curls into the smallest shadow of a smile for the briefest of seconds, and I have no doubt now that he's not just her bodyguard.

As I watch them go, Luis starts chatting loudly in Portuguese to another man who just joined the group. A couple of men have stayed back whilst two others, along with Katya, Matteo and two other women who looked like clones of Katya, have ventured off to their VIP night, wherever that might be. Jake does that thing that I've noticed he seems to do so often, where I think something in my head, then he answers it, out loud, as if I've asked him.

'Luis got them some tickets to the opening of a new bar on The Gap. Maya was telling me about it yesterday, asking if we wanted any tickets. The owner is an ex-boyfriend of hers.'

'And you didn't fancy it?'

'Not for me. I'll go sometime soon. Show my face. We all like to support each other, the businesses on the island, especially when it's a friend of Maya's too.'

'What's The Gap, by the way? I'm taking it you don't mean the clothes shop.'

'St Lawrence Gap. It's where all the bars and clubs are on the island. Well, not all, obviously, but the most popular. It's a bit of a tourist spot too. I'll take you one night, if you like?'

'Yeah, that sounds fun. Maybe Rachel can come too? And Dale?'

'I'll speak to Maya, see if she wants join us too. She grew up here so she knows everyone.'

'You must know everyone though? I mean, in your business.'

'I know a lot of people, our paths cross a lot, but Maya grew up with them. And you can't make old friends.'

'No, I don't suppose you can,' I say quietly, and I think of Emily. I feel a stab of hurt, as I realise that although I don't want to talk to her ever again, I do miss her. We spoke every day and suddenly, she's just gone.

'Sorry,' Jake says filling my glass again. 'I didn't mean... I don't...' He runs his hand over his chin. 'Listen, old friends are part of your past. And you will have memories with them that no one can take away from you, that you won't forget, even if you want to, but that's what makes you who you are now, and *that* you, well I think she's pretty incredible. You feel like the oldest friend I've ever had, when in fact you're the newest. Sweet cheeks, that makes you so damn special.'

I look up and meet his gaze, his blonde hair slightly blowing in the sea breeze. He is mesmerising. I drink in his face, his tan, his light blonde stubble and his yellow coloured eyes glinting at me, full of intent and promise. And it hits me then, like a ten-tonne truck. I am in way over my head already. Way deeper than I said I'd let myself get, and I can't seem to do anything about it. Time seems to have stood still, and I forget there is anyone around but me and him. I take a deep breath, as I feel his fingertips lightly brush over my knuckles sending a bolt through my body.

'Sweet cheeks?' he whispers.

'Yes?' I say, my voice croaky. But he doesn't answer. I reluctantly tear my gaze from his and look out to the inky black ocean. I close my eyes for a moment and breathe in the salty tang in the air. My senses feel alive like I'm waking up from a fog after years in a haze, and I know it's because of him. I'm suddenly beyond excited about taking a trip with him to Miami. Miami!

I let out a little laugh and the edges of his lips curl up. 'What's funny?'

'I'm going to Miami!' I say with a giggle.

'You are.' He grins at me looking very pleased with himself. 'Shit!' he exclaims and I start. 'Do you have a visa for the States? God, I never even thought about that.' He pushes his hand through his hair, looking worried.

'Jake, it's OK, I do, it's in date and everything.' He lets out a huge sigh of relief. 'Luke had been banging on about wanting to go to Vegas for our honeymoon, but Kate said it had to be a surprise, so she made me get one, just in case.'

'OK, great. Well, if it's alright with you, I'll get your passport details from Maya from when you checked in and make arrangements. You don't have anything planned the next few days, do you?'

'Nothing at all.'

'Perfect.' He looks excited, and I smile warmly at him. 'OK, now I have to go and do some mingling, and you have to keep me company. Shall we go?' And he nods in the direction of the bar as the party begins spilling on to the beach.

'Let's,' I agree. Jake turns to Luis and touches his shoulder to get his attention. 'Luis, we'll catch you later.'

Like the gentleman he is, Luis stands and shakes Jake's hand before kissing me on both cheeks. 'Look after him, my dear.' He smiles at me with a wink. 'And try to keep him out of trouble, no?'

I put on my most serious face and nod solemnly, 'I'll do my best, Luis.' And he laughs and claps Jake on the back.

'You are a very lucky man,' he says to Jake but with a slight bow in my direction. But Jake says nothing and simply flashes him a huge, winning smile.

Chapter Twenty-Three

That saying 'time flies when you're having fun', well tonight seems to be living up to that phrase. It's late, I'm not sure how late, as I left my watch in my room, along with my phone, but most of the guests have ducked out and it's mainly just staff left now. I think this is what they call 'island time', where no one rushes or worries about how late it is or what else they should be doing. It's so laid-back and relaxed, and I'm finding I love this slower pace of life right now. Although, given my relationship with Jake, I'm not sure I can allow myself the credit of taking things slow. I know, I know, nothing's happened. But I feel like we are on the edge of something, and I'm not sure whether or not to throw myself over the precipice or run back for the hills screaming.

I'm sat on a table with Jake, Michael, Maya, one of the chefs from tonight's BBQ called Aaron and two guys from the entertainment team, Pierre and Luca, who are like a double act and have had me crying with laughter at least three times this evening.

'No, really, I can't have any more,' I say, as I hold my hand over my glass. 'You're a bad influence,' I mock scold

Michael, as he attempts to fill my glass again. He gives me a sceptical look.

'Oh, go on then!' I say with an exaggerated eye roll.

Jake's hand is slung over the back of my chair and, every now and again, I feel his fingers lightly brush over the top of my shoulder, from the base of my neck and back again. It made me feel conspicuous at first, being amongst his work colleagues. And not only are they his work colleagues, they're his employees for goodness' sake!

But as I looked around the group and noticed that no one had batted an eyelid, I let myself loosen up a little, even though having someone else apart from Luke touching me in such an intimate way felt really, really weird at first. I also found it a little disconcerting how easy I relaxed into his touch.

I glance around our little group, taking in this group of strangers that I so easily fit into this evening and who have taken me in to the fold, no questions asked, no assumptions made. Although, I think that says more about Jake's relationship with them, than it does about his one with me. Maya and Aaron are having an in-depth and lively discussion about the merits of banana versus blueberry pancakes. Banana better texture, blueberry better taste according to Maya, and banana better to cook, blueberry more aesthetically pleasing according to Aaron. The way I shovel in pancakes I'd be hard pressed to examine them long enough to put up any sort of argument.

'Us Americans know our pancakes,' Aaron says. He has a shaved head and is built more like a wrestler than a chef.

'And I'm a diligent pancake consumer,' grins Maya.

'When I manage to get you to my place for breakfast, we can have a taste test,' says Aaron, as he stretches his hands behind his head earning him a playful whack in the stomach from Maya. He doubles over in laughter and shock, and gives a playful wink in our direction, as he sees us watching them. Maya shakes her head, but can't hide the smirk that's playing on her lips.

'I don't eat them for breakfast,' she challenges, with a defiant look on her face.

'Hell, baby, I can go any time of day!' drawls Aaron earning a raucous laugh from the table, Maya included.

Pierre and Luca are currently involved in a heated contest of flip the beer mat, and there are currently a dozen or so strewn across the table, on the floor and in the air. They've each lined up six mats in a row, at the edge of a table, and are having a race, which levels of competitiveness have reached Olympic standards, attempting to flick them and catch each one in their hands before moving to the next. Pierre lets out a howl of pain as he misjudges his flick and slams his fingers upwards on to the rim of the table. Obviously this fills Luca with glee, and he bounces up and down in his chair until moments later, on his sixth and final beer mat, he does exactly the same thing. They both start playfully shoving each other, trying to elbow the other one out of the way, and Jake has to sweep in and grab the jug of punch, sitting on the table, before it becomes a casualty of the game.

'I think we should just call this one a draw,' says Jake. Michael, who has been watching over the whole spectacle, gives a hearty laugh and claps his hands together.

'Ladies, gentlemen, I think it's most definitely time for me to bid you goodnight. I don't want to risk a scolding from my good lady wife.' He's met with groans of disappointment as he stands, but I notice that each one of us, including me, gets out of our seats to say goodnight to him, a real sign of the respect and fondness everyone here around the table holds for him. Jake, Pierre, Luca and Aaron all shake his hand and give him a clap on the back, and Maya leans in to kiss him on the cheek. I'm unsure if it's appropriate for me to do so as well, but it feels wrong not to, so I do and, luckily, he doesn't look horrified. As I do, he says very quietly in my ear so only I can hear, 'This island has a certain sort of magic about it. Make the most of it.'

He gives a small nod of his head and waves, as he heads off in the direction of the hotel, his feet giving a little dance in time to the slow reggae beat as he saunters up the path.

'He's really special, isn't he?' I say to Maya, as she watches Michael go.

'He's one of the kindest men I have ever met. Everyone loves him. Staff and guests alike. I know Jake feels an affinity to him, because he's the one person here who really knew his dad.'

'Isn't it time he retired?' I ask her.

'Ha! No way. He loves this place as much as it loves him. Plus I think May enjoys keeping him out from under her feet.'

'I can't imagine being married to someone as long as they have.'

Maya looks at me for a moment with a quizzical frown on her face.

'What?' I ask.

She looks a little nervous as she speaks. 'You... you *were* engaged, right?'

I feel my stomach drop, and I open my mouth then close it again.

'Er, God, right. Yes, I mean, yes, yes, I was but...' I get a strange feeling in my stomach, as it dawns on me that

I didn't even realise what I'd said before the words were out of my mouth. And I'm not sure if that makes it better or worse. Is this how I really felt? I mean feel. Feel? Felt? For God's sake, I don't know. But as I said it, the sickening truth is that I meant the words. I *can't* imagine what it must be like to be with someone that long. And especially not with Luke. I know that now. In spite of everything that's happened, I know I couldn't have spent the rest of my life with him.

Maya gives me a small smile and reaches out and gives my hand a squeeze. 'It's OK,' she nods, 'I understand.'

'It's...' I start, 'I think the word is complicated.' She laughs and, whether she means to or not, her eyes dart to Jake for the smallest of seconds.

'Isn't it always?' She gives me a knowing smile.

'Apparently so.' I reach for my drink, and we share a small laugh together. Right on cue Jake leans in and whispers in my ear.

'OK?' he asks, and I nod, feeling Maya's eyes on me, but she looks away when I glance back at her.

'So,' she says, addressing the group, 'do we think my brother is going to surface anytime soon, or should I make my own way home?'

Aaron opens his mouth, and Maya glares at him with a pointed finger.

'And don't even think about it,' she scolds him.

'What?' he laughs, trying and failing miserably to look innocent. 'I'll take you home, just home. I promise. Both hands on the wheel at all times.'

'Well, it doesn't really look like I have a choice, does it?' she says only half meaning it. 'Come on then. And I have everyone here as my witness that you have sworn to be a gentleman.'

'Like I know how to be anything else.'

They move around the table, saying their goodbyes, and I get a hug and a kiss from both of them. As Maya says goodnight to Jake, she leans in and says something I can't make out and then both their eyes flick to me. I see her place a hand on his arm and smile. After they've left, amid squeals from Maya as Aaron actually chases her up the path and across the terrace, I turn to Jake.

'What did Maya say just then as she left?'

'Hmm?' He tries his hardest to look like he has no idea what I'm talking about. I give him a look, and he unexpectedly leans forward and buries his face into my hair in a hug.

'She said she can see why I like you so much.' As he looks at me through his long eyelashes, I feel his stare burn through me.

'Oh. Right,' I say quietly, wringing my hands together and looking away. Despite his openness and the fact that he's been so touchy-feely with me from the beginning, it still takes me by surprise.

'Fancy a walk on the beach?' he asks and, instantly, my stomach flips and my heart starts to race all of its own accord.

'Yeah, OK.'

Jake pushes back his chair and stretches as he stands, downing the last of his drink.

'See you tomorrow, guys, have fun,' he says to Pierre and Luca who are currently balancing plastic cups on their chins. They both wave their arms around in what I can only assume is a goodbye gesture, and I burst out laughing as Pierre throws himself off balance and tries to grab his cup, managing to send it crashing straight into Luca's face.

'Sabotage!' yells Luca, as Jake and I leave them to it. I wouldn't be surprised to see them still here in the morning.

We make our way through the tables and down to the sand. There are no hotel guests left at this time of night, just a few staff members laughing and drinking on some of the tables. A few of them are clearing up the area, but no one seems in much of a rush and this way of life is so infectious, I can't believe I'll ever want to leave. We reach the sand, and I slip off my flip-flops, leaving them at the side of the decking, and Jake does the same with his. He's wearing dark jeans and a pale blue, short-sleeved shirt and looks effortlessly gorgeous. We pass just a little way from Luis's cabana, and I see no signs from them that they are stopping the party any time soon. Luis holds up a champagne bottle towards us, and Jake runs over and grabs it from him, as I give a wave as way of thanks. Luis blows me a kiss, and I pretend to catch it and clutch it to me which has him howling in laughter.

'You've got a fan there,' Jake says. 'In fact, I am starting to think the only reason people are being so nice to me tonight is because of you.'

'What can I say?' I shrug. 'I'm a crowd-pleaser.'

'Evidently,' drawls Jake, and I feel my cheeks heat up. We stay in silence, as we head out of sight of the bar and further down the beach. All the sunbeds have been stacked up for the night, but we take a spot on the sand under one of the cabana canopies and settle down, Jake pushing the bottle of champagne in the ground between us. It's dark, but there's a full moon and the lights from the hotel grounds cast shadows on to the sand.

'Tonight was fun,' I say and lift up the bottle of champagne taking a swig. Jake takes the bottle out of my hands putting it to his lips and taking a drink. There is something about his lips touching the bottle, right after mine have, that fills me with a hum of excitement. I don't know if it's the drink or the incredibly clichéd romantic surroundings of the moonlit beach, but I'm feeling emboldened and nod to the bottle.

'It's almost like we've kissed,' I say, looking sideways at him, and his gaze flits between my lips and the neck of the bottle.

'Almost,' he replies in a low voice that does nothing to quell the fire that's raging in the pit of my stomach, and that fast seems to be spreading elsewhere. He holds out the bottle to me, and I take it from him, our fingers touching ever so slightly.

'Are you cold?' he asks.

'Not at all,' I say, my voice soft and quiet. Then I take a drink from the bottle to stop my mouth saying anything else. As I tilt back my head I'm aware of my neck being exposed, and I see Jake watching me out of the corner of my eye. I quickly tip my head down, as if he's about to take his teeth to me, which right now, the way I'm feeling, wouldn't be the absolute worst thing in the world. I'm actually rather hoping he does. I feel like a sort of spell's been cast tonight. Like I've been accepted here, with all my flaws and past skeletons, and no one cares. They like me for me, *Jake* likes me for me. And I'm just going to say it now, because I know. I know he likes me, I can feel it, and I can't deny it any longer. This, this thing, this charge, this feeling running between us. It's there. I can feel it. I take another mouthful of champagne and hand Jake the bottle which he puts down in the sand between us.

'Sweet cheeks, I need to tell you something. I should have told you sooner. I should have told you right away, but I didn't want anything to ruin it.' He gestures between us. 'To ruin this.'

My heart beats faster, and not in the excited, nervous way it usually does around him but in a sick with dread sort of way.

'OK. You can tell me. What is it? You're not married are you?' I let out a nervous laugh, trying to ease the uncomfortable tension that's building and look up at Jake. His eyes are glinting, but even through his tan, I watch as the colour drains from his face. I stare at him for a second, but when he doesn't say anything, a horrible, cold realisation creeps over me, and I scrabble to my feet feeling suddenly dizzy.

'Oh God. Oh God.' The words are out of my mouth before I can stop them, and I instantly feel inappropriate. Why should he have told me? Who am I to him? No one. I am absolutely no one. But deep down I know it's not that simple. Jake rushes to get up and reaches for me.

'Carrie, please. *Please*,' he pleads, reaching for me, as I take a few paces backwards. 'Hear me out. Let me explain.'

'Wow. I really read this wrong didn't I? I thought... I don't know what I thought I just...' I run out of words, and I'm aware of Jake's arms around me despite my trying to push him off. I have a dull ache in the pit of my stomach and my chest. Jake's married. *Married*. He committed to someone, agreed to be with them forever, vowed to be with them. And the most ludicrous thing is, that all I can think of is that it wasn't me. Why would it be you, idiot? I scold myself. I met him this week, literally days ago. I could probably still count it in hours if I wanted to. Why the hell am I even thinking such a stupid thought? OK, now I really am losing the plot. Just because the connection I feel to Jake is new for me, doesn't mean it is for him. Is that why I am thinking so deeply about this? Because I know I've never had this feeling before. Not even with the man I was about to marry. I need to have a word with myself, I don't even know how old he is.

'We're getting a divorce,' he says quickly, interrupting my thoughts. 'We got married really young, and we've been separated for four years. We just never got round to the divorce, because she left for New York. She's engaged to someone else, sweet cheeks. Legally we're still married, but that's it. That's all it is, a legality. One we are trying to sort out at the moment, actually. I didn't tell you because of what had just happened to you. I thought the less marriage talk the better, and then because I hadn't mentioned it to start with, the more time that went on the harder it got to bring it up. And you seemed so happy. I didn't want to do anything to spoil it. I'm so, so sorry.'

He lets out a long exhale, and we are both still for a moment. I can feel his heart beating in his chest, and I'm aware of my own, matching his rhythm. We stay like that for a minute, and only when he's sure I'm not going to bolt, he very slowly releases his hold on me.

'Sweet cheeks, I'm sorry. It's honestly just paperwork.'

'So,' I take a deep breath and run my hands over my hair, 'secret job, secret wife. Anything else you need to tell me? Father of three? Secret agent? Undercover spy?' I'm making light of it to try and cover my own embarrassment about the huge, overwhelming sense of relief I feel.

'Nothing else. I promise. I should have said something. I just felt awkward. Again.' He takes my hand, running his thumb over my knuckles as he does, and I stupidly wonder if he did this to his wife. 'Can I tell you about it? I need you to know. Please?'

'OK. But don't feel you have to…'

'Explain myself to you?' he cuts in, and I blush because that was exactly what I was about to say. 'I think we both know I do.'

Actually, I really am interested. OK, nosy. We reclaim our positions in the sand, and I gratefully take the bottle of champagne from where it's sitting, this time taking at least three mouthfuls to steady myself.

'Her name's Megan. Our parents have been friends for ever. They met at university, and I've known her all my life. It had always been an unspoken presumption that we would sort of end up together, by our parents that is, not us. Anyway, we started dating, mainly just to shut up our parents, I think, and we got on really well. Because we'd known each other so long it was just easy. And then everyone started talking about marriage, and it all just sort of snowballed. It felt like it was the next logical step, and that I should want to get married too, and so I just proposed. And Megan said yes, because she felt the same, like it was the right thing to do. Well, our parents were over the moon, so we got married. I was only twenty-five.'

'How old are you?' I interrupt. He smirks and lets out a little laugh.

'How old am I? I'm thirty-six. Why, how old are you?' he asks accusingly, a smile playing on his lips.

'I'm thirty-one,' I say, sticking out my chin, and his smile breaks out causing one little butterfly to do a somersault in my stomach. 'Sorry, carry on.'

'We were married for six years, but the last two she was back and forth to New York with work, so we didn't feel remotely married. I was in London at the time. We hardly saw each other. I think there was a stint of about four months where we were apart, and we barely even noticed it. So after my dad died we both realised that life was too short to spend it in a half-arsed relationship. We weren't unhappy, it just wasn't a marriage. We were friends who'd tied the knot because we thought that's what we should do, because everyone was telling us it was. It sounds stupid, I know, but that's how it was.'

'Honestly, it doesn't sound stupid at all,' I mutter and realise how much of Jake's story I recognise as my own.

'What did hurt was that I found out she had been seeing someone else for almost two and a half years. Someone at her firm in New York, she's an architect. I just wish she would have said. Because, ultimately, we were friends, and I felt she betrayed our friendship more than our marriage. So, because of that, our friendship was pretty much ruined, and so we don't have any sort of relationship any more. Then about a year ago she told me she was engaged and that we should get a divorce, and we both agreed we would get it all sorted but life's been so busy, we've only just got round to it. We're working on getting the papers signed right now.'

'Gosh,' I say not sure how else to respond. 'Right.'

'Well, there you have it. That's all of it. Promise. You've shown me yours, and I've shown you mine.' I look up at him and see the corners of his mouth curling at the edges, suppressing a grin.

'Yes, we have.' He puts his hand over mine and, because it's so big, his fingertips rest on my thigh, and I bristle slightly.

'We're OK, right? You'll still come to Miami?'

'Yes, I'll come.' Then a thought comes to me. 'You know when you asked me to dinner? Was that a cover because you bottled it? Were you going to ask me then?'

'No,' says Jake, looking super sheepish.

'You were!' I laugh, shoving him.

'OK, maybe I was,' he admits with a grin. 'But I thought it would sound way too forward if I didn't give you some background first, so I thought I better fill you in on the situation out there and then ask.'

'What, so you waited all of, like, three minutes? Because then it wasn't so forward?' I can't help but giggle, and he holds up his hands.

'Alright, alright, you got me. I bottled it.'

'Ha! I knew it! You're not as smooth as you make out after all.'

'So you think I'm smooth, hey?'

'I never said that,' I try, but he sees through me in a second. 'So when do you think your divorce will be finalised?' Why the hell did I ask that? I can't seem to help myself.

'I don't know. Soon, I hope. I'm waiting for papers to sign, and once that goes through it's pretty much done. I should have had them by now actually, but there must be some sort of hold up her end. I'm not too worried about it, they have to be here soon because she's getting married at Christmas. At least she was when I last heard from her.'

'Did you love her?' I need to get some sort of restraining order on my mouth.

'Yes. But not in the way I should have. Not in the way a husband should love his wife. And she didn't either. She's always been quite...' He pauses while he searches for the word. '...selfish, I suppose.'

'Selfish?'

'Perhaps that's too strong, but she's pretty unemotional, quite... detached, I suppose is a better word. We are actually nothing alike.'

I try to picture Jake with this woman, Megan, who is so unlike him. His affection, his warmth.

'You don't sound it. I mean, not that I know you that well or anything,' I add hastily. He turns to face me, his whole body shifting in my direction.

'I think you know me well enough.'

He touches my face, and I close my eyes letting his fingers trail over my jawline and down my neck to my collarbone. I feel like someone is stoking a fire deep in the pit of my stomach. He runs his fingers back and forth across it, and my heart starts to race as my body reacts habitually to his touch. He shifts his weight towards me, as he turns his body into mine.

'You are like nothing and no one else I have ever encountered. What is it about you?' His eyebrows crease in the middle as he frowns, his eyes sweeping over every inch of my face. I don't know if he actually wants me to answer his question, but I am so caught up in his closeness and his touch that I can't seem to find any words. He leans towards me and, ever so softly, brushes his lips against mine, sending a bolt of lightning straight through me so strong that I fear I may be torn in two. My stomach flips, and I can't seem to focus on anything except the briefest touch of his mouth against mine.

'Carrie!' I hear a voice, but I can't work out if I'm imagining it or if it's real. 'Carrie! There you are!'

We pull apart, and my fingers instantly go to my mouth, to where his lips were.

'I thought you'd gone to bed, but Luca said you'd come to the beach.' I turn my head to see Rachel and Dale making their way across the sand. Dale looks sheepish, having obviously noticed what they may have interrupted, but Rachel is so preoccupied in her post-coital joy, she clearly hasn't a clue. I can't help but smile at her total ignorance. I turn my attention back to Jake, and his face is a strange mixture of anger and joy. Did we just kiss? Have I just kissed my second man ever? But, no. No, I haven't. I mean our lips touched, but it wasn't a kiss, not a real one. But it could have been, had we not got interrupted. It could have been more than a kiss. OK, let's not get carried away, our lips barely touched.

I chance a look at Jake and, as we keep our eyes locked, I have this feeling in the pit of my stomach that nothing is ever going to be the same again.

Chapter Twenty-Four

I wake with a start to a knocking on my door. I'm really disorientated. It was at least three in the morning before I got to bed. Alone. Me, Jake, Dale and Rachel stayed chatting on the beach for a long while once they interrupted our non-kiss, and I press my fingers to my lips again as I crawl out of bed.

Jake had sat behind me on the beach, his arms wrapped around me for the whole time, but we didn't non-kiss again. Even as he walked me to my room to say goodnight and held on to me for just a little bit longer than was completely necessary, he didn't try and kiss me. He stared at my face for the longest time, and I felt him watching me every second it took me to open my door to my room, which was actually an inordinately long time, as I couldn't seem to concentrate on swiping my key card and dropped it on the floor at least twice, maybe three times, I can't quite remember. Then once I was safely inside, I looked through the peephole in the door, and Jake was just stood, staring at my own door. Then he started walking towards it, and I jumped back, before I remembered he had no idea I was there, so I started peeking again. He walked towards my door, put out his hand to knock, but then stopped.

I held my breath for the entire time he was in such close proximity to me but watched as he paced up and down between our doors, ran his hands through his hair, opened his door, took another look towards mine and then stepped into his suite. I only dared breathe out once he was in his own room, and I immediately went out to the balcony and lay down on one of the loungers, just staring at the sky.

I wanted that non-kiss to be a kiss. I didn't want Rachel and Dale to walk on the beach, but I was also relieved when they did, because I'm nervous. I'm nervous of so many things. The way I feel when I'm around him, the fact I feel I have no control over what I'm doing and, most of all, the way I seem to throw all sense and reason out of the window when he's in my proximity. I mean, I'm not saying I would have ripped off all my clothes and rolled around naked on the beach there and then but, honestly, the thought may have briefly crossed my mind.

I suddenly realise that I'm still stood in the middle of the room, clearly lost in inappropriate thought, and leg it to the door. I half expect to see Jake, but it's Maya, looking bright as a button, with a beaming smile on her face.

'Morning!' She sounds incredibly chirpy for someone who got to bed at a fairly late hour and looks annoying refreshed and glowing. 'Here.'

She holds out a takeaway coffee cup and a bag bearing the logo of the bakery across the road. 'I thought you might need this. On me.'

'Oh my God, you're a lifesaver. Thank you so much.' I hold open the door to let her in, but she shakes her head.

'Can't stop, I have to check in a load of overeager holidaymakers desperate to get on the beach. Just wanted to give you those, and also these.' She hands over a white envelope she's been holding under her arm. 'It's your flight itinerary for Miami. Today.'

She grins at me, and my eyes widen in shock.

'*Today*?'

'Yep. Today. You leave at eleven thirty, so Jake asked if you could be downstairs for nine to get to the airport and get checked in and so on. Is that going to be OK?'

I feel a rush of excitement and nerves, as I take the envelope from her.

'Oh, wow!' I shriek. 'OK, thanks. I better get a move on. Oh God, what time is it now?' I add in a panic. Please don't be eight thirty, I think, but Maya gives me a reassuring smile.

'It's only seven, don't worry you have plenty of time. Jake said it was a late one last night, but I thought you'd probably appreciate the early wake-up call to pack and get yourself sorted. You know what men are like,' she shrugs, 'they think you throw a clean pair of panties in your bag and you're good to go.'

'Thank you so much. I appreciate that. Er, Maya, before you go, could I ask you something?'

'Of course you can.'

'What should I pack? I don't even know what we will be doing or what the hotel is like. I'm worried I won't have the appropriate stuff.'

She looks thoughtful for a moment.

'Well, you'll be back by tomorrow night. Your flight leaves Miami at four in the afternoon, but I know Jake has booked you dinner tonight so...' She taps her finger on her lips and tilts her head to the side, and I can almost hear the cogs whirring in her brain.

'OK, I can be really quick, Marie can manage for a moment,' she says to herself. 'May I?'

She nods inside the suite, and I step back.

'Please, by all means.' I watch her stride purposefully to the walk-in wardrobe and fling the doors open with all the flair and passion of Gok Wan.

'So,' she says, leafing through my clothes on the rail. 'Travel in this, and you can wear it for the rest of the day when you get there.' She hands me a navy swing dress with spaghetti straps and a cross back. 'Then you'll need something for dinner tomorrow night. Oh, wear this, this is perfect.'

It's a black body-con dress with a small slit up the back and a high neck, but has a lace back all the way down to the top of my bum.

'OK.' She carries on leafing and pulls out a pair of grey, frayed denim shorts and a black, shirred boob tube. 'You can wear these tomorrow if you go to the beach, and if not, you can wear this for some shopping and to fly home in,' she says handing me my short, floral print wrap dress. 'Perfect, take two pairs of flip-flops, one black and one camel coloured, if you have them, and one pair of heels that go with that dress. And a bikini just in case. OK, sorted. Right I best get back.'

'Maya,' I laugh, 'that was amazing! I am so impressed.'

'I like clothes,' she shrugs. 'And fashion. And shopping.' She sighs with laugh and a wistful look. 'Shame my bank balance doesn't.'

'You should totally go into personal shopping. I would have spent ages agonising over what to pick. Can you come and dress me every day please?' I laugh.

'I wish!' she groans. 'I love it here but personal shopping would be my absolute dream. One day maybe.'

'Well I think you'd be awesome at it, for what it's worth. And thanks for bringing all this up.' I gesture to the envelope and treats.

'It's got all the hotel details in there too, in case you need them. But he'll look after you, Carrie. Honestly, I can't think of anyone better. Have an amazing time. Miami's great.'

I return her smile and another flash of excitement jolts through me. 'Thank you so much, I owe you one.'

'Well, between you and Rachel, I have an incredibly happy brother *and* a boss who is practically skipping about the place, so I think we can call it even.'

I blush and can't help the smile that creeps on to my face.

'OK, thanks,' I say shyly and follow Maya as she heads to the door. 'Actually, Maya, sorry, do you mind if I ask you something? It's not technically work related, and I understand if you don't or can't answer because Jake's your boss, but I have no one else to ask.'

'OK,' she says slowly, looking intrigued.

'Jake told me about Megan.'

'Ah.'

'Yes. And well, God I feel so stupid asking this, I mean this *really* isn't anything to do with me, it's just because of everything lately...' She places a hand on my arm to stop me rambling.

'Carrie, I don't pretend to know all the ins and outs of my boss's personal life, but as far as I know and as far as Jake's told me, it's over. I think it's been a bit messy in the past, but it's very, very over. I don't think it was ever going to last, if you want my opinion, but she's getting married again now so it should all be finished and done with soon. And don't worry about asking, I would want to know too, but you have no worries there.'

I smile at her gratefully, relieved at both her answer and the fact she doesn't think I am some crazy stalker type.

'Just enjoy Miami. Don't worry about things too much. I hate to sound like a cliché, and this is really none of *my* business now, but sometimes, you've just got to go with it.'

'Thanks for being so nice,' I mutter, embarrassed that I can't seem to get any of my own shit together at the moment.

'Anytime.'

I watch her disappear in the lift before retreating to my wardrobe to throw all my things in the small carry-on case I brought for the plane trip over here. I figure it's only one night, and I have my capsule wardrobe, so this should suffice. I do a quick double-check through the stuff Maya picked out, and I am still mightily impressed she managed to pull this stuff together in a matter of minutes. I grab the other things she told me to put in and after a quick shower, and despite just being brought a pastry and coffee, decide to grab some breakfast before I set off. Well, I don't know when I'm next going to eat so it seems only sensible.

I pick up my phone to text Rachel, just on the off-chance she might be awake, and see she just sent me a message five minutes ago.

In the dining room if you fancy brekkie?
Saved you a seat. Xxx ☺

I notice another three messages and figure I should probably catch up on everything since I'm going away for a night. I reply to Rachel quickly telling her I'll be down in ten and, first things first, call my mum. She answers almost immediately.

'Darling! Hello, how are you? We were just talking about you and your glamorous trip.' Before I have a chance to ask who 'we' is, she says down the line, 'I'm just over at Jean and Alan's having a coffee. It's a lovely day here. We've decided to go to Stratford for a walk by the river.'

Jean and Alan are my mum's neighbours. They live next door but one and are a bit like an unofficial auntie and uncle to me.

My mum lowers her voice and adds in a hushed whisper, 'They've said they'll drive and Jean has a voucher for afternoon tea that she got for her sixtieth from the ladies at her aquafit class, so I thought why not? Anyway,' she says back in her normal voice, 'how are you doing, love?'

'Hi, Auntie Jean!' I shout down the phone. 'I'm good, Mum. Really good actually. Everything's fine. I'm having a nice time, and I've made some friends so I have had some company. I'm actually having fun.'

'Oh, darling, I am so pleased. I do worry about you. Dare I ask if you've heard from anyone here?'

'Only Kate,' I say popping her on loudspeaker whilst wriggling into the dress Maya chose for me. 'Actually, Mum, I've got to be quite quick. Would you believe it I'm going to Miami today, I just called to let you know.'

'Miami?' she squeals down the phone. 'What do you mean you're going to Miami?'

'Well,' I pause for a moment while I think this through.

I don't want to lie to my mum, but I really should have thought about what I was going to say when she asked before I called her, I don't want to freak her out, but I can't quite say, well I met this guy a few days ago, and it turns out he owns the hotel, and he's flying us to his other hotel in Miami. Yes, just the two of us. Oh, and he's ridiculously attractive, and we sort of non-kissed, and I think he fancies me. Did I mention he's married, by the way?

'It's a sort of organised trip,' I say, hoping this isn't too much of a lie. 'The owner of the hotel is arranging it, and we'll be staying the night in one of the sister hotels. It's only a night and should be fun, see the sights of Miami and stuff.'

'Right, well, just a moment, love.' I hear a muffle, and her voice is distant for a second as I hear her say, 'Yes I do, it's back at the house. I'll nip and get it now. Sorry, Carrie, Jean wanted a plastic-backed rug for us to sit on, I said I'd pop and get one. I say, Miami! Sounds very exciting. And the hotel's organising it you say?'

'Yes, you know, like a sort of added extra.' I wince at how stupid this must sound, but my mum doesn't seem to react.

'Well, you take care and be safe. Is someone you know going with you?'

'Yes,' I say brightly, knowing that while this isn't strictly true or what she means, it's not an actual lie, 'I won't be on my own.'

'OK, darling, make sure you text me when you get there, and let me know you've landed. I best go, I need to get the rug, and Alan's just started backing the car out now.' Thank God for the plastic-backed rug. It seems to have my mum a bit preoccupied, and I'm grateful she's not asking any more questions.

'Alright Mum, love you lots. Enjoy Stratford.'

'Love you too, darling. Miss you.'

'You too, Mum.' And we hang up. I glance at the little icon on my phone telling me I have two more messages, my thumb hovering over the button momentarily, then I decide not to look at them until I'm back. They can wait. I don't want anything to ruin my mood, which right at this moment is one of a slowly building excitement.

I can see Rachel balancing a plate, bowl and a cup of juice as she makes her way across the dining room towards the open terrace doors. I run over and relieve her of the cup quickly before she sends the whole lot crashing to the floor.

'Thanks,' she sighs, as we place them all down on the table, 'I took the liberty of getting breakfast for two.'

She nods at the crockery, laden with food, and I take a fork and stab some fruit.

'I'm surprised you're awake, to be honest, Rach.' Rachel shrugs and gives a coy smile that I know she doesn't mean for a second.

'Well, Dale had work first thing, so we were awake anyway.'

'I bet you were,' I say with a giggle. 'So you know I mentioned Miami last night?' I'd told her Jake had asked me to go, and from the look on her face she'd had a million and one questions she was absolutely desperate to ask.

'Yes lady, spill.' She takes a sip of juice and tears off a piece of croissant, shoving it in her mouth as she settles in for my reply. I fill her in on the whole Alexander Steele debacle (she also loves the movies) and the fact that Jake may have to go and do damage control.

'He asked me to go, and I just said yes. I didn't even really think about it until afterwards, but something just made me agree. This is so not like me. What the hell is going on? Am I mad for saying I'll go?'

She looks horrified at the suggestion.

'Er, no, not at all. If some hot, rich man wants to take me to Miami and stay in his swanky hotel, I'm all in!'

'Yes, but I hardly know him.' I think I'm just looking to Rachel for some reassurance that what I'm about to do is actually totally well planned and thought out, and not a mental idea at all.

'Oh, who cares? I mean, I'm pretty sure he's not a serial killer, and he couldn't stop staring at you the whole time we were on the beach last night. I actually thought he was going to get up and drag you away at one point, he looked so frustrated to have company! I think this is his chance to get you all to himself.'

I can't pretend the thought hadn't crossed my mind, but now Rachel has said it out loud, I wonder how I'd feel if the opportunity ever presented itself. Which I'm sure it won't, but you know what if it *did*? I feel a bit sick at the thought, and it clearly shows on my face.

'Carrie, you know you don't have to do anything you don't want to. Jake isn't going to take advantage, that doesn't seem like his style.'

'No, it's not that,' I say honestly. 'I mean…' I look around to check no one is listening and lower my voice to a whisper, 'I have sort of thought about it.'

'Ha, I knew it!' Rachel claps her hands together excitedly and almost upends the table in the process. 'Well, you know what I say, get back on that horse girl!'

I can't help but laugh at her choice of words.

'I'm getting way ahead of myself, I know I am.'

'You're not at all. I saw your heads together when we showed up on the beach last night. Don't think I didn't notice.'

I feel my face burning and suddenly become very interested in the strawberries I'm pushing around my plate.

'We didn't kiss,' I say remembering the feel of his mouth on mine and getting a little flip in my stomach. 'Well, we didn't *not* kiss but it wasn't a proper kiss.' Rachel squeals, and I start shushing her and waving my hands up and down as she bobs around in her chair.

'Well a non-kiss is still a kiss in my books,' she says wisely with an air of finality.

'How is it?' I laugh popping some pastry into my mouth.

'It just is,' she shrugs, and I shake my head.

'Well, if I'm not back tomorrow night he's obviously kidnapped me and sold me to some drug cartel, so call the Feds, OK?'

'Promise,' she nods.

'You'll be OK while I'm gone?'

'Oh, I think I'll be just fine,' she says with a knowing smile. 'Dale has tomorrow off, so he's taking me on an island tour to make up for the one I missed with you and Michael, but somehow I don't think we'll get very far.' She has the good grace to at least blush slightly and lets out a very girly giggle, which I can't help but join in with.

There's something infectious about Rachel and her easy-going ways. No pretence, straight up honesty, what you see is what you get, and it's so refreshing. I can't think of anyone better than her to hang out with at this time in my life.

We stay out on the terrace, nursing coffees, until I head upstairs to collect my stuff. I take a sweeping glance around the room, making sure I remembered to put my phone and my charger in too, and head downstairs to the lobby for just before nine.

Maya is nowhere to be seen, but the tall blonde, I now assume to be Marie, is busy on the phone while a guy, I was introduced to last night as Andrew, is pointing some guests in the direction of the beach. I'm not entirely sure what to do with myself, so I take a seat across from the reception desk on one of the sofas and try to look as relaxed as possible. I take out my sunglasses and put them on. There. I am cool and calm, and I know exactly what I'm doing. The sunglasses are actually a really good call, as I can get away with doing some people watching. I love people watching. Luke always thought it was weird and nosy, and now that I think about it I suppose he had a point but, really, is there anything more interesting than other people? Look at my life lately. And Rachel's. And even Jake's. I bet you someone would think that was all really juicy if they were a viewer from the outside.

I reach in my bag and pull out the bottle of water I've taken from the fridge in my room. I'm really just looking for something to occupy my hands and stop me fidgeting, when I hear a pair of heels clicking towards me across the lobby.

'Jake's making a call in his office,' Maya tells me. 'He said for you to go through to the back.'

'Great, thanks.' I reach for my overnight bag, and she puts out her hand to stop me.

'Eric?' she calls to the front doors, and one of the burly security guys gives her a nod. 'Put this in Jake's car for me please, they'll be leaving in a few minutes.'

Eric swaggers over and takes my bag without a word, disappearing back through the doors and outside. I feel like a bit of a mini celebrity. Being close to Jake gives me access to certain little perks I wouldn't usually have, and I could really get used to this. No, Carrie, don't get used to it. This isn't real life, I have to remind myself.

Maya leads me behind the desk, to the door to the back offices, and I suddenly feel self-conscious that I'm crossing a line and glance around to see if any of the other guests are looking at me, wondering who I am to be getting special treatment but, of course, as usual, no one is bothering at all.

I follow her through the door, and my eyes fall instantly to Jake's office, where I can see him sat behind his desk. His face looks serious, and he has his hand on his forehead as he speaks into the phone. I can see young Barack Obama guy sat in an office to my right and two people I recognise from the catering team are sat poring over some paperwork in one of the offices to my left. Maya ushers me round the room and gestures to Jake's door.

'Go on in, he said it's fine.' I hesitate momentarily and shift my bag on my shoulder, slightly unsure if that's the right thing to do, but Maya obviously senses my hesitation. 'Really. He said for you to go straight in, even if he was on the phone.'

'OK, thanks, and thanks for this morning too. See you when we get back I guess.' *We?* Why didn't I just say *I?* Apparently I'm speaking on behalf of us both now.

'You're very welcome, my pleasure. Have a great time. You'll love it.' She reaches out and gives my arm a squeeze and couples it with a reassuring smile that I appreciate, before heading across the room and back out to the front desk. I push open Jake's door, and his head jerks up with a frown then instantly transforms into the most disarming smile. He stands up, still on the phone, and beckons for me to sit on the sofa, so I perch on the edge, clutching my bag. I don't know why I'm so nervous all of a sudden. Perhaps the fact I'm about to embark on this spontaneous trip is just sinking in. I can smell Jake's aftershave in the air and take a deep breath, as I try to look like I'm not listening in, which I clearly am.

'Uh-huh. Yes. Yes. No, not right now, let's wait and see.' I can see the concentration on Jake's face as he speaks. 'Let's see how it pans out. No, definitely not. Yes, this evening. No, I have plans, but I'll see you before. Yes, her name's Carrie.' He looks up at me and smiles making my insides do a little dance. 'OK, thanks Jackson, that's great. We'll see you later.'

I flush slightly. He said we as well. He hangs up and makes his way around the desk towards me. He's in a white shirt with light grey trousers and brogues.

'Hey,' he says softly, as he reaches me and instantly takes my hand in his, briefly stroking it. 'Ready to go?'

'Yep!' I say excitedly. Because I realise I *am* excited. So much so that I'm actually bouncing a little on the spot. 'Everything OK?' I ask Jake, as he shuts down a sleek, silver MacBook on his desk and slides it into a leather bag.

'Yeah, it will be. I know Jackson and Anna are great, but I just want to get out there and see for myself that it's all under control. I hate being forced into these situations, but I have to be visible to the staff and also the press, let them know it's all under control and there's nothing to worry about.'

'But doesn't it look more worrying if you rush off there? Like something really serious must have happened for the owner to fly out?' I'm not sure why I'm trying to talk myself out of a trip here. 'Sorry, I'm not helping, am I? Ignore me, I don't know anything about it, Jake, sorry.'

'No, it's OK. And I understand what you're saying, but I want to have a proper meeting with Anna and, if possible, I'd like to meet with Alexander Steele. I know both his and our PR team are trying to set it up, so hopefully it'll happen. I know he's been at the centre of this mess, but I need him on side, he's a huge name and if we handle this badly, it could really damage us. People want to stay at the hotels the celebrities do. No matter how they bloody behave,' he adds angrily with a roll of his eyes. I reach out and give his arm a small squeeze thoroughly enjoying how firm his biceps feel under my touch.

'It'll be fine. It's Miami, right? How bad can it be?' I say trying to lighten the mood and his face softens.

'I'm so glad you agreed to come. I really want you to have a good time.'

'And I will.' I nod towards the door. 'Shall we?'

'I can't wait.' He grins and gives me a wink that would look creepy on someone else but just looks irresistibly sexy on him, and I wonder again what the hell I am getting myself into.

Chapter Twenty-Five

'Oh my God,' I squeal, as I step out on to the balcony, 'Jake, this is amazing!'

The Palm Bay Grove hotel is in the Coconut Grove area of the city and is set a small way back from the marina, which I can see from my suite. Jake made sure I got the best available room left in the whole hotel, and his is the room next door to mine. I wasn't sure how the sleeping arrangements were going to work and was slightly apprehensive that he might have booked us into the same room but, of course, I was worrying for no reason at all. Why would I even think he would book us into the same room? I take a deep breath and slide my shades up on to my forehead, peering up and down the road to the line of other hotels and feel another buzz of excitement.

'Seriously, Jake, this is so cool. I can't believe this is yours!'

He laughs and steps out on to the balcony, leaning against the railing.

'Well, technically it's the group's.'

'Yes technically, but you know what I mean. Technically, you're still the owner.'

'OK, *technically*,' he grins. 'I do sometimes sit back and think, how did I get here? It doesn't even seem real to me some days. Then I remember all the ridiculously long hours, airport trips, hiring, firing and so on I've had to do and think that, yes I did actually work for it. Well, me and my dad.'

'He would be unbelievably proud of you.' I link my arm in his and lean into him giving him a supportive nudge. 'So, what now?'

He pushes his sunglasses on to his head and gives me a look.

'Well, I can think of a million and one things I would love to do but, right now, I'm afraid I have to go to work.'

'Oh, of course, that's fine. I'll amuse myself.' I try to hide the disappointment in my voice. I know it's the only reason I'm here, but there was a small part of me that had forgotten Jake was actually here to work.

'I need to speak to Anna and find out what's happening. Let me make a couple of phone calls, and I'll be back to you ASAP. I won't be any longer than half an hour. I'll order some food and drinks, what would you like?'

'It's your hotel, what do you recommend?'

'Ah, so you trust me enough to let me order you dinner? OK then, a surprise it is. I'll get room service to send something up for you.'

'Perfect, thank you.' I hesitate as I'm not sure how to broach the subject. 'Er, Jake? Sorry, this feels a little awkward.'

'Are you OK?' he looks concerned all of a sudden.

'Yes I'm fine, it's just… I need you to tell me how much this is all costing, I need to pay my way.'

He suddenly looks a bit angry, and I bite my lip, worried I've offended him.

'You're my guest here, don't you dare offer to pay for anything again,' he says sternly. 'I invited you here and won't hear of it.'

'Sorry,' I say, chastened. 'I just…' I stop as he holds up his hands.

'Don't you dare, not another word. And you don't have to be sorry.' He pulls me into his arms. 'Just relax, OK? This is my treat, I want to treat you.'

'OK,' I say relaxing into his arms ever so slightly, before pulling away. 'I mean, thank you. Very, very much.' I smile up at him, and he leans down towards me.

'You're welcome, sweet cheeks.' He kisses my forehead, and all I can think about is the moment on the beach and his mouth touching mine. I blush again, and this time I know he notices, but I know he won't know what I'm thinking. Unless he does? He seems to have a way of reading me I can't quite explain.

'I'll be back soon.' He leaves, and I walk back inside to take in the room and hang up the things I know will crease in my bag.

The layout of the suite is different from its sister hotel in that it's one huge, open-plan room with the biggest bed I've ever seen, raised on a small platform in the centre. It's directly in front of the balcony door so the first thing you see, as you wake up, is the vista out to the marina and the brilliant, bright, blue sky.

The hotel is even more modern than the Palm Bay in Barbados, with a black leather sofa, headboard and chairs punctuating the crisp, white walls. My favourite bit of the room are the two massive, bright orange, star-shaped cushions on the bed and one single high-backed, velvet armchair in the same vibrant colour. This suite is called *Seville* and in the slick, black Mercedes on the way from the airport, Jake told me the suites are all a different colour theme. He's staying in *Lux*, which is accented with gold and the red suite that got trashed by Alexander Steele and co. was ironically called *Rage*. I liked the sound of *Rosé*, which Jake tells me has a gigantic beanbag shaped like a candyfloss and hot pink, flamingo cushions.

I walk into the bathroom and let out a laugh. Every inch of the room is white apart from the jet black towels and the free-standing, roll-top bath that's again bright orange. I also notice the complimentary toiletries are filled with an orange liquid to match. I wonder who thought of this theme, I wonder if it was Jake?

I run my hand over the edge of the bath and perch on the side. Jake wonders how *he* got here, well right now, I'm wondering pretty much the same. If you had asked me two weeks ago, God one week ago, where I thought I would be right now, I certainly wouldn't have said here. But despite not being where I thought I would be, I feel more and more like this is where I'm supposed to be. And I don't mean sat in a bathroom in a swanky hotel in Miami. Although I most certainly wouldn't have thought that either.

I have to admit, it is pretty cool. If a little bizarre. I pick up my phone and snap a picture of the room and send it to Rachel along with one of the view from the balcony. I've made myself a promise to not look at my other messages until I'm back in Barbados tomorrow, and I know this is mainly because I don't want to have to lie to Kate if one of them is from her. I'm pretty sure she will have texted, and I don't know how to say I've swanned off to Miami for the night with Jake without making it sound, well a bit dodgy, I suppose. I mean, I don't think it's dodgy, but someone who is looking in from outside might. Especially the sister of my ex-fiancé who I broke up with a week ago, albeit with damn good reason.

I look at myself in the mirror and feel a surge of pride flood through me. My skin is tanned and glowing, the sun has lightened my hair slightly in places, and my dusting of freckles stands out across my nose. I hardly recognise myself from the girl who arrived in Barbados a week ago. In such a small space of time, my whole life has turned around and, despite the degree of uncertainty my future holds, if I can get through week one, I know I'm doing OK.

My thoughts drift back to Jake as they so often seem to do. Now he is certainly something I didn't count on. Not even in the deepest corner of my thoughts was the possibility that I might meet someone who has the effect on me that he does. We both know there is something happening, and I know neither of us can put our finger on it, but we can't deny the intense chemistry between us. I can't think like this, I just can't. This time last week I woke up ready to marry Luke. How can it all be so very different and yet so very right? But that's just it, it does feel right with him. *He* feels right, and I can't explain why. Because it shouldn't so soon after, should it? A knock on the door makes me jump, and I hurry towards it. Blimey that was quick. I yank open the door to see a table full of room service to greet me.

'Good afternoon, ma'am,' a young man says, in a spritely American accent. 'My name is Chad. I do hope you're enjoying your stay so far.'

'Your name is Chad?' I say stifling a giggle. *So American!*

'Yes, ma'am, that's correct.' He grins at me clearly just thinking I misheard him. 'May I come in and deliver your room service today?'

I realise how rude I must seem and open the door to beckon him in.

'Sorry, yes of course. Thank you, please come in. Just set it anywhere you like.' He wheels the trolley over to the sitting area and opens the leaves on the table, spreading out the platters as he does so. He slowly removes each cover with a flourish, looking at me for a reaction each time, which I oblige with 'oohs' and 'aahs', much to his delight.

'Enjoy your meal, ma'am, and please don't hesitate to call us if there is anything at all we can do for you. You have a great trip and a very pleasant stay with us now.'

I suddenly realise I'm supposed to tip him, aren't I? I scrabble to my bag and realise I don't have any dollars. Only some Barbados dollars and about twenty pounds. Oh God, how embarrassing.

'Er...' I look around as if a wad of dollar bills is likely to materialise from thin air but, as I look back to Chad, he is shaking his head looking horrified.

'Oh no, ma'am. You're here as a guest of Mr Holden. Everything has been settled on your behalf. Everything. I've been instructed not to take a cent from you ma'am,' he adds looking a little awkward. 'But please don't say I've said that.' Poor Chad, he looks momentarily mortified as his professional masks slips ever so slightly for a second.

'Of course I won't. And thank you, Chad, you've been very kind. I'll make sure Jake, sorry, Mr Holden knows how well you've looked after me.' Chad looks like he's just been told he's won the employee of the year award and smiles at me so widely he looks slightly mental.

'Ma'am, you are too kind. It's my pleasure. No problem at all, no problem at all.' He's slightly bowing as he backs out of the suite and closes the door behind him still bobbing as he goes.

I turn back to the food and see that Jake's ordered me calamari for starters, steak frites for main and what looks like New York-style, baked cheesecake for dessert. How does he do that? He's never seen me eat any of these things, and yet he's got it spot on. I settle down on the orange chair and lay my napkin across my knee spreading my hands on the table in anticipation. The smell is incredible, and I can't believe room service here looks so good. I squeeze some lemon on the calamari and spear a piece with my fork popping it into my mouth. I roll my eyes and let out a small groan. Heaven. I should probably go easy, seeing as I know we are having dinner later, but I've not eaten since breakfast and this just tastes too damn good.

I'm just mopping up the last bit of raspberry coulis on to my final forkful of cheesecake when there's another knock at the door. I suspect it's probably room service come to clear the plates, so am very pleasantly surprised when I see Jake standing there.

'Oh, ru-ro!' I mutter holding my hand over my mouth to avoid spraying him with cheesecake. He laughs and steps past me inside, running his hand down my arm, and I feel all my hair stand on end.

'I see you've enjoyed the food then,' he laughs, as I hurriedly try to finish my last mouthful as quickly as possible. I swallow and feel a little out of breath.

'It was delicious! Seriously good. Thank you.' I narrow my eyes at him. 'How did you know how I liked my steak cooked?' I ask.

'Call it a hunch. Something about you just said medium rare to me.'

I smile, still eyeing him with suspicion. 'Well, it was gorgeous. Thank you. Oh, and I met a lovely young man called Chad who was so nice to me and, quite frankly, is an asset to your hotel.' He takes a step closer to me, and takes my hand in his, as his eyes darken.

'It seems I need to get some charm lessons from Chad then, doesn't it?' He presses my knuckles to his lips, and my stomach leaps. I wish that it wasn't my hand he was kissing right now and then get embarrassed that I'm thinking about the non-kiss again, and my cheeks flush. I'd fit right in the *Rosé* room at this rate.

'Listen, I've spoken to Anna, and they've managed to set up a meeting with Steele and his people. He's going to be here in the next hour if you'd like to come with me and meet him?'

'Really?' I say, unable to keep the excitement out of my voice. 'Would that be OK? I mean, is that appropriate?'

'Well, you can't stay for the whole meeting, but there's no reason why I can't introduce you and then you can go do some exploring until I'm free. I don't think it should take more than about twenty minutes, to be honest, then some photos for the press release, and I need to have a sit down with Jackson and Anna. I've booked dinner for nine p.m., so hopefully that's enough time for you to have a little wander around.' I glance at my watch. It's quarter past five.

'That's great. So I'll be ready for eight thirtyish, yeah?' And Jake nods. 'You don't have a guide book or map or anything do you?' I ask him. 'I didn't have time to do much reading up on what to see and where to go.'

'I thought you might like to have a wander along the South Beach area. It's so classic Miami, and it's all everyone talks about when you mention the city, so I thought it would be pretty cool to be able to say you've been there.'

'That is a very good idea. That sounds brilliant,' I say smiling at his thoughtfulness. 'Can I walk from here or...' Crap. I don't have money for a cab, and I don't want to ask Jake to call me one because I know he will want to pay, but he interrupts me.

'I've got a car for you. It's yours for the afternoon, and Peter will take you anywhere you want to go, then pick you up and bring you back here later.'

'Oh my God, wow. That's great, thank you. Are you sure that's alright?'

'Of course it is, I'm not about to let you wander round a new city on your own. Peter's great, he will show you all the spots, as you drive around, and knows the city like the back of his hand. He's usually my driver when I'm here.'

Jake has a driver. That's pretty impressive. The more time I spend with him the more I realise that actually, he's kind of a big deal. He's thirty-six and is the CEO of a major hotel group. He employs hundreds of people and is responsible for, what I'm sure is, a multimillion-pound business, but he never acts like it.

'Do you have your phone on you?' Jake asks, and I pick it up from the bed. 'Here, take my number and, if you need to, at any time, about anything at all, call me.'

I unlock it, type *Baywatch* into my contacts and pass him the phone to enter his own number. He bursts out laughing and shakes his head, entering his number before he hands it back.

'Call me now so I have yours. Is that alright?'

'Of course it is,' I say and do just that, listening to the familiar iPhone ringtone emanate from his pocket.

'Nice one. Right, you ready? I have a movie star to go and make nice with.'

I assume we will be heading to the bar or restaurant, so I'm surprised when we walk down the corridor, and Jake stops outside a room with *Rays* written on the door. I look up at Jake with a questioning look on my face that he understands. Of course he does.

'It's more private than the bar and less formal than one of the meeting rooms. We get to keep it low-key.'

The door opens, and we are greeted by a tall, willowy, redhead with thick-rimmed glasses and her hair cut into a short, sharp bob. She's wearing a figure-hugging black dress and has on a pair of skyscraper heels I recognise as Louboutins. In her hand is an iPhone I can see flashing with a call that she's totally ignoring.

'Jake,' she says, a little breathless. 'We're all set, come in.'

Jake moves aside and holds the door for me, as I step into the suite. I can see a gigantic, yellow sofa across the other side of the room. *Rays.* Of course. Yellow suite.

'Anna, this is Carrie. Carrie, Anna Anderson.'

'Hi, nice to meet you,' I say, holding out my hand with a smile. I see her give me a quick once-over and find myself on the end of a very cool smile.

'Likewise,' she replies smoothly, before turning to Jake. 'Jake, we are really pushed for time, it would be great if we could get on with this.'

She moves through the room in the direction of the sofa but not before giving me another look, one I don't find at all welcoming. Quite the opposite in fact. She turns on her heels and, as I follow her, I feel Jake's hand on the small of my back as we make our way through the suite. I'm instantly surprised at how many people seem to be in here and, although it's huge, it feels a little crowded. I do a quick headcount.

There's me, Jake, Anna, one, two, three guys, who look like security, a balding man in a suit, some guy in a checked shirt and yellow braces with a huge beard who's holding a camera and, finally, two other men and a woman, in what looks like her gym gear, stood around the bed. On the end of the sofa is a young guy with cropped, black hair, chiselled cheekbones and dazzling, blue eyes. He's wearing black skinny jeans, Converse and a white shirt, and I recognise him instantly as Alexander Steele. He looks up as we enter, and I have one of those strange moments where I want to say 'Oh hi, how are you?' because he looks so familiar I think I actually know him, when in reality he has no clue who I am. He stands and rubs his hands on his jeans before extending one to Jake.

'Jake, mate, how are you? Good to see you again.' He has the grace to look somewhat sheepish and gives a little, nervous laugh at the end.

'Alex,' Jake replies a little coolly. 'How have you been?' No one could miss the hint of sarcasm in his voice, and Alexander rubs his hands on his thighs again nervously.

'Look man, I'm really sorry about what happened. You know Cara,' he laughs, 'she's fucking mental. I don't know what got into her. I'm not one for trashing hotels, mate, you know me. Not with the movie coming out soon. I'm really fucking sorry.' He glances over to the guy in the suit who gives him a small, encouraging nod. 'We're going to sort you out with the damages and all that. I just wanted to clear the air, face-to-face. You've always been top-notch at keeping my stays private and looking after me.'

The more he speaks, the more I notice his British accent coming through. He might be a Hollywood A-lister but right now, in front of Jake, he looks like a naughty kid being forced to apologise to his head teacher. Jake's features are stony, as he pauses for a moment, but seems to recover himself and breaks out into a smile, even if it does look a little forced.

'Alex, I know how it gets. We love having you here, we really do, and I know how things get out of hand sometimes. No need to apologise further. We'll have our people mop it up, there'll be no repercussions from our side. I appreciate you taking the time out to come and have a chat.'

Alex looks to his team by the bed, and the woman and Anna exchange glances.

'I think we would like to get some photos, just to show all is well between the two camps, if that's OK with everyone?' says Anna, and the woman gives Anna a grateful nod. I realise that Alexander's team are working even harder than Jake's to keep his public image in favour. Suddenly, and for absolutely no reason at all, everyone turns to look at me. I'm not sure if they think I'm part of the photography team, but it's only then that it dawns on me that I should have left as soon as Alexander started talking. I was only supposed to come and meet him, not stay for the whole thing. But, in my defence, he didn't really give me much chance. Thankfully

Jake stands up and comes over to my side before turning back to Alexander.

'Alexander, I'd like you to meet Carrie Kingston. She's staying here with me for a couple of days.' I smile nervously and am glad when the rest of the room seems to spring back to life, organising furniture and lighting for the photos. As Alexander comes to greet me, his undeniably handsome face and boyish grin put me at ease straight away. He holds out his hand, and I take it.

'Carrie, nice to meet you. First time in Miami?'

Oh. My. God. This is Alexander Steele. The last time I saw this guy's face was in the bloody cinema, and me and Kate were swooning over how fit he was. He's got such a charm about him, and I find myself forgiving him for trashing the hotel room instantly. I mean, I think it was pretty much Cara Porter anyway, by the sounds of things. God, look at me, defending him. He clearly does know how to turn on the charm.

'Yes, first time. I'm only here for a couple of days, but I intend to make the most of it.'

I feel Jake's stare boring into me, but I deliberately ignore it, already knowing the exact look he'll have on his face.

'Wow, you're British!'

'That I am,' I laugh. 'From Warwickshire.'

'No way!' says Alexander animatedly. 'I was born in Birmingham. Not been back in a long time though,' he adds with a hint of sadness.

Out of the corner of my eye I see him get a signal from one of his team.

'Well, have a wicked trip won't you. Miami's great! And you're in good hands with this guy.' He jerks a thumb at Jake and gives me another flash of his Hollywood smile. 'Sorry, lovely to meet you. Excuse us won't you?'

He turns and strides across the room but not before he leans into Jake to whisper something, which I just manage to make out as 'Wow. Lucky guy.' He turns and gives me a wink. I manage to stop myself, just in time, before I start giggling like a schoolgirl. Jake lays a hand on my shoulder and runs it all the way down the length of my arm, then takes my hand in his.

'I'll see you later on. Please call me if you need anything.' He looks down at me, his eyes square on mine. 'I'm already looking forward to later.'

'Me too,' I say, just as Anna coughs impatiently and looks at her watch before giving me a glare.

'I'll come and get you at eight thirty, OK sweet cheeks?'

'I'll be ready,' I reply, feeling like there's a tense kind of anticipation in the air and time seems to slow for a moment. Jake breaks our gaze and turns to Anna.

'Can you show Carrie to the lift for me?'

I already know how well this is about to go down, so I step in before she can throw any comments my way, but she still manages to get out a derogatory huff.

'Jake, it's fine, I know where it is. I'll ask for Peter at reception, yeah?'

'OK. And yes, he's expecting you.'

'Thanks, I'll see you later.' And with that, I leave, without a second glance at Anna the Awful.

Chapter Twenty-Six

Peter, it turns out, is an absolute gem and our drive around Miami reminds me somewhat of my island tour with Michael. He's funny, easy to chat to and really good company.

'So I told him,' he bellows from the front seat, 'I don't care who you are, young man, you don't put your feet on my upholstery y'hear?'

It turns out the young man was in fact Leonardo DiCaprio, and he'd hurt his knee doing a stunt for his latest film. Peter's had me roaring with laughter for the whole car ride. So much so I was tempted to get him to just keep driving round and telling me his stories.

'You must have seen some things,' I say wiping my eyes. 'Who's the most famous person you've driven?'

'Once, back in the eighties, I had Muhammad Ali in the back of my limo. I worked for a private company back then, and I drove him from a press conference back to his hotel. I didn't talk to him, we had the screen up for most of the way, but he said hello to me, and I got a glimpse of him. Legend.' He shakes his head as if recalling the memory. 'They don't make 'em like that any more.'

'Wow, that's amazing. Sorry that you got stuck with just me today, not half as exciting, I imagine.'

'Well, you're the first girl Mr Holden's ever asked me take such good care of, so I'd say you're one of the biggest VIPs I've met.'

I open my mouth to reply but realise I don't have anything to say. Peter raises his head and catches my eye in the rear-view mirror. I can tell, from the creases at his eyes, that he's grinning, and I bite my lip, suppressing my own smile.

'That's alright, ma'am. I promise I won't tell him how you blushed.'

Peter drops me at the top of Ocean Drive, and we agree to meet back here in an hour. It's not long, but all I want to do is walk along one of the most famous streets in the world and soak it all in.

I walk on the street side, passing the art deco frontages of numerous hotels and street-side restaurants. There's a strong sea breeze but it's so warm, brushing the hairs on my skin so gently and blowing against my face. I suddenly feel a rush of pure affection towards Jake for bringing me here. The colours seem so much brighter, like everything is in high definition. So clear and crisp that it feels as if it's all been finely tuned.

I hear an almighty roar and spin my head in its direction behind me. A yellow Lamborghini blasting Latin rap comes into view, as it crawls down Ocean Drive. I feel like I should perhaps do some Miami bingo. Supercar, check.

I make my way further down the street and pause outside Versace's house. There are a number of people crowding in front the gates, on the steps and some even taking pictures. The house is beautiful, and I just enjoy staring at it in a quiet contemplation that life, is in fact, incredibly short.

I walk all the way down to the corner of Ocean Drive and 5th at the bottom of Lummus Park, which separates the beach from the road. I decide to walk back along the beach path and smile to myself, mentally ticking off my bingo card as I see an incredible, fit-looking couple on Rollerblades cruising down the pavement. Ah Miami, you're already so fun!

South Beach is perfect like I imagined. White sand, palms and tanned, toned bodies. I slip off my shoes and make my way to the beach, doing exactly as I did in Barbados and wriggling my toes deep into the sand. There. I've touched the sand on South Beach. I reach down and scoop up a handful, letting it run through my fingers and blow away back on to the beach.

I climb back to the path, which I want to call a promenade, but that just sounds way too British. Sidewalk? Promenade? I'll ask Peter. Speaking of which, I glance at my watch. Oops, I better start making my way back, I've only got just over ten minutes.

I turn my back to the land and look out to the sea. My little Warwickshire village seems a world away right now, and I can't even begin to consider how it might be when I eventually return. Except I know at some point I'll have to face it all. I just don't want to right now.

I meander back up to my meeting point with Peter ticking off a couple more Miami bingos off my list as I go (shirtless man jogging wearing headphones, woman in a thong on the beach). Before I reach the corner of Ocean and 13th I can see the black Mercedes pulled up waiting for me. It's a beautiful car, probably one of the fanciest I've been in, but out here, amongst the Hummers, Lamborghinis and Ferraris, it just looks like any other saloon. Peter is leaning against the bonnet, waiting for me, and opens my door, as I walk up beside it.

'Hello,' I say cheerily. 'Oh, thank you very much. You don't have to do that for me, you know?' I gesture to the open door but climb in anyway. Peter walks around to the driver's seat and starts the ignition.

'You'd better get used to this sort of treatment,' he replies and pulls off into the traffic.

'What do you mean?'

'Well, ma'am, if you're with Mr Holden, you won't be getting cabs anywhere any more.'

'Oh, we're not...' I start then stop myself. Perhaps I should just keep quiet, I'm sure Jake doesn't want all his personal life being chatted about across his hotels. When I first met him, I thought he was the handyman for God's sake. And he still feels like that down-to-earth guy. No ego, no showing off, no air of superiority. He's just Jake. Except that's what he is to me. Not to Peter, or Chad, or even Maya or Dale, although I know he considers the latter two as good friends too. Here in Miami, it all seems much more professional. But then I suppose it has to be what with things that have happened lately, and I remember he said this is where the head office is for the group so it's most certainly going to be a different feel to the one big, happy family vibe I get in Barbados.

I have to admit, being chauffeured around and staying in stunning hotel suites in exotic locations doesn't seem like much of a hardship right at this moment. Don't get used to it, Carrie, not real life. Not. Real. Life. OK, now that's not totally true because it is actually happening to me so this bit is very real. I just need to remember it's not forever.

I use the time in the car to soak up the city, and Peter doesn't interrupt my thoughts apart from to point out things coming up that I might want to see and, as we get closer to the hotel, I begin to think about the evening ahead with Jake.

This will be our first real date. I don't mean date. It's just dinner, no one's actually called it a date. Apart from me, just then. But we've spent plenty of time together, just the two of us, so I don't know why tonight's making me feel so nervous. Actually, I do. There seems to have been a slight shift in our relationship since the non-kiss. And I know I'm probably completely overthinking it, but I know I'm nervous because there's the prospect of an *actual* kiss. God, get over yourself, Carrie! I'm sure he can manage to resist you. But a niggle in the back of my mind asks can I resist him? And more importantly, do I want to?

'Ma'am? Ma'am, are y'alright now?' I can suddenly hear Peter's voice.

'Peter, gosh I'm so sorry, I was absolutely miles away.' I have no idea why I've suddenly become very British. Jolly good show, Peter, simply marvellous journey! Bravo!

'That's alright, ma'am.' He steps out of the car and comes around to open my door. I manage to regain my manners and sense of propriety.

'Thank you so much. I had a really nice afternoon. Thanks for being my impromptu tour guide.'

He doffs an invisible chauffeur's hat towards me and gives me a huge grin.

'It's been my pleasure. Mr Holden keeps excellent company, I'll give him that.'

'That's very kind of you to say so, thank you,' I laugh. 'Speaking of which,' I nod towards the sliding doors of the hotel, 'I should go. We're having dinner at eight thirty.'

'Good evening to you, ma'am. All the best now.'

I see Peter beckon to one of the doormen, and they shake hands before they begin chatting together. I make my way up to my room, passing by Jake's door and pausing briefly. I lean towards the door and listen to see if I can hear anything, but it's silent. I jump out of my skin at the loud *BING!* that sounds as the lift doors open and two young girls, no older than sixteen, step out, chattering away, arms laden with bags of shopping. They smile at me on the way past and, as they swipe into one of the suites at the end of the corridor, I hear one of them shout, 'MOM! DADDY! You're not going to *believe* who we saw in American Apparel.'

Ah, what it was to be sixteen, when the only thing you had to worry about was which Hollywood A-lister you were going to bump into on Miami Beach before traipsing back to your five-star suite. I laugh to myself then think back to my own sixteen-year-old self, a world away from these girls.

I was with Luke when I was sixteen. That seems like such a long time ago. Although, to be fair, last week seems like a long time ago now. The time when I was going to marry Luke seems like a totally different life that happened to someone else. It feels like that girl wasn't me at all. People say that when you've been with someone so long, you grow into one person, is that what happened to me? Did I stop being Carrie and became just Carrie-and-Luke? And not in a good, 'look how perfect they are for each other' sort of way but more of a 'I've not been able to grow up as my own person' sort of way. I guess my relationship with Luke has defined most of who I am up until now, and it might sound totally dramatic, but coming away feels like I've finally been allowed to be my own person and make my own choices. And right now, I'm choosing to put on my best little black dress and have dinner at a fancy restaurant with Jake.

I can't seem to do anything to quell the nervous anticipation I feel as I wait for Jake to knock on my door. I've smoothed my dress down a million times and keep fiddling with the clips holding back my hair. It's hot, but I've chosen to leave it down with a few pins pulling the front off my face. Again, thanks to my tan, I've managed to get away with minimal make-up, so I just slapped on a bit of highlighter and mascara with a splodge of Vaseline on my lips. I pop out to the balcony and take a quick selfie with the view in the background to send to Rachel. I notice another two messages but ignore them, knowing I've already texted my mum and she knows I'm OK. I plug in my phone by my bed just as I see a reply come back from Rachel.

OMG you look so hot! Have fun and promise NOT to behave yourself! LOL! Text me later with aaaaaall the details, lady… kiss, kiss, kiss! X x x

I grin and put my phone on the bedside cabinet, flicking it on to silent. This is the time I miss my old flip phone, it feels much less satisfying pressing a little button than slamming it shut in satisfaction. Maybe, now I think about it, that's why mine only lasted about six months.

A knock on the door makes me jump out of my skin. Jesus, Carrie, calm down. I'm a nervous wreck, but as soon as I open the door and see Jake's huge smile I relax. He's wearing a navy shirt, grey, slim fit trousers and brogues. He looks, and smells, divine. Suddenly his smile drops, and his mouth hangs open.

'Oh God, is it too much?' I mumble, smoothing my hands over my dress again. 'I can change, I have something less formal.' As I begin to turn back to the room, my face burning in a million mixed emotions, he gently grasps my arm, stopping me.

'No… no,' he stutters. 'You look incredible.' He pulls me into him, as if it's the most natural thing in the world, and kisses my cheek. 'Incredible,' he repeats, before his face becomes plastered in a smile again. We both stand grinning at each other like a pair of idiots, as I soak up his compliment.

'Well thanks,' I say, twiddling the ends of my hair, 'you don't look too shabby yourself.'

'Not too shabby?' he says with mock outrage, as he plays with his cufflinks and rolls his shoulders. 'I borrowed this shirt from Alexander Steele since you seem to fancy him so much. Thought it might not hurt my chances.'

I burst out laughing. 'You did not borrow it from him! For one, you're much bigger than him and two... OK, there isn't a two, but I know you didn't.'

'Oh, so you've been comparing our bodies, hey? I best get down the gym.'

I roll my eyes, and he laughs.

'And I do not fancy him,' I say, as I step out of the suite and close the door behind me.

'OK, so I didn't borrow it from him. And good. I'm glad you don't fancy him.' He pauses and lets me lead the way to the lift. 'Because he fancies you.'

I frown and look at Jake.

'What? Don't be ridiculous, no he doesn't!'

'Oh no, he does,' Jake says, totally serious. 'He told me. When you left, and after all the photos, we were chatting and he asked me how long we'd been together.'

'He didn't?' I say giggling at Alexander presuming we were a couple. 'And what did you say?'

'I said two years, and we were madly in love, and I was going to ask you to marry me.'

I punch him on the arm, but he playfully dodges it and grabs my hand kissing my knuckles.

'Jake! You did not?'

'Oh yes I did,' he says with a wicked glint in his eye. 'Then he said that he wanted to check before he asked for your number because, if he didn't mind me saying so, he thought you were sexy as hell. His words, not mine. Although I happen to wholeheartedly, one hundred per cent, agree.'

My whole face turns pink, and I can feel the heat spreading through my chest. I bite on my lip and not because Alexander Steele thinks I'm sexy as hell (although that's a bit of a confidence booster), but because Jake does.

We take the lift to the ground floor, and the warm breeze hits me as soon as we cross the lobby and go through the doors to outside. Jake's hand is on the small of my back, again, gently guiding me the whole time. Although he still makes my skin prickle with electricity every time he touches me, I'm getting more and more used to his tactile ways and am finding I miss it on the times he's *not* touching me, even though I still can't control my constant blushing.

Jake stops, as we reach the street in front of a gleaming, bright red Ferrari, which I presume belongs to one of the guests. I push my hair out of my face and turn to Jake.

'Are we going with Peter? He's great, by the way, you do have excellent taste in staff.'

'I'm afraid you're stuck with me tonight, no Peter. In fact, I thought when in Miami…'

He stops, and I follow his gaze to the Ferrari in front of us, as I realise what he's planned. I can't help myself, as a grin spreads across my face from ear to ear. I let out a bark of laughter.

'You didn't?'

'I did,' he says, rubbing his hands together, as a young valet from the hotel runs down the steps and holds out a key to Jake. With a satisfying *beep, beep,* he opens the car and repeats even louder, 'Oh, I did!'

I do a little hop from foot to foot, throwing back my head in more laughter.

'Can I just say, this is completely brilliant and totally cringeworthy, all at the same time. And I love it!'

'I'm glad,' says Jake, clearly so happy that I've taken this gesture in the right spirit. 'In you hop.' He nods to the door that's being held open for me and adds, with a wiggle of his eyebrows, 'I'm driving. We have a car to pick us up later. Peter was more than happy to let me take this if it meant he could come and drive it back. I think we both deserve a drink.'

'Sounds good to me. But there is no way I will be hopping into this. You may have to get me out with a winch at the other end.' As ladylike as I can manage, I wriggle myself in the low, bucket seat and feel like I'm almost lying on the floor. I clip in my seat belt, as Jake takes his seat next to me, firing the ignition and the engine roars to life. I let out a small squeal of excitement, as we pull off at what feels like full throttle. Not that I know anything about cars, except that this one is very fast and very expensive.

'So you like your surprise?' Jake asks, grinning as he takes the car through the Miami streets with a cool confidence.

'I do. In spite of myself, I love it.' A thought suddenly dawns on me. 'Jake... is... is this *yours*?'

He grins. 'Is what mine?' he asks innocently.

'It is, isn't it? Oh my God!' I get a fit of the giggles, and he joins in with my laughter.

'What can I say?' he shrugs his shoulders. 'It was a childhood dream of mine. As a kid, all I ever wanted was a red Ferrari. It was *the* car. I watched my dad work his ass off for years, followed his work ethic and when I could, I bought one. It was a gift to ten-year-old me. I leave her here though, because there is really nowhere else I could drive her, except maybe Dubai if and when we open there. Now that's something I'm excited about.'

'A new car or Dubai?' I ask, and he laughs.

'Mainly Dubai, but yes, also maybe the car a little bit.'

'I didn't have you down as a petrolhead.'

'I'm really not, you've seen me in Barbados. I like to...' he searches for the word, '...blend in.'

'I'm not sure, looking at you, you blend in anywhere, Baywatch,' I say with a wry smile.

'I guess in Miami, even a red Ferrari doesn't stand out *that* much.'

'Well, I like her,' I say, stroking the dashboard which earns a laugh from Jake.

'I like her too,' he agrees. 'Maybe I'll call her Carrie.'

'Don't you dare!' I say, and he lets out another roar of laughter.

'I don't think I've ever laughed as much as I do when I'm with you, sweet cheeks.' He reaches over and takes my hand briefly before returning it to the gearstick.

'Yes, but at me or with me?'

'Oh, definitely with you. That's what makes it so great.'

As I process his words, I realise I've never really been complimented by a man. I'm sure Luke said some nice things to me in his time but, right now, I can't remember one of them. For some reason they all seem to mean so much more coming from Jake. Maybe because they just feel like he really means them, and not like he's saying them because he feels it's the right thing to do.

'So, where are we going?' I ask, as we drive across the water, and I recognise that we are heading back towards the South Beach area.

'Prime 112, it's a steakhouse at the end of Ocean. It's classic Miami scene.'

'How do you mean?'

'Well, let's just say the Ferrari will fit in perfectly. But I figured, in for a penny, in for a pound. The food is great, and you usually get some celebs in there, so I thought it might be fun for tonight. Plus, I know the manager, so he always gets me a good table and looks after me.' Miami bingo, flashy restaurant, check!

'Do you go there a lot then?' I'm really hoping this isn't some sort of date night special I'm being taken on, that hundreds of other girls have seen.

'Not socially, no, but I bring work business here a lot. Out-of-towners like it because it's so well known.'

'Well, you know me, I love a Hollywood A-lister,' I say, deliberately trying to wind him up after he thought I fancied Alexander. I give him a sideways glance to see him fighting a smile, trying not to rise to the bait.

'Clearly I'm going to have to try much harder than a fast car and a swanky restaurant to float your boat, Miss Kingston.'

'Boats! Ooh, now you're talking!' I say with a laugh. 'Seriously though, I think you know I'm more than happy with a plate of chips on the beach.'

'I do. And that's why I adore you so.'

His words send a rush of butterflies through me as I take them in. I'm sure it was just a passing turn of phrase, but I can't stop running them through my mind until we arrive at the restaurant. Which, incidentally, is absolutely buzzing with people. There are Hummers, limousines and some other very expensive-looking sports cars that I have no idea what they are.

'Wow. You weren't kidding, were you?' I say to Jake, as he pulls up in a space dedicated to valet parking in front of the restaurant. He gets out, and hands his keys to a valet, before coming to my side and helping me out of the car. Which has him laughing hysterically, as I pretty much have to roll out on to the pavement, with him catching me, before he stands me upright again.

'Next time warn me not to wear such a tight dress,' I huff, as we make our way into the restaurant.

'Absolutely not,' says Jake, his eyes twinkling as they wander over my outfit. He starts chatting to the first member of staff we see, shaking his hand with gusto. The music is loud in here, especially for a restaurant, and I'm surprised by its humble, painted wood exterior. I expected something much more in your face but, once inside, I see why Jake said it was flashy. The place is heaving with people, some sat at tables, but many crowded around the bar waiting for a table. It's dimly lit with low lights casting a soft glow across its many patrons, and a heavy, deep bassline thrums out of the speakers. The whole place is quite intoxicating. We're escorted to a table at the far corner of the restaurant, and I take the seat with my back to the wall facing out to the restaurant whilst Jake sits opposite me.

'Sorry,' I say, 'I took the best seat.'

His eyebrows raise ever so slightly.

'I think you'll find I have the best seat in the house, sweet cheeks.'

I bring my eyes back to meet his and feel a jolt inside of me. I clear my throat and drag my eyes away to the menu.

'What do you recommend?'

'To be honest, it's all good, but the steaks are pretty damn special.'

'Hmm, I had steak at the hotel earlier.' I scroll my eyes down the menu and try to take it all in but, for some reason, I'm having a hard time concentrating tonight. 'I think I'll have the salmon,' I say closing my menu with an air of finality. 'I can't manage a starter after lunch.'

Our waiter comes over, and I watch as Jake chooses a suitable wine from the list.

'I'll have the steak, so you can try some,' he says, relaying his order to the waiter, who confirms how Jake would like his steak cooked (medium rare), and it doesn't pass me by that he takes it the same as me. Or did he just say that so I can try some? Before I have a chance to ask, the waiter turns to me expectantly.

'I'll have the salmon please.'

He nods to us both with a 'Sir. Madam.' and hurries off. I fiddle with my knife and fork, realigning them on top of the napkin, even though they were perfectly straight already. I look up at Jake, and he's watching me with a huge grin.

'You've come on a date with me.'

I roll my eyes and try to stop myself from grinning back.

'This isn't a date,' I say calmly, my insides churning like a washing machine.

'Oh, sweet cheeks, I think you'll find it is.'

'I've never been on a date,' I say simply, and Jake's eyes fly open in shock.

'What?'

I shrug, realising that it probably is a bit weird getting to my age and not having been on a first date. 'Well Luke and I were so young, we just sort of, hung out. We didn't go on a first date, like this, or anything.'

'Ah, so you admit it's a first date.' Jake pounces on my words as soon as they're out of my mouth. 'And by first date it implies there will be a second.'

I look at him and can't help but smile. His mouth is curling at the edges, and something in his yellow eyes glints at me. His blonde hair is pushed back giving me a clear view of his ridiculously handsome face that, tonight, is almost clean-shaven but just showing signs of short stubble. I wonder if the novelty of his face will ever wear off. God, he's sexy. I try to stop conjuring up images of him with his shirt off.

'Well, I guess that depends how tonight goes, doesn't it?' I say brazenly, taking a sip from the glass of water the waiter filled for us as we sat down.

'Oh, challenge well and truly accepted.' And his face displays his semi-permanent air of absolute shamelessness.

'So did today go well?' I ask, instantly feeling a little like a nineteen fifties housewife, and wish I hadn't.

'I suppose so, yes. I don't really like all this PR bullshit which is why Anna gets so frustrated with me half the time. I just want an easy life, but I suppose my job pretty much rules that out. But no, today was good, I'm glad I came. And I'm extra glad that you came, you're the perfect end to my day.'

He reaches over the table to take my hand, and I just enjoy the feel of his hand on mine for a moment. I don't feel as self-conscious here as I do in Barbados. I'm not worrying about what anyone else might think. Here, we're just two people out on a date. People might even think we're a couple, and my insides warm a little at the thought before I push that idea out of my mind. Just dinner, Carrie. It's just dinner.

'What do you think of Miami?' Jake asks, as the waiter comes over and pours him a taste of the wine. Jake nods, and he fills my glass before placing the bottle in a bucket next to us.

'I love it. It's so… bright,' I say enthusiastically.

'Bright?' Jake laughs. 'What exactly does bright mean?'

'I don't know,' I say giggling at my own phrase. 'Just everything here seems so rich, and not just in money terms. Am I making any sense at all? Well anyway, to sum up, I love it. And I know I only had a few hours here, but it was perfect to just wander and take it all in. And the hotel is amazing, by the way.' I take a breath and grin at him.

'Do you like it?' Jake asks, clearly buoyed by my compliment and thankfully ignoring my rambling. 'I wasn't sure about it at first, but people seem to love the whole design and theme of it.'

'What? That's my favourite bit!' I interrupt him loudly, raising a curt look from the table next to us. 'I love the suites and the colour themes. I think it's brilliant. Who came up with that, by the way?'

I take a sip of wine, and Jake mirrors my action and does the same. It's cold and crisp and, as it slides down my throat, I feel another rush of intense joy.

'How's the wine? Do you like it?' he asks, almost as an aside to our conversation.

'It's excellent, thank you.' I take another sip. 'Going down far too easily.'

'Good, tonight is all about you.' I can feel his gaze burning into me, as I try to look anywhere but at him. I realise he's taken hold of my hand again.

'So you like the hotel?' he says gently after what feels like the longest pause in the history of pauses.

'It's brilliant, I love my room. So was it your idea?'

'It was. I don't know why, but I always loved the idea of different rooms being different colours. To be honest, my dad thought it was ridiculous when I mentioned it to him years ago, but people seem to love it. My favourite is yours, of course, and I did like *Rage* but that's been kind of tainted now.'

I wince slightly at the grim look on his face.

'Is it bad? Have you seen it?'

'It's pretty bad,' Jake replies with a heavy sigh, as he drains his wine glass before pouring another and filling up mine as he continues. 'There's no structural damage, and some of the furniture can be saved, but all the décor will have to be redone. Plus the bathroom mirrors are both smashed. God knows how. And two of the tiles on the bathroom floor have been cracked, so it's likely we will have to redo the whole lot. It's fixable, and the insurance will pay out, but it's just the hassle. And our bloody reputation.'

'But you've smoothed it out, right? With Alexander I mean?'

'Yeah, and he's said that if it gets mentioned in any interviews, which I mean, come on, that's the first thing they're going to ask about, right? He said he'll mention how great the hotel was and try and give us as much free publicity as he can drum up. And the good kind this time, the sort we actually want. Anna's already managed to line up a fashion shoot in some of the rooms for one of the big glossies, I forget which she said, that's happening next week, and we've got Lissy Davis booked in for a few nights next month too which will help. I guess I can't complain too much, I just want everyone to know it's business as usual. And that usual isn't movie stars and models doing drugs in my fucking hotel.' He rubs his hand over his face. 'Sorry, rant over. I won't mention work again, I promise.' He links his fingers in mine across the table, and I let him.

'Don't be silly. I asked. I want to hear about your day. I like hearing about your job, it's novel to me, I've never met anyone who runs a hotel chain, and it's completely different from what I do. Lissy Davis, well that's good exposure for you, and she's perfect for the kind of publicity you need right now I'd say.' Lissy Davis is the teen pop queen who's taking over the world one sickly-sweet melody at a time, but she's a super wholesome, all-American, Christian girl who is more angelic than Britney, you know, pre head shaving and umbrella wielding, obviously.

'Tell me more about your job,' Jake says, the stress on his face visibly melting away. 'I seem to do nothing but talk about the hotels with you. I want to know about your work.' He turns my hand over on the table, exposing my wrist, and begins drawing small circles ever so slowly with his index finger. It's incredibly distracting, and I feel a rush of heat run through my body as he trails his finger around and around. I struggle to focus on his question, and he notices.

'Sorry, am I putting you off?' Jake asks with another one of his devour-you-whole looks. I can't seem to tear my eyes away from his, as he moves his fingers up my arm to the sensitive crook of my elbow. I feel my heartbeat quicken.

'You always seem to put me off,' I say slowly feeling each brush of his fingertips on my skin.

'And you me.' His voice is thick and low. 'Sweet cheeks, I think by now, you know how much I want...'

'Salmon?'

What? Did he just say salmon? I barely register the person beside me, until I realise it's the waiter looking at me expectantly.

'Salmon. Right, yes. Yes please!' I say, all too enthusiastically.

I can see Jake's mouth curling into a smile, as the waiter places his steak in front of him and hurries off. Jake's face is full of suppressed laughter, and just the sight of it makes me grin.

'Oh, stop it,' I say, 'you're disgraceful.'

We stare at each other, both knowing his unfinished sentence hangs heavy in the air. I'm pretty sure he was going to say what I can't even imagine him saying right now, but my pulse is racing nonetheless. I decide to risk it.

'So,' I clear my throat, 'you were saying?'

He pauses briefly, his fork halfway to his mouth before popping in a piece of steak and chewing ever so slowly. I watch him swallow and take a sip of wine. The whole, usually mundane, process has me mesmerised. I can't take my eyes off him.

'Was I? It's completely slipped my mind,' he says playfully, it not having slipped his mind one little bit. 'Perhaps you could remind me?' I decide to play him at his own game.

'Oh, I think it was about you wanting something?'

Jake fills our glasses and returns the bottle to the wine bucket. He regards me for a moment, his head tilted, a smile playing on his lips, before he picks up his knife and fork and slices off a small piece of steak, spearing it on to his fork. He leans over the table, holding the fork out to me. I look at him, my face not giving anything away, even though I can feel my skin prickling all over my body. I lean forward and, oh-so slowly, open my mouth. Without taking his eyes off mine, he places the steak on my tongue, as I close my lips around it. I sink my teeth into the soft flesh and chew it, savouring its taste, before swallowing, keeping my eyes on Jake the whole time.

His mouth is slightly open, his face a mixture of shock, pleasure and an unmistakable look of desire. He drops his fork on the plate with a huge clatter, earning us a few questioning looks from the other diners. He pushes back his chair and stands up abruptly, taking a step towards me, and yanks my hand, tugging me out of my chair. He pushes his body into mine, and I forget we are in the middle of a restaurant and that everyone is probably staring at us. He lowers his face until we are nose-to-nose and slowly tilts his head, so his lips are millimetres from my mouth.

I can feel his breath warm on my lips, and I'm breathing heavily in time with his own deep, slow breaths, and he pushes his hand into my hair. Then, just as sudden as it happened, he lets me go and sits back in his chair, draining his glass of wine. I sit down and do the same.

Did that just happen? Did we just have our second non-kiss? Jake's yellow eyes are boring into mine, as we steady our breathing. Neither of us speaks for a moment before he reaches for my hand once more, his now oh-so familiar fingers tracing their usual path along my knuckles.

'I don't ever want to do anything to make you feel uncomfortable, sweet cheeks. You know you can trust me, but I hope you know I struggle to keep myself in check when I'm around you. I can't explain it, to you, me or anyone else for that matter. It's as if we're already connected on a level I can't even begin to make sense of.' He pushes his hair out his face with his free hand and fixes his gaze on me again. 'I know the situation you've left behind, and this is not, for one moment, about me, it's all about you. But I won't stay away from you, not unless you tell me to. I can't.' The noise of the restaurant drowns out, and it's just me and him. 'Just so we are both clear on what I possibly could want.'

Something grips tight in my stomach, and I know then. I know what I want. I push my plate away.

'I suddenly don't feel very hungry,' I say quietly, and Jake's head shoots up, a look of fear on his face that he's gone too far. I stand up and hold my hand out to him. He pauses for a moment before he takes it and stands to meet me. I reach up on my tiptoes and whisper in his ear, breathing in his scent and feeling the briefest brush of his face against mine. 'Let's go.'

Chapter Twenty-Seven

As we leave the restaurant I stand patiently by Jake's side, as he speaks to our waiter. I watch as he hands over a black Amex card, and he shakes his hand to reassure him that there isn't anything wrong with the meal, but our plans have changed unexpectedly and we have to leave. I wonder if he needs to call our car but, sure enough, when we leave the restaurant, the valet points us in the direction of the black Mercedes just across the road.

Our driver, who I don't recognise, steps aside and holds open my door to let me in before Jake and I settle in the back seat. My earlier bravado has been replaced with a barrel of nerves, and I'm surprised Jake can't hear my heart beating. It feels as if it's about to burst out of my chest, it's pounding so hard.

As we pull away, Jake takes my hand but continues to look out of the window and doesn't make eye contact with me for the rest of the journey. We sit in silence for the entire drive back, neither of us speaking a single word, but the air between us is charged with a tangible energy. I stay rooted to my seat, as Jake gets out and our driver comes to open my door.

Jake takes my hand again to help me out of the car, and our eyes meet for the first time since we left the restaurant. My stomach lurches, as he leads me inside, and we make our way across the lobby to the lift, where he presses the button and the doors spring immediately open. We step inside, standing side by side, millimetres away from each other, but just far enough so that our bodies aren't touching. We stay looking forward until we reach our floor, where I chance a small sideways glance at Jake, careful to move only my eyes, not my head.

We walk down the corridor, and his hand gently skims down my back, guiding me towards our suites. We reach his first, and he pauses, as if giving me a moment to reconsider. But I don't need to. I take a step towards my door, pulling out my key card and turning the handle. I turn to look at Jake in silence. He's stood a few paces away from me, outside his own suite, waiting for my next move. I push open the door and hold it ajar, as I keep my eyes on him, my intention loud and clear. He hesitates for the smallest second before walking towards me and stepping inside.

I shut the door behind me and turn, expecting to see Jake making his way across the room, but he's stood right behind me and the second the door clicks into its frame, his lips are on mine. My entire body thrums with desire as a million bolts surge through me, and I realise how much I've been longing for this, as our kiss becomes more urgent, more desperate.

He gently pushes me back against the door, and his hands are at my face as I place mine at his waist, taking in his huge frame, and I open my mouth to his. This time there is no mistaking. This is a kiss.

He lowers his hand to my waist and pulls me towards him, his other hand finding the back of my head, as he laces his fingers into my hair at the nape of my neck and gently pulls my head back exposing my throat.

He takes his lips from mine and trails a soft, gentle line of kisses down from my ear and across my collarbone, as I let out a long, languid breath. I bury my face in his neck as, unexpectedly, he lifts me in the air, my arms gripping around his body, and carries me across the room, placing me upright at the foot of the enormous bed. I stand on my tiptoes and link my hands around the back of his head, as he kisses me again, slower this time, his tongue gently skimming over my bottom lip. He reaches round and as his fingers find the zip of my dress, he pauses and looks at me carefully before he speaks, the first thing either of us have said since we left the restaurant.

'Sweet cheeks, is this OK? I've told you, I won't do anything you're not comfortable with.'

'This is more than OK.'

'There is no point of no return, alright? If you want to stop, we will. Immediately.'

'Please,' I say, my voice thick with longing, 'don't stop.' And I pull his head down to mine to kiss him again, reaffirming my words.

This is all the signal he needs as, ever so slowly, he pulls down the zip of my dress, and I roll it off my shoulders. On a surge of newly awakened confidence, I push him back so he's watching me, and I pull down my dress, letting it pool on the floor at my feet and leaving me facing him in nothing but my heels and underwear.

Jake lets out a small moan of appreciation, and he reaches for me, his face buried in my neck, his hands skimming down my back, stopping just short of my black, lace thong. The feel of his hands on my body has me reeling with desire. I'm desperate for him, aching for his touch.

I run my hands down his shirt setting to work on undoing his buttons. My hands are shaking slightly, as I fumble in my haste to rid him of his shirt and feel him, skin to skin. I push it back off his broad, tanned shoulders and, even though I've seen his body plenty around the pool and beach, it still surprises me just how perfect it is. I reach out and run my hand over his abs, and I see his lips form the beginnings of a smile. He puts his hand over mine and moves it to the middle of his chest, holding it there for a moment, before he takes it to his lips and kisses my fingertips in the most tender and gentle way. I take my hand and lift it to his face, as he takes a step towards me, closing the distance between us.

'You're incredible,' Jake says, as he takes his hand to my back and unhooks my bra, sliding it down my arms and letting it drop to the floor. I stand here before him, a small scrap of lace is all that's left of my clothes, and I feel no shame whatsoever. This is the first time I've let a man see me like this, and I always thought I would feel embarrassed but here, with Jake, I feel the exact opposite. I feel beautiful, but it's more than just that, I feel sexy.

I step out of my heels, and we smile at the now even bigger height difference between us. His hands slowly skim the curves of my naked breasts, and my breath hitches in my throat, as I feel a pang of lust rush through me. His hands settle on my waist, and he lifts me on to the bed behind us, placing his hands either side of my head, as I unzip his trousers, and he kicks them off on to the floor.

Our eyes meet as his hair hangs around his face while he gazes down at me, framing his intense, golden yellow eyes that are burning into my own. It causes a ripple of heat to flash down my body settling somewhere just below the waistband of my knickers.

I feel Jake hook his thumbs into the waistband of my thong and slowly pull it down over my legs. He pauses to take in the sight of me, naked, lying on the bed in front of him, eager and wanting. He hesitates briefly once again, to check he's not crossing a line, before he pulls down his boxers, stepping out of them and moving back on to the bed, gently nudging my knees apart with his own. His body presses down against mine, and he hoists me further up the bed, our breathing quick and heavy. He leans back, reaching into his trousers for his wallet before I hear the rip of a condom packet, and I watch as he rolls it down over him. Jake takes his hand to my face and strokes it so softly, so tenderly, that I feel tears spring to my eyes causing him to freeze instantly and lift his weight slightly.

'Carrie, I… If this isn't OK…?'

I lift my head pressing my mouth hard against his, my tongue pushing gently between his lips, feeling gratified when he responds in the same way.

'It's perfect,' I say on an exhale of breath, which catches in the back of my throat, as he lowers himself down towards me, and I feel him slowly and gently easing into me. He lets out a low, guttural moan, giving me a moment for my body to accept him, before he begins to move. A slow but purposeful rhythm as our bodies move in perfect sync, our mouths clashing and my pulse racing.

I lose myself in him, totally and completely, my mind and every fibre of my body full of only him. His touch, his taste, his smell, the way his body feels against mine, his breath against my skin. Every second is a moment of complete ecstasy.

He takes one of his hands from beside my head and slides it between us, roaming over my breasts and tucks it beneath me, briefly cupping my bottom before he winds it around my waist and draws me to him, driving deeper inside me, as he quickens his pace. I wrap my legs around him and splay my hands across his shoulders. Time stands still as we move, it could be one minute or one hour, my mind is dizzy and body feels more alive than I ever thought possible.

'Jake,' I whisper, as a warning, as I feel myself building, his movements taking me higher and higher until I'm teetering on the edge. 'Jake,' I cry more urgently.

'You are so beautiful,' he murmurs into my hair. Each stroke he makes takes me closer, and I feel his body tense. 'Carrie…'

And hearing my name on his lips is the final nudge over the edge, and I can't hold it any longer. The spiral of desire releases, as I feel a million volts course through me, sending me dizzy with pleasure just as I feel Jake thrust forward, his body rigid, before he stills, and we lie, our breathing ragged, our hearts pounding, entwined on the bed.

'Well, that was quite a first date,' Jake says, as we lie face-to-face on the bed, my skin still tingling, and Jake's damp hair, flopping down into his eyes.

'Well, it was very good steak,' I counter, and he bursts out laughing.

'Oh, so you only slept with me to get to my dinner?'

I prop myself up on my elbows and lean down to plant a kiss on his mouth, not quite believing I'm somehow in a position to do so.

'I think we both know that's not true. But I must say, I am totally starving.'

'Now that I can fix,' he says and pads across the room. He picks up the phone and reels off a mammoth list of food before replacing the receiver and heading back towards me. I watch his naked body greedily, his firm bum, the tanned, muscular back, his enormous shoulders. I tilt my head and grin to myself, biting my lip, and my eyes follow him back to the bed.

'Enjoying the view were we?' he says with raised eyebrows.

'Maybe,' I say with a shrug, despite us both knowing the ship has well and truly sailed for me to be playing it coy. He dives back on to the bed and rolls on top of me, pinning me to the mattress by the wrists.

'You,' he says, through a huge ear-to-ear grin, as he nips at my neck with his teeth, 'are fucking perfect.'

I let out a giggle and, in this moment, I feel the happiest I can ever remember.

'Anything you want in particular?' Jake asks, as he continues to work his way down my skin, tantalisingly close to my breasts.

'Hmm,' I murmur contently, 'are we talking food or otherwise?'

'I don't see why it has to be either or…' he purrs into my bare skin. He releases one of my wrists, and his hand travels over my chest, down past my waist, and settles at the top of my thighs, causing my knees to fall ever so slightly apart. My body bows to meet the touch of his hand, and I'm propelled right back into a world of pleasure under his languorous, rhythmic touch.

There's something about the way he touches my body. He makes me feel I have nothing to hide, nothing to be ashamed of, and I find myself losing any previous inhibitions, growing more confident and feeling sexier than I have ever felt. After sex with Luke, I was rushing to pull my underwear and pyjamas back on but here, with Jake, I don't feel the urgent need to cover up my body and am quite happy, more than happy, to lie here, totally sated, for the second time, skin to skin, with him.

'So…' I say, not even really sure where I'm going.

'So indeed,' Jake replies, grinning. 'You OK?'

I'm touched that he feels the need to keep checking I'm alright with the speed at which things seem to have escalated, although I can't deny I haven't wondered, on more than one occasion, what this would be like.

'Honestly, there is nowhere I would rather be right now. Thank you for being so…' I search for the word, 'I don't know… so… so *you*.' Jake laughs and kisses my forehead.

'OK, now I don't know if that's a good or a bad thing.'

'Definitely good.' My hearts swells with affection for him, and I struggle to keep myself from letting out a little sob.

'Hey,' he says softly, 'what is it? I have to say, making someone cry after sex isn't usually considered a good thing. My confidence is taking a bashing here.'

I giggle. 'Oh, I'm being ridiculous, I just… God, you're going to think I'm some sort of nutter, but when I'm with you none of the other crap seems to matter. You just make everything feel so…'

'Good?' Jake suggests.

I pull back from him and look into his eyes. 'Yes,' I say honestly, 'good.'

'I know. Because that's exactly how I feel. I'm not going anywhere, sweet cheeks. I want you to know that.'

'Yes, but I am.'

Jake kisses me again. 'Let's not think about that now.' He rolls out of the bed and moves towards the bathroom. 'Back in a mo.'

Just as the bathroom door closes there's a knock on the door of the suite. I glance around nervously, suddenly aware of my nakedness, even though there's a door between me and the person on the other side. Unsure what to grab, as Jake's in the bathroom with the hotel issued dressing gown, I pull on his shirt and wrap it around me. I expect to see a huge table of room service so find it very hard to hide my shock and horror when I come face-to-face with, none other than, Alexander Steele.

'Well, hello!' he says gleefully, giving me a full once-over and leaning on the door frame. 'I was looking for Jake but, I must say, you're a much better surprise.'

My face turns instantly pink, and I cross my legs, pulling Jake's shirt tighter around me.

'I thought this was his suite?'

'No, his is next door.' I'm unsure what to say to Alexander, who will surely be wondering by now that if Jake and I are a couple then why the hell aren't we sharing a room, but I quickly realise he seems much more interested in my current state of undress than our sleeping arrangements. 'But, he's actually here so…'

'I can come in and wait, if you'd like?' He gives me a lopsided smile and raises his eyebrows.

'No need.' Jake's voice comes from behind me, as he places both hands on my shoulders. I glance back at him, his face stony, his chest bare and a white towel hanging from his hips. 'I'm here now, how can I help?'

He physically takes a step in between me and Alexander, shielding me from his eyes, but Alexander just grins even harder.

'Just wanted to stop and say bye, mate. My schedule's changed, so we're getting the red-eye to London tonight instead of tomorrow. And y'know, thanks for being so sound about everything, yeah?' His turn of phrase is undeniably British, and he holds his hand out to Jake, who takes it somewhat grudgingly.

'Not a problem, always a pleasure to have you here.'

'Pleasure's all mine,' drawls Alexander, as he leans brazenly to one side to peer round Jake's bulk causing him to shuffle in front of me another inch or so.

Alexander lets out a small chuckle and raises his hand.

'See you again soon, mate. Take it easy, yeah?' Then in my direction with a wink he adds, 'G'night, sugar.'

Jake shuts the door with more force than is quite necessary and rounds on me, his eyes blazing, as he raises his brows.

'I believe that's my shirt,' he says, his deep voice resonating through me.

'Well, he liked it,' I giggle and sprint past him to the other side of the room before he can grasp me, the shirt slipping through his fingers as I bolt past him.

'Oh, I see.' He stalks across the room, fixing his towel and making his way towards me, his mouth turning upwards into a smile. 'You won't win.'

I jump on the bed and he laughs.

'It's almost like you're trying to get caught.'

'Maybe I am,' I pout at him and, with a new-found flurry of confidence, I peel off his shirt and throw it at him, laughing in delight at the stunned look on his face.

We both freeze at the sound of a loud knock on the door and a cry of, 'Room service!'

'Give me your shirt!' I say in a panicked voice.

'Ha! Not a chance!'

My eyes dart around looking for another suitable option, but I can't see my dress from earlier or anything else.

'Oh, for God's sake!' I hiss at Jake, jumping off the bed and sprinting into the bathroom, as he howls with laughter behind me. I close the door and can hear Jake making small talk, as the table clatters into the room. I unhook a dressing gown from the back of the door and snuggle into it catching a glance of myself in the mirror. I stare at myself. I still look the same, I'm not different in any way. Except that I am, I *feel* different. I just had sex with my second man *ever* and it was the most intense, sexy, mind-blowing experience of my life. I didn't know sex could be like that. I feel turned on right now just thinking about it, and the thought that Jake is just on the other side of that door, half-naked, does nothing to quell that feeling.

I rake my fingers though my hair, the pins from earlier long gone, and smooth it down before splashing my face with water. I hear the door of the suite close followed by a knock at the bathroom door.

'You OK in there?'

I open the door and let Jake in.

'I'm fine, just freshening up a bit.'

'After we've eaten I'll run you a bath,' he says, backing me towards the countertop. He lifts me up on to it and stands between my legs.

'Oh, that sounds lovely,' I manage to murmur between his kisses, and he reaches up, undoing my dressing down and letting it fall open. He skims his hand down my bare flesh, and every single hair on my body stands on end.

'Our food will get cold,' I giggle, as he cups my bottom pulling me to the edge of the counter. He pushes his body to mine, and I feel his intention loud and clear against my thigh.

'I don't care.' He nips at my ear with his teeth, his huge hands kneading my bum firmly as he grips my hips. 'I'm never leaving this hotel room.' He pushes my dressing gown off my shoulder and moves his mouth to my bare flesh.

'Put me down,' I say with a giggle and gently push him aside not meaning it at all. 'Actually, scratch that, pick me up. I can smell that food.'

He groans his resistance and sighs.

'OK, OK. What the lady wants, the lady gets.' And he scoops me up, as I squeal with delight, and carries me out to the bedroom placing me down on the sofa, as he begins to spread the food out.

'Jake, can I ask you a question?' I say, as I reach over to a plate and pick up a chip, blowing on it before popping it in my mouth.

'I think you just did,' he says with a smile, and I pick up a chip and throw it at him which, much to my annoyance, he catches in his hand and then shoves into his mouth.

'OK fine, another one?' He opens his mouth to speak, just as I realise my mistake. 'Don't you dare!' I yell, as I throw another chip at him which he isn't quite quick enough to catch this time, but manages to swat it straight back at me so it lands in my hair. He doubles over in laughter so infectious that I find myself joining in. He walks around to where I'm sat and takes the chip out of my hair.

'Sorry,' he says and kisses me firmly on the lips, 'go on.'

'No you're not.' I fail to hide my amusement. 'Look Jake, I'm sorry for asking, but I just need to know, have you ever… you know, with a hotel guest before?'

His eyes crease up, and he suppresses a smile, as he repeats my words back to me, 'Have I ever, you know?'

'Yes,' I say, my cheeks heating but this time with embarrassment. 'You know, have you ever… slept with a guest before?'

'You mean before you just now?' he answers trying not to laugh.

'This isn't funny!' I berate him and reach for another chip, now my apparent weapon of choice, but he's too quick and stops my hand, taking it in his.

'No. I've never slept with a hotel guest before.' A feeling of complete relief floods through me. I'm not just another name on a list. 'OK?' he asks, his face searching mine.

'Yes, sorry, I didn't mean to question you. I'm sorry, I just…'

'You just needed to know this wasn't my thing? Sleeping with the guests? A new woman every fortnight, that sort of thing?'

I nod silently, feeling ashamed of myself for even thinking it, and I'm worried I've offended him, but his voice is soft and sincere.

'That's not my bag, sweet cheeks, I like my sex to have meaning to it. I don't sleep around. I love sex, don't get me wrong, but not without feeling. For me, there's no point without that.'

I take in his words. Feeling. Does that mean, he has feelings for *me*? I can't go there right now, as much as I have a desperate need to know but, by his own admission, he must do, mustn't he? And once again, he answers my question without me even having to ask.

'Which I think tells you all you need to know.' He pulls me on to his lap, feeding me a chip. 'Now, what would you like?'

I position myself astride his lap and trail my fingers down his chest, all the way to the soft line of hair that disappears into the top of his towel.

'I thought you said the food would get cold?' Jake says, looking up at me with raised eyebrows. I push my hands through his hair and tug on the corner of his towel.

'Yeah well, now it's my turn to not care.' And, as I let him wrap his arms around me and I lose myself in him once again, it's only him I care about.

Chapter Twenty-Eight

'I can't believe we've only been away a day! It feels like a lifetime since I was here. Although, I guess a lot's happened since then.'

My hand is in Jake's, as we sit in the dark in the back of Michael's car on the way to the Palm Bay, Barbados.

'Well technically, one thing happened a lot of times,' grins Jake, and I feel myself blush. I'm suddenly glad it's night-time and glance at Michael who, the height of professionalism, has his eyes fixed on the road and gives no sign that he's heard a thing.

'Jake, back at the hotel, I know it won't be like this. I mean, I understand, it's your place of work, you're the boss. You can't be seen to be, you know... *with me*.'

'I'm not. You're with me. And you're right, I am the boss and if there's any issue, which there won't be, but if there is, I'll be the one to handle it. There is nothing for you to worry about. Not a thing.'

I smile to myself in the dark. Actually, it's more of a manic grin, I feel so elated right now.

'OK, that's... thank you.'

'No, thank *you*,' he says, 'this has been the best trip to Miami I've ever had.'

'And as my first time there, it was pretty awesome.'

We spent last night lounging around the suite, drinking champagne, kissing, talking and a few other things, a few times. Jake ran a bath, like he promised, which I let him share (oh the hardship!), and we settled back on the bed picking at more of the food we'd had delivered. It was the best time I've had in a long time and a little lump springs to my throat just thinking about it.

Jake had some work calls to make and needed to have a sit down with his team today, so I had the morning to myself. He was heading to a meeting with Anna when we parted ways and, much to my pleasure, he landed a huge kiss on my lips just as she walked through the lobby. The look on her face was completely priceless, like I'd just stolen her favourite toy and, I have to admit, it left me with a feeling of smug satisfaction.

While Jake was in work mode, Peter drove me back to the beach for a long walk, the opposite way to what I went yesterday, stopping at the Ritz-Carlton at the top of Bal Harbour beach for him to collect me again. I stopped for a coffee and pie along the way, not feeling hungry for anything more. After my night with Jake, all my senses seemed to be on high alert. The sun on my skin, the bitter taste of the coffee, the sweetness of my blueberry pie and the heavy, hip-hop beat coming from a Hummer that cruised down Collins. It's as if I've been living life through a fog that's suddenly and spectacularly cleared.

We pull into the hotel turning circle and as we get out of the car, watching our bags being ferried inside, I catch Michael's eye, and he gives me a wink and a small nod of his head. I smile back at him, trying to resist the urge to break into a huge grin. I follow Jake into the hotel and notice a very discreet glance at our linked hands by the two doormen. We head to reception where the statuesque blonde, Marie, is busying herself with some papers.

'Evening, Marie, any messages while I've been away?'

'Good evening Mr Holden, Miss Kingston. No, no messages, but Maya was quite keen to speak with you when you got back.'

'Oh? Did she say what about?' he asks, distracted as he pulls me closer to him.

'I'm afraid not. She'll be back on shift at six a.m. and asked to speak to you as soon as possible.'

'If you see her before me, just let her know I'm back, and I'll come and speak to her in the morning. I don't want to bother her on her night off, she works too hard as it is. I need to check on a few things myself, but it can wait until tomorrow.'

'Sure.' Marie gives me a quick glance and a smile before she turns back to Jake. 'Anything else I can help you with?'

'Not at all, thanks Marie, have a good night.' Jake gives her a winning smile and, even though he's her boss, I see her blush ever so slightly.

'Goodnight Mr Holden.' She turns to me and nods, politely but not unfriendly. 'Goodnight.'

We take the lift up to the top floor and, once outside the doors to our respective suites, we grin at each other, shuffling awkwardly like two teenagers at a school dance, and then suddenly Jake starts to laugh. And so I start to laugh. And then we stand there, laughing our heads off for no reason at all. And it's so stupid and yet so, just, funny. When we manage to compose ourselves, Jake takes out his key card and holds open the door to his suite.

'Oh, for fuck's sake,' he says still laughing, 'just come in will you?'

'Go on then,' I shrug, 'I suppose I've nothing else to do.'

'Oh, I can think of plenty of things we can do, sweet cheeks, don't you fret about that,' he says with a smirk, and I step inside.

Jake's suite is an exact mirror image of mine except with a few more personal effects, although not that many to say it's his home.

'Nice room.'

'Thanks.' He flicks on the lights and heads over to the fridge, pulling out two bottles of ice-cold water. 'I would show you around, but I think you know where everything is by now.'

He takes a step closer to me, and I flinch as the cold of the bottle hits my back as he curls his arms around me. He notices and pushes the freezing cold bottle between my shoulder blades causing me to throw my body forward into his, as I let out a little yelp.

'I'm sorry, is that cold?' he says, not sorry at all. I shriek and try to wriggle free, but he clamps me to him, his arms tight around me, a look of overwhelming longing in his eyes. Just then, his phone starts to ring.

'Saved by the bell.' He releases me and grabs it out of his jeans pocket, checking the display.

'It's Maya. I'll speak to her tomorrow,' he says and throws the phone on to the bed.

'Shouldn't you get it, if it's urgent?'

'If it was that urgent, she would have left a message with Marie. You hungry?'

I nod. 'Actually, yes. Why is it all I seem to do around you is eat?'

'Well, technically you've yet to finish a meal with me, for some reason we keep getting distracted.' And he runs his fingers down my arm, kissing me softly.

'You are very distracting.' I murmur through his kisses. 'I don't even know what time it is, let alone what day.'

'Ah, I could trick you into staying forever then?' he says happily, but I can't hide the sinking feeling in my stomach at the mention of leaving. The look on my face must give me away, and he kisses me again, pulling me tightly to him.

'Don't,' Jake whispers. 'Like I said, we'll think about that later. I'll order up some food, and then I want to jump into the shower.'

'Me too,' I say pulling at the bobble holding up my hair. 'Shall I meet you back here in a minute?'

Jake looks briefly dismayed.

'Don't be ridiculous, get your ass in that bathroom.' He nods towards the door with a delicious smile, and he gives my bum a little squeeze, just to reinforce his words. 'I'll be back in a minute.'

I smile sweetly and do as I'm told but not before he's grabbed me back towards him and given me another heated kiss.

'I can't get enough of you, sweet cheeks,' he says with a groan, and I look up at him, my heart swelling with an exhilarating, yet slightly unsettling feeling.

'Me neither.'

'I should really call my mum,' I decide, as we lie in Jake's huge bed, post-dinner and shower and dreamy, dreamy sex.

'Feel free if you like, I don't mind.' His fingers are tracing small circles on my back, and I nuzzle into him. 'Are you guys close?'

'Yeah, I'd say so. I mean, much more so since my dad died, but we've always got on, even before that. I was a complete daddy's girl, but she never resented it or felt pushed out, not that she ever let on, anyway. I thought she might have a bit of a meltdown about the whole wedding fiasco, but she's actually been great. She seems to thrive in a bit of a crisis, by the looks of things. She's a coper, that's for sure.'

'Like you.'

'I don't know, am I a coper?' I consider his statement. 'Maybe I am.'

'You absolutely are. How many other people would have faced things like you did? I've said it before, you're incredible.'

'Yes, but that was when we were in bed...' I point out.

'In *and* out of bed.' He kisses my cheeks where they've turned pink.

'Stop, you're making me go red.' I push him playfully on his chest, not moving him an inch.

'You? Go red? I hadn't noticed,' Jake says smoothly through a thinly suppressed smile.

'Oh God, I knew it was so obvious.' I bury my face in my hands mortified. 'I can't bloody help it!'

'I like it. Plus it makes me feel good about myself. I like that I have the ability to make you blush. What must you have been thinking about all those times...?'

'Never you mind.'

'Maybe you could show me...'

'Maybe I'll try and make *you* blush.'

How does this escalate so quickly? We can just be talking and the next minute we're writhing around on the bed. There's something animalistic about my attraction to Jake. Something so urgent, so desperate about the way I need him, the way I want him. And I think if it had been only that, then I wouldn't feel so nervous about our current situation but, as it stands, I have feelings for him that I can't put into words and no amount of pretending will hide the fact that I'm falling, fast and hard, for this man.

I wake the next morning, lying with my back pressed into Jake and his arms closed around me. I stir and he murmurs in my ear, 'What a way to wake up.'

I feel desire surge through me, and he brushes my hair from my neck, pulling me firmly towards him, hooking his legs in mine.

'You have to go to work,' I tell him, giggling as his hands make their way down my body and settle at my hips before pulling me back towards him, circling his hips against me as he does so. Who am I kidding? I'm powerless to resist him. 'Oh, why do I care? It's not my job!' I roll over to face him, gently taking his bottom lip in my teeth, as I stretch up to align our faces. 'And you're the boss after all.'

'I love it when you say things like that to me.'

A feeling of contentment and happiness washes over me again, and I press my lips, and my body, against his decisively. I am on holiday after all.

As Jake and I get ready to venture out of his suite I realise, guiltily, I still didn't call my mum and scrabble in my bag for my phone.

'Damn, it's out of battery.'

'Use the one on the desk if you want. Instructions are on the front,' Jake calls through from the walk-in wardrobe.

'OK great, thanks. Remind me to put it on charge before we leave.'

I punch in Mum's mobile number, which I know off by heart, and it dawns on me that hers and Luke's are the only two numbers I know by memory. It rings and rings and goes through to voicemail, so I leave her a quick message.

'Hey, Mum, it's me. I'm back in Barbados safe and sound. We had an amazing trip, but I'll tell you all about it later.' I definitely won't tell her *all* about it later but some of it. 'My phone's out of battery, so I'm leaving it in my room to charge and will try and call you later. Hope everything's OK and you had a nice time with Jean and Alan. Talk to you soon. Love you lots.'

I hang up, as Jake makes his way towards me looking drop-dead gorgeous in flip-flops, blue beach shorts and a white T-shirt. His hair is still messy from bed, and I walk over to him and push my hand through it instinctively.

'Ready for breakfast?' I ask.

'I need to catch up with some stuff and try and speak to Maya, so I'll come and find you later, OK?'

'Sure, no worries.' I glance at my watch, loads of time left for breakfast. 'I need to find Rach and have a catch up with her anyway, see what I've missed. She'll probably be at breakfast, so I'll come down with you.'

'Perfect. I wish I could stay in bed with you all day.' And he runs his finger along the waistband of my shorts.

'So do I.'

'This last couple of days have been perfect, I'm so glad you came.'

I raise my eyebrows at him, and he lets out a bark of laughter.

'To Miami. I'm so glad you came to Miami.'

'I'm so glad I came to Barbados.' Of all the things I could have chosen to do after everything went tits up, this was by far and away the best idea I had.

I stop off at my room, quickly change into my bikini and beach dress, grabbing my bag with sun cream and headphones in, remembering to stick my phone on charge too, before we head down to reception. I'm a bit nervy that people will look at me and automatically know I've had sex with the owner of the hotel they're staying in, but I realise I'm being ridiculous. Some of the staff may have cottoned on to something, but I'm pretty sure we have Maya, Dale and Michael on Team Carrie, so I doubt it will turn into a rumour mill. At least I hope not, for Jake's sake as much as mine, although I'm starting to realise I care more about what people here think than he does. We spot Maya behind reception, and as we approach her eyes widen and a look of relief washes over her face.

'Jake, I need to speak to you. Now,' she says breathlessly.

'Fire away. Are you alright?' he asks, glancing to me and looking puzzled at her obvious panic. Maya's eyes flit between us for a second.

'Could you come to the back? Carrie, I'm really sorry, but I just need to speak with Jake in private.'

I'm not offended at all, but I am definitely worried. Maya's usually so composed, but she seems really uneasy.

'Of course! That's fine, I'll go to breakfast and see you later on. I guess I'll be by the pool or on the beach.'

'See you later. Enjoy breakfast.' Jake kisses me briefly, but tenderly, and I smile at his openness. As I thought, he really doesn't care who sees.

'Oh sorry, Carrie, I almost forgot. Rachel came down and said she would be in the dining room and then heading to the pool if you wanted to look for her. She said she tried to call you but your phone was off,' Maya relays to me, still looking flustered.

'Great, thanks Maya.' I turn to Jake. 'See you later. I hope everything's OK.'

'Can I take you for dinner tonight? See if we can actually get you to finish a meal,' he adds with a wink.

'Well, we can but try,' I reply, smiling.

'Well, well, well. I turn my back for five minutes and everyone's making plans without me!'

I follow the very posh, British voice that drifts my way and turn in the direction of its owner, a tall, stunning blonde wearing nothing but a black bikini and floor-length, orange kaftan barely covering her slim, toned body that's almost Victoria's Secret perfect. I see Maya's eyes fall to the floor, and Jake's body goes totally rigid, his fists balled at his side. The woman struts over to us and leans back against the reception desk lowering her Chanel sunglasses and flipping her long hair over her shoulder.

'Well?' she says, looking back and forth between us all. 'Is no one going to introduce me?'

Maya's face blanches, and Jake's is set in an angry frown, as he says grudgingly through gritted teeth, 'Carrie, this is…' He stops and can't bring himself to say the words that I already know are coming. She extends her hand to me and gives me a satisfied smile.

'Oh Jakey, please,' she tuts. 'I'm his wife, darling. And you are?'

Chapter Twenty-Nine

I honestly don't know what the hell I'm supposed to do now. Megan stands there, her hand out to me, a pout on her lips and a whole bucketload of confidence oozing from her every pore. I look to Maya, who is holding her breath and looking totally stricken, then to Jake, who is breathing deeply, trying to keep his composure, his face a picture of anger. I put out my hand and shake hers, not knowing what else to do.

'Megan,' he begins in a slow, measured tone, and I can tell he's struggling to keep his temper under control. I've never seen him angry before, and it's quite unnerving as well as being just a little bit sexy. 'OK, two things, Megan. Firstly, what the hell are you doing here? And secondly, you are *not* my wife.'

Megan looks not in the least bit bothered by the fact that he's clearly livid.

'Well actually I am, darling, which is why I'm here, but we'll get to that in a sec. Maya, could you have some fresh towels sent up to the room, you know how I like new ones every day.' She turns to me and whispers to me as if we're best friends, 'You know, my skin just can't handle it otherwise, it's a nightmare.'

I have literally no idea what she's on about but nod slowly and plaster a smile on to my bewildered face. So she's staying here too. Oh Jesus Christ.

'Anyway,' she carries on, totally ignoring Jake's exasperation, 'I'm guessing you two are…?' She flicks a finger between me and Jake, as she raises her eyebrows, a playful smile at her lips.

'Megan that's none of your fucking business.' Jake takes a deep breath. 'I'll ask you again, why are you here?'

'Oh, Jakey, don't be tetchy, darling, we're all friends here.'

Are we? I think to myself.

'I'm getting married, sweetie.' She holds out her hand and flashes us all a glimpse of the biggest rock I've ever seen in real life. 'Water under the bridge and all that now, isn't it?' She lets out a little giggle and drapes her arm around Jake's shoulder. 'I could give… Carrie, was it? I could give her some tips on how to handle you! He's quite something, isn't he?'

I want to curl up and die on the spot, and Maya suddenly looks very interested in some paperwork on the desk. Jake glowers at the ceiling and takes Megan's arm, removing it firmly from his shoulder.

'For God's sake, Megan! You can't just show up here…'

'I'm just teasing, darling, calm down,' she interrupts him. 'I'm only here to sort out some paperwork. I don't know what's been going on, but it's all been taking ages, so I thought I'd pop down here and you could sign it all, and we could get this whole business sorted out.'

She stands there beaming like this is the best idea in the world, and she can't understand why we aren't all whooping with joy at her genius. Megan waves her arms in the air.

'But anyway, shall we have breakfast?' I don't know who she's addressing, but I'm certainly not swapping notes with Jake's wife over a bacon sarnie. As if she eats bacon sarnies anyway, I mean, look at her.

'I have work to do,' Jake says quickly and firmly. 'Give me an hour, then we can meet up and I'll sign the papers so you can be on a flight back to New York tonight, alright?'

'Well, for starters there's no flight out until tomorrow morning, but Andre is away on business, so I'm here for a few days!' She announces this like it's the best news ever, but my heart sinks at the idea of having her around. 'I thought it would be nice to relax and get some sun. Kill two birds with one stone, as it were.'

I suddenly feel a bit awkward so touch Jake's arm. 'Er, I think I'm just going to go and get breakfast.'

His eyes are full of regret and worry, as he looks at me. 'Carrie, I'm so sorry. I had no idea.'

I smile at him.

'I know you didn't. It's OK, I'm fine.' I force a smile on to my face feeling distinctly not fine. 'I'll see you later on. Definitely for dinner if not before.'

'Ooh, where are we going for dinner?' Megan butts in, looking excited.

'*You* are going nowhere for dinner, I'm taking Carrie out. Not us we, me and her we!'

She flicks her hair and holds up her hands. 'Fine, fine. I know when I'm not wanted! Come on then, Carrie, let's go?'

'Go?' I stutter, utterly confused.

'To breakfast!' I freeze, and Jake puts his head in his hands.

'Megan…' he growls, in a warning voice, but Maya comes to the rescue.

'I'm so sorry to interrupt, but Rachel said she had something private to discuss with you Carrie, so it might not be quite appropriate for Megan to join you this morning. I'm sorry to disappoint you both.' I look at Maya, and she winks at me before I mouth '*thank you*' at her, and she smiles remorsefully. I glance at Megan who is busy cleaning her glasses on her kaftan.

'Oh well, not to matter. I'll grab a smoothie from the bar later, and we can all catch up afterwards.' The awkward tension in the air goes completely unnoticed by her, and she places her shades back over her eyes, giving us all a wave. 'Ciao, ciao, folks.' And off she strides out towards the beach.

We all stand there momentarily in shock my mouth slightly agape, Jake looking at the floor, his fists still clenched by his sides, and poor Maya looking like she's about to be sick.

'Jake, I am so, so sorry,' she says looking distraught. 'I did try and get a message to you. I'm really sorry. I didn't want to say anything to Marie, you know how she struggles to keep this sort of thing private, should we say.'

Jake pinches the bridge of his nose and steadies his breathing.

'Maya, it's not your fault. Sorry you had to deal with her.'

'It's fine. I should have done something else, got a message to you somehow…'

Jake turns to me and scoops me in his arms.

'I am so sorry, sweet cheeks. God, the woman is a bloody nightmare! I'll get rid of her, I promise.' He holds me at arm's length and looks deep into my eyes. 'And we are still going for dinner later, I promise.' He sighs and rubs his hands over his face. 'At least I can sign the papers and get all this shit done once and for all.'

'Look at the positives, then. It's not all bad.'

'Why are you so great?'

'I ask myself the same thing every day,' I say, and Jake finally cracks a smile. 'To be perfectly honest, as much as having your wife staying at the same hotel make me feel slightly ill, she's actually hilarious. At least, she probably would be if the situation wasn't quite so cringe-inducing.'

But she certainly doesn't seem remotely interested in Jake in anything other than a let's get divorce kind of way, which I have to say is a huge relief. Jake looks at me deadpan.

'She is not hilarious. Oblivious, irritating, arrogant, inappropriate... all of the above.'

I laugh in spite of the awkwardness of the whole situation.

'I hope it goes OK with her later. And now I'm going to spend the day hiding from your wife. Maya, thanks for saving me from the breakfast from hell. Did Rachel actually need to speak to me about something?'

'No, but it was the first thing that came into my head!'

'Well it did the job, so thanks.'

'I would say anytime, but hopefully it's not a regular occurrence. Excuse me.' And she picks up the phone that's begun to ring on the desk in front of her.

'I better go too,' Jake says, sounding like he would rather do anything but. 'I'll see you later.'

'You will.'

Feeling brave, I lean up and plant a swift kiss on his cheek, then looking around to see if anyone's noticed, I turn on my heels and scurry to the dining room leaving him standing there with a smile on his face. I glance over my shoulder, and he's still watching me and, even with the events of the last few minutes, I can't shake the feeling of happiness still simmering away inside of me.

As I make my way to breakfast, I can't help but run over what's just happened. Never in a million years did I expect to meet Jake's wife. Looking at him, I should have known she would be stunning, but I didn't expect her to be quite *so* gorgeous, and I did feel self-conscious stood next to her. But then again, I can't think of anyone I know who wouldn't. Suddenly I hear a loud squeal from behind me, and I turn to see Rachel hurrying towards me, her arms outstretched and a massive smile on her tanned, little face.

'You're back!' She pulls me into a tight hug and then holds me away from her like my mum used to do after Brownie camp. 'You look fab! So come on, tell me all about it.'

'So do you want the good news or the bad news?'

Rachel looks grave for a second before pulling a regretful face and putting her hand on my arm. 'Oh no, was he shit in bed?' she asks seriously, and I burst out laughing.

'We definitely need coffee for this,' I warn her. 'We might even need rum punch.'

After I filled Rachel in on the events of the last forty-eight hours (was that really all it was?), we headed down to the beach where we spend the morning horizontal on a sunbed. I caught a brief glimpse of Megan reclined by the pool on our way out of breakfast, but I've managed to avoid her since, although at one point I was sure I heard her high-pitched giggle and promptly decided to take a swim in the sea.

As I knew she would be, Rachel was, once again, the perfect audience to my story. She actually screamed when I told her me and Jake had slept together and then again when I said it happened again. And again. And… well, she was excited anyway. At one point, she leaned over and said she was pleased I'd taken another step forward, and she was happy to see me smiling so broadly. We had a hug and welled up a little bit which we blamed on the bright sunshine.

The sun has beaten down all day and even though we sat in the shade to share a club sandwich and chips for lunch (OK, we may have had a cocktail, but that was Dale's fault), it's still been scorching. I take myself off to the sea for a dip, while Rachel spends far too long picking up some bottles of water at the bar with Dale. The water is chilly but not freezing cold, and I grow a few inches as it hits my warm skin and dips into my belly button. There's a distant beat of music that drifts on the breeze from the hotel, and I can hear laughter coming from a family with small children. I recognise them as the ones I saw in the dining room on my first day, and I smile as the little boy splashes his sister, their dad chasing them through the shallow water, whilst their mum watches on, laughing. They look so happy.

I think back to that morning of the wedding, the day my life did a complete U-turn. It doesn't seem real, even though it's only a week later. I try to imagine myself and Luke, on a beach in the sunshine, watching our children, but I can't, the image won't come. All I see is Luke and Emily's faces, with *their* baby. I press my eyes shut and try to picture myself, here, but as future me, and every single time I do, all I see is Jake.

I move through the water, shivering as I dip my shoulders under the surface, and float face up in the sea, letting the waves rock me back and forth as I keep my body afloat. I sense a movement in front of me and, being instantly terrified I'm about to get eaten by a shark, whip my body upright and see Jake smirking, as he stalks towards me through the water. His tanned body is glistening from the seawater, his hair is damp and he's wearing his classic red Baywatch shorts. I have had sex with that Adonis. I give myself an internal little cheer, as my face breaks out into a huge grin.

'Damn,' he says punching his fist into the water and sending up a fresh spray into his chest, 'busted!'

'I thought you were a shark.'

'What and I was going to devour you whole? Don't tempt me, sweet cheeks.'

As he reaches me, he draws me to him, kissing me in such a way that causes goosebumps to ripple all over my body. He dips down in the water, scooping up a handful and splashing his face before pushing his hands through his hair, slicking it back. I reach up and link my arms behind his neck before he lifts me slightly, and I wrap my legs around him as we bob up and down in the water.

'So, did you talk to Megan? Sorry your wife,' I ask, stressing the word with more jollity than I actually feel, and Jake groans.

'Yes. And don't call her that. She is not my wife.'

'Technically she is…'

'On paper only,' he mutters through gritted teeth. 'But yes, she came to see me. Basically, she just wanted me to sign the papers ASAP, because Andre has his parents coming over from Germany. She wants to be able to say she's actually divorced and not engaged to their son while she's still legally married to someone else. I think they are struggling enough with the fact she's been married before, they're quite traditional from what I could gather, so I think she was getting a bit anxious they would kick up a fuss.'

'Which is actually not a bad plan on her part,' I add, and Jake sighs.

'No, to be fair to her, I see why she's done it and, trust me, there is no one happier than me to see an end to this. I just wish she had done it from afar, rather than swooping in on precious time with you.'

'Well, hopefully, she'll stay out of your way now she's got what she wants. Are we still on for dinner tonight?' I try to steer the conversation away from Megan. Although I know there's nothing between her and Jake any more, I would prefer not to dwell on the subject too long.

'That's what I came to say. I'm taking you out. Be ready for seven, and I'll give you a knock.'

'Where are we going?'

'Never you mind, I'll see you tonight.' Jake presses his mouth to mine, his tongue venturing between my parted lips, and I feel my pulse quicken as I wrap my legs tighter around him. His kiss deepens, as he tugs playfully on the tie of my bikini top.

'Don't you dare, mister!' I warn him flicking seawater up at him, which I instantly know is a mistake. He gives me the biggest smirk, and I momentarily think I've got away with it, but he plants his hand on the top on my head and dunks me straight under the water. I pop back up, my mouth open in shock, and push the water from my face. Jake is laughing hysterically, and I desperately try to do the same to him, but have absolutely no chance. Despite just being plunged into the sea, the sight of him relaxed and laughing is enough for me.

'I like you in Barbados,' I say to him, wringing out my hair.

'Oh, gee thanks!' he replies, pretending to sound offended but still smiling. 'I'll tell you now, sweet cheeks, if that was hating me in Miami I can't wait to see how much you like me here.' He gives me a wink as he stands, the droplets of seawater running down his perfect chest into that little line of hair that I'm now much more familiar with.

'No, you idiot, I meant you seem much more relaxed here. Well, you didn't this morning, but you do now.'

'I'm sorry, sweet cheeks. Megan's alright really, she's just… so bloody annoying! And turning up like this, with you here, was really a testament to her impeccable timing.' He shakes his head and gives a small scoff. 'I was worried about work in Miami, I wanted to see it for myself and get things smoothed over, get plans in place. I don't usually worry, but this just felt bigger than what we've dealt with because of his high profile. I needed us to come out of it on the right side.' He pushes his hair back from his face and rubs away the drops of saltwater that have fallen on to his forehead, as his frown melts away. 'And I wanted to make sure you were OK. I think we know each other well enough now for me to say this, but I didn't want you to feel any pressure, being there with me.' He gives me a sheepish, lopsided grin, and my heart contracts a little.

'Jake, I didn't, not at all. I promise.' I take his hand in mine, linking our fingers together.

'Good. But I was also aware that you might not have had very many… first times… with a guy.' I can see where he is going, so I help him out.

'You were my second, in case you were wondering.' Any embarrassment I could have felt at this topic of conversation just falls away under his gaze, my soul opening up to him.

'I kind of guessed.' He looks suddenly shy, and a heartfelt sensation creeps through my chest. 'Not that it showed!' he jumps in, 'I mean… you were incredible but…' he looks at me, a grimace on his face, but it instantly turns to relief as he sees I'm smiling,

'You really are very sweet,' I say, as we push our way back through the waves and head to shore.

'Ha!' he hoots. 'I'll have to do something to put that hideous slur on my character right then, won't I?'

Without waiting for an answer he picks up his knees and sprints through the shallows on to the beach.

'See you later Baywatch,' I shout towards him, and he turns, jogging backwards, with a salute in my direction. I watch as he veers to the right and gives the small boy a quick high five and a ruffle of his hair before he heads towards the hotel. He jogs past Rachel, who's returned with two bottles of water, and she does a fake swoon, flinging her arm across forehead and pretending to stumble backwards. As I head back to our beds, I take a moment to reflect. The sun is shining, I'm making memories, friends and even the arrival of Megan can't sour my mood right now, not one bit.

'Well, do you want the good news or the really good news?' Rachel asks, as I pick up my towel to dry my hair.

'Good news.'

'Amy and Bryony are checking out. Au revoir, bitches!'

'Ha, no way? Oh, how we'll miss them! So what's the really good news then?'

'The really good news is that she came down to the bar to try and find Dale, say goodbye or whatever, basically to get one last dig in I think, but she full-on fell over on her wedges and face-planted into the bush.' Rachel's face is one of unbridled, smug joy, and I burst out laughing.

'Oh, she didn't?'

'Did, did, did, my friend. And the best bit was she was so ashamed she just turned around and scurried back to the lobby.'

'What a perfect exit for her.'

And with that piece of news, I feel even better than I did moments before.

Chapter Thirty

'Are you going to give me any clue where we are going?' I ask Jake, as we sit in the back of a darkened car that evening.

'You'll see soon enough. God, are you always this impatient?'

'No, but I am nosy,' I concede. 'I can't help myself, I like being in the know.'

'You should hear some of the stories from the hotel, you would not believe some of the stuff we've dealt with. Housekeeping in particular have some excellent stories.'

'Oh, go on, please!'

He shifts his body towards me ready to tell the story. 'OK, this is one of my favourites, because I was actually there when it happened. We had a couple of honeymooners staying with us who were a bit experimental in the bedroom, and this one night they'd been out for dinner and she had so much to drink, I mean, she was smashed. Anyway, they went up to their room, and I don't know how she managed it in her state, but she'd handcuffed him to the chest of drawers in the room, except that, and I don't know exactly what happened, she was so drunk she passed out, and he couldn't find the key anywhere. Apparently, he looked for like an hour. So this poor guy comes down to reception, shirtless, but he'd luckily managed to put some shorts on somehow, and he's got these two, big towels over his hands. We all thought he'd burned himself or something, but under these two towels are the drawers from the chest still attached to the handcuffs.'

'You are joking? Oh my God!' I snort and my hand flies to my mouth, as I try to stifle a laugh, my mouth agape.

'Nope! He had to literally yank them out of the unit and carry them down to reception, still attached, so we could cut him out. He was so mortified they checked out the next day. I don't know if the marriage lasted, but that's one to tell the grandkids.'

'That is too funny, awful, but funny.'

'I could write a book, sweet cheeks, honestly.'

The conversation flows easily as we drive down the coast, I'm not even sure what direction we go in but after around twenty minutes, the car pulls into a bay at the side of the road. Next to it, I can see a small bar and restaurant, and there's a path that leads down to the beach illuminated by flaming torches. As I climb out of the car, I can hear the waves breaking and soft jazz floating on the breeze.

'Wow, is this where we're going?'

'Almost.' Jake leans his head in the car to chat to our driver before he heads off. 'Follow me,' Jake says, and we make our way down the path, completely bypassing the restaurant.

We walk down the wooden beach path, and I'm thankful I wore flats with my loose, linen shirt dress, as we make our way a little farther across the beach, away from the restaurant and towards a small cluster of palm trees. And that's when I see it. A small table and two chairs, nestled in between the trees, which are covered in fairy lights and hanging lanterns.

Four large torches, like the ones on the path, stand proudly around the table. It's magical.

'Oh, Jake.' I press my hands together and touch them to my lips.

'What? This? Oh, this isn't for us! I've got a picnic rug and a pack of Scotch eggs for us on the other side of these trees.'

I punch him on the arm and he slings it over my shoulder, drawing me into him.

'If you had, that would be fine too,' I say.

We walk across the soft sand and, as we are about to take our seats at the table, Jake pulling out my chair for me, a tall, athletic-looking man with a completely bald head comes across to us and shakes Jake's hand.

'Carrie, this is the man of the hour, Sal, who made this all happen.'

'This is wonderful, thank you,' I say sincerely to Sal.

'My pleasure. Jake told me he had a VIP guest, so it's my pleasure to host you tonight. Please, take a seat and enjoy, Amelia will bring your food out shortly. The wine's chilling already. May I, Jake?'

'Please do.'

As Sal pours us a cold, glass of white, Jake leans over to me. 'There's no menu, Sal has a set menu each night, it's his and chef's choice.'

'Sounds perfect,' I smile, my eyes passing from him to Sal, who nods to us both and heads back to the lights of the restaurant. 'Do you know *everyone*?' I ask Jake narrowing my eyes at him.

'Not everyone,' he laughs, 'but, as you'll have noticed, I do know a lot of people who know good food!'

'And selfishly, I'm very pleased you do. This is really, really lovely, Jake. Thank you. See, I told you you were sweet.'

'Well, I can't say it was a totally selfless move, I didn't want to share you.' He gives me a lopsided smile, as he raises his glass. 'Cheers, angel, to you.'

'And to you,' I say.

'So to us, then?' He licks his lips and gives me a challenging stare.

Why not? 'To us.'

'To us.'

We take a sip of wine, our movements mirroring each other. Slow, deliberate, Jake's eyes never leaving mine. Us. One word, two little letters but such meaning. Us. How can there be an us? But we both know there is, we just don't seem to know how it's happened, or where it's going. I get a sinking feeling in my stomach. Where can it go? There is a chance Jake and I will never see each other again once I leave here, and I can't imagine a time when that's the case, not right now, here with him.

'Jake?' I can't not ask him about it, not when it's weighing so heavy on my mind, but I don't want to put a dampener on this evening. It wouldn't be a dampener as such, it's more like I'm about to lob a huge, great bucket of cold water over it. 'Jake, I really don't want to say it, but…'

'So don't,' he shrugs. 'Just don't say it.'

'You don't even know what I'm about to say.'

'Yes I do.' He looks so annoyingly smug that I pout my lips at him.

'Go on then.' I sit back in my chair and fold my arms waiting for him to elaborate.

'If I'm right you have to kiss me,' he challenges, and I roll my eyes, but my mouth curls into a smile.

'And if you're wrong?'

He thinks about this for a second then a grin spreads over his face.

'I'll take off all my clothes and run into the sea.'

'Oh Lord,' I giggle. 'And anyway that's not a fair bet because that's the sort of thing you'd just do anyway, bet or not. But go on then, what was I going to say?' Jake leans back in his chair and spins his wine glass with his fingers. He takes a deep breath.

'You were going to say, I'm leaving soon, you were going to ask what's *us*. You were worrying that in a week you'll be gone and that will be that.' He gestures between us, 'That this, will be all over. Sweet cheeks, do you think I'm going to let that happen? Honestly? No chance. This isn't just some fling for me, you know that, although you do have me well and truly flung!'

I laugh and drop my eyes, suddenly a bit embarrassed. He stops talking, so I'm forced to look at him and as soon as our eyes lock together, I feel it again.

'I'm not ready to let you go, Carrie. Whatever happens, when you leave, it won't be the last time we see each other. I don't have it all worked out, but I don't need to, I just know it will.'

'I wish I looked at the world the way you do. You're so sure of things, so confident, so laid-back. I can't seem to get through one day without a heap of doubt and freaking out about something.'

'Well, I think you could be excused for that lately. Anyway, I don't see that in you, that's not who are you, it's who you think you are, maybe, how you think you should be, but I haven't seen that since that first day when you chucked your shoes at me.'

'That's because of you,' I say softly, and he reaches across the table for my hand.

'No, sweet cheeks, it's because of *you*.'

My eyes sting with the threat of tears, and I blink them back rapidly as a young girl, dressed in a white shirt, black trousers and black tie, approaches our table with a tray full of food. She places it between us and sets down a small, white plate in front of each of us, giving us a polite smile as she backs away to the restaurant, the moment between Jake and I temporarily over.

'Bloody hell,' I say, taking in the tray, 'this looks incredible.'

There's a huge array of different seafood dishes ranging from calamari, grilled prawns, scallops, whitebait, a small bowl of what looks like flaked, white fish with seasoning and a dressed crab atop the lot. Jake leans forward, picks up the platter and places it in front of him. He looks at me innocently.

'Right, I'm set. What are you having then?'

'Get your fork out of my cheesecake!' I yell at Jake across the table trying desperately to shield my plate.

'I bet you say that to all the boys,' he fires back, forking off a chunk and demolishing it in one bite. This is pretty much the way the whole of the night has gone.

We were presented with a huge tray of grilled salmon to share for the main course with a side of creamy potatoes and vegetables. There was something so intimate about dishing up our own food together. It felt less like a formal date and more like we were hanging out at home, having a meal together after a day at work. Dessert was the only part of the meal that wasn't chosen for us, so I went for a peanut butter cheesecake and Jake opted for chocolate torte.

'Come on, tit for tat, send over the torte, mister.'

'Give me your plate.'

'No chance,' I scoff knowing full well I'm in danger of losing my entire dessert if I do.

He sighs, slicing his torte in half with the side of his fork and pushes it towards me.

'I thought you didn't like to share?' I say, remembering his earlier words, as I do the same with my cheesecake and we do a dessert swap, our plates chinking together in the middle as we slide our respective puddings over to one another.

He crumbles off a small piece of cheesecake and pushes it on his fork, before scooping up a piece of torte to join it and places the combo into his mouth. He swallows and tilts his head to the side, his blonde hair slightly ruffled in the breeze.

'That very much depends on what I'm sharing. And who I'm sharing it with.'

The way the words roll off his tongue send a rush of heat over my skin, and I feel myself blushing in that oh-so familiar way. And he knows it.

'Fancy a sleepover tonight?' he asks casually, and I squeeze my thighs together as my body reacts instantly to his words. I am utterly useless in controlling its behaviour when he's around.

'Your place or mine?' I ask him, and he leans back laughing.

'Fancy finishing up here and getting a cocktail back at the hotel? Dale's working so I guess Rachel will be there too.'

'Yes, let's do that,' I say feeling the warmth from my skin seep down to my insides, and we grin at each other. Who knew cocktails and the prospect of a sleepover could ever seem this perfect?

Chapter Thirty-One

'I am only having one. Do not let Rachel convince me otherwise!' I instruct Jake firmly, as we walk across reception and outside towards The Coconut Shack.

'I won't, don't you worry about that, one drink only.' He snakes his arm around my waist and murmurs into my ear, 'I have somewhere to be.' And he holds me close all the way to the bar.

Rachel is perched on her usual stool, while Dale serves a customer a couple of beers. The bar's busy, but not overcrowded, and feels like it's got a particularly good vibe about it tonight, or maybe that's just me, revelling in my evening with Jake and the prospect of what's to come. Rachel breaks into a huge smile as she catches sight of us and beckons to the two stools next to her.

'Hey, how was dinner?' she asks, and looks at us expectantly, as we slide up on to the seats. Jake holds up two fingers in response to Dale's brandishing of a cocktail glass with a hopeful smirk in our direction.

'Delicious. I'm absolutely stuffed. You'll have to get Dale to take you, it was amazing, wasn't it Jake?'

'Yeah, it was alright I suppose, company was a bit crap though.'

Rachel giggles, as he gives me a kiss on the top of my head, before she catches my eye and gives me a look that says 'I want to hear all about this later'.

'Yeah, I'm not sure Dale and I are in the whole going out for dinner type of place,' she says spreading her hands out in front of her, as she leans back on the stool and crosses her tanned legs. 'We're really more about the breakfast than the dinner.' Dale gives her a wink, right on cue, as he brings over two mojitos, placing one in front of me and Rachel. Jake turns to say something to Dale, and I lean towards Rachel whispering so only she can hear.

'Seriously, dinner was so romantic, I'm proper falling for him, Rach,' I say, biting my lip and giving her an apprehensive grimace, and she puts a reassuring hand on my leg.

'Aw, honey, I know you are. But he's falling for you too. Dale told me that he was talking to Maya the other day and both of them said how he's been working really random hours so he can spend as much time with you as he can. I mean, I know I said he liked you, anyone can see that but seriously, babe, from what I've seen and heard he seems head over heels.'

'Rach, what the hell am I going to do?'

'Don't worry, we will have a proper chat tomorrow. Let me know when Jake leaves in the morning, and we can get in the hot tub and hash it all out.'

'That sounds brilliant, thank you. Hang on, what do you mean when he leaves?'

'Pah! Don't give me that.' She glances around me at Jake and rolls her eyes. 'Like he's going to leave you alone for another second that he doesn't have to.'

Just as Dale comes back with Jake's mojito, and Rachel starts telling us about their plans to go jet-skiing tomorrow, if we want to join them, a shrill laugh cuts through the air and Jake winces.

'Megan?' I ask.

He groans by way of a reply. 'Do you want to go?'

'No,' I say, 'it's fine. We can drink these and go after.'

'Do we have to?'

'Yes! Stop being such a wimp, this is your hotel.'

'And your wife…' Rachel interjects bravely, as Jake gives her a cold stare which she bushes off with a laugh. 'She was in here earlier, actually, flirting her knickers off with some guy I've not seen before. Sorry Jake, I know you're married to her.' Jake rolls his eyes at Rachel and opens his mouth to say something before she ploughs on, 'OK fine, almost *not* married but, seriously, you wouldn't have thought she was about to get married again the way she was carrying on. The poor guy looked a bit shell-shocked to start with, but seemed to be absolutely loving it by the time they left.'

'Oh, here you are! Hi guys! Jake, I forgot how good the food is here. You're going to have to fly me home in the hold at this rate,' chirps Megan and lets out another raucous laugh. I catch Dale's eye across the bar, and we quickly look away, both of us trying our best to hold in a giggle. She is like no one I've ever met before, the confidence just radiates from her, and I can tell her skin is thicker than the gold Cartier cuff hanging on her tiny, tanned wrist.

'Dale, I'll have what everyone else is having thank you, darling,' she says, giving him a little wink and blowing him a kiss, as she pulls up the stool next to Jake. I look at Rachel, who's shaking her head, but clearly she's not too bothered about Megan's flirty display towards Dale. She did see off Amy and Bryony after all.

'Gosh, what a day. How are we all?' Megan proclaims, making it sound as if she's done a shift down the mine and not just been lounging by the pool. 'Where have you two been hiding this evening, hey?' she asks, wiggling her perfectly groomed eyebrows towards me and Jake in a suggestive manner.

'For dinner,' Jake says with a tight smile, politely but curtly. Ever the saviour of an awkward moment, Rachel leans forward and extends her hand to Megan.

'Hello, I'm Rachel, nice to meet you.'

'Lovely to meet you, any friend of Jake's is a friend of mine. Speaking of which I saw Luis earlier, Jake darling, such a lovely man. He spoke very highly of you Carrie. But then he's always been a sucker for a pretty face.'

Megan crosses her legs in front of her, and the split in her dress reveals long, tanned, flawless limbs I could only dream of. But I'm fairly sure Megan just said I was pretty, which I'll take as a compliment coming from her, Jake's almost-ex-wife or not.

'Where's your date, Megan?' Rachel puts in, but if Megan picks up on her implicit tone, she doesn't let it bother her.

'Oh, he's just gone to the bathroom. He is *such* a nice guy.' She lets out a little giggle before lowering her tone slightly. 'I know I'm a happily married woman… Oh, don't look so grumpy Jake, I don't mean you, darling, I'm talking about Andre, but I quite fancied him to be honest, he's a bit of a dish! But get this, he was telling the most incredible story about why he's in Barbados… Oh look, here he is now!' she halts and looks behind us all, waving her arms excitedly, and Rachel, Dale, Jake and I all turn to look in his direction. Megan jumps down off her stool and strides towards him, taking him by the arm and squeezing it to her. 'Let me introduce you to everyone.'

'He is quite dishy actually,' admits Rachel, but my mouth has gone dry and my heart's stopped beating as the earth shifts beneath me. Megan launches into conversation introducing her new friend, as I slide off my stool, my legs wobbling under me, clinging to the bar, as Jake looks on, his face full of concern.

'This is Rachel and Dale, they're... well I don't know who they are *exactly* but anyway, whatever, and this is my almost ex-husband, Jake and his girlfriend, Carrie. Everyone, this is Luke.'

As soon as she says his name Rachel, Jake and even Dale, turn to look at me. I feel the blood drain from my face as the bottom falls out of my stomach and hits the floor.

'Oh fuck,' I hear Rachel say, but her voice sounds like it's a million miles away. My eyes look to Luke and he's stood, arm in arm with Megan, surveying our little group with an equal look of horror on his face. For a brief moment no one says anything, but I can feel Jake's body next to mine, as my head swims and I try to make sense of what's happening.

'Luke?' I whisper, his once familiar name feeling so alien on my lips.

'Yes that's right, Luke,' replies Megan, as Luke and I hold each other's gaze. 'I was just telling them about why you're here, Luke. His girlfriend, well fiancée, ran off on their honeymoon without him after she cancelled their wedding because of a row. Talk about an overreaction, but anyway, he's come all this way to win her back, isn't that romantic?'

I hear movement behind me, as Rachel climbs off her stool and comes to my side. 'Now I know it's nothing to do with me, but I don't think it was quite like that, was it?' she aims at Luke. He frowns, and I feel a surge of affection for her.

'Rach, it's OK,' I say, my voice quiet and croaky.

'Is it?' Jake leans in and says to me softly.

Luke takes a step towards me and, instinctively, I back away and bump into Jake's body wedged just behind me. Luke stops and doesn't move any closer.

'Carrie,' he begins. He looks the same, a little tired but the same. His black hair, strong jaw and swimmer's body. He's the boy I fell in love with all that time ago. He was the man I was going to marry, but everything is different now. Everything. And I feel like I don't know the man standing in front of me at all.

'Sorry, what on earth is actually going on? Am I missing something here?' says Megan loudly, holding up her hands to halt proceedings, her face in a deep frown with a look of utter confusion.

'You have no idea,' groans Rachel, earning her another dirty look from Luke which she bats right back with one of her own. Luke turns to look at Megan, her earlier words clearly only just catching up to him.

'Hang on, that's not his girlfriend, that's my fiancée, the one I came here for. Carrie, I came for *you*. I want us to talk, can we leave? Please?'

Jake puts his hand on my back, the reassuring pressure momentarily quelling the sick feeling rising through my body. He looks down to me, his gaze strong and steady.

'You don't have to do anything you don't want to do, you know that. Just say the word.'

Luke gives a scoff, and we all look at him.

'I'm sorry, who the fuck are you?' he snaps at Jake, who instantly steps forward, and I see a muscle twitch in his cheek as he holds out his hand to Luke.

'Jake Holden, I work here at the hotel.'

I smile, on the inside at least, at the fact he didn't roll out 'CEO of Holden Hotel Group'. I realise now, he's been so quiet to try and control his temper. He's only holding it together because of his position in the company and the fact that Luke must be staying here, although every inch of his body and face are screaming that he wants to drag him down to the beach and throw him into the sea.

'Well maybe I could have a word with Carrie alone, if that's alright with everyone here?' Luke says sarcastically and everyone seems to hold their breath.

'Actually, sorry, I'm not sure I'm OK with this,' Rachel says, stepping forward. 'Sorry Carrie, I'm so sorry, but I can't just say nothing.' Part of me wants to grab her and wrestle her to the floor, but the other part, the part of me that's winning the argument right now, wants to see what's going to happen. I feel, just for this moment, like I'm a spectator in my own life and this particular episode is about to take an interesting turn.

'I don't know you,' Rachel says calmly, 'and, quite frankly, I have no intention of rectifying that, but over this past week I have got to know this wonderful person pretty well. She is one of the most brilliant people I have ever been so lucky to meet and you, Mister can't-keep-it-in-your-pants, have behaved like a twat of epic proportions. You slept with her best friend and, if that wasn't bad enough, she's now having your baby and Carrie found out on your wedding day.'

'Carrie, what the hell have you been telling these people?' Luke interrupts, his face livid. I am about to pull him up on the 'these people' comment, but Rachel jumps straight back in, a sweet but deadly smile on her face.

'Oh sorry, my mistake. Please tell us all which part of anything I just said was incorrect?'

Dale lets out a long breath and a small laugh behind the bar, before we all look at him, and he quickly scurries off to serve a well-timed customer that's appeared. Luke looks at the floor, and I see his cheeks flush slightly, as he shuffles on the spot, and for a slow, extended moment no one says anything until Megan loudly shatters the silence, shaking out her blonde mane as she speaks.

'Sorry, you did *what*? Is that *true*?' She looks between me and Luke and Rachel and then Jake, and I can't seem to summon the words, so very slowly, I nod my head.

Megan gasps and physically recoils from Luke looking him up and down as if he's going to have passed on some hideous disease to her. But then, much to everyone's surprise, and no one's more than mine, she walks over to me and stands by my side, linking her arm through mine.

I'm flanked by her, Jake and Rachel as she physically crosses the battle line to my team, or perhaps that should be our team by the display of solidarity I'm experiencing, then she shakes her head and says with utter disgust, 'And I had *dinner* with you.'

Jake steps forward, his huge bulk making even well-built Luke look small.

'Perhaps this is a discussion for another day,' he says in a measured tone. 'Rachel, I suggest you take Carrie inside.

Luke, please feel free to enjoy a drink at the bar, Dale will be happy to serve you.'

We all hear a loud 'humph' come from Dale's direction, indicating he would not be happy at all, before he recovers himself and simply says, 'Of course.'

Jake gently touches my forearm, and I feel Rachel's arm around me as she steers me in the direction of the hotel. Megan is still by my side, shaking her head, her arm still through mine and I don't bother to remove it. Right now, I'll take all the support I can get.

'Don't you tell her what to do!' Luke says in a sudden outburst. 'I don't know what the fuck's been going on or who you think you are but she's my fiancée.'

'You sure about that?' Jake says, without missing a beat, his face set and his eyebrows slightly raised as if daring Luke to challenge him. I can't stand it any longer, and I turn, breaking free from my chaperones and rounding on Luke, hot tears stinging my eyes.

'I have nothing to say to you, Luke. You shouldn't have come. I don't want to talk, don't you understand? Nothing you say will change what you've done!' My voice is raised, causing a few guests to cast curious glances in our direction. 'Get away from me Luke, you disgust me.'

'And me,' adds Megan, as she strokes my hair, and the tears fall thick and fast in rivers down my cheeks. Rachel wipes her hand across my face in an attempt to brush them off, but they are just replaced with a fresh deluge.

'Come on, sweetie, let's get you inside,' she says softly, and I let myself be led to the hotel.

Chapter Thirty-Two

I sit on the balcony, my face still wet with tears and my head thumping. I'm nursing a glass of neat rum that Rachel has poured me, which tastes vile but I drink it anyway. I've been sat here for a good hour, I would guess. After Rachel and Megan brought me up to the room, Megan slipped off quietly, but before she left I heard her and Rachel have a very brief, whispered conversation.

'I've got a good mind to get Jake to throw him out of the hotel! Rachel, did he really do what you said?'

''Fraid so. Look, Megan, I know this is nothing to do with you, and I'm sure Jake is keeping an eye on him, but could you just do a bit of low-key recon and make sure he doesn't try and come up to Carrie, and if he does just keep him at bay somehow, I know she doesn't want to see him.'

'I will do it!' I could hear Megan reply forcefully, as if she was donning her camouflage and warpaint at that very moment.

After she left, Rachel brought me my drink, or anaesthetic as it's currently proving to be, and has sat next to me on the balcony in silence. I didn't need her to say anything. I don't even know what to say myself, so how could I ask anyone else to help?

There's a soft knock on the door, and I jump out of my skin. Rachel puts her hand on my leg.

'I'll go,' she says, then adds quickly when she sees the panic in my eyes, 'don't worry, I won't let him in. I promise.'

I face out to sea as I hear the door open, my heart thumping out of my chest at the potential of Luke being this close to me again, but my body sags with relief as I hear Jake's voice, quiet and instantly calming.

'Can I come in?' There's a pause as Rachel hesitates, clearly unsure what to do.

'Sorry, let me speak to Carrie, I don't know... I'm not sure if...'

'It's OK,' I call to her. My voice sounds raspy and my throat is scratchy and sore from my crying. I feel Jake's presence at my side, and I glance up at him, his face breaking out into a look of pure anguish as his eyes meet mine.

'Jesus.' He sinks to his knees, at my side, and clasps my face in his hands.

'Do I look that awful?' I sniff with a hollow laugh.

'You are beautiful, always, but I much prefer to see you not in tears.'

Rachel clears her throat and points to the door.

'I'm just going to be outside, OK? I'll come back as soon as you want me to.'

Jake reaches into his pocket and pulls out his key card, handing it to her.

'Use my room, Rachel. Help yourself to anything in the fridge or whatever. If you want, call some room service for anything the two of you might need.'

'Thanks,' she says and takes the card, planting a kiss on my head before she goes.

Jake pulls the other sunbed over and sits on it, placing his hands over mine.

'I know you're not alright, sweet cheeks, and I don't blame you. I'm sorry I didn't come sooner. I wanted to give you some space, and I was checking some things with reception.' He cups his hands on my face for a moment, and the way he looks at me makes me eyes fill with tears again. 'I am so sorry no one could warn you. No one made the connection between your names, and he booked it so last minute. Maya hadn't even seen the booking yet, even then she might not have realised.' He pauses, and I can tell he's considering his words. 'He's booked in for a week.'

'A *week*?' I cry, feeling fresh tears threaten and my chest tighten at the thought.

'It's OK. I've made some calls, and there is a hotel just down the road that we have a deal with if we can't accommodate guests and vice versa. They have room for him, so we can ask him to move to somewhere else due to unforeseen circumstances. Don't worry about that bit, that's for us to figure out. The main thing is he doesn't have to be here if you don't want him to be. I wanted to speak to you before we did anything.'

I take a deep sigh and close my eyes, pressing my fingers to my temples.

'Jake, I have to talk to him. I don't want to but, sooner or later, I will have to talk to him. I was an idiot to think I could run away and never have to face it. I ran all the way here and what happened? All the shit just followed me and turned up on my doorstep. Well, your doorstep. What did I think was going to happen? That I could just stay here forever and never go home? That a few text messages were going to get rid of it all?'

I ball my hands into fists and then spread my fingers in exasperation while letting out a shout of frustration.

'I'm so angry, Jake. I am just so angry. Angry about how the two people who were supposed to love me and support me betrayed me. About how I was humiliated in front of my family and friends and that now, as a result of *that* union, there is going to be a constant, living reminder of what they did who is related to my best friend, Kate. Who, incidentally, desperately wants a baby and can't even have one. I'm angry that I care so much, when what I should do is tell them all to go to hell and move on with my life. I've tried so hard this week, Jake, so hard, but then what happens? Luke shows up and I go to pieces.

'And then there's you. I can't pretend I don't feel something for you, because I do, and it's so confusing because at the start of this week, my heart felt broken and then you stroll into my life and suddenly I feel something I've never felt before, and I don't understand how that can happen.' My eyes are streaming with tears, as I bury my face in my hands. A silence hangs in the air, and the noise of the night seems suddenly louder. The rush of the waves, the music and laughter from the bar, the breeze rustling the palm trees.

'Carrie,' Jake tentatively lays his hand on my arm, 'it's OK. It's OK to not have the answers...'

'Answers?' I interrupt him with a bitter laugh. 'I don't even have the questions right now, Jake.'

'Do you want me to get Luke to leave?' he says, ignoring my outburst. God, he is frustratingly calm and composed, and I'm here acting like a complete psycho.

'I don't know,' I say honestly. 'I have to talk to him. I can't see him tonight, I'll have to speak to him tomorrow.'

I sag back on to the sunbed, deflated, defeated and feeling broken.

'Do you want me to go?'

I look at him, taking in his face, watching as the breeze ruffles his hair and his eyes seem to glow.

'Yes. No. I don't know. I just…' I stop and sniff loudly, giving a small laugh. 'Well, if you wanted to see me again earlier this evening, you certainly won't after tonight's display.' There are so many other things I know I should say but, right now, I've run out of words and energy.

'Sweet cheeks, it's fine.' A small smile crosses his face. 'I'll send Rachel back in, and I'll see you tomorrow. Just say the word and he's gone.' He takes his massive hands and rubs them across his face before reaching out and cupping my face in his palm. 'And, for the record, nothing and no one will ever stop me wanting you.' He leans forward and kisses my cheek with a tenderness that brings more tears and a heavy ache into my chest. 'Get some sleep. You'll feel better tomorrow.'

'You sure about that?' I ask, repeating the words he said to Luke earlier this evening. His face breaks into a smile, as he stands to leave, and I unfold myself and get up too.

'That's my girl.' And with a final wink as a sign off, he leaves.

I walk inside and pull the doors closed behind me, sinking on to the bed. I look to the side and see my phone still plugged in where I've disregarded it when I left this evening. At home, it barely leaves my side but here, I feel like there is no one, except perhaps my mum, that can't wait. I unplug it and turn it over in my hands, feeling its smooth, curved edges, the lamplight of the room reflecting off the surface. Then, with all the strength I can muster, I hurl it at the wall.

I wake up, hot, confused, my eyes stinging and my head pounding. God this feels worse than any of the hangovers I've had this holiday. I glance at the lump under the duvet next to me and see Rachel's dark mane strewn out behind her on the pillow like a mermaid, her body gently rising as she breathes in her sleep.

After I decided it would be a good idea to smash my phone's screen so I can barely see it, let alone use it, I cried some more, and Rachel found me curled up on the bed and just sat with me until I eventually fell asleep after a very long time.

I find my watch in the bathroom and, even though it tells me it's only five thirty a.m., I know I can't go back to sleep, so I put on my bikini, that's been hanging to dry over the side of the bath, dress in my denim shorts and vest and shove my towel under my arm. I slip the room key in my back pocket as I gently open the door, careful not to wake Rachel as I leave.

As it closes behind me, I stand and stare at the door to Jake's suite. It takes every ounce of restraint I possess not to knock on his door and curl up next to him in his bed, breathing in his scent and feeling his skin next to mine. I walk over to the door and very lightly place my hand on the wood, taking a deep breath. Even from here, I can feel him. Feel his presence and that constant tug towards him. I tear myself away and make my way through the deserted hotel, and out towards the beach, without meeting a soul.

I feel calmer once I'm outside and find myself almost jogging to get down to the sea. The early morning sun is just breaking through the clouds, and the sand is cold and damp under foot from the night's rain. I take off my shorts and top, dropping them to the sand on top of my towel, and jog into the sea.

The water's cold but I push on, gasping, and thrust my body forward through the waves to dive head first under the water. The instant silence, the cold on my scalp and the tingle on my warm skin bring me back to life, the images of the last few hours rushing through my head. I rise to the surface and take a deep breath, as my face pushes out of the water into the warm, morning air. I squeeze out my hair and lick the salty water from my lips, relishing the tang of the sea on my tongue, as I begin to swim away from the shoreline, stretching my arms out in front of me and pushing hard with my legs. It feels so satisfying to glide through the water so effortlessly, the blood rushing to my muscles as I power on, cutting through the waves. I come to a stop, treading water for a moment where I can no longer reach the bottom, before making my way back to shore at a more leisurely pace.

The sun is burning away the cloud already and, by the time I reach the beach, I have to squint against its brilliant rays as they break through the leaves of the palm trees that are dancing in the wind. I wrap my towel around me and sit on the sand, staring out to sea. How is it that in some moments everything seems so simple and then in others, life's the most complicated thing in the world? My dad always used to tell me that nothing worth having ever came easy, but this morning feels like it doesn't come easy, whether you want it or not.

'You always did love the beach, didn't you?'

I jump out of my skin at the sudden interruption to my thoughts, and my body tenses at the familiar, yet so strange, sound of Luke's voice. I don't turn or make any movement to get up from my current position so, after a pause, he comes and takes a seat next to me. I turn my head towards him but can't quite bring myself to look at his face.

It's so strange him being here. Like my little bubble of protection has been burst by his sudden, unexpected arrival. Never in a million years did I think he would come out here. Part of me realises that I should probably be glad he's come to fight for me, but I'm not, not at all. I don't fill the awkward silence that settles between us, not wanting to make it any easier on him, and stare back out to the horizon.

'It's really nice here, isn't it?' he says, almost cheerily.

I turn my head towards his, meeting his eyes for the first time, and repeat his words slowly.

'It's really nice here, isn't it? *That's* your opening line?' But he ignores my venomous tone, as if I haven't spoken.

'I couldn't sleep and saw you come down here from my balcony. Carrie, we need to talk.'

'Do we, Luke? What would you like to talk about? Please go on, I am all ears,' I say sharply. We're not even thirty seconds into the conversation, and already I'm losing my cool. He winces at my tone before taking a deep breath.

'Please, can you just listen before you say anything? I know it doesn't change anything, but I am so sorry. I know what a mess this is and how badly I've fucked up. But Emily and I, we're not going to be together. I've said I will help with the baby, but I don't want to be with her, Carrie, I want to be with you.'

'Luke, can't you see that makes it worse, not better?' I yell, unable to help myself. 'The fact that you threw it all away on something that meant nothing to you. And now there's a baby on the way you still can't be bothered to even try.'

'Why would you want me and Emily to be together?' he asks confused.

'I don't, Luke, I just… It feels like it's all for nothing. And a child gets dragged into this whole mess as well, with parents that aren't even together, and it has a whole, dark cloud hanging over it all. It just all feels so wrong and mixed up.'

'Carrie, I want you back,' he says hurriedly, like he's desperate to get the words out before he loses me completely. 'I want us to be together. To have our own family, a proper one.'

I let out a bitter laugh and shake my head at him.

'Luke, forget about the baby for a second. Even if it didn't exist, even if a baby wasn't in the equation, you cheated on me. With Emily. I was supposed to be able to trust the two of you more than anyone else in the world, and you will never be able to rebuild that, no matter what happens. Not now, not in a year's time, not ever. I will never be able to trust you again, don't you see that? Imagine it was the other way round. Imagine it was me and Dan.'

He puts his hand to his forehead and rubs at his temples, as if trying to remove the image from his mind, but I carry on.

'Luke, think about it. You find out on our wedding day I've slept with Dan and now I'm having his baby. Put yourself in my position, what would you do? You'd just forgive me and marry me? Would you Luke?' I'm trying to keep calm but can feel the tension in my voice rising as I struggle to hold it together. He sits there for a moment, and I see tears in his eyes.

'I would want to make it work…' he whispers.

'So you'd be OK with it then, would you? That Dan had kissed me, touched me, seen me naked, had sex with me, that his baby was growing inside me? You'd be completely fine with that?'

He slowly shakes his head. 'No. No, I wouldn't.'

'Thinking about what you did makes me feel physically sick, Luke. I can't bear to look at you, let alone have you touch me or even think about being in any sort of relationship with you. I don't want you in my life any more.' Tears are rolling down my face as I say the words with more strength than I feel, but with complete conviction. 'We are over, Luke. Over. It's done. You shouldn't have come here, I don't know what you thought was going to happen.'

He wipes his own tears away and tries to reach for my hand before my warning look sends him into retreat.

'I just wanted to…' He lets out a long sigh. 'I think I already knew it, but I couldn't let you go without a fight. I needed to know I'd done everything I could to make it right.'

'Luke, have you even listened to a word I've said? You will never make this right. Nothing will fix it, you have to understand that, surely? Let me make this perfectly clear for you, once and for all. I am not your fiancée. We are never getting married, and I don't love you any more.' I say the words and can't quite believe the truth I feel in them as they leave my lips.

'Carrie, don't say that,' he says, as a look of utter panic spreads across his face. 'Of course you love me! We've been together forever, and it's only been a week! You don't just fall out of love with someone in seven days.'

I push my hair back and take a moment to think about what I'm about to say next. Not that I need one to make sure I'm doing the right thing, but because I feel like it demands a moment of silence for the life I'm about to bury, never to return to.

'Despite hating you right now, Luke, you can't just switch off your feelings for someone so, yes, you're right, there is something still there. But any love I had for you died that day I found out what you did. I loved you for the man you were, but the man I fell in love with, the man I loved for all those years, would never have done this to me, to us. You're not that man to me any more. He doesn't exist. So, no Luke, I don't love you.'

Luke shakes his head and runs his hand through his hair. I look at him, studying his face, the face I've looked at for so many hours, woken up to so many times, that now seems so, so different.

'We should never have been getting married anyway,' I say softly, as I trace a circle in the sand with my finger. 'If we had the sort of relationship we should have had, none of this would have happened, let's be honest. I think we just got carried away with it all. I hate you for what you did to me. And I won't ever forgive you, but I can see now it wasn't right. It wasn't how it should be.'

We are both quiet for a long moment, the breeze whipping around us, the noise of the waves breaking on the sand seeming louder than I've ever heard them.

'Carrie, I need you to be honest with me. It's been bothering me since last night. Megan called that Jake guy your boyfriend. Why?'

I can't deny that I thought this question might come up, and yet I still didn't prepare myself for what I would say but I think, all things considered, it doesn't really matter now. My heart beats a little faster, as I think about Jake and the fact that I really don't want to be talking to Luke about him. Jake is nothing to do with Luke, and I don't want Luke to have anything to do with him. I feel like even hearing him speak Jake's name taints it somewhat.

'We've…' I stop, looking for the right phrase, 'we've been spending a lot of time together.'

Luke laughs bitterly. 'Have you now? Well isn't that all very cosy? Who the fuck is he, anyway?'

'He's someone who's been there for me when you weren't, Luke,' I say angrily, seriously irked that I'm suddenly becoming the bad guy, yet I can't help but feel a pang of guilt for what's happened between me and Jake, even though I know I shouldn't. 'When you had no regard for me at all, he came and picked up the pieces.'

'Isn't he just the knight in shining armour then?' Luke says, heatedly.

I know my face is going red at the thought of Jake and, as I struggle to meet Luke's eye, I realise that, despite it being over with me and him, I can't hide that fact that he knows me all too well.

'Oh my God, did something happen? Has something happened between you?'

His face contorts into a horrified look as the possibility dawns on him, one that I don't think he ever considered. I can't speak for a moment, and my throat is dry as I remember Jake kissing my neck, his hands on my bare skin, our bodies moving together in a perfect, steady rhythm.

'It did, didn't it?' Luke shakes his head, and I hear his breathing deepen. 'Did you kiss him?'

I know there is no going back from what I say. I don't want Luke any more, but the fact that he might not want me brings such an air of finality to the situation that I hadn't really considered. But as my thoughts drift back to Jake, I know that's what I want.

'Yes,' I say, the word hanging in the air. 'Yes, I've kissed him.'

'Jesus Christ, Carrie! What the fuck? You didn't waste any time did you?' Luke replies, his voice raised and angry.

I turn on him, absolutely livid, a new-found rage rising up in my body. 'Hang on a minute, I don't think you're in any position to lecture me! So you're telling me it's absolutely fine for you to sleep with someone else when we were actually about to get married and were still together but not for me, even when we're broken up?'

Luke stares at me, a shocked look on his face, and I suddenly realise why. Shit.

'I'm sorry,' Luke says in a slow and strained tone, raising his hands, 'what did you just say? You *slept* with him? Are you fucking joking? You actually slept with him?' He spreads his hands in front of him as if looking for an answer to appear out of nowhere.

'I don't have to explain anything to you,' I retort heatedly. I feel momentarily flustered but quickly regain my composure. 'You lost that right when you decided to throw our relationship away for a one-night stand with my best friend!'

'Oh yes you do!' he shouts. 'I want to hear you say it.'

'You know what, Luke?' I scrabble to my feet clutching my towel to me, and he immediately gets up as well, 'Yes, I slept with him, and you know what else? It was fucking great! And I didn't do it because I wanted to hurt you or to make you feel like shit or to prove a point. I did it because I wanted to. I really, *really* wanted to.'

We stand there, glaring at each other, both equally as furious as the other.

'Right,' Luke says, matter-of-factly, 'well I guess that's that then.'

'I'm sorry, *what*?' I say my eyes wide. There is no way in hell he is going to slut-shame me into being the one to end this relationship, just because I slept with someone after I broke up with him for sleeping with someone. God, even I can barely keep up.

'Well, I mean you've clearly made your choice and moved on without a second thought, haven't you, jumping into bed with some stranger!'

And for a moment I feel like I'm going to punch him in the face.

'Oh my God, Luke, listen to yourself!' I yell in frustration, not caring if anyone overhears us, although the beach still seems totally deserted. 'Firstly, Jake is not a stranger…'

'No? So you didn't meet him a week ago then?' Luke interrupts. 'What's his last name?' Oh for God's sake, this is ridiculous, but I can't help myself.

'Holden,' I say smugly. 'And before you ask, he's thirty-six.' I can't quite believe this has spiralled to this level of petty, yet here we are. I let my towel drop to the floor and feel suddenly self-conscious in front of this man who's seen me naked thousands of times, the first man that ever did, in fact. I quickly pull on my shorts and vest over my still damp bikini and stand with my arms folded across my chest.

'Look, Jake… Luke!' I amend hurriedly, as I realise my mistake. 'Luke!' Oh shit. As soon as the words spill out of my mouth I want to curl up and die. Well, that was completely unintentional, but I bet that hurt him. Luke throws his hands into his hair with a horrified gasp, as he looks at me in utter contempt.

'Are you serious right now? Carrie, I don't even know who you are any more.'

My face falls, and I look at the ground, covering my eyes with my hands, before I sigh and look at him. 'You know what the saddest thing is?' I ask him quietly. 'I feel like, after all this time, perhaps we didn't really know each other at all.'

Luke's eyes meet mine, and I can see the hurt in them. The defeat, the sadness and finally, the realisation that there's no coming back from this now.

'So that's it then? Over. Just like that?'

'No, Luke, not just like that. If only it *was* just like that. I'm hurt, I'm angry, everything I knew has been turned upside down. I came here for space and you couldn't even give me that. You didn't come here for me, you came here for you, to try and relieve some of your own guilt. If you ever loved me at all you would have left me alone to get my head around things, but you had to push it. You came here to try and get to me to say it's OK. Well it isn't. You couldn't just be strong enough to let me hate you, could you? Even though I was the one who was betrayed, you had to make it about you. I'm so angry with you Luke, and Emily, but now, I'm not even sorry it happened. If that's the kind of people you both are, I'm glad I found out now rather than after we were married. I just wish I hadn't wasted sixteen years of my life. I know you're hurt too, but I'm not sorry for what happened with me and Jake. That wasn't about me and you, it was about me and him.'

Luke meets my tearful eyes and gives me the most sorrowful look I have ever seen.

'I can't believe there's even a you and him. A you and anyone else. I'm so sorry. I know this is all my own fault, but... I just... I just can't believe this is it.'

'This time last week I would have said the same, but it is Luke. It has to be. We can't be friends. You and Emily, you're having a baby, for Christ's sake. I can't be around that. I don't want to be. I think you should just go.'

He's silent for a second as if weighing up his options, but really, he doesn't have that many.

'OK. I'll book the next flight back home. I guess there's probably one I can get tomorrow, maybe the day after. I don't suppose you'll come with me? We still have stuff to sort out. The house, the wedding refunds, bills. All that sort of stuff.'

'The house is mine, in my name. You never paid anything towards it therefore we have nothing to sort out where that's concerned. You get your stuff out and that's that. The next set of bills we pay out of the joint account, then whatever money is left in there we can split, and I'll close it down. What else... the wedding refunds? Well, Kate said she cancelled anything she could and whatever money gets refunded will go into the joint account anyway, so I guess we just split that too. I'll speak to her and see what the suppliers have said, but I don't think we will get any money back from anyone. You know, seeing as we cancelled with a couple of hours' notice.'

'Wow, you've really got it all worked out, haven't you?' Luke says with a sad laugh.

'Well it's not like I had a choice, is it?'

Luke looks so ashamed of himself, and I'm glad. Glad that he's finally realising the magnitude of his actions and also relieved that this is, hopefully, the only time we will have to have this conversation. But I recognise that if it is, I'm not quite done.

'You know what, Luke? I thought that after all this time, even if you didn't love me, that you at least respected and cared for me on some level not to do what you did. I'd rather we'd broken up before any of this happened, than have to go through it.'

I take a deep breath and square my shoulders before I ask him for one final truth, if he can manage it.

'I need you to answer me a question, and be honest. Quite frankly that's the least you can do.'

'I will,' he agrees nervously. 'What is it?'

'If I hadn't found out that day, would you still have married me?'

Every fibre of his body freezes as the colour drains from his face. He clearly didn't expect that.

'Well? Would you?' I say, louder this time, and he flinches slightly.

Luke can't bring himself to say the words, so he just gives the smallest nod of his head.

'Eugh!' I yell, in frustration, kicking at the sand. 'You really are a complete shit. Go Luke. Just go. I don't ever want to see you again.'

'When are you coming home?' he asks feebly.

'I don't know. And even if I did, that is no longer your concern.'

And with that, I stalk up the beach away from the hotel, fresh tears brimming at my eyes. I round the corner, where he can no longer see me, and crumple to my knees, the sand grazing against my bare skin, letting loud sobs wrack through my body until there are no more tears left to cry.

Chapter Thirty-Three

I walk further and further along the beach until I realise it's probably time to go back. I don't have my phone or my watch, so I have no idea what time it is, but the sun's gradually getting higher and hotter. There are hotel workers dragging sunbeds around the beaches and early morning swimmers and joggers are starting to appear between the buildings, down the little alleyways that lead from the main road on to the sand. I feel like I need to talk to Jake, but now it seems like he's somehow involved, I don't know if I can, or if I should.

Back at the hotel, the beach is quiet, but there are a few people moseying around, walking on the beach, getting breakfast or swimming in the pool. The gardeners are tending to the plants, before it gets too hot, and sweeping down the paths, ready for the guests to start spilling out. Everyone's lives are going on as normal, but here I am, not knowing which way is up or down, left or right, if I'm coming or going.

I'm desperate not to speak to anyone so keep my head down and my pace quick as I slip through the doors of the lobby, but am greeted with the dazzling sight of a shirtless Jake, leaning over the reception desk talking to Maya in a hushed tone, his face set with a deep frown. He double takes as he sees me and immediately strides over, stopping just in front of me. I can see from his body language he wants to reach out and close the gap between us, but he doesn't, and I'm not sure if I respect him for it or if I'm disappointed. I think probably both.

'Coffee?' he asks me tentatively.

I nod.

'My office.'

I nod again and let him lead me through the door to the back offices, Maya giving me a sympathetic smile as she chats away on the phone. The offices are empty, which I'm thankful for, and Jake ushers me inside, closing the door behind him. He immediately goes over to the coffee machine on the side and presses some buttons so it whirrs to life. He doesn't ask me anything or make any movement to try and press me for info, he just sits on the sofa opposite me, as the coffee machine works its magic, giving me a small, reassuring smile.

The silence is killing me, but I'm not sure where to start. 'Jake, I'm sorry.'

'Well, you should be,' he replies and my head, and heart, drop. 'You've been in my company for at least three minutes and you've not once looked at my chest.'

I snap my head up to meet his smile, and instantly feel better, for the first time that morning breaking into a smile of my own.

'Sweet cheeks, you have nothing to be sorry for. Why on earth do you need to be sorry?'

'For Luke turning up. And making it awkward.'

Jake holds up his hands and leans back on the sofa.

'Hey, it's not awkward for me, I'm only worried about you. I thought you were going to pass out when you saw him.'

'And I thought you might knock him out.'

He laughs and stretches his arms on the back of the sofa, opening up his gorgeous torso for me to gaze upon at my leisure. He clocks me looking, and I can't help that my lips curl up slightly at the corners.

'It was somewhat tempting but, you know me, I'm a lover not a fighter,' he says with a wink and any tension I felt starts to ebb away at his relaxed, easy attitude.

'Why are you just what I need?' The words leave my mouth before I've had chance to think about what I'm even saying. A grins spreads across his sun-kissed face, and my cheeks flush with embarrassment at my candidness. 'Sorry, I didn't mean... I just... OK, maybe I do mean it.' I wring my hands in my lap. 'I'm sorry, I can't help how I feel. I thought I was over Luke and, in a way, I am, I want to be, but I'm still hurting, Jake, and I'm still so angry with him. I don't think I love him any more. Well, I know I don't, and I told him as much. But to have it out there, and to actually say it, it was scary because it's all I've known. And then you're here, and all I want to do is be near you. All the time. I know it sounds crazy, but you just...' I pause to catch up as the words come tumbling out, 'you make everything make sense.'

I look up at him, a smile still on his beautiful face, his eyes burning into mine, as if he's reading the words written on my heart. He stands up and, in total silence, goes to make up two coffees before bringing them back to the table and setting one down in front of each of us. He leans forward, resting his forearms on his knees, and shakes his head to remove a stray strand of hair from his eyes.

'I don't want to turn this into to some sort of serious chat because one, I think you've probably had enough of those for one day and it's barely even breakfast time and two, I'm shit at big speeches, but I think it's only fair you have all the facts.'

My stomach lurches, and I take a deep breath, unsure whether or not this is going to be bad or good news.

'As soon as I saw you in reception, I haven't been able to get you out of my head. You're there when I wake up on a morning, when I'm supposed to be working, when I go to bed and all the moments in between. I love my life, I was quite happy plodding along, doing my own thing and then suddenly there you were. All freckles and magical smile and beautiful laugh. Sweet cheeks, you're the most unexpected inevitable I've ever encountered. And I say all this without any underlying intention or hidden agenda.'

He reaches for his coffee and takes a sip, replacing the cup on the table, and looks at me through his rogue strands of hair that, like their owner, seem to have trouble behaving.

'Just promise me that you won't settle. Not for anything less than incredible, no matter who or what it is. Because this is all we get. And you're just too damn special.'

I want to throw myself into his arms and kiss him, but my legs have turned to cement and I'm rooted to the sofa. My mouth and throat are dry, as I clear my throat.

'Jake, you're just so distracting. I can't think straight with you here. I don't know how to sort my thoughts out into sensible, rational ones.'

'They don't always have to be sensible, rational ones, you know?' he says with a soft smile, but my face is far from smiling.

'But that's just it, I have such a mess to sort through, they do have to be. I can't make sense of anything with you so close, because all I want to do is…' I blush and he suppresses a smile, as he knows exactly where my thoughts were about to go, '…all I want to do is be around you, and I can't think straight when I am. I thought being here would help me sort out my feelings about Luke, but never in a million years did I think I would have to sort out my feelings for you too.'

Well this has taken an unexpected turn to the serious. Admitting I have feelings for Jake was never on the agenda and that includes admitting it to myself, let alone admitting it out loud to him. I take a sip of my coffee. It's the perfect drinking temperature, plus frothy, creamy and bitter. I take another mouthful, cradling the smooth, warm cup in my hands for comfort.

'Do you want me to get Luke to leave?' he asks. The only question he's put to me so far. My heart says yes, but I shake my head.

'No, he knows it's over between us. He said he was going to get the next available flight.'

'Well, like I said, if you want it, he's gone. No fuss, no drama, I promise.'

We both pick up our cups and simultaneously lift them to our mouths draining the last of our coffee before returning them to the table, in absolute, perfect symmetry.

'Jake, I think I need to go.'

'I understand. It's fine, sweet cheeks. Would you like to get dinner tonight? Room service maybe, then you don't have to worry about bumping into him.'

'No,' I say quietly, 'I mean go home.'

I see a look of something flash across his face. Sadness, panic, anger? I can't place it, but he's shaken by my words and momentarily loses his calm composure.

'What?'

'I'm sorry, Jake. I never expected this to happen with you, but it has, and I need to work things out. I realise I have a life I need to sort out at home.' I gesture my arms around me. 'This, this isn't real.'

He pushes his hands though his hair, breathing deeply before he finally speaks. His voice and smile are tinged with sadness as he looks at me, that familiar spark of energy surging through me under his stare.

'It feels pretty real though, doesn't it?'

My heart aches and tears burn at my eyes. I feel one escape and roll down my cheek, as Jake moves around the table to my side, brushing it off with his thumb as he cups my face.

'Baby, please don't cry. I didn't want this to be that sort of conversation.'

I take his hand and gently move it from my face, holding it in mine, examining his fingers and the lines on his palm.

'I'm so sorry, Jake. I never meant to get involved like this. I just need to work things out, and I think I need to do it alone.'

'I've told you, don't apologise to me. I don't want you to leave, but I do understand, and please don't think the fact that I'm not trying to stop you means I don't care. It's the absolute opposite. It's not easy for me to see you go. No matter what happens, I will always be happy that you came to stay.'

He kisses my fingers to his lips and murmurs on to my skin, his gaze locked on to mine.

'There's something I want to say to you, but I don't think you're ready to hear it right now. But if and when I see you again, I'll tell you, OK?'

I nod and sniff away my tears. This is so much harder than I thought it would be. My heart aches at the thought of never seeing him again, but I realise this is a distinct possibility.

'I'm going to go and make another cup of coffee, because I don't think I can actually watch you walk away from me, even if it would give me an excuse to check out your bottom.'

I laugh, sniffing through my tears.

'Bye, Baywatch. You've been the best.'

He treats me to the parting gift of his brilliant smile that, this time, doesn't quite meet his eyes but still, he gives me that wink I'm now so well acquainted with.

'You've been better. I'll see you around, sweet cheeks.' And, as promised, he turns to make another coffee.

'You don't know how much I wish that was true,' I breathe, and I walk from his office feeling an overwhelming sense of unhappiness that I didn't feel at the end of my first life-changing conversation of the day with Luke. This feeling now, that's how it should have felt with Luke, how it should have felt to end my relationship with my fiancé, not with Jake. With Luke, I felt relief. Now, I just feel heartbroken.

'Promise you'll text me when you get home?'

'Of course I will. Thank you so much, Rach, you've been amazing.'

'And here I was thinking I was going to be in for a boring holiday sat by the pool. I honestly haven't ever had as much fun as this in my life! It's been an absolute pleasure to share this complete madness with you. I can't believe you managed to get a flight out tonight, I've had no time to prepare myself for this!'

'Me neither,' I say, honestly. I only started looking this morning but spoke to the airline and they had a few spare seats for the night flight back to the UK so here I am, packed and ready to go. Well, as ready as I'll ever be. Which despite my earlier conviction that this was the right thing to do, it now feels like I'm not remotely ready at all. I'm more than a little worried that Luke might have booked himself on this flight but there were hardly any seats left. At least I hope not.

I checked out with Maya just a few minutes ago, and the whole time I felt like she wanted to say something to me but couldn't. We stuck to some somewhat awkward, stilted chit-chat, but she gave my hand a squeeze as she handed over my paperwork and simply said that she hoped she would see me again. Then I ran away before I started crying again.

'Have a good last few days. What time do you fly on Friday?' I ask Rachel.

'At like twelve something, so I should be back home by teatime. God, I'm going to be so bored without you!' She pulls me into a huge hug. 'And I know my instructions, I won't tell Luke you've gone until you've taken off, I promise to wait. Despite wanting to run up there to him this instant, laugh in his face and tell him you've buggered off back home just as he's arrived.'

I've basically hidden from Luke for the whole day and even switched off my smashed phone so he can't call me. There was no way I wanted him on the same flight, and I know he won't even have considered I would leave.

'Look after Jake for me, won't you?' I say to her, and I can feel myself close to tears again. She gives a little laugh and a cough, looking at me with raised brows.

'I think we both know there is no one else on this planet who can possibly come close to you when it comes to Jake. But yes, I promise to make sure he doesn't throw himself into the sea.'

'Oh, Rach, don't say that!' I rub my hands over my face in despair. 'I can't get my head straight here with him,' I groan, and she takes my hands in hers, holding them in front of her.

'Honey, you have to do what's right for you. And, anyway, something tells me Jake isn't going to forget about you in a hurry. Don't worry about him, he's a big boy. Or so you told me,' she giggles.

'I'm going to miss you so much,' I laugh.

'Me too. But Northampton isn't far, we can see each other loads.'

'I would love that.'

'Oh my God! I know you weren't going to try and sneak off without even saying goodbye, Maya just told me you were leaving. And here I was hoping for some cocktails and a bit of a girls' night to cheer you up!'

'Megan, will you shut the hell up!' reprimands Rachel. 'This is supposed to be a covert operation here.'

Megan pulls a guilty face and lowers her voice to whisper. 'Sorry, sorry,' she hisses. 'Roger that!'

She straightens herself and shakes out her ponytail, her short, navy blue sundress swinging around her lithe, tanned frame as she does so.

'Carrie, good luck.' She pulls me into an unexpected hug and squeezes me tightly. 'I know we don't know each other all that well, but what that hideous Luke fellow did to you was simply awful. No matter how good-looking he is,

I'd have dumped his cheating behind sooner than you could say divorce. You deserve so much better.'

'Thanks, Megan,' I say and mean it. Who knew Jake's wife would be someone I will actually be a little sad to leave behind too? She might be totally mental, but she is good entertainment value, I'll give her that. 'Good luck with the wedding. I'm sure you'll look amazing and it will all go brilliantly.'

'Oh well, naturally,' she says, no hint of irony in her voice at all. 'And I hope it works out with you and Jake. I've known that man a long time, and I can see why he's in love with you. You really are perfect for him.'

Time seems to slow for a moment, as I process her words.

'Sorry, what did you say?' Rachel says grabbing Megan's arm.

'What?' Megan replies, extracting her arm from Rachel's grip, looking horrified.

'About Jake being in love with Carrie?' Rachel's voice is high-pitched, and she sounds slightly hysterical.

'Oh that. Well yes, I mean, just that he is, isn't he?' she says nonchalantly. 'Come on, you'd have to be blind not to notice!'

We all stand there, Rachel staring at me intently, waiting for something to happen, so I suppose I better say something.

'He's not, Megan. We're close that's all. He definitely isn't in love with me.'

'No, he loves you, darling, trust me, I know. He's never loved *me* that way, and he married me for goodness' sake! I can see it a mile off. Plus, you know, he told me.' Megan seems to be completely unbothered that her husband is in love with me, and her eyes flick between me and Rachel, taking in our shocked expressions. 'What, you didn't know? God, you really have had your head in the sand, haven't you? Bless you, darling. But yes, totally head over heels,' she laughs.

I can't speak, but luckily Rachel seems to be acting as my emotional translator.

'Jake actually told you he was in love with Carrie?' Rachel says, far too loudly for my liking, and I dart my eyes around the front of the hotel, checking no one's overheard as she carries on grilling Megan. 'OK, so what did he say? And I mean, like, the actual words. You can't give us half a bloody story!'

I roll my eyes and huff at the pair of them. 'For God's sake, stop saying that, both of you. Jake isn't in love with me, Megan. He might… like me, or maybe even fancy me, but he can't be in love with me.' Even to my own ears, my voice sounds slightly freaked.

'Except that he is, though,' she says matter-of-factly. Rachel opens her mouth to say something, but Megan cuts her off. 'Yes, *alright* Rachel! Will you calm down? I'm getting there if you would let me finish.'

Megan spreads her hands in front of her, a delighted look on her face, clearly thrilled she's the one in the know.

'Well, Jake and I were sorting out this whole divorce thing and we were talking, as you do with your almost, nearly ex-husband, and so I asked him if you and him were serious, and he said no but that if things were different then maybe you could be. He didn't elaborate, obviously, otherwise I would have known who that scummy little toad Luke was but anyway, so *I* said the problem with me and him was that no matter how hard we tried we just weren't suited, and then Jake said that the thing with *you* two was that you didn't have to seem to try at all.' Megan pauses for dramatic affect and leans in towards us. 'So, me being me, I just said that it sounded like he'd fallen in love, and *he* said,' she falls silent looking pointedly at Rachel, 'and these are his *exact* words before you start off again, *he* said that he thought he had. Fallen in love with you, I mean. So there you go.'

My voice comes out small and croaky as I speak. 'Megan, is that true? Did he actually say that? You've not just got the wrong end of the stick?'

'Absolutely not, I am an architect you know,' she says, as if this explains everything, her tone slightly offended.

'Carrie, are you still going to go?' Rachel asks carefully.

'I… I…' I had never considered this as an outcome. Never in any possible conclusion did I think Jake would fall in love with me. And despite it sounding like the most absurd thing I've ever asked myself, I am in fact debating the question in my head. Do *I* love him?

'Carrie,' Rachel's voice is almost a whisper, she asks me the very same question I'm trying to make sense of, 'do you love him?'

'Oh well, of course she does, don't you?' Megan interjects, as she gazes distractedly at her huge engagement ring.

A heaviness hangs in the air between the three of us, Megan and Rachel staring at me expectantly. What the hell am I supposed to say? Obviously, I'll say no, won't I, because I don't love Jake. I mean, how could I? It's only been a week. I know we have this ridiculously supercharged chemistry between us but that doesn't mean I love him. Just because I was more upset about leaving him than I was ending things for good with Luke, that's just because Jake's been the good to his bad, the light in the horrible darkness I faced. The laughter to my tears, the feeling, the warmth and the completeness when all I felt was hollow and empty. Oh shit. My heart beats faster as the words come to life in my head. I can't love him, I mean I *can't*.

'Carrie?' Rachel looks at me concerned.

I start to panic, and all I want to do is get away from this conversation. You know, because running away is apparently my new thing.

'Rachel, I have to go.'

'Go?' she says her voice surprised. 'But… but what about Jake?'

'What about Jake? He hasn't told *me* he loves me.'

'But he did tell me, and I'm the next best thing,' interrupts Megan.

'And even if, by any stretch of the imagination, he actually does, that just makes all this harder, not easier. How would it even work? I can't even think about it right now, I need to go, Rach.'

'Oh for goodness' sake, you can't leave us on a cliffhanger, Carrie, come on!' Megan wails, as my taxi pulls up outside the front of the hotel. I couldn't risk taking a hotel car in case it was driven by Michael and I spent the whole time crying or totally regretting my decision to leave. I give Rachel another tight hug.

'It will work out, babe,' she says sympathetically.

'Of course it will. All you need to do is go away, miss Jake terribly, realise you did actually love him all this time and voila! I've saved the day again. What?' asks Megan, as she pulls me into her and squeezes the life out of me. 'Then at your wedding you can tell everyone it was down to me.' She giggles and gives me a wink, batting her long mascaraed lashes up and down.

'I never thought I'd say this, but I'm actually going to miss you, Megan.'

She frowns and scoffs, sliding down her sunglasses from her head. 'Naturally, darling. At least now I'm here Rachel has a new pool buddy.' And she links their arms together.

I laugh out loud at the look of horror on Rachel's face, and I turn to her. 'Please say bye to Dale. Oh, and Michael, of course. Will you tell them...'

'I'll explain it all,' she says holding up her hands and shooing me into the car. 'Now go before I do actually cry.'

As the taxi pulls away, and I clip in my seat belt, I wave to Megan and Rachel, both of them standing there looking forlorn. Just as I turn my head away I see a flash of blonde and do a double take to see Jake run out of the doors and come to a halt, as the taxi pulls away. His face is full of regret for a moment, before he smiles and gives a salute at the car. Tears fill my eyes and I turn away, unable to watch his figure disappear behind the walls of the hotel entrance.

'Good holiday, miss?' the taxi driver asks, making me start at the interruption to my thoughts. I let my head fall back on to the headrest and press my lips together fighting back the tears once more.

'Life-changing,' I sigh.

'Ah well, you know you can always come back,' he says happily.

Can I? I wonder and close my eyes, letting the events of the last few hours run wild in my mind. So much has happened I don't even know where it begins and ends, but there's one thing that I keep coming back to. My stomach lurches at just the thought of it. No matter how stupid it is, how far-fetched, how insane and probably totally untrue,

I just can't keep it out of my head. It's the slim, and albeit it very faint, possibility that Jake might actually be in love with me. And the more solid, ludicrous and terrifying one, that I'm not entirely convinced that I'm not in love with him too.

Chapter Thirty-Four

Six months later

'I'm just getting on the train now, so I'll be about an hour,' I say, wrestling my way through the bunch of Friday evening commuters, clutching my bag to me like a shield. My fingers are numb from the January cold, and I look up at the sky, convinced it's about to snow. 'And I swear to God, Rachel, this hotel you've booked better have central heating because I am freezing my pale bum off!'

'What, you think I'm about to book you into some dive? I saw your suite in Barbados don't forget, lady!' she laughs.

'Yes, but that was technically for my honeymoon.'

'And you don't think I'm going to be able to tempt you to a little romance, hey? Well your loss, babe.'

'Who knows? It's been a while,' I reply glumly, and she laughs.

'I'll see you shortly. What carriage are you in?'

I look around me, trying to find the letter on the side of the doors, as I'm jostled forward.

'Er, C, carriage C, providing I can get a seat,' I groan, as I shove my elbow into a dark trench coat and heave a man, who is trying to push in front of me, out of my way. 'Lord, this is brutal, see you soon. Don't get on the wrong train!'

'Would I?' Rachel scoffs before we both say a resounding 'Yes' at the same time.

I ring off, chuckling to myself. Since I got back from Barbados, Rachel and I have seen each other at least twice a month. As much as I love Kate and she will always be my best friend in a certain way, it's been hard to keep as close to her as I have been because of Luke. I know she's super excited about becoming an auntie, and she's finally started to come to terms with the fact her and Justin won't ever have a baby biologically, but they've started looking into fostering to adopt and have had a couple of initial meetings. Everything seems to be going the right way for them, but I know, deep down, she can't wait for the baby to arrive.

Me, on the other hand, not so much. I'm not angry like I was or even sad about it as such, but I just don't want a reminder of that time and what they did to me. Because that does make me sad, to know Emily is gone from my life for good. I don't hate them, I just don't feel anything for them now.

Strangely, given his closeness to Luke, the person I've kept in touch with most, almost on a daily basis, is Dan. I think it's the reason that him and Dani broke up, to be honest. She was convinced something was going on between us, and that I was trying to get him to sleep with me in some sort of twisted revenge plot directed at Luke but, obviously, it's nothing of the sort.

Dan's been perfect at relaying just the right amount of information, so that I'm not shocked and unprepared if someone happens to mention any Luke-based news in passing, but not too much that I feel like it's being rammed down my throat all the time.

Speaking of ramming things down throats, things between him and Rachel seem to be progressing nicely since we all got together on Halloween for a fancy dress party at Rachel's house.

Halloween was always a big thing for our friendship group, and every year Luke and I would always host a scary movie night for everyone. We'd make themed drinks and snacks and get everyone huddle up on the sofa. So this year Dan said he would spend it with me, and when Rachel invited me to her party, he was happy to come along as my purely platonic plus-one. They hit it off in a ridiculously big way, and I'm pretty sure the bite marks he had on his shoulder the next day were not part of his costume. I know he's been to see her a few of times since then, and he's been out with us the last few times she's been up to see me. The last time she visited, he managed to end up staying for breakfast with us the next morning.

I think Dan felt a bit guilty to start with, as his allegiance lay with Luke to a certain degree, but once he got to know Rachel I don't think the fact that she was the self-appointed deputy of Team Anti-Luke actually ended up mattering one bit. I don't think Luke was whooping for joy at their union, but I don't think he dared say anything to anyone about their relationship status after the situation he created for himself. Which is still a mess, but at least I'm not part of that mess any more.

I've been told by Dan that Luke's planning to move in with Emily in the next week or so, so he can be there for about a month before the baby arrives to help out as she gets closer to her due date. As it stands, they aren't together, just trying to get along for the baby's sake and, to be honest, if they can do that, at least I think I can find it a bit easier to think about.

Am I over Luke? Yes, definitely. Am I over what happened? Or maybe that should be, am I over Emily? Almost. And for now, that's good enough.

I settle into my window seat, placing my weekend bag on the aisle seat next to me, hoping no one asks me to move it before Rachel gets on at Northampton. It was Rachel's birthday on the twenty-ninth of December, so we are taking a little weekend trip to London to celebrate now the Christmas rush is over and to give ourselves something to look forward to in dreary, skint January. She's booked us into a swanky hotel, we have some indulgent Covent Garden spa treatments on Saturday before doing some sightseeing and shopping topped off with dinner and cocktails. Then Sunday will be a recovery brunch and maybe some more shopping before we get the train back on Sunday evening.

I have to say, I've been looking forward to it all Christmas holidays. It was very strange to just be me and Mum this year for Christmas. After Dad died, I made sure there was always loads of people around but that was the last thing I wanted, so it was quite a quiet and somewhat sombre affair. Although we did consume about eight thousand mince pies and at least twenty bottles of Prosecco over the course of the festive period, so it wasn't all bad times.

Thinking of my mum reminds me I should text her to let her know I'm on the train. I swipe open my phone, my heart tightening a little, as it does every time I see the background picture; a sun-kissed, white, sandy beach, framed by palm trees, the sea blue and clear in the distance and a brown, wooden sign that reads *To The Beach*. The place that, sat on a stuffy, grey train, seems a million miles away. But in my head and imprinted on my heart, it's still absolutely, breathtakingly crystal clear. I still remember everything about taking that photo, and I press my lips together and unashamedly let a wave of fresh thoughts about Jake skip through my mind.

As soon as I landed back in the UK I had a message from him that buzzed up on my phone before I'd even left the plane. It's still on there now, sat in my messages, and I go back to it almost on a daily basis. OK, definitely on a daily basis. I know it off by heart and could recite it in my sleep if I was asked to which I know is totally weird and borderline creepy, but it's all I have of him. And even after all these months, it's still not enough.

Well, sweet cheeks, it's not half as fun here without you, and you've only been gone a matter of hours. I just need you to know that I understand. And that you leaving doesn't change how I feel or anything that's happened between us. I would love to say that we'll talk soon but, as much as it's what I want, I know it's not what you need and, like I said before, this is all about you. Just know that over the next however long it might be, I am going to want to call you every day, want to message you every day, but I won't because I know it won't help you, sweet cheeks. You were right to leave (and you have no idea how tough it is for me to write that!). I'll be here, just working on my tan until you're ready for another jet ski ride. Who knows where that one could lead? (The last one is pretty unbeatable as jet ski rides go.) Right, I'm off for a cold shower because the thought of you straddling me on a jet ski is all too much right now. Stay smiling, it suits you more than you know.

J xxxx

I wrote and rewrote my message back to him about ten times and, in the end, all of them felt wrong so I just wrote what I felt right there and then.

I wish you weren't so lovely, it would make all of this so much easier. I miss you. Already. And I will continue to miss you until I see those red shorts again. Thank you. I will come back, I promise. C. xxxxxxxx

Except, once I realised that I'd left behind the most real thing I'd ever experienced, it was too late. I remember the exact moment I knew what an idiot I had been, it was on the August bank holiday, a few weeks after I got back, and I was at a BBQ at Rachel's. I had tried to convince myself that I would forget Jake, and that I just had to give it time, but then I ended up being stuck in the world's most depressing conversation with some guy telling me all about his recent break-up because, apparently, when I said I was just out of a relationship he took that to mean I would obviously want to hear all about his.

He was going on and on about how he had missed her

and how it had all been so difficult having to plan his own meals now she no longer cooked for him, even though they weren't living together, and he had no idea why she had been so offended when he said he didn't want to move in with her because it was too far away from his favourite pub, where he spent most nights with the boys. What a catch he was! He was saying how he was totally fine now because it had been at least two weeks, and he hadn't thought about her once. That was, until that afternoon, when he'd microwaved a Pot Noodle and melted all the plastic. But then he said something that made me realise I had just been kidding myself.

'Well that's just what happens, isn't it?' he'd chortled to himself. 'Out of sight and out of mind until you forget they ever existed at all.'

When I left Barbados, I already knew I'd fallen for Jake in a big way. A way bigger way than I ever thought I could. But stupidly, and I see that now, I thought that once I left the feelings would fade over time and I'd forget. Because that weirdo man was actually right, that's what happens, isn't it? The less you see someone, the less you think about them and the less you feel for them. But with Jake, the exact opposite happened.

Since the moment I left him I've felt an ever-present longing, like a hunger that, no matter what I do, I can't satisfy. When I'm working, I think of him, when I'm lying in bed at night, I think of him, and when I'm out having fun, or at least trying to, I constantly watch the door in case, by some miracle of God, he walks in. Except I know he won't. Poor Rachel must be totally sick of my despondency about the mistake I made with Jake, but what else could I do? I couldn't stay forever, and I didn't want to get into something when I knew I still had the whole Luke fiasco hanging over my head.

Especially since I could already feel that what was between me and Jake wasn't just some holiday fling.

'You could just text him, you know?' Rachel told me one day when I was feeling particularly sorry for myself.

'And say what? Oh, hi Jake, I know I haven't been in touch with you for weeks, and I know I ran out and left but, just to let you know, I'm not actually an emotional wreck any more and, great news, I'm over my ex, so I wondered if you might fancy hanging out? Oh except... yes that's right! We live thousands of miles apart, and how the hell would we even begin to make it work? He'd think I'm more unhinged than I was when I last saw him.'

'He does not, nor will he, think you are unhinged!' she had said, crossly. 'He loves you.' Which I met, once again, with a roll of my eyes. 'He would be so pleased if you got in touch, and I know you want to. His message said he wants to be in touch with you, he's just giving you the space you asked for.'

'I just feel like too much time has passed now. I don't know what I would even start with.'

'How about, hi, how are you? I've missed you. That would be a start.' She said it as if it was the most obvious thing in the world.

'He's probably moved on, Rach. I doubt he's even still thinking about me.'

'Oh, come on!' Rachel had yelled, throwing up her hands in exasperation. 'We both know that's not true, and you will never know unless you text him!'

I've lost count of the number of times we have had different variations of this conversation, and each time it comes back to my fear that he may have moved on, and I feel like I've left it so long, I actually can't get in touch. Thinking that I may have lost Jake forever makes me sick to my stomach, yet I still can't bring myself to get over my fear and just send that text. I hate to admit it to myself, but I also know it's down to a horrible, niggling feeling that it may have all been in my head. That he didn't feel about me the way he said he did, despite what Megan and Rachel thought, and that I would be rejected by him. The thought of that is too much to bear. I would rather hold on to the amazing memories I have of our short time together, than to have it ruined forever.

I close my eyes, letting the motion of the train lull me into a sleepy daze and dream of cool oceans, sandy beaches and Jake.

Chapter Thirty-Five

Rachel does in fact manage to get on the right train, and we get to into King's Cross and take the Tube to Leicester Square, where we drag ourselves, and our weekend bags, into the cold night air.

'Rachel, do you actually know where you're going?' I ask sceptically, the freezing wind biting at my cheeks, as she stops in her tracks and looks from left to right, a puzzled look on her face.

'Yes, of course I do, we just need a cab. It's not far, but it's too cold to be trailing around London.'

'You do know that's what we are going to be doing for the entire weekend, don't you?'

'Oh shut up, smarty-pants,' she laughs. 'Ah! There! Grab that taxi.'

Once settled into our black cab, she hands the driver a business card, and he nods in understanding as we set off through the Friday night traffic.

'Rach, you'll have to let me know how much the hotel cost so I can pay my half. I know you're a control freak and like to book everything yourself, but you're not paying for me too,' I remind her.

'Thanks, sweetie, I will do once we pay up on Sunday. Shall we check in and get settled then have a drink in the hotel bar before we decide what to do for dinner?'

'Yep, sounds good to me. You, Rachel Hart, are the perfect date,' I reply, a happy feeling glowing inside me, warming my chilly bones, and as the lights reflect on the windows, we watch the city come to life for a Friday night.

'Bloody Nora, Rach! This is a bit fancy, isn't it? Are you sure I'm going to be able to afford to pay you half?' I ask her worried, as we pull up outside the hotel that's situated somewhere between Covent Garden and Leicester Square, according to the ever-vague Rachel.

'I got a good deal, don't worry. Anyway, we deserve a treat.'

I pay the taxi driver, as Rachel gets the bags out and goes over to speak to the doorman, dressed in a thick, black coat and leather gloves, who stands outside a silver and frosted glass revolving door. Bay trees covered in fairy lights stand in huge, mirrored pots framing the doorway and a sleek, black awning overhangs on to the street. As we push our way through the door the whole place instantly reminds me of Barbados, my stomach clenching at the unexpected memory and, as I look around me at the marble, the muted colours and the sleek furnishings, I suddenly understand why. I scurry to catch up with Rachel who is stood at the reception desk, chatting to a good-looking, young guy in a grey suit, black tie and white shirt. She's laughing away, and I presume she's checking in, not just trying to pick up a date for the evening.

'Rachel? *Rachel!*' I hiss at her, trying to get her attention. She turns slowly, her face in a grimace that knows she's been busted. 'This is his hotel, isn't it?'

'Maybe,' she says quietly.

'Oh my God, Rach! I can't stay here!'

'Why not?' she laughs. 'Of course you can. I knew it would be nice and, like I said, I got a cheap deal. I don't know anything about London, or where to stay, but this hotel was always going to be decent.'

'It's more than decent, look at it,' I whisper, gesturing around the lobby. 'It's bloody palatial!'

'Well, we both know he has good taste,' she says with a knowing look.

'Stop that right now!' I say crossly, then add more calmly, 'Why didn't you tell me? You could have given me some warning so I could have prepared myself.'

'Calm down you, weirdo! Let's go get changed, and you'll feel better after a glass of wine.'

'OK sorry, I'm fine. I don't even know why I'm freaking out.' And I don't. I take a few deep breaths to calm my hammering heart.

Our room, as expected, is decadent. Soft grey carpet, large, silver-framed, free-standing mirror, black, wooden bed frame and crisp, white bed sheets with a grey, quilted throw and pillows laid across it. We hang up our dresses for tomorrow's night out and, after a quick shower, I change into a pair of black, skinny jeans and cream jumper with some jet-black, suede heels, and we head down to the bar for cocktails. Rachel is in a soft grey jumper dress and black, knee-high boots, her hair twisted up on top of her head, and I laughed at her for matching the décor.

The first bottle of white goes down far too easily, and we are both giggling away before long. As I do anywhere I go, I glance at the door occasionally, mind, body and soul longing for Jake to walk through it. But of course, like always, he doesn't. It's worse here though. This is actually *his* hotel. The Holden. If he was ever going to walk through any door, this one here is the most likely. I catch Rachel watching me, as the barman pours us each a glass of champagne out of a chilled bottle of Dom Pérignon. Her mouth is curling up into a smile.

'Go on, say it,' I groan at her.

'You should text him,' she says smugly. 'What's stopping you?'

'Me! *I'm* stopping me!'

'But you could just *not* stop you.'

'He will have moved on, Rach, it's been six months. I've missed my chance.' I take a big gulp of dry, fizzy champagne. She considers me for a moment and then asks me a question she hasn't asked since the day I left Barbados.

'You did love him, didn't you?' The words hang in the air, as I look anywhere but at her before I sigh heavily.

'I don't know, Rach. Maybe. At times it felt like I did. But what does it matter now, anyway?'

'Come on, don't be sad. I'm sorry if the hotel was a bad idea.'

'It's fine,' I reassure her, reaching over to squeeze her hand. 'It's actually kind of nice. I feel like I'm closer to him in some weird way.'

'Shall we have dinner in the restaurant here tonight?' she says, changing the subject before I can lament my sorrows any more. 'I'm pretty shattered and could do with saving my feet for tomorrow. And the restaurant's meant to be amazing, there's even a waiting list apparently.'

'Then how on earth are we going to get a table?' I ask her, as she begins gathering up her bag and wine glass.

'Oh, I think that's just if you're not staying at the hotel, I'm pretty sure they reserve a section for guests. Would you mind getting someone to bring this bottle to the restaurant when you get a minute?' she says addressing the barman. 'I don't want to drop it.' And she holds up her bag and glass in way of explanation.

'Of course, no problem at all,' he says with a long, lingering smile at Rachel, and she grins sweetly back at him.

'Don't tell Dan I flirt with hunky bar staff so I don't have to carry my own stuff,' she whispers to me on our way through the lobby to the restaurant.

'I think that's probably the only time it's allowed,' I say.

'What, when they're hunky or I need stuff carrying?'

'Both,' I giggle at her, and she snorts into her champagne flute. 'Thank you for this weekend, Rach, it's just what I needed. And I'm sorry for freaking out about the hotel.'

'Don't apologise you daft thing, I'm used to you freaking out by now.' I give her a little shove, and she has to put her glass to her mouth quickly to stop the champagne spilling over the edge.

By some total fluke, the restaurant do actually have a table for us, and we're ushered to the back of the heaving room and shown to a table that already has our champagne bottle icing in a bucket.

'Well that's impressive!' I say, as we take our seats.

'Get us, pair of fancy-pants.' Rachel lets out a little giggle and clinks her glass against mine. 'Cheers, sweetie! To getting over our fears. And when I say ours, I mean yours.' She laughs at my sigh and the shake of my head.

'Don't you ever get bored?'

'What, of trying to make you see sense? Nope, never. You deserve him.'

I push the thought of Jake out of my mind, as Rachel takes a big slug of champagne before clearing her throat.

'Carrie, I need to tell you something, and you have to promise not to totally freak out. Again.' She pulls a face and looks at me apprehensively.

'OK.' I regard her suspiciously before snapping my eyes wide open. 'Oh my God, you're not pregnant, are you?'

Rachel actually guffaws. 'What? No! But I am going to throw this dress away!'

'Sorry,' I wince. 'Apparently now anyone has news I just presume they're pregnant. Go figure. Sorry, go on.'

She takes a deep breath, about to speak, just as a waiter comes over and gives us a nervous smile.

'Rachel Hart?'

'Yes.' She looks at me, and I shrug my shoulders.

'You're needed at reception, would you mind?' He gestures towards the door of the restaurant looking at her expectantly.

'What, *now*?' Rachel says with a frown and a glance in my direction. 'Are you sure it's me?'

The poor waiter looks between us both. 'Yes, ma'am, quite sure. It won't take a moment.'

'Er, OK well… yes, OK. Sorry, I'll be back in a mo.'

'Do you want me to come?' I ask concerned, lifting myself slightly out of the chair.

'No, no, no, I'm sure it's nothing. I won't be a sec.'

'Alright, well if you're sure?'

She waves her arms in a dismissive gesture. 'Course, back in a mo.'

She struts off behind the waiter, and I watch her go before turning back to my glass, turning its stem in my fingers. I glance past some tables to my right and out of the huge floor-to-ceiling windows to the people bustling past on the street. It's a Friday night in one of the busiest cities in the world, and there's people flagging down cabs, some hurrying along the pavement to get out of the cold and others huddled together outside bars and restaurants planning their next move, all of them, their faces laughing and smiling. Now, happiness seems synonymous with Jake, and I automatically turn to the doorway only to find it just as it always is. Perhaps it's because I know that this is his hotel and that at some point he must have been here, walked this floor and been in this space, that I find it hard to tear my eyes away, my gaze lingering on the spot.

'Looking for someone?'

My fingers slip on my glass, almost sending it toppling over, but I manage to recover it just in time and then my whole body freezes. My heart is beating so hard I think it might burst out of my chest and the blood rushing through my veins seems suddenly hotter. The room spins momentarily, as I carefully stand up, my legs shaking underneath me and, breathing as steadily as I can manage, I turn around. My hands fly to my mouth as I see him, hair just as blonde, eyes just as golden and his smile, just as perfect, just as I remember. I don't know whether to laugh or cry, so I do a little bit of both, as I stifle a shocked burst of laughter with my hands and feel the tears well in my eyes.

'Hello, sweet cheeks,' he says taking a step towards me. Oh his voice. To hear his voice again.

'Hello,' I sniff, still frozen to the spot.

'Were you looking for someone?' he repeats, closing the gap between us.

I nod, my lips pressed tight together, as I struggle to believe that it's him. He's wearing a light grey jumper over a white shirt and blue jeans with tan brogues. He looks heavenly, and my breath catches in my throat as I speak.

'You,' I say, my voice a whisper.

'Good,' he replies as he reaches me, his hands suddenly in my hair and his lips pressing hard against mine. I react to him immediately, every single part of my body firing, as his kiss deepens and I snake my arms around his neck. He breaks away, our breathing heavy, and I giggle, embarrassed that I seem to have forgotten we are in a restaurant, although it is *his* restaurant so we might be excused.

'I wasn't planning on that being my opener...' Jake says looking not one bit sheepish but totally smug.

'I'm glad it was.'

'I was worried you might slap me. God, you have no idea how much I've missed you.' He pulls me to him, and I breathe in his scent, revelling in the feel of him, his touch, his smell.

'I think I do. Jake, I'm so sorry I haven't been in touch...' He puts his finger to my lips stopping me.

'There will be plenty of time for that. Can we go somewhere quieter?'

'Let me guess, I don't suppose you might happen to have a suite here, do you?' I ask him, and he laughs. It's the most comforting sound.

'Maybe,' he shrugs with a smile. 'Come on, let's go rescue Rachel from the wild goose chase I sent her on.'

'That was you?' I say my face a picture of shock. 'Wait a minute... Oh my God, Jake, does she know?'

'Of course she knows,' he says grinning. 'Who do you think set this whole thing in motion?'

'Wait, what?' I say stopping in my tracks. 'You being here, us, this was all Rachel?'

He nods. 'She was terrified you were going to freak out. The original plan was I was going to see you tomorrow, but I couldn't wait. Plus I knew she wouldn't be able to keep it a secret from you, and I wanted it so be a surprise so I could see your reaction without you having time to think about it. Your genuine reaction. And I have to say, I am incredibly relieved.' He lets out a long exhale and the hair that's fallen on to his forehead lifts slightly.

'I bet that was what she was going to tell me just now, the sneaky thing!' I say my mind racing.

'God, I've missed you,' he says kissing my head and laughing into my hair.

As we leave the restaurant, my hand in Jake's, I feel like I'm floating. He's here. I keep repeating the words in my head. He's here. He's here. I can see Rachel's back as she leans on reception, her foot tapping impatiently, and Jake gives a loud cough. She turns and, as a look of recognition dawns on her face, she breaks out into a huge grin.

'Oh my God! I *knew* something was up, you sneaky shit! You're here!'

She punches Jake on the arm and then turns to me, grabbing me by the shoulders.

'I am so sorry! Please don't be mad I kept it a secret! I was going to tell you, literally *just* then, because I was worried you would freak like you freaked out about the hotel, but clearly this one couldn't wait. Do you hate me?' She gives me and Jake a once-over, noting our linked hands and the beaming smiles on our faces.

'Of course I don't.' And I pull her into a hug whispering in her ear, 'Thank you.'

'You freaked about the hotel?' Jake looks at me, an amused smile playing on his lips.

'No,' I lie. 'OK, I may have freaked a tiny bit. But good freaked!' I blush, and Jake grins. 'Oh, but...' I look from Rachel to Jake, totally torn. 'Look, I know I'm in the dark here, and I don't know what's being going on, but I know Rachel had this weekend planned out and...'

I really don't want to offend Rachel since she's been so bloody brilliant, but I really, *really* just want to spend some time with Jake.

'Calm down. Dan's coming first thing in the morning,' Rachel says, putting me out of my misery. 'We had this whole thing planned out that Jake was going to surprise you at breakfast tomorrow.'

'But I got an earlier flight to catch up on some work here and, well I just couldn't wait. I saw you in the restaurant, and I couldn't help myself...' The way he's looking at me, his eyes wide and eager, makes my insides squirm and melt away into pools of hungry desire. Rachel snorts and holds up her hands.

'OK, so I now officially feel like I'm third wheeling. I'm going to get an early night and will see you guys tomorrow. I'll pack your bag up for you, don't worry. Jake will you get someone to collect it and take it to your room?'

He nods and turns to speak to the guy on reception. With him out of earshot Rachel turns to me speaking in hurried but excited whispers.

'Carrie, are you OK? Please tell me this was the right thing to do? I didn't want to interfere, but I couldn't see you torture yourself any longer! I thought if you just could see him again, at least you know then, either way, if it's worth giving it a go or not...' She trails off looking guilty, but I grab her hand.

'No, *I'm* sorry! For being such a nightmare then not doing anything about it. I needed this push, Rach, I really did. I just couldn't see it. Thank you. So much.'

'Oh thank God, I almost had a coronary when I first saw him!'

'You and me both, chick,' I giggle, as Jake comes over.

'You set?' he asks and I nod, before the three of us make our way upstairs in the lift, saying goodbye to Rachel at the third floor. After she gives us both a huge squeeze, Jake and I thank her again for interfering in a good way, and then we stand, face-to-face, grinning at each other, as we make our way to Jake's suite.

'This is us.' He swipes us in and pushes open the door.

I let out a long whistle at the incredible room. 'Woah.'

A massive leather sofa with coffee table and two matching chairs are in the centre, and I can see a huge four-poster bed off in a room to the left, through some double doors. There's a rooftop balcony leading off the sitting room and a plush, grey rug with some huge cushions and beanbags in one corner next to a fireplace.

'Drink?' Jake asks, coming up close behind me.

'Please. I need something to steady my nerves.'

'Why are you nervous?' He goes over to a cupboard, opening it to reveal a fully stocked minibar, and pulls out a bottle of what looks like more champagne, followed by a corkscrew, and gets to work.

'Because I have so much I want to say, and I don't know where to start.'

'You know you don't have to say anything, don't you? You have nothing to explain.' He pours two glasses and beckons me over to the sofa. We sit side by side, my legs curled up under me, and stare at each other again, huge smiles plastered on both our faces.

'I do, Jake, I really do. If not for you, then for me. Please, just humour me?'

'I will, I promise. But can I just say, it's really, really difficult for me not to pick you up and carry you through there.' He nods towards the bed room, and I bite my lip, giving a tiny nod.

'OK…' I start to speak, but a knock at the door interrupts me. 'That'll be my bag.'

Jake gets up to answer it, thanks the mystery person behind the door as he places it by the entrance to the bedroom and comes back to the sofa to join me.

'Good old Rach.'

'Indeed,' he agrees and settles back on the sofa. 'She first emailed me in November, basically saying that she knew you wanted to get in touch, but felt like you couldn't so she was taking your life, rightly or wrongly, in her own hands. She said you'd told her you missed me, but that you didn't know how I felt about things, but if I felt like she thought I might, then would I want to see you again. Obviously I said yes, and we arranged this whole weekend. Like I said, it was supposed to be tomorrow but…'

As I process his words, he takes my hand and rubs my knuckles like he used to in Barbados. Such a simple thing that to me, here in this moment, fills me with joy. I sigh and begin to explain myself.

'I felt like I'd upped and left you, Jake, and how could you possibly have been bothered about me still? I thought I'd left it too late and now it would seem ridiculous if I got in touch. Like, hi, remember me? I'm that girl you spent a week with who legged it back to England and hasn't spoken to you since, how's things? Weather been nice? I didn't know what to say. I don't even know *what* we had in Barbados, I couldn't work out what it was,' I take a sip of champagne to steady my nerves, 'I just knew it was something. And now,' I look around and spread my hands, 'now I'm here, and you're here, and I can't quite believe it, but it feels just like it did, just like we haven't been apart at all.'

Jake leans forward and kisses me gently before drawing back, watching me as he does, as if he's taking a moment to consider his words.

'That day you left, as soon as I saw the taxi pull away, I knew what mistake I'd made not putting up more of a fight for you. But honestly, sweet cheeks, I could see you were torn, and I needed you to get there on your own, not have me pushing how I felt on you in the hope you might start to feel the same. That's why I let you go, because it was the right thing to do. And you were right, you would have never been able to get over what happened properly if you and I had been in the equation.' He drains his glass and places it on the table before pushing his hands through his hair, a look of exasperation crossing his face. 'God, you have no idea how much I wanted to get in a car and come to the airport. You have no idea how much I wanted you, how much I *want* you.'

I put down my glass and place my hand on his face, his short stubble brushing coarsely against my skin.

'I do know because I wanted it too. I was too scared to admit it, Jake, too scared to face up to what it was. I just knew I had to be over Luke and be able to give myself to it one hundred per cent.'

'And now? Are you over Luke?'

I don't even hesitate.

'Yes.'

We sit in silence for a moment, Jake looking down at my hand as he cradles it tenderly in his, and I take a moment to absorb him. The familiar lines, the strong jawline, his huge hands and muscular, broad shoulders. The air between us is thick and heady, humming with anticipation. It feels like I only saw him yesterday, and that the last few months without him have all been a dream. He suddenly pulls me towards him, my body pressing on top of his, as he murmurs a single word into my lips.

'Good.'

I part my mouth, our kiss immediately becoming hungrier, more impatient. His hands travel beneath my jumper and run up my back, as it arches under the touch of his fingertips. I hold my arms aloft for him to slide off my jumper, as I do the same for him, and I begin to unbutton his shirt, my fingers fumbling in my haste. He sits forward, and I push it down across his shoulders, giggling as it gets stuck around his biceps.

We stand, and he yanks it off, as I unbuckle his belt, pushing down his jeans and he steps out of them before slipping off his shoes and socks. Jake drops to his knees, and pulls down my jeans, before he cups my bottom firmly, pulling me towards him as I step out of them. His eyes never leave mine, as his warm breath skims across my hip bones. He takes hold of the lace edge of my knickers and, at a slow, tortured pace, drags them down my legs. His fingers run from my ankle all the way up the inside of my leg, stopping just before he reaches the top, my head lolling to one side in unashamed longing.

I hear the sounds of a packet tearing open and reach for my glass to moisten my mouth that's become so suddenly dry. Jake takes a seat on the sofa and tugs my hand towards him, my thighs settling either side of his. His mouth places a line of kisses across the top of my shoulder, and I bend my head down to nestle my face into the crook of his neck. His hands find my waist as he lifts me up, allowing me to gradually lower myself on to him. He groans before finding my mouth with his once more and kissing me as if his life depended on it, and I know I'm no longer lost, no longer scared. I'm right where I should be.

Chapter Thirty-Six

My head is resting on Jake's chest, as we curl up together on the sofa in our underwear, a throw from the bed wrapped around us. Well, wrapped around Jake, who's wrapped around me.

'I suppose I best go,' he says, stretching out beneath me, so I look at him confused, a frown on my face. 'See you in another six months, yeah?'

I pick up a cushion and beat him across the head with it as he tries to defend himself, laughing heartily.

'You are not funny!' I say but can't help the smile in my voice. He wraps his arms around me, trapping me to him, and kisses my neck making me giggle as I snuggle back down under the throw.

'Don't worry, I'm not going anywhere. And neither are you.' And he squeezes me to him.

'Jake?'

'Yes, sweet cheeks?'

'When I left Barbados, you said you had something you needed to tell me but that you didn't think I was ready to hear it and you'd tell me next time you saw me.'

'I did.' The corners of his mouth turn up into a smile.

'Well?'

'Well, what?'

'Come on spill!' I say, hitting him with the cushion again before he grabs it out of my hands and throws it across the room.

'What, you mean you couldn't possibly think of what it might be I wanted to say?'

I bite my lip embarrassed. I didn't have a clue at the time, but since Megan let loose the 'L-word', as stupid as it was to even *think* it, I couldn't help but wonder. Jake shifts his body slightly so we are face-to-face as he speaks.

'That day in the lobby when we first met, there was something about you. I just didn't want to keep away. I *couldn't*. Even right back then I felt something I'd never felt with anyone. By the time we'd finished on the jet skis, I was done. You have no idea how much I wanted to kiss you that day. So badly it was almost painful.'

'I might have a tiny idea,' I say quietly, and he smiles as he continues.

'By the time we got to Miami I knew I was into something I couldn't stop. And well, yeah, then Miami happened and that was TKO,' he laughs sheepishly. 'You're funny and brilliant and sexy and… and everything I could ever imagine wanting.'

He rubs his hand over his chin and grins, a little embarrassed. It's gorgeous.

'So what I wanted to tell you before you left, was that I'd fallen for you, in a big way. And that, despite our circumstances and the distance and everything else, I was, actually, in love with you.'

'Jake…' Tears prick my eyes, and I blink to fight them away, and my heart swells to a hundred times its size inside my chest.

'I know it's mental,' he laughs, 'but it's true.'

'And now?' I ask.

'Not that I ever really doubted my feelings had changed, but seeing you tonight, I know what I felt was, well, just that.'

I steady my breathing, that has become increasingly more rapid in response to his words, and take a deep breath before I speak.

'I think I tried to pretend to myself that it wasn't happening, but I knew deep down it was,' I say.

'That what wasn't happening?'

'That I wasn't falling. It had only been a week, and I was in a really weird place. I was worried that what I felt wasn't real.' I reach for his hand and link our fingers together. 'But it was, and I did fall for you in a big, big way. And not just because you saved me from going mad that trip. These last few months have been torture without you, I couldn't get you out of my head. I knew as soon as I got on the stupid plane that I was actually a little bit in love with you too.'

He smirks. 'Only a little bit?'

'OK, maybe quite a big bit.' We beam at each other, the words we have both known for the last six months finally becoming real.

'Sweet cheeks?'

'Yes Baywatch?'

'This might be jumping the gun a bit, but how do you feel about Dubai?'

Epilogue

'Hurry up, we're going to be late!' I yell to Jake, as he climbs out of the pool. I'm totally distracted by the water glistening off his pecs, and I tilt my head to the side, hands on my hips, trying to be mad but not really meaning it at all. He struts over to me and shakes his hair in my direction, purposefully flicking water all over me.

'Let's be even more late,' he growls, pressing his wet skin against mine.

'Jake!' I squeal. 'Get off! You'll ruin my hair. Go and get dry will you, everyone will be here soon.'

'Yes boss,' he grins and slings a towel over his shoulders, sauntering with no urgency at all inside the Palm Bay Hotel. Maya comes running out, shaking her head and huffing as she passes him.

'Is he joking?' she says in a high-pitched voice, looking horrified at Jake's state of undress. 'And you, go get ready, now! Not another word!'

'OK, OK I'm going. I won't take long, don't panic.'

'I am not panicking!' she snaps, her voice full of panic.

'Blame Jake,' I laugh. 'This is all his fault trying to distract me with his shirtlessness...' I trail off into a daydream and sigh.

'And I am so, so happy for you but, please, I am *begging* you, go get ready.'

I skip inside and up to Rachel's suite, the one I stayed in my very first time here.

'Where the hell have you been?' she shouts at me, the second I creep into the room.

'I'm here, I'm here. Sorry, I was hurrying Jake along.'

'Get that dress on now, Carrie Holden! I am not walking down this aisle without you!'

'On it. Oh my God, Rach, you look amazing.'

'I know!' she whimpers. 'Don't I?' She looks down at herself. 'Do you think Dan will like it?'

I smile at her, reaching out and giving her hands a squeeze. 'I *know* he will love it.' I slip into the pale pink, silk bridesmaid's dress hanging up on the door of the walk-in wardrobe and slide my feet into my heels. 'Right, come on. Let's get you married, shall we?'

'Ah, there's my wife!' Jake shouts way too loudly, as I make my way over to him after the ceremony.

'Jake, most of these people know we're married, you don't need to yell it every time we're in public,' I laugh, secretly loving that this is actually what he does.

'It never gets boring calling you my wife.' He plants a huge kiss on my lips. 'Everyone…' he bellows, and a few people turn around, as I grab the hand he's raised in the air and shush him with a giggle. 'You look sensational, Mrs Holden,' he says giving me an appreciative once-over with a look in his eyes that makes my insides melt.

I feel my cheeks heat up, smiling at the effect he still has on me.

'And you don't look too bad yourself,' I grin back, nudging him with my shoulder, and I go a bit misty-eyed looking at Rachel and Dan kissing on the beach as their photographer snaps away in the background, with Maya ordering the guests around, in her new role as wedding planner for the hotel.

Rachel and Dan turned out to be the biggest surprise for all of us, including them. We all thought it was a bit of fun, but oh, how wrong we were. They went from strength to strength, with him moving down to Northampton to be with her, and the fact that we're at their wedding says it all really. They are so good together, and I see the looks of contentment on the faces of their friends and family who all know it too.

Luke isn't here today and neither is Kate. Dan's friendship with me somewhat got in the way of him and Luke, and I think Luke ended up being a bit pissed off that Dan had kept in touch with me, even though our relationship goes way back and we're pretty much like brother and sister. Then Dan's relationship with Rachel only seemed to add to Luke's assumption that Dan was *taking my side*, so despite their history, they very rarely see each other any more. Which Rachel is thrilled about because she said she would never get past what Luke did to me, and she secretly believes that Dan won't either.

Kate and I still keep in touch every now and again and, despite the fact I will always care about her, our friendship, sadly, just isn't what it was. She's thrown herself into the role of doting auntie, and rightly so. She was so excited that we found it hard to have a conversation without her constantly talking about the new arrival, so our chats got less and less frequent, to the point where they've pretty much stopped all together, and now we only communicate with the occasional text.

Emily had her baby, a boy, four weeks early, which caused another big hoo-ha as Luke wanted a paternity test to prove it was his. I actually felt quite sorry for Emily at that point, just for maybe a minute, with a newborn and being accused of lying about who was the father. To me, Luke's doubt made no sense at all. I think if it had been someone else's, then she probably wouldn't have gone to the effort of upending all our lives as we knew them. I mean who would *choose* Luke as the better option if she had another one? After everything that's happened, I take a deep breath and feel so glad that it wasn't me to be honest.

My attention comes back to the present, as Jake hands me a chilled glass of champagne from a passing tray and drapes his arm over my shoulder.

'You know, I always get a bit nostalgic coming back here,' I say wistfully, leaning into him. 'Can you believe it's actually been two years since I first threw my flip-flops at you on this very beach?'

'I think about it every day, sweet cheeks. And I thank God you did.'

I lift my head up, giving him a gentle kiss. 'Hmm, I love you,' I murmur into his lips, contently.

'And I love you, Mrs H.'

Thinking back, it's hard to believe it was only two years ago. So much has happened and sometimes, even though it's my life, I still can't get my head around it.

After Jake showed up in London, we knew then we were a done deal and spent the next six months flying back and forth between our respective locations, doing the whole long-distance thing. Something that we both hated, but that was somehow made easier by getting to fly first class (at Jake's insistence) and knowing we got to see each other at the end of it.

We made the move to Dubai, together, six months later, almost a year to the day from when we met, and I honestly never knew life and love could be this way. Jake's working from Dubai, getting the new hotel up and running, which should happen in the next twelve to eighteen months, and the nature of my job means I've been able to carry on pretty much as before, although I find I take less on than I did previously, because quite often we are back in London or Miami and, sometimes, even make it over to Barbados.

Jake often finds me looking out over the pool from our bedroom balcony, pensively gazing at the view, and I think, *How is this my life?* Yes, we have a pool, and yes, our bedroom has a *balcony!* Sometimes I have to pinch myself. I'm not quite sure I understood just how successful The Holden Group was until I got to experience it first-hand. I love to tease Jake by telling him that I have no idea how he makes any money, since he pretty much spent the whole time I was in Barbados hanging out with me in a pair of shorts, although he promises me that was an exception he made just for me, and I have to concede that, seeing it for myself, he does work incredibly hard.

I glance down at my Tiffany engagement ring, a yellow diamond surrounded by a cluster of smaller, white diamonds, and my simple, plain wedding band nestled next to it. Rachel actually googled it and is convinced it's worth about fifteen grand, but I told her I'd rather not know and felt a little bit sick at the thought. Jake said he picked it because when I was around the sun always seemed to shine, and even after twelve months of wearing it, it's still a surprise to me to see it on my hand, even though being Jake's wife seems like the most natural thing in the world.

When he asked me to marry him, it was the easiest decision I had ever made. Just after we moved to Dubai, we had to be back in Barbados for Dale's leaving party, as he's moved to Miami to work at the hotel there. Which, now I think about it, was probably a good thing seeing as Rachel and Dan are now getting married here. We took a break from the party to walk along the beach and have a little reminisce about where it all started.

'I'm so glad you came here on your honeymoon,' Jake said to me, as we strolled along the beach, past the spot where we sat drinking champagne out of the bottle, the night he told me he was still married to Megan. Luckily, I find it easy to laugh about that now, and she still remains adamant that her revelation of Jake's feelings for me is the only reason we're now married.

'Me too,' I grinned.

'Would you like to come here on your next one?' he asked me.

'I… What?'

He confused me with his question, and it took me a moment to process it before he said, 'Just wondering where you'd want to go on our honeymoon?'

I remember not being sure what to say at the time, as I pretty much thought he was just making conversation, but then he got down on one knee on the sand and turned to me, my ring, just for me, winking at me from its box.

'Sweet cheeks…' At which point I started bawling my eyes out, and he had to stand up and give me a hug because I couldn't control myself. 'Sweet cheeks, you have brought meaning to my life, unbridled happiness to my heart and fire to my soul. So I wondered, you know, if you've got nothing else planned for the next fifty years or so, if you might fancy marrying me?'

'I… I…' I stammered.

'Is that a yes?' he said, his voice thick with a smile.

'Yes! Yes!' I nodded furiously, as he slipped the ring on to my finger, and my eyes tripled in size as I took it in. It still gives me goosebumps thinking about it, and I smile up at my husband, my *husband*, not quite able to believe my luck.

I still can't quite fathom how, what should have been, the worst week of my life did a full one-eighty into the best, but I think it's down to some inner strength we call on when we need it most. Well, that and the man stood next to me now. The one I know will stand beside me through the ups and the downs, no matter what, for the rest of our days.

Jake looks down at me giving me a wink. Funny, isn't it? How the best things really do happen when you least expect it.

The End

Printed in Great Britain
by Amazon

13521346R00263